Beneath Sleepless Stars
Elizabeth Cole

ALSO BY ELIZABETH COLE

Honor & Roses
Choose the Sky

A Heartless Design
A Reckless Soul
A Shameless Angel
The Lady Dauntless
Beneath Sleepless Stars
A Mad and Mindless Night

Regency Rhapsody:
The Complete Collection

Love on the Run

Beneath Sleepless Stars

Elizabeth Cole

SkySpark Books

PHILADELPHIA, PENNSYLVANIA

Copyright © 2015 by Elizabeth Cole.

All rights reserved. No part of this publication may be reproduced, distributed or transmitted in any form or by any means, including photocopying, recording, or other electronic or mechanical methods, without the prior written permission of the publisher, except in the case of brief quotations embodied in critical reviews and certain other noncommercial uses permitted by copyright law. For permission requests, write to the publisher, addressed "Attention: Permissions Coordinator," at the address below.

SkySpark Books
Philadelphia, Pennsylvania
skysparkbooks.com
inquiry@skysparkbooks.com

Publisher's Note: This is a work of fiction. Names, characters, places, and incidents are a product of the author's imagination. Locales and public names are sometimes used for atmospheric purposes. Any resemblance to actual people, living or dead, or to businesses, companies, events, institutions, or locales is completely coincidental.

Ordering Information:
Quantity sales. Special discounts are available on quantity purchases by corporations, associations, and others. For details, contact the "Special Sales Department" at the address above.

BENEATH SLEEPLESS STARS / Cole, Elizabeth. – 1st ed.
ISBN-10: 1-942-31611-9
ISBN-13: 978-1-942316-11-4

Chapter 1

♋

January 1809

"What do you think of this one?"

Alexander Kenyon, the seventh Duke of Dunmere, braced himself as his uncle pushed a small portrait toward him from across the vast desk of his study.

The miniature portrayed a young woman from the waist up, sitting demurely in front of a woodland scene. The subject was pleasant enough, Alex thought. Ash brown hair framed delicate features, and brown eyes gazed placidly at him. If the artist was honest, she was a slip of a thing.

"Who is she?" Alex asked.

Uncle Herbert checked a small notebook he was holding. "Lady Violet Holloway. Good family, though not nearly so wealthy as in previous generations. Impeccable bloodline, though. By all accounts a perfect lady. Most importantly, the Holloway women are known to be fearsomely good breeders. Twins as often as not." His uncle nodded significantly.

Alex sighed. Of course. The fact that he was now thirty-four with not a single heir was clearly weighing on his family's minds. His heirless, childless state was not for lack of trying.

Now Alex needed to marry again. His uncle Herbert Kenyon took on the duty of sorting through potential brides to suggest. It was not an enviable task. There were few eligible ladies who actually possessed all the qualifications necessary to be considered as the next duchess of Dunmere. The obvious choices—the daughters or sisters of other dukes, and earls, and viscounts—were assessed and discarded one by one. Many were too old or too young. Even more were already promised to others. Several had scandals attached to their names. Of the small number of ladies who somehow managed to cross all those hurdles, none were willing to marry him specifically. They knew better.

Alex's bad luck in brides was now infamous. He'd married no fewer than three times, and each time, his wife had died within the year. Rumors had fanned out among the ton, growing worse over time, hinting he was cursed. Despite his title, Alex was not sought after now. It made finding a willing bride rather challenging.

Other than the inconvenient curse, Alex should have had no trouble finding a wife. Dark haired, tall, well-shaped by constant exercise and work around the estate... He was as handsome as any woman could ask for.

Well, he used to be. Two years previously, he lost his right eye in an incident he would never discuss with any of his family. He wore a patch over the ruins of his eye socket, and tried not to care that his new appearance made his life even more difficult.

Learning how to see with only one eye hadn't take too long, though he still sometimes doubted that he was truly seeing properly. Of course, a portrait wasn't a person, but this little painting was quite pretty.

But the question was not whether he wanted this particular woman, but whether *she* was willing to marry him. He'd do what he must for his family and the future of his line. Now it was up to this unknown woman.

"She'll be amenable to the match?" he asked skeptically.

"I have not spoken with the lady herself yet," Herbert said, "since I wanted to get your approval first. Her guardians assure me that she trusts their judgment, and that she is perfectly accomplished in all the ways a lady must be. I imagine they are eager for her to wed, seeing as she's twenty-five."

Alex frowned at the picture. She looked younger than that. His uncle saw the look and interpreted it correctly. "The picture is a little old, but there was none other to be had. She's been more or less out of society for the past few years, tending a close cousin in her last illness, then a period in mourning. She's not had the opportunity to be in the social circle, that's all. I am assured that she is not lacking in any way. If she's too old…"

"No." Alex put the portrait down. "The last thing I want is some nineteen-year-old, novel-obsessed girl."

"So you do think she might suit? You'll at least meet her and consider?" Herbert asked.

"How many other options are left?" Alex retorted.

Herbert closed the notebook. In the dull winter light of the day, his faded blue eyes and grey hair made him appear older than his fifty-five years. "At the moment, she is the only one. I'm willing to find more names if you prefer. Perhaps there's something I've overlooked."

"No, you haven't," Alex said. "You're as methodical as I am. She's the only one left for me to ask, isn't she?" He took another look at the little portrait, at the calm, clear gaze of the lady. It was only paint, and it told him nothing. Only when he met her would he know what sort of person she truly was. Whether she'd flinch at his face, or be scared of the rumors...

"Very well. I'll arrange to meet her."

"Thank you." Herbert gave a sigh of relief. "She's been living near Colchester with family for some years. I'll send a note to her guardians, advising them of developments." He reached for the portrait, but Alex stopped him.

"I'll keep it until a decision is made," he said. But rather than looking at the portrait again, he placed it face down on the desk.

* * * *

Letters were sent back and forth over the next weeks, primarily between Herbert Kenyon and Judith Peake, who seemed to be the power behind the throne. A date in mid-February was agreed on for a meeting.

Alex directed his valet to pack his bags for a journey to Hawebeck Place, the estate of the Peake family, who took Violet in after her father's death. He dreaded the idea of meeting this young lady so abruptly, but there was little point in doing anything else. She wasn't in London for the Season. She scarcely seemed to leave her family's estate. So a less orchestrated encounter was unlikely. And if he hated her on sight, or if she hated him, well, social visits were only about a quarter hour. A long way to go for a fifteen minute chat. But a marriage would last far longer.

He resigned himself to going. But on the morning before he was to leave, a message arrived at Dunmere Abbey. Alex ripped open the sealed envelope and read the contents.

"What's that?" Herbert asked. He'd come into Alex's study again to discuss the sort of last minute details that always came up when a master left his domain.

"Bad news," Alex muttered, though he felt relief inside.

"Are the Peakes having any difficulty?" Herbert asked anxiously.

"This isn't from them," Alex explained. "I'm afraid I have to go to London immediately."

"What? Do you mean immediately after you visit the Peakes?"

"No. I mean I must go into London this moment. Good thing I'm already packed."

Herbert frowned. "But what of the meeting? We spent weeks arranging the time! Lady Violet will be waiting to see you, and she'll be dis—"

"Disappointed? At not meeting me, a man she doesn't even know?" Alex shook his head. "I doubt that." He held up the letter. "This, however, is imperative."

"You always say that when you dash off to the city. What can possibly be more important than the continuation of your family name? The lineage of Dunmere?"

The safety of the whole nation, Alex thought. He memorized the brief note, then threw it in the fire. "I have no choice in the matter. Why don't you go to her on my behalf? They're expecting a Kenyon of Dunmere Abbey. You are one. Meet the lady and decide if she'll be suitable."

"Be reasonable, Alex," Herbert protested. "What good is it to her to meet an old man?"

"We're not pretending this is a love match, are we?" Alex straightened his cuff irritably. "She's buying a title, and I'm buying an heir. Or a path to one. I don't want some absurd notion of romance to enter into it. The idea of some flighty, starry-eyed wife in love with love is not going to work. You can evaluate her just as well as I can. Probably better, considering my history," he added, not able to keep the bitterness out of his voice.

"Alex."

"Just…" Alex shrugged. "I have no time. Do this for me."

"Very well. I will take care of everything," the older man said, turning to go out.

"Uncle," Alex called, stopping him at the doorway. "When you meet her, don't sugarcoat this. Don't hide anything."

"I have no doubt the Peakes are acquainted with your past, just as I looked at her very carefully. The lady must be aware of the situation. Who in England is not? But I do not plan to mention any absurd rumors or insulting names!" Herbert looked annoyed by the whole idea.

Alex nodded once and turned away. Whoever this lady was, she must already know she was being asked to marry the Duke of Death.

Chapter 2

♋

VIOLET WINCED AS THE CURTAINS on her bed were pushed aside, exposing her little nest to the harsh morning. Her lady's maid stood there with her arms outstretched, making her slight form seem larger than it was.

"Get up, get up, my lady!" Dalby urged. "It's nearly noon!"

"So?" Violet sat up unwillingly. The windows of the room let in a stream of winter sunlight bright enough to make her want to pull a pillow over her face. "You say it as if there's cause for concern. I always sleep late."

In fact, Violet's schedule was so well known to the household that she didn't understand Dalby's excitement. The girl had been her lady's maid for nearly six years, and it wasn't as if anything had changed recently. Violet rose late because she rarely fell asleep before dawn. When one chose stargazing as a hobby, late nights were inevitable.

"Oh, you don't understand, ma'am," Dalby said. "Your aunt will be here any moment and she'll be upset if you're still abed."

"Aunt Judith is coming up here? Why?" Violet slid out of the high bed, her feet going right into the slippers Dalby always laid out for her.

"You need to be dressed as soon as possible," Dalby said. She seemed out of sorts, her normally tidy brown hair now falling loose under her maid's cap. "Your aunt says a suitor is coming to call this afternoon!"

"I don't have any suitors," Violet pointed out. "So who could possibly be coming to call?"

"The Duke of Dunmere!" a new voice chimed out.

Judith Peake strode into Violet's bedroom with her arms and smile both suspiciously wide. She was the opposite of Violet in both looks and temperament, despite being related to Violet by blood.

"Good morning, Aunt Judith," Violet said.

Judith didn't lose her smile as she said, "Good afternoon, you mean. And it will be a good afternoon, since by the end of it, you will be betrothed to a duke! What a coup, yes?"

"One afternoon makes for a brief courtship," Violet said, nervousness starting to bloom within her. "You're being quite optimistic, don't you think?"

"Oh, I've been arranging the matter for over a month. This is a formality." Judith leveled her gaze at Violet, her eyes cold. "That is, it *will* be a formality so long as you present yourself as a perfect lady!" The false smile returned. "Which of course you will. Sweet, demure, polite. Accomplished—but not to excess. Charming—but not flirtatious. And above all, *alert*."

"Yes, Aunt," Violet said.

Dalby murmured next to her, "Don't worry. I told Cook to brew your coffee extra strong, ma'am."

"Thank you," Violet whispered back.

Judith walked to the wardrobe and flung it open. "Now then, what sort of gown would impress a duke? Dalby, what do you suggest?"

Dalby hurried over to discuss the matter with Judith. Violet reached for the breakfast tray and poured herself some coffee. Of course Violet's preferences would not be considered. Judith thought Violet was an oddly behaved irritant, and she would no sooner seek Violet's opinion on a matter than she would ask a tea table.

So Violet was draped and primped and styled and adorned under Judith's sharp eye. She wore one of her best gowns, a blue and white striped silk creation that showed off Violet's delicate coloring and further heightened her slim figure. A cropped white jacket covered her arms and the top of the dress. Pearls at her throat and ears completed the ensemble.

"Well done, Dalby," Judith said. "Open your eyes wider, Violet. You must look attentive when the duke arrives."

"And *why* is he arriving?" Violet asked, feeling sharper after her second cup of coffee. "What possible interest could a duke have in me? I'm only the daughter of a second son of a baron. Papa was never even expected to get the title."

"But he did, and of a barony that goes back over five hundred years!" Judith reminded her. "Your blood is as noble as Dunmere's, even if your title is less distinguished. This is a great opportunity. This may come as a surprise to you, but not *every* man in England is a duke."

Violet was aware of that, but she knew better than to say so out loud. "Yes," she said patiently, "but why come at all? Why should a duke go in search of a bride? Surely there are families campaigning for the honor."

Judith sighed in exasperation. "What do you think I've been doing all this time? I keep my ears open, I hear of an opportunity, and I seize it! Marriages are not random occurrences, my dear. They require effort and skill to arrange."

And to endure, Violet thought, again keeping her thoughts silent. She looked out the window over the grounds of the Peake estate. It was not extensive. Over the years, parts had been sold off or rented as the Peake fortunes declined. Roger Peake was wealthy, but not as wealthy as he'd been when Judith married him thirty years ago, largely because Judith was good at spending her husband's money. However, the main house was large and gracious. Even a duke might be a little impressed.

That afternoon, Violet sat in the parlor with Aunt Judith and Uncle Roger. She held a recent pamphlet on astronomy in her hands—comets were a particular interest—but she was unable to concentrate. Her mind was too busy considering all the possibilities of this potential suitor. If Judith was telling the truth, then he must be serious enough about a match to come to Hawebeck Place and meet Violet in person.

But then why had Judith kept the plan secret till the last minute? Perhaps she thought Violet would object. Or was there something wrong with him? Why choose Violet out of the blue? She was not popular. She had one Season among society, which garnered no proposals, and certainly Violet was not known for her wit. Yes, she was considered fair. But she froze up when asked to speak in front of more than a few people, and it was worse with strangers in the room. Nor was her dowry impressive. No, not even Violet would have chosen Violet for a duchess. So why did this man?

She glanced over at Judith suspiciously. Her aunt had a predilection for fortune telling. Was it possible a coincidence of birthdates or names or something more absurd—

like favorite fruits—could have started this mess? What if Judith pressed the issue and made a fool of herself and the family by claiming that Fate decreed the match? Violet shivered. She despised such nonsense, and she hoped the real story was more mundane. If she got up the nerve, she'd ask the duke...assuming he ever arrived.

Uncle Roger was moving nervously about the room. He'd sit for a moment, then get up, then move to the window, then to the fireplace. Then he'd sit again. To Violet's sharp eyes, he looked as though he very much wanted a drink. It was not a difficult guess. Roger Peake found solace in a wine bottle far more frequently than anywhere else.

For her part, Judith embroidered with stoic resolve, and the clock ticked onward. She sat tall and straight in the chair. She wasn't a beauty, but she was a woman people listened to, especially when she chose to use her charm.

"Of course a duke keeps his own schedule," Judith muttered then, after looking at the clock. She'd made a similar statement every quarter hour.

Violet considered ringing for more coffee, but then looked down at her already trembling hands and thought better of it. Too much coffee made her quite odd. And though she knew nothing of this Duke of Dunmere, she knew a marriage was her best chance to escape her aunt's home. Could she endure much longer with Judith sniping at her and making her feel like a failure every day, in a dozen little ways? Violet had to find a better place.

Then a footman entered. "The Honorable Herbert Kenyon," he announced.

Roger rose immediately, and Judith did too, out of sheer eagerness. Everyone expected the name to be followed by another, more illustrious name, but it wasn't, and only one man entered the room.

He was an older man, dressed simply but well, and everything about his appearance suggested wealth.

"Mr Peake," the gentleman said. "Mrs Peake."

He then bowed in a courtly fashion. "And, of course, Lady Violet," the man greeted her. "I am here on the behalf of my nephew, Alexander Kenyon, Duke of Dunmere. He regrets very much that he could not come in person. At the last moment, he was unavoidably detained."

Judith reacted in her typically dramatic way. "Oh, that is most unfortunate! We have been so looking forward to meeting his grace."

Indeed, the best tea had been prepared, with especially expensive food purchased for the dinner Judith hoped the duke would remain for. This might be an expensive misfire, Violet thought.

Kenyon gave a little shrug. "Alas, events did not fall out as planned. His presence was demanded in London."

"Well, a duke must have many demands on his time," Judith said, more smoothly now that she recovered from her first shock. She gave a significant look to Violet, who understood she was now to perform.

"My aunt has informed me that you have spoken to my uncle and guardian," she said, not mentioning she was informed only hours ago. "So it is the case that Dunmere has offered for me?"

"Yes, my lady," said Kenyon, "after great consideration."

"Forgive my confusion, sir, but I do not see precisely what consideration was taken. I have never met the duke," Violet said, fearing even this statement would be too bold.

"Violet," Judith said, in a tone that was nearly a hiss.

Kenyon, however, only smiled sadly. "Not romantic, I admit. A proposal by proxy is surely not what young ladies dream of. But the duke is an honorable gentleman and I assure you he has the means to give you a comfortable life." The last part of his phrase had to be a vast understatement. Only a fortune could have made Judith's eyes light up the way they had.

He went on, "The duke did wish to learn more about you, my lady, which is why I am here. Of course, I can also answer what questions you may have."

Violet looked at the older man, who seemed sincere. "I would appreciate that, Mr Kenyon."

After being seated and offered tea and cakes, Kenyon asked her, "Where to begin, my lady? Let us start with something simple. What are your pastimes?"

Violet opened her mouth, intending to explain about her interest in astronomy, when Judith interrupted.

"She is a great reader, Mr Kenyon. Her adorable nose is nearly always in a book."

"Novels?" he asked, with interest. "Radcliffe, perhaps?"

"Certainly not," Judith said with a slightly nervous laugh. "If you're asking if I would permit her to read that horrid stuff, I assure you dear Violet is not so frivolous."

"I asked merely because I saw a few of her titles on the shelf over there, including the last one—*The Italian*?" Kenyon said mildly.

Judith made a half turn in her seat, spied the offending books, and turned back to him with wide eyes. "My goodness. I haven't the slightest idea how those got there. I shall have them disposed of immediately."

"Seems a shame. I quite liked *The Italian*."

Violet hid her smile before Aunt Judith could see it. But Mr Kenyon did, and she caught a tiny answering smile.

Judith recovered quickly enough, and praised Violet's many accomplishments, which was a shock to hear. She didn't exactly lie, Violet had to admit, but she embellished.

"And I do not need to point out that our dear Violet is as lovely as a spring day," Judith was saying. "She takes after her mother."

Her aunt gestured to a portrait to the left of the fireplace. It was of Violet's mother just after her marriage, and the artist did a fine job in capturing the subject's vitality. The soft brown hair was artfully curled and coiffed in the style of the time, but the glow in the woman's cheeks was rich and natural. High cheekbones and a slender nose did much to convey an aristocratic air. Only the mouth, with the pink lips and the slight curl on the side, just short of a smile, hinted she was someone who laughed easily and often. Violet remembered that laugh from very long ago.

Kenyon rose to examine it more closely. "Ah, I think I can see the resemblance." He turned to Violet. "Would you humor an old man, and pose next to the portrait? My eyes are not what they once were."

If so, he must have once possessed the eyes of an eagle. Violet didn't think he missed a thing the whole visit.

Violet joined him at the portrait, and let him compare the image and herself.

"You're older now than she was when this was painted," Kenyon said. "But I imagine you were the mirror image. But no, your mother had blue eyes. You must have your father's eyes."

Violet smiled. "Yes, sir, I do. As well as his interests, which he shared with me through my childhood."

"You must miss them very much," he said softly, looking keenly at her, "for your own eyes to be so glassy now."

Judith joined them, afraid to leave the conversation to Violet. "Can I offer you more tea, Mr Kenyon?"

"No," he said. "But I would like speak to Lady Violet for a few moments. Perhaps a brief turn around the garden. Alone."

Judith's thoughts were plain. She wanted to hear everything, yet she didn't dare annoy the man, who could easily quash all her careful maneuvering. "Why, certainly. If Violet is not too tired."

Violet said, "I would be glad to, Mr Kenyon."

Coats and hats were fetched, and soon they were in the gardens. Although the winter day was brisk, it wasn't too cold, and the fresh air was a pleasure.

When they were out of earshot of Judith, Kenyon said, still in that mild voice, "Avoiding her conversation is reason enough to accept any proposal."

Violet wholeheartedly agreed, but she couldn't let him insult her family, no matter how correct he was. "I am grateful that my aunt and uncle have taken me in," she said. "If not for them, my situation would likely be far less comfortable than it is now."

He nodded. "They should be grateful to have such a well-spoken young lady in their home."

"Was there something in particular you wished to discuss, Mr Kenyon? Something you felt my aunt would not be qualified to answer?"

He gave her a brief smile. "It was evident to me that

you were not aware at all of the arrangements made by your aunt." He did away with the fiction that Uncle Roger was in any way involved.

"No," she said. "Of course, she has been attempting to arrange my marriage for some time, and with particular zeal since the death of my cousin, Madeline Peake. I was her companion while she was ill, you see. I fully expected news of a match at some point. Though…" she stopped.

"You also expected to meet the gentleman in person first."

"Yes," she admitted.

"I thought so. So I must ask candidly: do you wish to marry the duke? He would hate to think you were forced into it. And he would not be insulted if you were to tell me now, in confidence, that you have doubts." He saw her expression and hurried on, "Don't have any fear about your aunt. I would certainly devise a story which leaves you innocent of her wrath."

"Before I can reply to that," said Violet. "I wonder if I might ask a few questions about the duke, since he could not be here himself?"

"Please do, but," here he raised a hand to forestall her, "let me answer your first question before you ask it. All the Kenyon men are incredibly handsome, as my own appearance proves!"

Violet laughed at that, and thought Herbert Kenyon must have been quite dashing in his youth.

"I thank you for the information, sir. But looks are a poor measure of suitability, and I should not like to base a decision on something so fleeting."

"Wise words, my lady," Kenyon said, more soberly.

Violet paused, collecting her thoughts. She knew so little of the duke, it was hard to know where to begin.

"He lives close to London?"

"Yes. It's a beautiful estate in Kent, well cared for and quite sufficient to support the duke and his family. The house, Dunmere Abbey, is quite impressive."

"And how…old is he?" she asked timidly.

"Thirty-four."

"Thirty-four," she repeated. "May I ask why he has not married before now?"

Kenyon frowned for a split second. "Your family has not told you about the situation at all?"

"Situation? No."

"He has married before," Kenyon said, after a slight hesitation. "He is a widower."

"Does he have a child?"

"No. He does have charge of a ward. Millicent Sherwood is a second cousin, and sixteen years old. But he has no children of his own."

Violet nodded. So Dunmere needed an heir. And Violet had sufficient pedigree to qualify as a suitable wife, though… "Are you certain he does not consider me too old?" she asked.

"He views the prospect of a nineteen year old wife with horror," Mr Kenyon said. "He values competence and good moral character above a pretty face."

"Ah."

"Though, if I may flatter you for a moment, Lady Violet, your face is prettier than the miniature portrait conveyed."

Violet looked down, unused to flattery of any sort. "If your nephew is half so kind as you, I should expect to be quite content. Can you tell me something of his character…his personality, that is?"

"I can tell you I am proud of him," Kenyon began.

"He is, of course, very conscious of his lineage and his name. He assumed the title just over five years ago on his father's death. Before that he was Earl of Waring. He has always been most proper in his dealings with people. Though he traveled abroad very frequently until last year or so, he pays attention to his favorite home—that's the Abbey—and has improved it considerably. Not that it was in poor condition before, but he's a careful steward."

Violet said, "Why did he travel so much? Does he have interests abroad? Uncle Roger spent some of his youth in Antigua, on his family's sugar plantation there."

"Well, his grace does not own land in the new world. His travels mostly took him to Europe, and I am not privy to his reasons. I do know that he was always happy to come home."

"It sounds as if he has all he needs."

"Except a wife to share it with," Kenyon countered. "Owning half the earth would get quite dull if one had to roam it alone."

"I see." Violet wasn't sure she did understand, but she thought that she might begin to. The duke actually sounded rather lonely.

"He is a good man," Kenyon said in conclusion. "And he would treat you honorably, I assure you."

She took a deep breath, considering. Accepting a proposal sight unseen might be mad…but it also might be the best decision she could make to improve her life. "Then I agree to the proposal," Violet said. "I hope I will not disappoint him."

Kenyon told her she had nothing to fear. In fact, he said those very words in such a way that Violet wondered—too late—if there *was* something to fear. Yet how could she ask such a question immediately after agreeing to a marriage?

"I expect to meet the duke before the wedding," she said quickly.

"Naturally! He would not neglect such an important step. It is merely an inconvenience that called him away."

They walked back to the house. At hearing of the successful agreement, Judith was all smiles, and practically doted on Mr Kenyon. Uncle Roger, who looked as if he'd a few glasses of wine while they were out, also added his slightly slurred congratulations.

Kenyon took his leave, again bowing to Violet. Judith could barely wait till the door closed to sigh in relief.

"Ah, that's done. The words are spoken, and we may as well start packing your trunks, Violet," her aunt said. "You performed better than I hoped, I do say. Look at you! Soon to be the wife of the Duke of Dunmere. And I'm told he's a very striking man, despite his injury."

"Injury?" Violet asked, puzzled.

"Lost his eye. He wears a patch now. Not that it will matter in the dark," her aunt added crudely.

Violet winced. She had only the slightest notion what Judith's words actually meant, but the whole tone made her shiver. The eye must have been what Mr Kenyon was referring to when he asked if she knew about the *situation*. Well, she had been honest. Looks mattered little to her. All she wanted was a life far from this house. Whoever this duke was, and no matter why he was so odd in his method of courtship, he was her path out.

* * * *

That evening, the Peakes enjoyed the special supper intended for the duke. It was recast by Judith as a celebratory family meal—mainly celebrating her own success as a matchmaker and businesswoman.

"All my hard work and faith rewarded," she said ecstatically. "Nearly everything occurred just as he said. Oh, I knew it. Once you see the path laid before you, all that remains is to walk down it."

"Who said?" Violet asked.

Judith glanced at her husband, who was well into a rather full glass of brandy. Then she said, "Just one of my good friends in London, you know. Mr Hanchett always gives me the very best advice."

"He's one of your little club," Violet concluded. Judith had long chased fads relating to the occult, and she was forever trying out new ways to divine the future or the past or other people's purses. Violet went on, "What was it this time? Cards? Divination by smoke? Did someone see me married to the duke in dark water by midnight?"

"It is rude to mock another's interests," Judith said, "especially as those interests have helped secure your marriage. If you followed my friends, you would know quite a lot more about the world than you do."

"I am quite content to study the world I see through the lens of my telescope," Violet retorted. "Papa taught me how beautiful the night sky was all on its own. Must you always look for meaning beyond that? Isn't it enough to see the beauty of the world?"

"My little Violet." Judith took a gulp of wine from her own rather full glass. "*You* look, but you do not see. That's the difference between us!"

Not the only one, Violet thought. Aloud, she said, "Please excuse me."

She rose and made her way to her room. She positioned her telescope, put on a heavy robe, and opened the casement window. Cold air rushed in, but Violet didn't care. It was the only way to see properly through the instrument.

Someday she'd have a real observatory. Her father had one built at the old family home, long ago. Violet promised herself that she'd replicate it someday. She renewed that promise whenever she had to suffer in the cold for hours as she worked. Lovely summer nights were one thing, but it took true dedication to stargaze in winter. Yet the sky changed throughout the whole year, and she wanted to understand all of it. So she ignored the icy breeze, and the freezing cold metal of the telescope barrel. She only saw stars, and she talked to herself as she made notes about her study.

The winter sky was absolutely clear, with none of the haze that sometimes rose up in warmer, more humid weather. Now the stars shone steadily, barely winking as she gazed through her scope. The faint tinge of blues or reds marked each star she gazed at, making them as familiar as old friends. And there… She smiled as she set the viewfinder on the slightly blurry object she was looking for. Its smudged appearance wasn't the fault of the glass. Violet suspected it was the tail of a comet, just beginning to grow more visible as the object neared the sun.

"Please let the next few nights be clear," she whispered. She so wanted to find a comet of her own.

No matter what, she swore, she'd never give up her study of astronomy. This man she was newly betrothed to wouldn't know a thing about the night sky, and he probably wouldn't care. But he couldn't stop Violet from pursuing the one thing that made her happy.

Chapter 3

♋

ON THE WAY TO LONDON, Alex was considering the Zodiac.

Not the one in the sky, true, but the one hidden within the power structure of Britain, the one that sent signs all over the country and the world to bring back knowledge others wanted to hide.

Alex arrived at his townhouse in the city with almost no warning, but his household staff were of the highest quality, and they had everything in hand by the time his coach pulled up to the door.

"Your grace," the butler said with a little bow. "A pleasure to see you back in London. Will you be going out?"

Alex nodded. His time in London was defined by "going out." Sometimes that meant official functions or social duties, but it was just as often connected to more esoteric work he could tell no one about. "Almost immediately. I'm not sure if I'll be back for supper, so just tell Cook that some cold food left out will suffice."

"Yes, sir."

Not long after, Alex walked through the streets to the Whitby Club. It was a long walk, but he preferred to move at his own pace rather than be driven around in a carriage. He also didn't like people to connect him to the place too strongly. After all, when one dabbled in espionage, it made sense to be discreet.

In fact, Alex was more than a dabbler in espionage. He'd been a spy for over ten years, serving as one member of the group called the Zodiac. It was so clandestine that even most people in positions of government deeply concerned with espionage didn't know it existed. There were only twelve agents active at any time, each given a zodiac sign as a code name. Alex's was Cancer.

All the agents took orders from the Astronomer. Almost no one knew who the Astronomer actually was—orders came through Aries, the first sign, a post currently held by a man named Julian Neville. Alex had his theories about the Astronomer's identity, but he also understood that saying those theories out loud was a stupid thing to do.

The agents were selected by a rather unconventional method. Many came from the military, where they had proved themselves to their superiors or otherwise attracted the attention of the Zodiac by some extraordinary feat. But that was certainly not the only path. Alex himself was approached by a well-traveled peer who was quite familiar with politics, yet never took part in them. That man turned out to be Julian's predecessor. It wasn't long after Alex lost his first wife, when Alex was desperate for anything to distract him from the blow. He was deeply frustrated and angry at life, and the Zodiac managed to direct that ire toward a better goal: protecting Britain.

Alex had several qualities useful for espionage. First, he was well born. Commoners deferred to him, peers respected him, and foreign agents thought twice before tangling with him. Second, he was intelligent—Waltham said it was harder than one might think to find both qualities in the same man. Finally, Alex just saw things in a different way than other people did. When he looked at a scene, he noticed far more than what was there. He could guess—very accurately—what happened before, and he could predict what might happen next. After he joined the Zodiac, he became known for being the man to send into the most puzzling situations. Alex would find the missing pieces of the puzzle and see the truth.

For about a decade, Alex relished his role, especially as less and less tied him to his home and his family life. Meanwhile, he embarked on two more marriages, both of which ended with death. He'd certainly learned not to grow too attached to anyone.

But as an agent, where personal connections were a danger, he excelled. He saw other agents come and go, even saw the first sign change hands. Alex never stopped taking assignments.

Until one brought him a little too close to death. Alex must have grown careless. Or he miscalculated. But he ended up in a very dark place, far outnumbered, and with no one to call for aid. He did climb out, leaving several bodies behind. But he also left behind a lot of blood, his eye, and his confidence.

Alex took a long while to recover. He couldn't tell anyone other than the Zodiac what happened, of course. The story of being attacked by a gang while traveling in a city abroad worked just as well, though. No one really wanted to know how his eye was ripped out.

Though still a sign, he could no longer go on just any assignment. Alex's face was now quite distinctive. There were some situations where being a man in an eyepatch didn't seem out of place. The courts of Europe were *not* those places. So Alex accepted more and more tasks that relied solely on his deductive ability. He became, in short, an investigator who worked for spies. He took the assignments given to him and tracked down loose threads, potential scandals, secret embarrassments, and suspicious events.

Tonight he'd get another one. He arrived at the Whitby Club just as the winter sun was setting, and he was grateful to be inside again.

"Dunmere!" a voice called out as he entered the large room of the first floor. "Join me." It was Julian, and his invitation carried an undertone of command.

Alex strolled up to the other man. "Are we making time for small talk?" he asked in a low voice, wearing a smile he didn't feel.

"Do you even know how to make small talk anymore?" Julian asked, his eyebrow raised.

"Come to think of it, no." Alex said. "What happened?" Privately, he mulled over Julian's offhand comment. What did he mean by *anymore*?

But Julian was all business now. "I need you to get to work. There's been a murder."

"A murder," Alex repeated. "Who was the victim?"

"A James Galbraith. Have you heard the name?"

"No. Should I have?"

"Not necessarily. He was a politician, representing a local borough."

"When did the killing happen?"

"Last night," Julian said. "I sent for you as soon as I could. The whole thing is a mess, top to bottom."

"Were there witnesses?" Alex asked.

"None so far. We're working on it."

"I'll investigate myself," Alex said. "Give me the details you have of the victim and the location of death. I'll have a few questions for the local magistrate, as well." Alex watched Julian's expression, noticing the other man's clenched hand. "What else? This isn't something that would attract the attention of the Zodiac, unless there's more to it."

"There is more." Julian handed him a square of paper with two wavy parallel lines on it. "This was found near the body, drawn on the stone pathway—in blood."

Alex recognized it as a zodiac symbol, and felt an immediate chill. "Aquarius. Is this a message?" he wondered out loud. "Something about an old assignment? Something left behind, perhaps?" He imagined how dangerous it could be if some foreign agent started taunting the Zodiac in such a public way. Or if this man, a politician, discovered a secret he should not have. "This also might be a warning," he guessed. "But if it is, who sent it?"

"That is what we would dearly like to find out," Julian said. His tone was mild as ever, but Alex now understood the agitation underneath. "The local authorities have no idea of this line of questioning, of course. But we *need* to know if there's a connection. If there is, you are the only man with the knowledge—and, quite frankly, the social standing—to pursue it at the highest levels, should it come to that."

"And I will." Once Alex got his hooks into an assignment he didn't let go until it was completed. That dedication cost him an eye. "Tell me now if you know whether Galbraith was connected to any agent's work. I'd rather not start cold."

"If I knew, I'd tell you," Julian said. "There might be a link, but we haven't found one yet."

Alex tested the obvious idea out loud. "It could be a coincidence."

"It could be," said Julian. "But coincidences make me extremely suspicious."

"You're not alone. I'll get to work."

"Thank you for looking into this."

Alex waved Julian's comment away. The polite phrase was unnecessary. He was a sign, and Julian was the first sign. He gave the orders. Despite Alex's higher social rank, in the Zodiac, it was Aries who commanded.

"Let me or Miss Chattan know if you need anything. The Disreputables are available for small jobs," Julian added, referring to a group of once shady criminals who now often helped the Zodiac.

Alex stood up. "Until I get a better sense of what's going on, I wouldn't know what to ask for. I'll keep you informed."

"Where are you going?"

"The scene of the crime, naturally."

"Nothing's left. The local authorities cleaned everything up. After they mucked it all up, of course."

Alex gave a little smile. "There's always *something* to find."

* * * *

When Alex reached the scene of the murder, it was indeed scrubbed clean of its worst gore. The blood was gone, and the area was quiet. Alex looked around the street and the buildings nearby. He noted the entrance to the building where Galbraith had his offices. He had apparently been there later than usual.

He checked the few notes Julian provided him, and

soon found the spot where the body was discovered. Nothing marked it, but the space was suspiciously clear. No dirt, no leaves... "No blood," he said. If Galbraith was killed here, there would be a stain on the ground where the blood seeped in. But there was nothing. However, Alex did see the faint image of the astronomical symbol for Aquarius. Someone tried to scrub it away, but didn't get it all.

So Galbraith was dragged here, possibly after the symbol was created. Yes, that made sense. The killer left the body nearby but hidden till the space was ready. Then he dragged the body to the spot to be found. But *why*?

"You looking for somethin'?" a voice asked.

Alex glanced up, where an older woman stood watching him. Her clothes hung on her loosely, and her teeth and hair were a fright.

"This is where the body was found," he said.

"Sure enough," the woman said. "Saw the law come running once everyone started shrieking."

"You live around here? Did you know the man who was killed?"

"He didn't invite me up to tea, though he weren't a bad sort," the woman said with a cackle. "But I seen him more than once. Worked over there." She pointed to the building Alex noted earlier.

"You were here the night of the killing. See anyone else?"

"No one I'd remember."

Alex pulled out a coin. "Is your memory improving?"

She reached for it, but he closed his hand around it before she could take it.

She sighed. "I saw...someone. But it won't help you find the killer. Who you with?" she asked suddenly. "Why do you care?"

"You have questions for me?" Alex opened his hand again, just a little. "Answers cost money. Or you can provide the answer, and take the money."

She pursed her lips, whistling softly through her teeth, evidently a habit of hers. "I'll tell you what I saw. But you won't think it's much."

"Go on."

"It was after midnight, but the moon was so bright it might have been day. I was over on the bench," she said, jerking her head toward another building wall. "And I saw this man bending on the ground just here. It looked like he was scratching in the dirt. I thought he'd dropped something and was trying to find it in the dark. Well, I didn't worry too much about it. I was nodding off, to be truthful. But the next thing I knew, someone was screaming. I looked and the man was laying flat on the ground. I hurried up to look, and he was dead. More people were around by then. They could all see he'd been killed. Stabbed right in the heart, he was."

"What did he look like?"

"Older man. White hair, and no beard," she said. "Very tidy. Clothes all neat, except for the blood. And not a very big man. When I first saw him, bending over, I thought he was a big man, and younger. But when I got closer, he wasn't much taller than me."

"You say he had white hair. Did he have a hat?"

"Well, it had fallen off."

"So you saw it by him?"

She frowned. "No. Can't say I did."

"But he was wearing a hat when you first saw him... looking in the dirt? You'd have remarked on it if a gentleman was outdoors without a hat, particularly on a cold night."

"Oh, yes. He was wearing a black hat then."

"Black hat over white hair?"

She paused. "Now that you say it like that, I'm not sure his hair was white after all. It seemed much darker when he had the hat on."

Alex handed her the coin. "Thank you."

"I didn't tell you a thing you didn't already know."

"You certainly did. You told me the color of the killer's hat and hair."

"No, the dead man's hat," she corrected. "I only saw one man."

"You saw two men," Alex said. "You saw the killer, a dark-haired man with a hat on, as he painted in blood on the ground. Then you saw the older, white-haired victim, *after* the killer dragged his body out to be found."

"I saw the murderer?" She put a hand to her mouth.

"You did. Be grateful he didn't see you." Alex bid the older woman goodnight and continued on. He poked around the area, searching for where the body could have been hidden. In an alley, he discovered a dark, sticky patch that was almost certainly where James Galbraith lay breathing his last. Alex hoped it was quick.

Armed with this new information, Alex went directly to the offices of the Zodiac. Though it was nearly midnight now, he was certain he'd find someone there. The offices were tucked away in a handsome but bland structure in London, located nowhere near any government offices or seats of power. The Zodiac's goal was to be ignored completely, and it had succeeded so far. Alex negotiated the many twists and turns, the stairways that never seemed to end up where one expected, and the corridors of unmarked doors. It took determination and patience to find the Zodiac, even when someone knew where to look.

Alex knocked on one door and waited patiently. After a minute, he knocked again, fighting the urge to question his judgment. This *was* the right door, and someone *would* answer it.

Finally, someone did. A woman looked out at him with no trace of curiosity. "Ah, you'd better come in," she said.

Inside the office, she offered a warmer greeting. "Good evening, your grace. I thought you'd come by eventually."

"You're never surprised, Miss Chattan," he said. Indeed, Alex had never seen Miss Chattan act anything other than cool and efficient. The woman had worked alongside Aries since he became Aries, and she was likely why the Zodiac ran so smoothly. Her capabilities didn't seem to extend to her personal appearance, though. Though blessed with pretty eyes and thick ash blonde hair, she was always a little disheveled and never fashionable.

She indicated a chair near her desk. "Julian is not here just at the moment."

"No matter," said Alex. "I spoke to him earlier. It's your assistance I need."

Miss Chattan sat down and waited for him to do likewise. "Have you found something already?"

"I may have," Alex said cautiously. "The victim was moved. Which means that it wasn't a casual killing, but rather planned at least a bit ahead of time."

"Why do we know that?" Chattan asked, playing the devil's advocate. "Perhaps a mugger saw that he'd gone too far and killed when he only meant to knock him out. So he moved the body somewhere in a panic."

Alex shook his head. "There was nothing in the scene to indicate panic. The body was deliberately placed in a spot where it would be *found*. If the killer wanted to keep it hidden, he wouldn't have moved it from the spot where Galbraith died, which was hidden fairly well. And, of course, the murderer also took time to paint a symbol in blood next to the body. Casual killers don't do that."

"They don't. And they certainly don't use the symbol of Aquarius." She was worried about that in exactly the same way as Julian had been.

"Yes." Alex frowned. "So that's what I have to go on. I don't think this was isolated. It makes no sense. Why that victim? Why that time? Why that place? Why a zodiac symbol, unless it's a message for us?" Alex shifted in his chair. "Right now, all I have is a new question every minute."

"So what do you want me to find?" Chattan asked, dipping her pen in ink.

"My first thought was that perhaps this wasn't the first murder. Try to find any mentions of past deaths with similar aspects. Same type of victim, meaning male, and that station or position in government." He shook his head slowly, thinking. "I'll use my connections to find out if Galbraith's home or offices actually were broken into lately. And if anything was taken."

"Anything else?" she asked.

"No, but while you're looking, see if there are any other deaths where something was painted in blood—anything, mind," Alex said. "Not just a symbol. And don't assume the death will be called a murder. Perhaps some magistrate wrote up a report and called it an accident, just to avoid the work of reporting and dealing with a crime. Find out if there's been any gossip surrounding symbols written in blood over the past few months."

Chattan nodded as she wrote. "I'll send word as soon as I have something. You're staying in town?"

"For a few days at least. I can't make any more guesses until I have more facts. But even if this hasn't happened before, I think it will happen again."

"Why?"

"There are twelve signs in the zodiac. What if our killer is hoping to use them all?"

Chattan shivered. "Well, with luck, you'll get to him before he has the chance. It's lucky you're available," she added. Chattan had actually been the one to convince him to stay on as a sign after his injury. *Even with one eye, you'll still see more than most*, she'd said. *We need you.*

"Yes, I'll keep working at it," he said. "I likely have a wedding to attend soon, but that will only occupy a day or so."

"At least that will be a more pleasant event. Who is getting married?"

"I am," he said.

"Oh. And who is the bride?" Chattan did not say *this time*. She let an eloquent pause say it for her.

"I believe her name is Lady Violet Holloway."

"So you haven't met her," Chattan surmised.

"Not yet."

"You will take the time to meet your bride before you see her in the church, won't you?" Chattan asked. "A lady likes a mysterious gentleman, but there's a limit."

"I'll consider your advice."

"Do that, your grace."

Alex did intend to follow Chattan's advice…after he learned all he could about James Galbraith's life and death, which took a few days of intensive work.

Though personally rather wealthy, James Galbraith was a politician who represented some of the poorer parishes in London. By all accounts, he was something of a reformer. He took the side of the exploited and the weak over and over. He railed against landlords who charged high rents for housing in the slums, and he advocated for better treatment of the insane and indigent. His death shocked those Alex spoke to, but only a few suggested it might be motivated by his politics. Most people thought he was the victim of a random, violent drunk...or someone who ought to be put away in Newgate.

"Galbraith was never shy about walking the streets of his parish," said one man who knew him. "Even at night. Perhaps he should have been."

As Alex put together all he learned of Galbraith, the killer remained a shadow. The old lady he talked to at first was the only one who seemed to have noticed anything. No one else saw any figure who might match the description of the killer. And what was Alex to do with what he had? A strong, rather young man who wore a black hat and dark clothes? That description fit half of the men in the city.

He went out every day in an attempt to scare up some detail or clue left behind, though memories were fading fast already. But Alex didn't give up.

However, one afternoon, Alex received a letter from Herbert. His uncle reported that the Lady Violet seemed entirely suitable and possessed of a quiet charm. She had agreed to the match, so Herbert declared his mission—the mission Alex had dropped on him—completed. *I await your instructions*, the letter ended. It was a not so subtle reminder that Alex was the only person who could actually conclude this business. Herbert worked very hard to find a suitable bride this time, and he succeeded in spite of Alex's lack of enthusiasm. Now Alex had to accept the reins and actually marry her.

"Quiet charm," Alex said to himself. What did that mean, exactly? Then Chattan's tart advice came back to him. If he wanted to find out, he only had to meet the lady. How difficult could that be?

* * * *

Alex returned from London very late, so he didn't have the chance to speak to Herbert until the next day at breakfast.

Also at the table was his ward, Millicent Sherwood. She was sixteen, and just emerging from the awkward transition of child to adult. Her frame was still decidedly slender, but no longer girlish. Alex suspected that was one of the reasons Millie had taken to wearing black for the past few years—people noticed the unusual color of her gowns, rather than the figure underneath. He was perfectly content for that to be the case, and never objected to her sartorial quirk. Alex dreaded the idea of suitors courting Millie. He still saw her as a precocious and talkative child. He didn't want to think of her being courted and married, and having children of her own, as she inevitably would.

Someday, Millie would have her pick of suitors. She had a compelling sort of beauty, bright hazel eyes, and a tongue that was often quicker than her better sense. When she did stop to think, she had a clever mind, always keen to learn. At present, she was rather obsessed with poetry and the theater, and was always pestering Alex to bring her the latest plays and new poetry collections from London.

But all that was not at the top of Alex's mind today. He pushed his plate away and focused on Herbert, ready to discuss the results of the older man's visit. "Well?" he asked. "I read your letter, but I'd like a bit more insight. What did you conclude?"

Herbert waved an impatient hand. "What else can I tell you other than what I wrote? I met the lady, I spoke with her privately, and she assured me she agrees to the marriage."

"Of course she would," Millie broke in. "Who turns away a chance to be duchess?" No one told Millie of the situation, but that hadn't stopped her from gleaning nearly all the details about it.

Herbert looked at Millie disapprovingly. "I can discern the difference between a social climber and a sincere agreement."

"Good thing Alex sent you, then," Millie countered.

"Enough, Millie," Alex said. He turned to Herbert. "Go on. What did you think of her? Be honest."

"Honestly? She is a very quiet woman. Obviously of good breeding and morals, despite a less than congenial atmosphere in the home. The aunt is rather overbearing. She, however, was the soul of politeness, and very pretty in the bargain. I think she'll be quite suitable."

Alex nodded curtly. "Then set a date with the Peakes. As early as possible. By the end of the month. We will be married here at the Abbey, with only close relatives invited. We'll have a dinner for the family afterward."

"By the end of the month? Surely, this event calls for more preparation…" Herbert trailed off when he saw Alex's face.

"I have had quite enough of extravagant weddings. It

will be here, with only our families, or it will not take place. I have other things to worry about, and the faster this is finalized, the better for all concerned."

"Of course." Herbert swallowed. "The Peakes will understand."

Alex didn't give a damn if the Peakes understood or not.

"Are you sure you do not want to invite anyone else?" Herbert ventured. "It's expected, and some people will be put out. Your mother—"

"—is in Bath, and quite happy to remain there," Alex said. "She hates to travel. The news alone should be sufficient to entertain her. Those other people have seen me wed three times before. They won't object to missing the fourth."

Millie laughed. "The fourth for *you*, Alex. But the first for this Lady Violet. Oh, well. I suppose gaining the title of duchess will offset the disappointment of the ceremony itself!"

"I'm not particularly concerned about that," he said.

Mille laughed again. "On that point, Alex, no one is confused. You're not concerned with the lady at all."

He was offended for a moment, until he remembered that he'd done precisely nothing to oppose that notion.

Alex knew he should meet with his new bride, but he suddenly found a thousand other items to put his attention to. The matter of the murder was obviously more important than Alex's personal life—even though there was little new information coming to him, and certainly not enough to warrant his complete attention.

He did send a few letters immediately. One he wrote to Lady Violet. That was an excruciating exercise. He wasted many pieces of paper before he produced a missive that didn't sound completely incoherent or glacially cold or absurdly familiar. What does one say to a total stranger? The final letter was only a page. He expressed an apology that he hadn't met her already, mentioned that he intended to visit her next week, and hoped that she'd be happy at Dunmere Abbey.

He sealed the letter, feeling that it was a poor effort. But it *had* taken most of the morning.

The second letter was far easier to write. He addressed it to Judith Peake and merely asked what day next week would be best to journey to Hawebeck Place.

Finally, he wrote to Chattan, asking why no new information on the murder had been sent.

The days slipped by as he waited for replies.

Chattan's arrived first. It was one line: *Marriage has also been called an excellent mystery.* He sighed in frustration. The message was clear to him. Chattan was hoarding whatever information she found until she decided he should hear it, undistracted by personal matters.

Judith Peake wrote back, filled with regrets. The Peakes would be entirely occupied with preparing for the wedding and marriage. There were people to visit, items to be purchased, and so much to pack. But she was certain that Lady Violet would become well known to him via her letters before their arrival at the Abbey. Lady Violet, she added, was a charming correspondent.

But no letters from Lady Violet arrived, charming or otherwise. He wrote once more to her, but that letter went unanswered, too.

And then the date of the wedding arrived.

Chapter 4

♋

ON A COLD, DRIZZLY DAY at the very end of February, Violet and her guardians arrived at Dunmere Abbey. They should have been there yesterday, but Judith had one minor crisis after another, causing them to delay their departure from Hawebeck Place, and then to waste time along the road, even to the point of staying one more night at an inn than originally expected.

It was maddening, and uncharacteristic of Judith. Was the woman trying to delay them? At least Judith had the sense to pay for a boy to ride ahead, so the duke would know what was happening.

"Don't worry, Violet," Judith said. "We'll get there just in time for the wedding. You won't miss a thing."

Except meeting my husband beforehand, Violet wanted to snap. The man hadn't even bothered to write to her, or answer her own letters, which Violet spent considerable time on, in an effort to introduce herself via her words.

All she got in return was an icy silence.

But what was to be done? She was bound by her promise.

At last they arrived. Judith pressed her face to the

rain-spotted glass in an effort to see every inch of the estate. Violet sat back on her seat, watching the few glimpses slide by through the other window. She was not nearly as excited as Judith to see her new home, since her stomach was tied up in knots at the idea of first seeing her new husband. Everything was happening far faster than she had expected.

"Oh, there is the Abbey itself," said Judith. "How positively elegant!"

"Half a ruin, I'm sure," her uncle guessed. "These old places always are."

"Oh, shush, Roger. The duke is a wealthy man. He understands the need to keep up appearances."

Violet peeked toward the house. That was a lot of appearance to keep up, she thought. The main house was four stories tall, and multiple wings spread out over the grounds. The countless windows gleamed, even in the dull cloudy day. Beyond the house, she could just see a lake, the surface as grey as the sky. At the far edge of the lake, a strange outline caught her eye. It looked like a ruined tower. The top was ragged, but it was still quite tall. If it was stable, she could set up her telescope there, away from any possible light.

Then the carriage pulled up to the house, followed by a second vehicle that held only trunks and crates—all of Violet's possessions. An army of footmen immediately went to work unloading it, hurrying to get the items out of the rain. Violet looked over anxiously.

"Be careful of that red wood case!" she called.

A footman looked over at her, the case in his hands. "This one, my lady?"

"Yes. It's fragile." She hated to think of someone dropping it, but she couldn't offer to carry it. Soon-to-be duchesses did not carry their own luggage. "Just be mindful of it. Have it sent to my room."

"Yes, my lady!" He bobbed his head.

"Come along, Violet." Judith grabbed her arm. "Fussing over luggage when you're about to be married. People will think you're touched in the head."

Violet turned to see Herbert Kenyon walking toward them. "Welcome!" he called out, smiling in particular at Violet. "We are so glad you have arrived at last."

"We were lucky to make it today," Judith said. "Though travel by coach is horrendous in the best of conditions."

"Good day," Violet said quietly. She looked past him, wondering why the duke wasn't even there to greet them at the door.

"Come in, come in!" Kenyon said, with somewhat forced cheer. "You must want to refresh yourselves after the journey."

The inside of the house was opulent by any standards. Violet quailed at the notion of becoming the chatelaine of such a place, but Judith made a satisfied little cooing sound in her throat. "How charming," she said.

A woman in a grey gown curtseyed to Violet. "Good day, my lady. I am Mrs Simpson, the housekeeper. Let me show you all to rooms where you can rest and change for the ceremony. A longer tour will have to wait, as will the introductions of the rest of the staff to the new duchess."

Mrs Simpson did not waste time, but led them up a massive marble staircase at the end of the foyer, and into a newer wing of the house. She first showed the Peakes to a large room and left them in the care of a maid who'd been tailing behind.

Violet kept on as Mrs Simpson advanced down the

hall, turned a corner, and kept going all the way to the end. Along the way, they passed portraits and landscapes hung on the walls, and seemingly innumerable little tables holding statues or vases of flowers or other objects of curiosity. The duke certainly did not lack for wealth.

At last, the housekeeper paused.

"These will be your rooms," she said, opening the door. "We call it the blue suite."

"Rooms?" Violet questioned the plural, but as soon as she saw the space, her mouth dropped open in astonishment. Even though the day was grey and rainy, light illuminated the blue silk wall hangings and the oriental carpets laid out everywhere. The bedroom was larger than half her uncle's house, it seemed, and that was besides the other rooms leading off from it. But the most amazing part of the room was the vast set of windows that took up almost one whole wall.

"That view looks out onto the main lawns," the housekeeper said. "You can see as far as the lake."

"It's beautiful."

"There is also a study off this room," Mrs Simpson went on. "And here is a dressing room and wardrobe. Conveniences through here. A closet for additional items out of season."

Violet saw another door opposite the wall with the massive window. "Where does that one go?"

"That connects to the master's suite," Mrs Simpson said.

"Ah." Violet swallowed, not quite prepared to think of the ramifications of that yet.

Then Dalby walked in, followed by a few of the footmen, who were all bearing various trunks. She directed them about, while Violet stood there feeling useless. Apparently, duchesses did not do anything for themselves.

The servant holding her red wood case approached her. "Ma'am? Where would you like this?"

"Over by those windows," Violet said, pointing.

He put it down with obvious care and then bowed to Violet before leaving. At least the servant took her instructions seriously, she thought. That was something.

Judith appeared in Violet's suite not long after, rubbing her hands together. "Well, let's prepare the bride, shall we? Lady Violet needs her wedding gown, Dalby."

"I know where it is, ma'am," said Dalby, as she unlocked a trunk.

Over the next quarter hour, Judith ordered the girl around, directing her to press the gown, and find the matching slippers and petticoats. Violet stood at the window, but turned when Judith snapped at Dalby for dropping a slipper.

"Dalby knows her duties, Aunt," she said. "Why don't you go to your own room to freshen up before the ceremony?"

Judith sniffed as she left, complaining of Violet's ingratitude for her careful oversight.

Dalby watched her go, then shrugged and continued her work. Even the maid found Judith's behavior appalling, Violet thought. "She's concerned that the ceremony goes well," Violet said out loud.

"She's concerned that it goes at all," Dalby muttered, in a low enough tone that Violet could pretend she didn't hear.

Luckily, Violet's gown had fared well in the trunk. Dalby checked it carefully, but there were no rips or stains. "Good," the maid said. "I worried the rain would leak in."

If it had, the dirty water would have destroyed the lovely white fabric. Dalby draped Violet in the simple, flowing gown. She tied a wide silk ribbon at the high waist, and let the tails of the ribbon trail down the back of the skirt to Violet's feet. The dress had delicate little sleeves, and Dalby handed Violet the long white gloves to cover her arms to nearly where the sleeves began. A strand of modest pearls completed the look.

Dalby was just arranging her hair when a knock came at the door.

As soon as Violet called for whoever it was to come in, a slender, dark-haired girl entered. She was dressed in black, which Violet felt boded ill for the day. Her pale skin and high forehead did much to lighten her appearance, as did her eyes, which were hazel and mischievous. She appeared to be about sixteen. She must be the ward Mr Kenyon talked about.

"I'm Millicent Sherwood, my lady," she introduced herself. "But call me Millie. Everyone does. I'm his grace's cousin. Did he mention me?"

"Mr Kenyon did. I'm afraid that his grace and I have not yet met."

"Yes, but not even in his letters?" the younger girl pressed.

Violet's expression must have revealed that she received none.

Millie rolled her eyes. "He swore he wrote. Oh well, it's too late now. Are you ready? Do you need anything?"

Violet thought about asking for a few years, or a fast horse, but the words died in her throat when she realized that this wedding was real, and she had no time left. She shook her head mutely at the younger girl.

Dalby gave Violet a quick kiss on the cheek. "Off you

go, my lady! When I see you again, I'll have to call you your grace!" She beamed at Violet and sent her on her way.

Millicent walked her to the chapel, which was in a much older wing of the vast house.

"Are you nervous?" she was asking, her eyes locked on Violet as though she were an exotic creature of some type. "You don't look scared. You're obviously too smart to heed the rumors."

Violet shook her head. "The eye? I was told. I certainly don't think that a significant issue."

"Not the eye. The *rumors*."

"What rumors?" Violet asked, puzzled.

Millicent stopped short, staring at her. "You don't know?"

"What should I know?" Violet asked, her nervousness growing into real fear.

"No one told you?" Millie went on, her voice growing disbelieving. "Not Uncle Herbert, or your family, or *anyone*?"

"Told me what?" Violet demanded.

"Oh, there's no time. The ceremony will be starting soon. You must come now."

"Told me what?" Violet repeated to the now moving Millicent. She hurried to keep up.

Millie grabbed her arm, saying, "There were some rumors going round about the duke. They scared some ladies away. Alex will explain everything, I'm sure." Millie's reassurance only had the effect of frightening Violet further.

They reached the old chapel of the abbey, an ancient space of cold stone with somber light spilling in from the stained glass windows. Violet took a quick glimpse in.

Candelabra were lit throughout the church, but the light did not seem to penetrate the gloom. There was only a small gathering of guests in the front pews. The rest of the rows were empty. Not the high society wedding gathering she would have expected of a duke.

Uncle Roger stood at the door, waiting to lead her down the aisle to give her away. Violet thought wryly that it was good he was there, since she'd be too paralyzed to walk down the aisle by herself.

"Come on," he muttered worriedly as Millie handed her off. "Your aunt doesn't want the slightest misstep—"

"Give me a minute to take my seat!" Millie ordered.

Violet was passed from Millie to Roger. She wanted to ask him if he knew about those rumors, but she could barely speak now, she was so nervous. Her throat was tight and dry. She would have paid in gold for something cool to drink—and even more to escape this contract.

But it was too late. "The march is starting!" Uncle Roger said.

Music from a violin and flute began the traditional air. She walked in time to the music, feeling her uncle pull at her elbow. He was certainly eager to get the ceremony concluded, to get her safely married off.

Then Violet caught her first clear glimpse of the Duke of Dunmere, standing at the head of the aisle. She inhaled, now even more confused. Why would *he* have trouble finding a bride? To say he was handsome didn't do him justice. He was more impressive than everyone else there, looking as if he was perfectly cut from stone. Dark hair, only hinting at grey, crowned his head. And yes, he wore a patch over one eye, but that did little to take away from his presence. It actually made him more arresting. A single, dark eye surveyed her as she approached, but she could read no expression in that otherwise perfectly formed face.

He descended one step when they reached the end of the aisle—like a god descending from Olympus, she thought. He took her hand, and if he noticed it was trembling, he said nothing. The couple ascended the step to the altar and faced the priest.

Violet tried to focus on the ceremony, but she was too intensely aware of the man beside her. He looked so cool and above everything, but she could sense the heat of him, almost searing her. She didn't know why he should be so warm, or was she imagining things? She began to feel light-headed.

Don't faint, she told herself. Whatever you do, don't swoon.

The ceremony proceeded quickly, without a long sermon on the virtues of marriage. This was a business arrangement, she realized anew. She was being sold.

The duke repeated the words he was prompted to say, without inflection. She glanced at him, wondering if he even thought about the vows he'd just made.

Then the priest prompted her to say the same words. She did so in a tiny voice, so softly she doubted the guests could hear her.

They were pronounced man and wife. The priest did not suggest that the duke should kiss her, nor did he appear to want to. The duke took her by the arm and presented her to the guests in the pews. They descended and began to accept the congratulations of the families.

She was married, Violet repeated to herself over and over. But she didn't have the slightest idea to whom.

Several guests surrounded her, separating her from her new husband, who was walking toward Millicent.

48 ❧ *Elizabeth Cole*

Violet tried to keep the new names and faces straight. Out of the corner of her eye, she saw Millicent talking with the duke in a low and urgent manner, though she could hear nothing of the conversation. The duke certainly didn't look pleased.

Then another guest besieged her, and Violet lost track of the duke.

"Gwendolyn Kenyon. I'm so glad to meet you, my dear. I knew that his grace would find a young lady who wouldn't listen to all those nasty things the gossips say."

"Of course not," Violet murmured encouragingly. At last, someone to tell her what Herbert and Millie had only hinted at, if Violet played her hand carefully. The woman would only tell her if she thought she already knew. "People are so silly, don't you think?"

"Silly is the very word. The Duke of Death, indeed! That's what the ton ladies were calling him, and no wonder they frightened their daughters. He's had bad luck in brides, that's all. It could happen to anyone."

"Henry the Eighth, for example," Violet said before she could stop herself. Inside, she was reeling. The ton called her husband *what*?

"Exactly!" Gwendolyn said. Then she frowned. "Wait, that's not the same at all! Henry wasn't cursed. He just chose to do all those horrible things, even if he was a king."

"And he had six wives, after all. Hardly the same situation," Violet said, hoping the hysteria beginning to creep over her wasn't obvious to anyone watching.

"And Dunmere has only had three, so there. Until you, of course."

Violet couldn't even answer at this point. She was the fourth wife of this man! And no one thought to tell her?

But her rational mind came back with a sharp rejoinder. She should have asked more questions. She was so desperate to escape her uncle and aunt's house that she didn't stop to wonder why a man would accept her for a bride. It figured that only someone called the Duke of Death would find a shrinking violet acceptable.

"Are you all right, my dear?" Gwendolyn asked. "You look a bit pale."

"Some punch, perhaps. I'm a bit parched," Violet said quickly. "It has been quite a day."

Her luck was going from bad to worse. She escaped the house where she'd been living miserably, but only by marrying someone feared by everyone else. Other guests glanced at her as if she were going to drop dead right there.

She sought out Aunt Judith, who looked like a cat with a fresh kill after the successful conclusion of the wedding.

"Congratulations, my dear," Judith said. "You are Her Grace, Lady Alexander, the Duchess of Dunmere now. How does it feel to be a bride?"

"I should congratulate you, Aunt," Violet returned, her throat dry. "You did an excellent job of keeping me in the dark about the details of my new husband. It is not surprising that a man who suffers with the title Duke of Death would have a tiny bit of difficulty in finding a fourth wife."

"All occurs as the stars intend, *your grace*," said Judith airily. "It was a lucrative enough arrangement to be well worth the difficulties I went to to preserve your, ah, open mindedness."

"You mean ignorance," Violet said. "And what could be lucrative? My dowry is modest at best."

"Yes, but it will help keep Hawebeck Place warm for

the next few winters."

"The duke is allowing *you* to keep my dowry?" Violet asked.

"Oh, yes. And a small, er, gift in addition. He needs a suitable wife more than cash. Money doesn't buy a name or a lineage."

"It did in this case," Violet said. Had she truly been purchased so baldly? What sort of man needed to do that?

Chapter 5

♋

ALEX LET VIOLET WALK IN front of him after the ceremony. No one cared about anything but the bride at this moment...as he knew very well. Guests surrounded the new Lady Alexander, the new duchess of Dunmere, his new wife. She accepted most of the best wishes with a smile and nod, or sometimes a few words spoken so quietly Alex couldn't even hear them.

Before he could quite decide what to do, Millie signaled to him. Her expression was anything but congratulatory, and her black gown looked ominous in the setting of the chapel.

"Alex, she doesn't know," Millie hissed as soon as she got within reach of him.

He frowned at her. "Doesn't know what?"

"About the rumors, or your previous marriages. God knows how, but they've kept it all from her."

"Are you joking?" Alex asked coldly. But something in his gut twisted.

"Of course I'm not joking," she said. "I was as surprised as you are. No wonder she agreed to it all. She didn't know what she was agreeing to."

He wanted to curse. Loudly. But he didn't.

"You have to tell her," Millie went on, "before someone lets a stupid comment slip."

They both turned, seeking out Violet.

"Oh, no," Millie groaned. "It's too late."

"Gwendolyn," Alex said, seeing who had his bride by the arm. He could see the frozen, stunned expression on Violet's face from where he stood.

"She knows," Millie said in despair.

"She knows," Alex agreed. What a mess.

* * * *

The wedding dinner was hideous. No, Alex amended, the dinner was delicious, as always. Rack of lamb, mint sauce, glasshouse vegetables, custards both savory and sweet…something for everyone's taste. If only the food was the sole criterion to judge the success of a meal.

It was the company that was hideous. The guests were obviously aware—on some level—of the divide between Alex and Violet. Though his new wife sat opposite him, she didn't look or act like a wife. She acted like a stranger, because that's exactly what she was.

The conversations around the table rippled uncomfortably, as odd silences broke through the words, and people struggled to find safe topics to discuss.

To make it worse, the Peakes swilled wine down like pigs, growing more querulous and nasty with every course. Mrs Peake, who seemed typical enough before, dropped her mask of the devoted guardian. She clearly considered her job done, and now did not have to treat Violet as a household member at all. Whatever tensions had been lurking between the two ladies before, they surged upward with every sip of wine Mrs Peake took.

After one comment from the older lady, Alex shot Herbert a look, not needing words to convey his thoughts. Herbert should have looked a lot more closely at the whole family of his potential match. There had to be a reason that Violet wasn't married before now—and they seemed to have found it.

Herbert knew exactly what Alex was thinking, but only offered a shrug in response, as if to say, if you want something done right, do it yourself. Alex frowned, annoyed that the other man was pointing out Alex's mistake.

And then, of course, there was Millicent. She viewed the whole dinner with a different perspective than anyone else. She was amused at the awkwardness, and often giggled to herself during the silences, making them even more awkward. When she saw Alex and Herbert's silent exchange, she laughed out loud, bringing all conversation to a halt.

"What are you laughing at, young lady?" Mrs Peake asked her, drunk and irritated and vaguely aware that she was part of the joke.

Millie only smiled at her. "Life, ma'am. I'm laughing at life."

The arrival of the next course helped smooth over that exchange, and provided a welcome distraction.

Through it all, Violet sat in silent mortification, so still she seemed to be willing herself to fade out of existence. Contrarily, her unnatural stillness made Alex look at her more frequently, trying to divine any of her thoughts.

His musing was interrupted by Mrs Peake's next words. "It was destined to be, so why should I question the wisdom of the stars?" she was saying. "The future belongs to those brave enough to grasp the serpent unflinching. That's why I made the match for you, Violet."

"It wasn't because of the stars," Violet said, her quiet voice nevertheless cutting through the whole table. "It was the money, according to you yourself, Aunt."

"You ill-mannered child!" Mrs Peake said spitefully. "You don't know a thing about it. What did I tell you? You look, but you never *see*."

At those words, Violet flinched slightly.

Alex placed his glass back on the table and looked directly at Mrs Peake. "That will do," he said.

The woman stared at him, apparently stunned he would object. Alex kept looking at her steadily, and she slowly realized the central truth of the day. Things were different now. Violet belonged to Alex, not to her. The Peakes were guests in his house, at his pleasure, and he far outranked them in every respect.

"Of course, your grace," she said finally. "One can't put aside the role of instructor and mother immediately, you know."

Violet looked at her aunt. Her brown eyes were wide with some emotion, but Alex didn't know her well enough to guess more. She stood up from the table. "Please excuse me," she gasped out, then turned and fled from the hall.

Millie half rose, intending to follow Violet, but Alex raised a hand to prevent her. "Finish your meal, Millie. I'll speak with her," he said calmly, setting his glass down. As he rose, he glanced at the Peakes, letting them see his contempt. "It seems *somebody* has to."

He left the room. The in-laws would have to go as soon as humanly possible. But first he had to speak to his wife.

Violet had barely reached the end of the hall when Alex stepped into it.

"Violet." He didn't say anything else, but that was enough to stop her progress.

She half turned. "Forgive me, your grace. But I had to get my breath."

"Come here," he said. "I'd prefer not to yell down the whole corridor."

Violet quickly retraced her steps. "Where would you like to yel—discuss things, your grace?" she asked, not looking at him.

"Follow me." Alex led her to a smaller room off the hall. Lit only by the sconces on either side of a small unlit fireplace, it was a gloomy space at the moment. The walls, paneled with dark wood, seemed to close in on them. When he shut the door and turned to face her, she took a step back.

"Charming family," he observed.

"The only family I have left," she said, then added, as if she couldn't keep the words in, "She never acted in the role of mother. *Never*."

"You actually lived with those swine?"

"Almost fifteen years."

"Dear God," he said, the full force of it hitting him.

"You must regret choosing me."

"I gather it's mutual," he replied.

Her eyes dropped to the floor, which was answer enough for Alex.

"You have heard about me," he said simply. "Though later than I would have preferred." He sighed. "If only we met sooner."

"Indeed," Violet said, a very slight reproof coloring the word.

Alex took a deeper breath. "All right. I deserved that. Though I'd point out that you didn't even respond to my letters."

"Because I received none," she protested, "though I wrote four to you…" Then she sighed. "Of course. Aunt Judith."

He understood Violet's conclusion immediately. "You suspect she prevented your letters from being sent?"

"And yours from reaching me. She was quite concerned that I know as little as possible, lest I change my mind."

"Now you do know. Tell me, are you frightened by these rumors?" The question had an odd quality in the little room. There was no echo here, unlike in the great hall.

"Whether I am frightened or not seems quite beside the point now," Violet said.

He heard a twinge of humor in her words, the gallows humor of one already damned.

"True," he noted, inwardly railing at this twist of fate. At least this one knew, he had thought, and was willing to ignore the rumors. But no, Fate had somehow managed to bring him the only woman in England who didn't listen to gossips. He would have let her go, if only there was an honorable way to do it. But he could see none.

"Your grace?" Violet asked, when he did not continue.

"Are you afraid of me?" he asked abruptly.

"It does not matter what the rumors say," she said finally. She did not actually answer his question, and they both knew it. "We are married. It is done."

"Not quite. The chief aim of any aristocratic marriage is to secure an heir to the title," he began.

"Yes, your grace," Violet answered, barely above a whisper. Alex saw her blush, and she would not lift her gaze from the floor. Such a quiet girl.

"But I'm not going to drop dead anytime soon, and neither are you," he added significantly. Violet looked as if she wasn't sure if she believed him. "I want you to be…" he paused. He'd been about to say *willing*, but he doubted Violet would ever have the spine to say no to anyone, especially not him. "I want to get to know you, and for you to know me better. I won't come to you until you ask me to. Is that fair?"

"More than fair. Yes, your grace," she whispered, still blushing violently. Her skin must be overheating at this point, he thought, fighting the sudden urge to touch her and find out.

"Violet, you haven't said the word *no* once since I've met you," he noted critically.

"No, your grace," she agreed quickly, but her comment was followed by a swift smile that was gone almost as soon as it arrived. Alex saw it, though, and felt strangely reassured. She had a sense of humor, at least. Perhaps she just needed time to become comfortable.

The prospect of not being bedded immediately appeared to make her more comfortable right away. At least some of the nervous tension flowed out of her. Looking at her in her pale wedding gown, he realized he had no idea what to say to this woman—his *wife*. He opted for a momentary escape.

"Let's rejoin our guests. They will be missing us."

"I doubt anyone in the room will miss me," she said. But she took his arm and let herself be led back to the dining hall.

The rest of the evening passed more quickly than the first part. Violet was still quiet, but the fight went out of her relatives, so the only conversation was awkward and desultory rather than abusive.

58 ☙ *Elizabeth Cole*

After the dessert course of a magnificent lemon cake which no one enjoyed, people passed through to the parlor. Violet declined to perform at the pianoforte, saying she did not feel ready to perform without some practice at the new instrument. "And anyway, I do not have a great talent for music."

"Other than the music of the spheres," Mrs Peake added absently, just at the edge of his hearing. Alex paused. What did that mean? But the thought of engaging Mrs Peake in conversation was enough to keep him from inquiring further.

So Millicent played her harp. She was quite accomplished, even though nearly everything she played was melancholy and in a minor key. Despite the beauty of the sound, it was not the sort of performance to energize people or encourage more revelry. Soon enough, the guests began to depart for bed or other pursuits.

The Peakes were led to their guest quarters. Alex watched as Mrs Peake nearly had to wrestle her husband away from a bottle of wine. The woman's practiced moves made him think it was a common occurrence, and probably accounted for Violet's own meager consumption of the wine at dinner.

Millicent left shortly afterward, after saying goodnight to Violet in particular. Then Alex caught Violet's hand and said in a low voice, "Come. I'll walk you to your own rooms now. For appearances, if nothing else."

She nodded quickly. "Yes, your grace."

He said goodnight to the few guests still in attendance and then passed through the great oak doors, with Violet on his arm.

The dim hallway ran from one end of the main building to the other. The stone walls sucked any warmth out of the air. Gloomy would be an accurate description at the moment, and he didn't much like the idea of Violet being afraid in the Abbey.

"It looks different in the daytime," he said suddenly. "The Abbey, that is. You should not judge it by what you see now."

"I saw a bit today. I look forward to exploring it," said Violet. "It's very different from what I'm used to."

He led her up the wide staircase to the next floor, where the main bedrooms were located. He walked all the way to the end of the hall, stopping at her door.

Violet opened it, but didn't step through.

They stared at each other for a moment in absolute silence, perhaps finally, fatally aware that they were officially married, though they had only met that day. Alex also remembered that he had not kissed his bride at the ceremony. It seemed too late to fix the omission.

"Good night," he said, somewhat stiffly.

"Good night, your grace," she returned.

Alex crossed the hallway to his own rooms. What had he done? Duty to his family was all well and good, but what did he have in common with that little slip of a thing in the next room? He could hardly imagine her acting as duchess, a position that required considerably more confidence than Violet seemed to have.

He sighed, then cautioned himself to not draw too many conclusions from a single day, and a very strange day for her. She must be feeling overwhelmed by events. They would talk in the morning. Everything could be sorted in the morning.

Pausing at his desk, Alex picked up his notes regarding the murder of Galbraith. Reading over them, he became absorbed in the clues again. He sat down to reconsider the case from every angle. Sleep was forgotten, marriage was forgotten, as he sunk into his work. This is where he could be effective, he thought. This was what was important.

But his concentration didn't last. He kept looking over at the connecting door, wondering about the stranger on the other side. He saw the light of a lamp burning from under the door. If she was awake, he could knock. He could speak to her, and learn something about her other than that she was shy and obedient.

And how would a shy, obedient woman react if he knocked and came into her room at this hour? Alex scared her just because of how he looked. Violating the sanctity of her room by entering without an invitation wouldn't help.

He stopped writing and fell silent. He listened hard, until he was sure he wasn't imagining it.

Crying.

His wife was crying on her wedding night.

So the curse was still going strong.

"Wonderful," Alex muttered.

Sleep was a long time in coming.

Chapter 6

♋

VIOLET SLEPT BADLY, AND ROSE late. Neither thing was unusual, but the reasons were new. During the late night hours, she lay awake, odd thoughts racing through her mind, destroying any attempt to sleep. For hours after he saw her to her room, she thought of the duke, and their marriage, and her future. She had stared at the connecting door for a while, seeing a light at the bottom gap. So he was awake, as well, though she doubted he was fretting over the marriage. He didn't seem the type to fret over anything.

At least she had a small reprieve from one thing she'd been dreading. She naturally had been nervous about her wedding night, more than most women, since she had no older sisters or close friends who might have reassured her. Aunt Judith's hastily offered instructions had been as cryptic as they were alarming, and Violet assumed her aunt was deliberately trying to scare her. The fact that she wouldn't experience that mysterious act right away came as a vast relief.

But she was left more curious than before. As she lay quietly in the bed, a heat rose in her cheeks as she thought of the duke—her husband, she corrected herself, trying to get used to the notion. He certainly was lovely to look at. What would a kiss from him feel like? Would she enjoy it?

Would he enjoy it? Violet didn't flatter herself that he was attracted to her in any way. And of course, her relatives were reason enough to regret marrying her. He must think she was just like them. That she was a crude, money-grubbing woman who didn't care who she married as long as it meant she would live well.

Panic rose in her breast as she thought of living in this house for the rest of her days, despised by her own husband. Overwhelmed at everything that happened, Violet indulged in something she rarely did, which was a cathartic bout of sobbing. But she did feel better afterwards, as if all the overwrought emotions fled along with the tears.

She must have fallen asleep at some point, because between one blink and the next, Dalby was suddenly there, the light was entirely different, and Violet felt a headache pulsing at her temples.

"Ma'am?" Dalby asked, concern all over her face. "What's the matter?"

"Nothing," Violet said, sitting up. "Why should something be the matter?"

"You were crying," Dalby noted. "Your cheeks are all blotchy and you've got salt stains on your gown." She paused, then said worriedly, "It wasn't *that* upsetting, was it? I mean, he wasn't cruel to you…last night?"

It took Violet a moment to understand what Dalby meant. She blinked several times—Lord, her eyes were dry—then felt a shock of comprehension. "No!" she burst out. "No. That…didn't happen. He didn't even step in this room."

"He didn't?" Dalby asked, taken aback.

"No. We spoke last night, and agreed that taking a little time to get to know each other first would be, um, wise."

"Oh." Her maid thought about it. "Well. Then why were you crying?"

"I don't know. I just was. Yesterday was not a good day."

"It wasn't such a bad day," Dalby said, trying to cheer her up. "You're a duchess now. And you never have to stay with your aunt again."

"True." Violet looked out the window. "And the clouds have moved off. That's something."

Dalby offered Violet a breakfast tray. She drank the coffee down and nibbled at the sweet, almost sticky bread on the plate.

After dressing, Violet found her way downstairs to the parlor where her aunt and uncle were sitting. They weren't talking. Roger was nursing the pains from his overindulgence the previous night, and Judith was embroidering again.

Her uncle greeted her with a slightly sick leer. "Up late as usual. Had a good sleep last night, missy?"

Violet guessed what he was referring to, and her mortification that he would even mention her "sleeping" with her husband seemed to be all the answer her uncle needed. He laughed, assuming her blush meant something different than it did. "So that's why he married again, is it?"

"Hush, Roger," Judith said mechanically. "No one is interested in your feeble attempts at humor."

For once, Violet agreed with her aunt. She didn't want to talk to them, however, so she quickly excused herself to find another diversion. Judith would stay at Dunmere

Abbey for as long as she possibly could, enjoying the better accommodations and abusing the generosity of the duke by eating his food rather than their own. Violet sighed. The next few weeks would be painful at best if the Peakes were going to be around for every meal and social visit.

She hoped to find Herbert, or Millie, or even Alex. But her search was in vain, so she returned to the bedroom, where Dalby was arranging her clothes in the wardrobe room.

Violet stared out the windows toward the lake she'd not even seen up close. She turned to Dalby and requested the maid to bring out her riding habit. Once dressed, she quickly strode out to the stables and asked for a horse to be saddled for her. One of the hostlers brought out a beautiful black one, who looked as eager to be outside as she felt.

"Will you want a groom, your grace?"

"Oh, no need. I only want to see the grounds and the lake."

The boy nodded in comprehension. "The grounds will be muddy and slippery, your grace, after so much rain. Mind how you go."

"Thank you for telling me. I shouldn't be more than an hour or so."

Then she was off. The cold air was glorious on her face. Winter hadn't let go entirely, but Violet could smell hints of spring in the air. Not of flowers, but of mud and earth, of clean running water.

Violet circled the main house, looking over the various wings. She tried to guess the age of the oldest parts of the building, and saw where the newer additions had been added. She always considered Hawebeck Place large, but it would fit into this place several times over.

She rode past a few gardens, the beds mostly free of snow and ice but still quite bare. In the spring, it would be lovely there.

Actually, the whole estate must be gorgeous in the warmer months. Even in the last, grey part of winter there was a certain charm to it. She liked how the Abbey settled into the landscape, and how the lawns changed to meadows and then into woods beyond. She was eager to see what the coming months would bring.

The lakeshore was barely fringed with ice, so pockmarked and thin it looked liable to crack under any weight. She gave the shore a wide berth, not knowing if the edge would be too muddy to ride through. But she could see how the water would reflect the image of the Abbey at one end, and the sunset when viewed from the other side.

She came to the western edge, and then rode on to the strange building she saw the previous day. It really did appear to be a ruined tower. She rode all around, and tried the one door, but found it locked. How very odd. And intriguing. She'd have to come back soon.

In the moment of silence before she nudged her horse forward, Violet caught the sound of rushing water. A stream lay beyond, perhaps draining from the lake to… somewhere. She rode on for several minutes, invigorated enough to investigate the mysterious sound. She found the little stream and followed it, approaching the line of trees in the distance.

Just as Violet was about to ride down a narrow path through the woods, she turned, hearing something behind her.

Hooves. Someone was riding toward her, fast. A moment later, she could see Alex, riding as if the devil drove him. In another moment, he was nearly on her. He slowed the horse with a sharp command, then circled her.

"Is something the matter at the house?" Violet asked nervously.

"Something is the matter right here," he growled. "What in the devil's name do you think you're doing?"

Violet, of course, had never seen Alex angry, and she had no idea how angry he was likely to get. The day before he'd seemed so cool, as if nothing could affect him. What had she done?

"I wanted to go for a ride, to see the grounds," she said nervously. "Why is that so strange?"

"It's been raining here for six days, and you are completely unfamiliar with the land. It's dangerous out here after so much rain!"

"How so?" She looked around, seeing nothing that hinted of danger.

"The riverbanks are known to collapse under even a little weight. The locals know enough to stay away until the ground dries. You should have a groom. Who let you go riding alone?"

"I refused the offer," she said. "I wanted to see the place for myself, and I'm not exactly riding off into the wilderness. We can see the Abbey from here."

He moved the horse closer, almost touching her own. "Don't make excuses. You could have been killed!"

"As if it would matter to you—you don't even know me," she said, her voice finally rising in response to his unreasonable, unforeseen anger. "Or do you only care that the ton will start gossiping about your curse again?"

The duke didn't even answer her. He instead grabbed her roughly and pulled her to him. Violet was too shocked to protest when he leaned forward and kissed her with punishing force.

It was not an act of love, or even passion. It was pure dominance. He wanted to show her she belonged to him. She could not leave him. She could not disobey him.

Violet felt the anger and power behind the kiss, and she wanted to melt away into a puddle to avoid the duke's wrath. But the kiss made it hard for her to breathe at all, let alone move. Her body began to arch toward him, even as she raised her hands to push him away.

"Your grace," she gasped, trying to catch her breath. "Please…"

He pulled away abruptly. "Never think I don't care where you are every second of your life. You are my duchess now, and you cannot scurry about like a country mouse. You belong to me and you will behave like it."

Violet dropped her head at the rebuke. She was not fit to be a duchess, and they both knew it. Her lips began to throb, unused to the kiss. Her first kiss from him. She had wondered if she would enjoy his attentions. It seemed she had found her answer.

"Look at me, Violet," he said quietly, coldly.

She raised her face, unwillingly. The outburst was over, and the man of stone was back.

"Never do something so foolish again," he warned. "And never go off alone. Do you understand me?"

"Yes, your grace," she whispered.

"Good. Follow me," he said grimly.

It was a silent ride back to the house. Violet didn't speak as Alex dismounted, then helped her down himself. He spoke sharply to the hostler who had come running out —it was the same boy who had saddled Violet's horse an hour ago.

The reprimand Alex offered was delivered in a perfectly normal tone of voice, but the boy looked as if he'd just been screamed at for allowing a murder to occur.

"It wasn't his fault," Violet said, as loudly as she dared. "He offered and I refused."

Alex didn't even turn back to her.

"The safety of the duchess is the duty of everyone who works on the estate. I should sack you," he said to the boy.

"Please don't," Violet said. "He is not to blame."

The duke paused, tense. The boy was terrified, his eyes flicking back and forth between them.

Then Alex shrugged. "See that she doesn't ride alone again."

"Yes, your grace!" the boy said quickly.

Violet rushed inside the house and up to her bedroom immediately, unable to stay and look her husband in the face. She was still burning with embarrassment over her own reprimand. She wanted to say something to him, but if she opened her mouth, absolutely nothing would come out. It never did when Violet was nervous. She would try to speak, she'd say nothing, and he'd be even more disappointed in her than before.

Perhaps if she wrote her thoughts down, it would help. Violet picked up a pen, then immediately put it down again. She was in too much turmoil to write down anything coherent. She had to settle her mind before she saw Alex again, or she'd surely say something she'd regret as soon as she managed to get a word out.

What had he told her? Oh yes. *You are my duchess now, and you cannot scurry about like a country mouse.* She was a mouse. Quiet all day, overlooked by everyone, and only up at night, when the rest of the world slept. Not at all what the duke thought he was purchasing.

But even if she was not a proper duchess at the moment, she could learn. Violet could learn anything if she put her mind to it. If she could calculate the paths of comets, she could certainly master whatever esoteric skills being a duchess required. She could be hostess for a party. She could meet with the village's matrons. She could see what Dunmere Abbey needed.

And she could be a proper wife to the duke, in time. Perhaps Alex would never love her, or even like her. But he'd tolerate her as long as she fulfilled her obligations.

Violet sat on the edge of the bed, thinking of one specific obligation. At some point, she'd have to say the words she dreaded.

"You may come to my room tonight," she whispered out loud, trying the words. That was the phrase a lady told her husband, according to Aunt Judith. Of course, Judith immediately added that a husband could legally do whatever he wanted to his wife, short of killing her, and no one would raise a fuss. So the words might not mean much in reality.

Then again, Alex did say he'd wait, and he didn't enter her room last night, so perhaps he was being sincere. All the same, Violet wasn't sure she'd ever have the courage to say the words, especially if it meant inviting attention like the kiss of that afternoon. Her lips still hurt, and Alex only held her for a moment.

It was all too much to consider. Violet summoned Dalby to dress her for dinner. "Maybe the dark blue dress," Violet suggested. "If I'm going to face my old family and my new family again tonight, at least it will be in my most modern outfit."

"Yes, ma'am," Dalby said. "A shame you won't fit

into that suit of armor down in the main foyer."

Violet smiled, happy she had at least one ally here. "Not this time, Dalby. I should be safe as long as Judith doesn't come to dinner with a sword."

Chapter 7

♋

ALEX WATCHED AS VIOLET FLED into the house from the front courtyard, and he couldn't fault her for it, not after what he'd done to her. Alex didn't even think about what he was doing. He just grabbed her, as if that could somehow keep a curse from taking her away. The next thing he knew he was looking at wide, warm brown eyes still stunned by his outburst, and saw how red her mouth was after he kissed her. His first instinct was to kiss her again, softly, to make up for the first, but he knew it would do no good. His wife feared him, and it was entirely his fault.

Thus, when he returned to the house himself, his mood was as dark as most rumors suggested. The first people he encountered, unfortunately, were the Peakes. Alex saw them arguing in low tones as they stood in the small ground floor library. Irritation welled up in him. If they had been more honest with Violet, none of this would be happening. Mrs Peake had angled hard for the marriage, stressing Violet's noble lineage, her biddability, and Alex's own desperation. She'd used the rumors to wring out several concessions that would have no place in a typical marriage agreement. And yet she kept Violet in the dark for her own convenience.

Alex took a deeper breath, then strode into the room.

Mrs Peake saw him and immediately gave a little curtsey. "Why, good afternoon, your grace."

Her bleary-eyed husband looked as if he might not be sober enough to bow without falling over, but Alex ignored him. Mrs Peake was the one who held the reins in their relationship.

"Get out," he told her.

"What?" Mrs Peake asked, blinking in confusion. "Do you require the room?"

"Not the room. The house. I want you gone in one hour."

She gasped indignantly. "We're not prepared to leave."

"I suggest you remedy that, because in one hour you'll both be seated in a coach leaving the estate, prepared or not."

"You truly expect us to go home so soon?" she asked.

"You can go anywhere you like," said Alex. "I can't begin to describe how little I care where you end up, so long as it isn't here. Fetch what you need. I'll direct the servants to pack up the remainder and send it via another coach. You now have less than an hour."

"Your grace, I don't think you understand—"

"I will give you one hundred pounds when you enter the coach," he said coolly, watching Mrs Peake's expression change. Mr Peake gave a strange snort that might have been a laugh.

Without further comment, Mrs Peake hauled her husband from where he was standing and left the room.

Alex was true to his word. He issued instructions to the majordomo, and the Peakes were helped efficiently and enthusiastically by several of the household staff.

They were ushered into a waiting coach precisely

fifty-five minutes after Alex's pronouncement. He handed Mrs Peake several folded notes. "Safe travels," he said shortly. "You may expect the other coach with your items to arrive one day after you do."

He shut the door before either Peake could reply. The coachman drove off with commendable speed, and Alex watched with no small satisfaction as the vehicle disappeared down the lane.

It was as if a plague was lifted from the house. At least that was one problem solved. With luck, he would never have to see that couple again. He glanced up at the brooding façade of the Abbey, wondering if he should have notified Violet so she could bid her family goodbye. Then he remembered last night's dinner and shrugged. Violet might feel a duty to see them off, but he didn't like the idea of her even interacting with the Peakes any longer. If she was upset about it, he'd simply add it to the ever-lengthening list of things he needed to apologize for.

Alex didn't seek Violet out again until dinner. It took that long to get all his emotions under control. He paced in his study, hearing her accusation over and over. *Do you only care that the ton will start gossiping about your curse again...?* Those were her words, and the worst of it was that it was partly true. He couldn't stand the idea of the gossips giving his name yet another round. But more than that, he knew how dangerous Violet's ride had been. The woods of the Abbey were unpredictable after heavy rains. The rocky soil along the gullies could collapse without warning, carrying a horse and rider into a stream, or down a slope, knocking a person unconscious. She couldn't know that, but one wrong step... He shuddered at the image of Violet lying broken on the ground. How could he bury yet another wife?

After a time, he regained his customary calm. He dressed for dinner and sought out Violet, after learning from a maid that she was in the library. He found her deep in a book, although she had changed into her evening gown before she started reading. The dark blue of the outfit emphasized her porcelain skin, and the very modern cut of the bodice definitely got his attention. It was perfectly ladylike, but still alluring. All that skin... Again, he regretted his thoughtless kiss from that afternoon.

"Good evening, Violet. May I take you in to dinner?" he asked formally, striving to forget his heated words from earlier that day.

Violet also seemed eager to forget, since she smiled at him when she raised her head from the book, laying it carefully aside. "Why, yes, your grace." She rose gracefully and took his arm.

"I want to apologize," he said before they started for the dining room. "I scared you this afternoon. That wasn't my intention."

Violet nodded, saying, "I know. It was most irresponsible of me to ride in an unfamiliar place, especially alone. I'm very sorry to have worried you."

Had she just turned the tables and apologized to *him*? Arguing with Violet might be a challenge. He liked a challenge.

He said, "I'll take you on a tour. It's your home now. You should know it."

"Thank you. I look forward to it."

He frowned. This reconciliation was going too easily. He was also distracted by her outfit. Lovely as it was, something was wrong about it. But what?

"I am intrigued by that ruin on the other side of the lake," she went on. "I saw it up close today, but the door was locked."

"The folly. Yes. It's not a ruin—it's just designed to look that way. There's a room on the upper floor."

"Oh, is there?" she asked, interest in her voice.

"Yes. You can see quite a distance from it." He looked at her. "That's really the purpose of the folly. The view."

"I would very much like to see it for myself," Violet said.

"Easily done. I'll take you there on the tour. Tomorrow."

"That would be wonderful." She smiled fully at him now, making him realize her earlier greeting was forced.

All the same, he found himself smiling back. Violet appeared to have forgiven him. Perhaps he could start over.

They arrived in the dining room, and Alex led Violet to her seat, determined to behave as properly as possible to make up for his beastly behavior that day. As he looked at his wife across the table, something niggling detail caught him again. What was *wrong* with her appearance?

Millie and Herbert were seated as well, and Alex signaled the butler to begin serving.

"Shouldn't we wait for the Peakes?" Herbert asked.

"They left this afternoon," Alex said shortly.

Violet looked up. "They did? I thought Aunt Judith would never—" She broke off.

Alex gave her a brief, slightly bitter smile. "Nevertheless, they left today."

"What good news," said Millie bluntly. "I suppose I'm too young for champagne."

"You're almost too young to sit at this table for dinner," Alex warned. "Particularly if you speak like that about houseguests."

"However hideous they may be," Violet added with surprising candor. She nodded to Alex. "Whatever you did, thank you."

That dinner was the first time Alex noticed something like natural grace from Violet. She spoke of little things, such as potential visits to and from neighbors, and asked about his plans for the estate. After her comment about her aunt, everything about her was calm and exceedingly polite. Was the removal of her family all it took? Alex could have simply paid a hundred pounds weeks ago and had Violet shipped over. He laughed to himself over the absurd thought. But all through dinner, something still bothered Alex about Violet's appearance. What was it?

After the meal, the family moved to the parlor. Herbert said he would teach Millie the intricacies of a few card games to ready her for such events when she joined society. It was plain he wanted Alex and Violet to remain apart, so they could talk and get to know each other better.

Violet refused an offer of wine, saying she'd have tea instead.

"Because of your uncle?" Alex asked, not wishing to circle around the subject.

"Partly," Violet admitted, her eyes downcast. "But I also find that wine doesn't agree with me at all."

"So no champagne toasts for you," he said.

She looked him shrewdly. "You paid her, didn't you? To leave the house."

"I did. A bargain at one hundred pounds."

Violet sighed. "Dear Lord."

"I suggest not thinking of it again," Alex said.

"I shall heed your advice, your grace," she said with a sad little smile.

Alex liked that she was honest enough to discuss it,

and willing to put it aside. In fact, he liked her quite a lot more than he did only a day ago. If things kept progressing at this pace, he'd fall in love with her before the week was out.

And that was something Alex had no intention of doing. He'd treat her well, and he wouldn't mind her companionship. But whenever Alex fell in love, death tended to follow.

Not that he'd tell Violet that, of course. He kept chatting with her, trying to keep the conversation safe. But he was also now close enough to her to smell hints of soap and lavender off her skin, which was a little distracting. All that skin. All that bare skin above the edge of the gown.

Then he knew what was missing. "You're incomplete," he said, enlightened.

"Excuse me?" Violet's eyes widened over her teacup.

"You're not wearing any jewelry."

"Well, I don't have much," Violet said, putting the cup back down.

"What do you mean?" How could it be possible for his duchess to have no jewels? "You mean nothing you had suited?"

"Not for this gown. I do have pearls, but I didn't like the look of them with this. I have my locket, and a few rings, mostly from my mother." Embarrassed, she gave a little laugh. "As you may have guessed, what money Aunt Judith controls is only spent on necessities…as she defines them."

"That will not do. Come with me." Alex rose, catching the attention of Herbert and Millie. "I'm going to show Violet something, and then we'll be back. Millie, why not tune your harp in the meantime?"

Alex led the way to his study, the same room where he first spoke to Violet privately. It was also where he kept the family heirlooms in a safe. Violet trailed along behind him, her curiosity evident.

He opened the safe with his own key, and removed a large box from it. "There should be something in here that will suffice until I can get you get your own jewels. Try this." He handed her a necklace.

Violet took it with considerably more care than he displayed. Diamonds lay in a glittering strand, accented by a large sapphire every two inches. Fastening it carefully around her neck, she walked to the mirror hanging on the side wall. The sapphires echoed the blue in the dress perfectly.

"They're beautiful," she said.

"They'll do," he agreed, secretly well pleased with the result. Violet would be a picture perfect duchess, if only she'd learn to stand up for herself.

"Is it too much?" she asked, plucking at the necklace.

Moving toward her, he reached out to adjust the stones lying on her breastbone, touching her skin, which felt exactly as soft as he imagined it would.

"*Too much* is not a term you'll be using as my duchess," he said.

"As you say, your grace." Violet lowered her eyes and looked away.

Alex lowered his hand to take hers, but he immediately noticed how tense her whole body was. Over the whole evening, she'd been projecting an aura of calm she didn't feel.

He stepped back, wondering if his nearness was making her even more nervous than usual. *Cursed*, he thought, unable to block the word from his brain.

Violet noticed the change in mood. "Shall we go back down?" she asked in a whisper.

"Yes. Follow me," he said, his grim mood returning.

"Should I not..." She choked on the words, but her hands flew up to the necklace.

"Keep it on. I gave it to you to wear, Violet. What the hell am *I* going to do with it?"

They rejoined Herbert and Millie in the parlor, but Alex felt cold the whole time. Violet sat by him, and most people would have said she seemed at ease. But she kept touching the necklace nervously, and smoothing down the skirt of her dress. She didn't want to be near him at all.

She excused herself after Millie finished her last song, and cast an uncertain look at Alex before she left.

He went to his study for a little while, and then after the rest of the house was quiet, he went up to his room, though he wasn't sleepy in the least.

Despite the late hour, he again saw the light in Violet's room from under the connecting door.

He knocked lightly. As soon as he did, he wished he hadn't. Perhaps she'd simply fallen asleep while a lamp remained on. Perhaps he was the last person she wished to see.

But then the door opened. Violet stood there, now in a dressing gown, with her hair down and merely tied back with a ribbon. He instantly wanted to touch it.

"Oh. I didn't expect you," she said.

"Who else?" he responded.

"Well, nobody, considering the hour...and the door." A little smile pulled at the corner of her mouth after she said it.

"I saw the light on," he explained. "You're obviously awake. You were up late last night as well. Is something wrong?"

She shook her head quickly. "No. I'm just, ah, acclimating, I suppose. It's quite different from where I used to live."

"You're sure? You're not ill?" Alex didn't like the tension wrapping around his chest. "If you're unwell…"

"It's not a cause for concern," she said. "I just have a different schedule."

"Will you be too out of sorts to ride tomorrow?"

Her expression brightened. "No, no. I want to see the estate. Truly."

"All right," he said, uncomfortably aware that he was hovering at his wife's door. "Get some sleep."

"You do the same," she said. "I wasn't the only person awake last night, or this one."

She smiled sweetly at him as she closed the door. So she'd noticed. Alex wasn't sure if he was pleased or not.

Chapter 8

♋

VIOLET DID NOT SLEEP WELL, but she rose earlier than usual in anticipation of the tour, and summoned Dalby to help her dress. She thought she was early. However, when she arrived in the breakfast room, she found Alex already there, sipping coffee.

"Good morning," she said. "I see I slept later than I ought to."

"Not at all. We're not in any sort of hurry," he said. "Did you sleep well after all?"

"I was…restless," she said, uncertainly. Restless wasn't really the correct word, but how else could she describe the wakeful hours and strange, barely remembered dreams that marked so many of her nights. Eventually, people would know that her sleep pattern had nothing to do with adjusting to life at Dunmere Abbey. It was simply how Violet lived.

Alex was surveying her carefully, but didn't say anything more about it. "Perhaps some breakfast will help set you to rights."

"Coffee will certainly help," she said.

She helped herself to some bread and jam from the sideboard, but discovered that Alex already poured her some coffee from the silver carafe near his place.

"Oh, thank you," Violet said. She sat and immediately drained the cup.

Wordlessly, Alex slid the carafe across the table. She looked up to see him hiding a smile.

"I like coffee," she said, feeling a bit defensive.

"Yes, I can see that. You might wish to tell Mrs Simpson—that's the housekeeper—to increase the next order."

Violet, who had just poured a second cup, felt a heat creeping up her neck. "I don't mean to be extravagant."

"If that's your definition of extravagant, then I have no fears on that account. Drink as much coffee as you like. There will always be more."

His casual tone reminded her of just how different her life would be in his house. Judith had always been so mean about finances, parceling out pennies only when she absolutely had to. Alex appeared not to think of money at all.

"Is this your customary hour for breakfast?" she asked. "I don't wish to disturb the schedule of the house."

"The house meets my...*our* schedules. And, yes, I generally rise early. I've never understood the attraction of dozing until noon."

"Ah." Violet's embarrassment didn't fade. He wouldn't think much of her own schedule.

"That reminds me of something," he said. "I've made arrangements for you to get fitted for a suitable wardrobe. The modiste will come tomorrow."

Violet guessed most of her own clothes would be inadequate for the sort of image a duchess ought to project. "That will be most appreciated."

"Doubtless you know what you like, but be sure you select several evening gowns. I am afraid we will both be victims of the ton whenever we go to town for the remainder of the Season."

"You don't sound thrilled," Violet observed.

"Society rarely thrills me. But I have a duty, and everyone will want to meet the new Duchess of Dunmere."

"What does thrill you?" she asked.

Alex glanced at her rather sharply.

"I thought we were meant to know each other better. Shouldn't I learn about your interests?" she said nervously, when he did not reply.

Then he nodded. "I'm interested in the Abbey, as you'll learn today. I'll probably tell you far too much about it."

Violet was happy to have found something he was willing to share. "I want to hear everything."

"You say that now," he warned. But he smiled at her, and Violet felt a little flutter in her stomach. Alex looked like a whole different person when he smiled.

They both mounted up and were soon riding away from the house. Alex stayed close to Violet and kept the horses' pace relatively slow. He told her some of the history of the Abbey, which had been seized during the time when many church lands were taken during the tumult of the Reformation. The Kenyon who had supported the king's efforts at the time was rewarded with the gift of the estate now known as Dunmere Abbey.

"There are many ruins and old villages still here on the land," Alex said, when they crested a hill and could look at part of the estate from that vantage point. "In some ways, little has changed, even after all this time."

"It's beautiful," said Violet. "I wonder that you would leave it for London at all."

He shrugged. "It's rarely by choice."

"But you're duke," she pointed out. "Who compels you to go?"

His expression went cold, making Violet wary. "It doesn't concern you, Violet. And you would not find it interesting in the least."

She wanted to protest that it did concern her, or else she would not have asked. But she remembered her intention to become a proper duchess, which of course would require graciousness.

"I understand, your grace," she said, keeping her voice even. "I'll not ask again."

He sighed, looking off at the land below. "What interests you, Violet?"

After the previous exchange, she was surprised he would ask, and she wasn't sure how to answer. For some reason, she felt too shy to mention her love of stargazing. He'd think it silly. "I like…being outside. This morning has been quite enjoyable. I spent most of my time out of doors in fact, when I lived with my aunt and uncle. And when that was not possible, I had books. I read quite a lot."

"So you stayed outside of your relatives' home when you could, and when you were forced to stay inside, you read so you would not have to speak to them," Alex rephrased.

"I…I would not put it like that," Violet said, blushing again.

"But you don't deny it."

"I don't like lying," she admitted.

Alex actually smiled at that. "Violet, I think we'll get along after all."

"Yes, your grace," she agreed.

"Call me Alex."

"Yes...Alex," she said. It was the first time she said his name.

He twitched the reins. "Well, let's keep on." He glanced down just as he was about to move forward, and pointed. "Watch out so you don't crush the snake."

"The what?" Violet followed his finger to where a snake slithered its way over a flat rock. Fear twitch up her spine. "I can't..."

He hadn't noticed her reaction yet. "Must be warmer than I thought, for it to come out for the sunshine so early in the year."

"Make it go away, please," Violet said tightly, feeling as if she were nine years old again. "Please."

Alex finally looked over at her. "It's harmless, Violet. Just a grass snake. Keeps the mice down."

"I don't care. I hate snakes."

"Really? Why? Were you bitten by one?"

She shivered at the thought. "No. I just...I've always been scared of them."

Alex moved close enough to take the reins of her own horse for a moment. She let him lead both horses away from where the little dark green snake was sunning itself. Violet turned her head to keep watching it. What if it suddenly followed her?

"You know it's harmless," he said again. "And you're a few feet above it. On horseback."

"I never said it was rational," Violet tried to explain, at last feeling the distance was enough that she could look at Alex once more.

His expression was concerned. "Are you all right? We could go back."

"No," Violet said, feeling foolish. "I'm sorry. I want to

see more of the estate. And you promised to show me the folly."

"So I did. Follow me." He led her down the hill, both horses moving into a canter across the wide meadow at the base.

They passed by the lake, the waters now blue, and the fringe of ice even narrower.

"There are swans in summer," he said. "They should return any week now. It's the best way to know spring is coming."

Violet thought swans would fit perfectly into the scene. They were as aloof and noble as Alex was.

A few moments later, they reached the odd structure Violet noticed before.

Alex dismounted, striding to her horse to assist her. Violet was acutely aware of his hands as he took her by the waist. Once her feet were firmly on the ground, his touch lingered for a moment, and Violet felt a little shiver that was oddly pleasant.

He offered his arm to her before they started to the door, saying, "The Abbey was so large at one point that they built little cells for the brothers so they could escape the bustle of the main building and pray quietly. Most have completely vanished by now, but one of my predecessors ordered this folly built with the same idea in mind —not that a monk would get a tower. But it's a place sort of separate from the world."

Even up close, it looked like the ruins of a very old building. Only the well-mortared walls and the newness of the wood frames of the door and windows revealed it as an imitation.

Alex unlocked the door with a key he held.

"Do you fear vagrants?" Violet asked.

He smiled. "No. Dunmere Abbey must be one of the safest places in England. I'm not sure why there's even a lock on it. Privacy for contemplation, perhaps."

He stepped through the open doorway, and drew Violet in after him.

A staircase wound up along the outer wall. At the first landing, there was another door, which led to a small room. Violet peeked in.

"Oh!" She was delighted. "This is darling."

In one corner, there was a small brazier, the sort that burned coal rather than wood. Near it was a teakwood desk, small but heavy. On the other side of the brazier was a sort of bed or couch frame, though there was no mattress or pillows.

"It's dirty," Alex noted apologetically. "I can't remember the last time I was in here. Years ago."

"It's a little untidy, but that's easily remedied. It's very charming."

There was a balcony, not visible from the lake side. Violet stepped out of the double doors to view the land beyond. The meadows past the lake rolled away toward a wood, and then down to a wide valley. In the far distance, she saw a ridge of hills. And above, there was only sky. She could put her telescope right out on the balcony and stargaze to her heart's content. "Oh, this is perfect."

"Do you like it?"

"I want to live here!"

"You do live here," he pointed out gently.

"No, *here*, here in this little room! I would sleep in that corner. And the desk just needs a chair and lamp. And the balcony—it would just be stars and moonlight, night after night."

"What if it's cloudy?"

"Then I will read."

"Do you want to see the upper level?"

She absolutely did. "There's more?"

"Follow me."

He led her up the winding steps again. He opened the hatch door in the ceiling, and then both of them were standing on the top level, which was just an open space, perhaps fifteen feet across at its widest point.

"I'm sure this was why the folly was really built," said Alex. "The view."

Violet spun around slowly, taking in the whole panorama. The bulk of the Abbey rose on the other side of the lake, and the sky arched overhead. The wall came to about waist height—enough to protect someone from falling, but not too high to inhibit the view.

"I was wrong before," said Violet. "*This* is perfect." She looked directly up at the thin clouds stretching across the heavens.

"So you like it," he said.

"I adore it. Can I come back some day?"

"Any day." He held the key out.

"Truly?" She reached for the key, but he quickly enclosed her hand in his.

"One small condition," he said.

"What's that?"

"The price of the key is a kiss."

Violet felt the key pressed between their palms. "Oh."

"Not like yesterday's," he said quickly. "Yesterday was a mistake."

"It was?" she asked. The flutter in her stomach was there again.

"Yes. Let me make up for it."

Violet nodded, rather flummoxed by his request. "All

right. I think so."

He reached out to touch her face. He bent then, his lips touched hers, and she forgot to think at all.

Violet warmed when he kissed her. He wrapped a hand around the back of her neck, the other threading through her hair. She didn't notice, lost in the exquisite feeling, so different from the harsh kiss before. No, this kiss melted her. She leaned into it, craving more.

Alex deepened the kiss slowly, and she was quite content to let him. But when he slipped his other arm around her, drawing her closer, Violet stiffened, pulled away from the kiss. "That's enough."

"Just a kiss," he murmured against her mouth.

"And what will it become?" she asked, gasping when he moved his lips to her neck, sending shivers down her body.

"Something more." He kissed her again.

She felt her body react to him, molding itself to his. But part of her still held back. "I just can't yet. I'm sorry."

He broke off the kiss, pulling himself away from her. "What are you afraid of?"

"Alex, I…" The words froze up in her throat. Violet tried to speak, but couldn't. She still barely knew him. She wasn't anything like the duchess he needed her to be. And she had no idea what she was doing. "Give me time. You said you would."

"I did," he agreed tonelessly.

She struggled to get the words out of her mouth. "I'll learn how to be a duchess. I will. But I'm not… I can't…" Violet's throat closed. She felt like she was choking. A hostile audience always did that, and Alex's expression could only be described as hostile now.

He let go of her hand, leaving the key with her.

* * * *

Violet rode back with Alex, but then didn't see him for the rest of the day. Dinner was largely a failure. Herbert and Millie tried to carry on normally, but Alex was distant and distracted. Violet kept as quiet as possible, feeling as out of place as she had the first day.

Violet stayed awake most of the night. She read a pamphlet from the Royal Academy of Natural Sciences on the topic of recent phenomena sighted in the heavens, and then tried to decide if she had sighted one of those things herself. Someday, she'd like to be mentioned in a pamphlet as the discoverer of a comet or a nova. Even if she was a woman, she was a duchess now. Would that allow her to publish? Or would it be even more shocking? Violet didn't know, then assumed the worst, and as a result she was miserable when she finally dropped off to sleep.

Dalby woke her at eleven. A tray stood nearby, with both toast and coffee. Dalby dressed her in a loose-fitting morning gown, meant for days without formal company.

Downstairs, Violet found only Millie in the parlor. She was dressed in black again, and she was reading from a volume of poetry.

"Good morning," Violet said.

"Oh, hello," said Millie, glancing up. "So Dalby wasn't exaggerating. You do sleep on in the mornings."

"I stay awake quite late," Violet said. "Do you happen to know where Alex is? I'd like to speak to him."

Millie put the book down. "Oh, he's gone off to London."

"He has?" Violet asked, surprised and oddly perturbed. "He said nothing about it."

"He never does. This happens all the time. He gets a

sealed letter, and then he flies off to London as though the devil were at his heels."

For someone who claimed that he didn't like London, he was certainly happy to go there at the least provocation. "What could possibly require someone of his rank to obey such a summons?" Violet asked, hoping that Millie would prove more forthcoming than her guardian. "Is he active in politics?"

"Oh, no. He claims it's personal business."

Violet tried not to think of one very plausible explanation for what constituted personal business. A mistress. She said casually, "And you've no notion of what it might be?"

"Not the slightest. It's been going on for years," Millie added. "I asked about it once or twice, and Alex told me it was nothing for a young lady to know about, and then he sent me to my room."

"Ah." Something stung Violet's heart. What else but a mistress, then?

She walked to the window, uncertain of what unwanted duchesses did in their spare time.

"Don't forget!" Millie said then. "The modiste is coming. Alex said you required a suitable wardrobe."

"I do indeed."

"May I join you for the fitting?" Millie asked, suddenly sounding shy. "I'd like to see the new designs. I never get to see what the ladies are actually wearing in the city."

Violet agreed to that readily, thinking that it would be pleasant to have someone around.

As it turned out, Violet had less spare time than she expected. Both the majordomo and the housekeeper wanted to speak to her, and Violet soon discovered that Dunmere Abbey was aching for the opinions of a lady.

"His grace never bothers about such things," the housekeeper confessed over a discussion of potential dinners. "But now that you're here, no doubt the Abbey will have more callers and you'll be hosting events, just as it used to be. The Abbey has been too quiet."

Violet did her best to answer the staff's questions, all the time feeling that she was not adequately prepared to take over the administration of the estate—though, of course, the household ran perfectly well before she ever arrived. But she did get the sense that most of them were happy the duke was no longer alone.

She sorted through some letters and invitations sent by neighbors, who had already heard of the wedding and sent congratulations. "Despite not being invited themselves," Violet murmured to herself. A small entertainment might be a good way to dip her toe in the waters of duchessing. A tea for the closest neighbors, perhaps.

A maid summoned her to her sitting room when the modiste arrived. Millie was already there, looking through renderings of new gowns and items that were most fashionable that year.

Fortunately, the modiste was an old hand at this business, and Violet more or less allowed the woman to do whatever was needed. She chose styles and colors that appealed to her, but she knew that it was better to let an expert work unencumbered.

Between measurements and fabric selections, Violet used her time with Millie to ask about Alex.

"Millie, can you tell me about the duke's previous marriages? I don't mean to pry…"

"It's not prying, Violet. He should have told you himself," Millie added with a huff.

"What happened? From the beginning?"

"He married for the first time to a Lady Catherine, who he knew quite well. I was only a baby and not living here yet, but I've heard the stories from Uncle Herbert and others. He was nineteen, I think, and she was about the same age, because it was her first Season when he proposed. They were married in September, and seemed quite happy. But Catherine died in childbirth, along with the child. It was less than a year after the wedding."

"He must have loved her, to marry so soon."

"I don't know," Millie admitted. "They said he was infatuated with her, and she with him, but perhaps that's only time talking. Anyway, he spent a year in mourning. But he was young, and rich, so he was still a catch on the marriage mart. Two years after Lady Catherine's death, he married again, this time to a very different type of woman. He was twenty-two by that point. The girl was only eighteen. They didn't get on well. Some lively fights, according to those who were around. Marianne had a temper when she didn't get her way. She also hated the Abbey. She insisted on spending as much time in town as possible. But Alex loves this estate, so sometimes he would send her to London and remain behind."

Millie then clapped her hands together. "Oh, that's a lovely gown you've got on now!" She told the modiste to have one made for her as well. "But in the black silk, please."

"Why do you wear black so often when you're not in mourning?" Violet asked her.

"I just like it," Millie said. "It goes better with my poetry."

Violet tried not to laugh, and then recalled that she was still in the dark about Alex's history. "So you were discussing Marianne."

"Oh, yes." Millie's face grew serious again. "One day, they had a huge row. Marianne stormed out of the house and took her horse for a long ride. She did that from time to time, and by that point Alex refused to chase after her. He just let her come to her senses on her own. Well, she didn't come home that evening, so he finally went in search of her—accompanied by all the men in the household. He was certain she was staying away to needle him further."

"And they found her?"

"Not until the morning. She was in the river downstream of the estate. Mind you, all this is just what I was told. They never knew if it was an accident, or if she drowned herself…"

Or perhaps murder, Violet thought. The duke rode out in the evening, after all. Maybe he *had* found her. Then she shook herself. She was being unfair, just like the gossips. And that did explain Alex's reaction when *she* went off riding on her first day at the Abbey. Of course he'd fear a repeat of the past.

"But he had a third wife," Violet recalled.

"Yes. Several years passed since Marianne's death. He didn't want anything to do with wives after her. But he was still going to become duke, and an heir is expected. His mother lives in Bath now, did Alex tell you that? She'd have come to the wedding, but she hates to travel. Anyway, he married again, mostly because his parents begged him to. Lady Virginia."

"And what happened to her?"

Millie went on with some reluctance. "After Marianne's death was when some people started talking about a curse. They said the Abbey was haunted. *Some* said—" Millie paused, glanced at the modiste, then shrugged.

"Some said Alex killed her in a rage." The accusations clearly bothered Millie. She went on, "Virginia heard some of the earlier rumors, unfortunately, and she believed them. Or seemed to. Alex was careful approaching that marriage. He spent a long time with her, getting to know her—"

"Good of him," Violet couldn't stop herself from saying.

Millie shook her head, remembering that he had not done so with Violet. "He liked her well enough. But she changed after the wedding. She became strange and moody. She took sick, but I think she wanted to die. Or she thought she was destined to die. She wasted away. She wouldn't even eat at the end."

"And then he chose me," Violet said.

"Not for years after Virginia."

"Did he ask anyone else?"

"I don't think so," Millie said.

Because he was afraid of the answer, Violet completed the unspoken statement. Until she came along, too ignorant and sheltered to question his interest in her. So he married his first wife for love. The next, for hope. The third for duty, and now her. Why had he married her... desperation?

* * * *

Over the next several days, Violet settled into a certain routine at Dunmere Abbey. Alex's continued, unexplained absence was a little hurtful, true, but it also gave her room to breathe. In between the many small duties she inherited as duchess, and the social calls people began to pay her, Violet also found time to set up the folly.

She ordered the building cleaned out and aired. As soon as the servants declared the folly fit for a duchess, Violet directed them to move several items into the main room, including a comfortable chair, some crates of books, and other items to make the space livable. The housekeeper had a few of the maids sew and stuff a new mattress for the built-in bed, and Violet spent a pleasant hour unpacking and rearranging books to fill the little bookshelves.

Millie came with her once or twice, curious to see the changes. "Is there anything better than unpacking a box of books?" the younger girl asked. "I don't think there is."

"Reading a book, perhaps?"

"Maybe," she said, "But there's something even better about deciding which one you'll read next." Millie paged through several of the astronomy books. "I say, you could do with more poetry. These are all pretty dull."

"A matter of taste," Violet said, unperturbed by the critique.

Finally, she carried the telescope case to the folly herself, as well as her special lantern.

"But there's already a lamp there, your grace," said one maid, as Violet left the house. "Brand new, and crystal clear."

"Thank you, I shall use it when I'm at the desk. But this lamp is particularly important." The chimney was made of red-tinted glass rather than clear. When it was the only light source, it was far less harsh to the eyes, and Violet could read by its light and then immediately look through her scope without fearing night blindness.

Violet opened the telescope case and carefully unpacked the telescope. It was a gift from her father. Along with the lantern, it was almost the last thing he gave her that seemed to be offered from the heart, before he'd descended into the madness that ended his life. Violet cherished it.

She was delighted when everything was set up to her specifications. All her stargazing equipment was in place, and she had her books and extra coal if the nights should be cool. The bed had a pillow and blankets if she decided to take a nap during the night. She could set the scope up on the balcony or the top floor. It could not be better if she designed it herself.

"I don't believe in fate," she murmured. "But I could almost believe someone built this place with me in mind."

Chapter 9

♋

WHEN CHATTAN SENT A LETTER to Dunmere Abbey, a few days after the wedding, Alex seized the chance to escape. He marveled at how that quiet slip of a girl managed to completely upend his life, just by existing. If only he knew a thing about her…but of course, he'd muddled that up already.

At least he understood murder. Alex went to the Zodiac's building as soon as he could. Chattan welcomed him inside the office. She wasn't alone this time. A boy sat in one of the chairs, kicking his feet at the rungs. When Alex entered, he stood up eagerly.

"This is Rook," Chattan said. She put her hand on the boy's shoulder. "One of the Disreputables."

"Rook?" Alex asked, thinking he'd misheard.

"Philip, really," the boy said. "But I've been called Rook for years. Long story." He was rail thin, and around twelve years old, but with an expression that seemed far older. A life on the streets tended to do that to even the most innocent of children.

Chattan said, "Rook's here because he knows about an earlier death that matches the one you're looking into. A homeless man was killed during the night in January.

When the body was found, it was next to a symbol drawn in blood." She pointed to a rendering of the symbol, one that looked just like the sign for Capricorn.

"I knew him," Rook said. "He didn't have a place to sleep most nights, but I saw him here and there. He never hurt anybody."

"Do you know his name?"

"Mr Lyle. He said his Christian name was Randolphus. He'd been a sailor. Full of stories."

Rook explained how the body had been found, stretched out on the front steps of a church still under construction. The bloody sign painted next to the body was assumed to be a random scrawl. "No one thought it had meaning—until the right people looked at it and recognized it." The boy looked at Chattan as he spoke, clearly impressed with her.

"A few newspapers reported on it," Chattan added, "but only that it was a particularly gruesome death—you know how sensational newspapers are."

"I certainly do," Alex said. He tended not to read newspapers himself, having seen his own name in them too many times. "They are not the first place I'd go for an accurate account."

"Nevertheless, it meant someone was asking questions." Chattan picked up another piece of paper. "I have the names of the journalists here, should you wish to follow up."

From the report Chattan made, both victims died in very similar ways—stabbed in the chest with a knife, and with bruises on the face suggesting that they were held so they couldn't yell for help.

"Exactly when was his body found?" Alex asked.

"The morning of the seventeenth of January, though

it's likely he was killed earlier, possibly the night of the fifteenth, to judge by how frozen the body was. But no workmen came to the site on Sunday, and Lyle was only discovered on Monday."

"Why kill a man like Lyle?" Alex asked. "What could a street beggar have done to attract a murderer?"

"He might have seen something," Rook offered. "Mr Lyle was old, but he was pretty sharp. What if he got the attention of the wrong person?"

"Maybe," said Alex. "In any case, I'll have to see where it happened."

After leaving Chattan, he took Rook along to visit both spots where the bodies were found, hoping for something new. Alex wanted to find other connections to Lyle, but it would be difficult for him to gain the trust of the sort of men Lyle knew.

Rook promised to gather information on his behalf. "Mr Lyle never hurt a soul," the boy said. "It's not fair that he was killed by some nutter."

There was still plenty for Alex to work on regarding both murders. From various authorities in the city of London to the underworld contacts who heard things the authorities never would, bits of information came filtering in. He heard more about James Galbraith's political leanings, who he tangled with in politics and business, and even some family history. Apparently, Galbraith had an illegitimate son who he tried to raise, though the young man turned to crime and cursed Galbraith's name.

Alex was the only one who had all the information. He tried to find a pattern in it, but so far, he had only hints.

So what did he know? There were two victims, at minimum. Each was killed roughly one month apart, a fact that seemed ominous, considering the symbols painted near each body. Alex worked at identifying a pattern in the dates of death. He thought at first it was the night of the full moon that tied them together. But only the most recent death actually occurred on the night the moon was full. The other was close to it, but not exact. And something told Alex that his killer would be exact.

The killer himself remained a shadow. Alex knew a few things. He was young enough to have dark hair. He was a larger man than Galbraith had been. He was strong enough to hold and kill someone without causing a struggle. And he wanted them to be found, along with the symbols he left nearby. Unfortunately, that wasn't nearly enough to go on.

Things began to stagnate. He rattled around his townhouse, a gigantic pile of bricks that was far too large for Alex alone. The servants kept the place running perfectly, which made Alex feel even more superfluous. He announced he would return to Dunmere Abbey. The air of London was getting to him. He needed to go home.

* * * *

Despite her days filling up with various small duties and diversions, Violet felt more alone than ever. Millie frequently provided her with company, and the weather improved, offering more opportunities to walk and ride through the grounds, which were slowly waking up in anticipation of spring. She lived for her long nights under the stars, happy at the folly. But she still felt adrift.

Alex was in London—so he said—and she wondered about him every day he was gone. She knew so little about him that she sometimes thought she'd dreamed the wedding. For the short time they were in the same house, he was alternately angry and kind; distant and cool one moment, then darkly passionate the next. He was the master of the estate, and then gone altogether. Violet had no idea what he thought of her, but she suspected he bitterly regretted his decision to marry her. In any case, by leaving he'd placed a barrier between them.

So she went on alone. She wrote letters to neighbors, then paid a few courtesy calls. She even attended church in the village, hoping that no one would find it odd that she attended alone. Though she met several new people, she felt no less lonely.

One day, when the sun shone brightly and the early March breeze was tantalizingly fresh, Violet was walking though the grounds and found a small graveyard under some trees. The ruins of a chapel stood nearby. This was a long abandoned place, and no one had been buried here for decades.

It was not entirely deserted, however. She found Millie lying on the fresh green grass of an old grave. The girl's legs were splayed out a bit, revealing slippered feet. Her arms were crossed over her stomach, and her eyes were closed.

"What are you doing?" Violet asked.

Millie answered without opening her eyes. "I'm imagining what it's like to be dead, of course."

"Why?"

The girl held up a slim volume of poetry, which had been lying at her side. "Wordsworth speaks so eloquently of finding repose among nature."

"And are you feeling repose?"

"I did at first. Now I feel a tree root in the small of my back." Millie sat up awkwardly, her black skirts pooled about her.

"Come on up," said Violet. "It's not as warm as it seems. And you'll get dirt all over you if you stay like that."

"No one cares what I look like," Millie groused. "Until my coming out, I may as well be invisible."

"That is not true," said Violet. "You must have plenty of friends."

"No," said Millie. "There's no one interesting around here. Alex won't let me go to London yet, and there are so many plays I want to see. But he's says I'm too young to risk the corrupting influence of the city. As if it's any better in the country, where there's nothing but gossip."

"But the gossip isn't about you."

"Some of it is," Millie said. She glanced sidelong at Violet. "You haven't heard what they say about me?"

"Does it have to do with your penchant for black clothing and graveyards?" Violet asked with a smile.

"No, not that. I mean…" Millie trailed off, then took a breath. "I didn't always live here, you know. I lived in Deal with my parents. But my mother died when I was six, and my father was not much of a father."

"I'm sorry to hear that," Violet said.

"Someone must have written to Alex about it. I've got Kenyon blood, and it reflected badly on the name, I suppose. My drunk father gambling away his money and my dowry when I was so little. How improper! Alex just showed up one day and announced that I'd be moving to Dunmere Abbey. He paid my father some money—told him he could do whatever he liked with it, for good or ill. But he brought me back here as his ward, hired a nurse and teachers and all. I've never been back to Deal. I don't want to either. This is my home now."

Puzzled, Violet said, "There's nothing wrong with that story. You're not responsible for your father's behavior. And it was kind of Alex to take you."

"But they say Alex only took me because I'm his," Millie explained. "His daughter, that is."

Violet blinked in shock. "What?"

"It's not true, of course," Millie said quickly. "I'm my father's daughter—got the Sherwood skull, he always said. And my mother barely knew Alex when they were children. Cousins, you know. Alex was abroad for the whole year before I was born, but does that little fact stop the gossip? No! They say the worst things they can about him, and anyone around him." Millie looked at her. "They'll say things about you, too. Just wait. Something horrible and cruel and utterly laughable, but people will still say it, because it's so salacious to say such things. All the scandal and none of the pain."

"Oh, Millie." Violet wasn't sure what to say. The younger girl suddenly seemed more worldly than her. In many ways, she was. "You must ignore it. Life here is good—let them talk if they want to. If you're happy, then their gossip will eventually be revealed as nonsense."

"I try," said Millie. "I never go to the village anymore. The other girls are beastly to me. But I'm happy here. Alex taking me in was the best thing to happen to me. I'm sure he regrets doing it every third day, but I try to be better."

"I understand," said Violet, struck by how similar the two ladies actually felt. "Now come back to the house with me. We'll have tea together. It's just about time."

After that, Millie became a sort of ally. Over the next few days, Violet's gowns began to arrive, as well. Every time she got the chance, she wore something different, just to see how it felt. She reveled in the novelty of having such a wardrobe. She appeared at luncheon in a gauzy linen gown with an empire waist and green ribbons at the neckline, feeling quite pretty. But then she ended up dining alone, which took all the joy out of it.

Violet went out to the folly every night after supper, and spent hours tracking something she suspected was a comet, as well as observing a few other phenomena. She even sketched a detailed map of the surface of the moon one night when it was half full. She felt such confidence when she found a star or planet just where her calculation said it would be. And no one bothered her or belittled her about her pastime, which was the most wonderful thing of all.

* * * *

Alex returned home from London on a bright afternoon, when the sky was so blue and clear that it seemed impossible anything bad could happen in the world.

He walked into the main foyer and stopped short. Violet stood at the top of the stairs, wearing a gown the color of the sky he'd just been contemplating. Her soft brown hair was done up in loose curls, and she wore pearls at her throat. Perhaps it was partly due to the fact that he had to look up at her, but the effect was that she seemed almost untouchable. She looked entirely like a duchess.

"Hello, Violet," he said finally.

"So you've returned from London," she said, without a trace of a welcoming smile. "Is your business there concluded?"

"No," he said, frustrated.

Violet paused, then said in a level voice, "So you'll be

going back."

"Inevitably."

"I see."

Alex stood there for a moment, unsure of her mood or in fact the actual meaning under her words. But when he walked up the stairs, she didn't move away. He should say something husbandly, but he was at a loss. Violet seemed more of a stranger than before.

"I'm happy to be back," he said, feeling like an intruder. "And I would like to spend some time with you while I'm here."

Her expression turned a little wary, then curious. "All right," she said. "You could begin by joining me on a few social calls over the next few days. I would appreciate your presence."

He nodded. Alex despised most activities like that, but he could hardly refuse after asking to spend time with her. And her hint about wanting his presence reminded him that one of the reasons he married her was to have a duchess again, partly to make him act more like a duke. He needed to reconnect with the social world around Dunmere Abbey, and joining Violet was the easiest way to do it.

As it turned out, the whole process was not nearly as bad as he remembered. Violet told him where they were going and when. He merely had to be ready to join her in the carriage, and they'd be off to another house or hall for a few hours. Violet had not been idle while he was away. She'd begun correspondence with several local ladies, hosted a tea for a few of them, received callers two afternoons a week, and gone to the church in the village once, in an apparently lovely gown, according to several people who'd seen her there.

In between the visits, Alex and Violet were thrown together, and they inevitably learned a bit more about each other. Violet became more assertive when she learned that Alex would not criticize her as her family had, and she told him a little more about her childhood. But on the subject of her parents, she would say nothing. She was never rude—Violet didn't know how to be rude—but she had a gift for gently deflecting questions.

Alex realized that only when they were at the Harleys' home one afternoon. Harley was the vicar in the village, and he and his wife quietly controlled much of the local society. Mrs Harley asked Violet about her parents, and Alex listened with considerable interest as Violet managed to completely avoid explaining anything about them. She did it so subtly that by the end, Mrs Harley decided she'd really asked about Violet's interest in heading up the committee for the improvement of the village green, which Violet graciously agreed to do.

A rumble of faraway thunder distracted him. "Ah. That may be our signal to return home now."

Harley turned to watch the stormy sky that had captured Alex's attention. "Perhaps you'd better wait it out here instead, your grace. Looks like a nasty cloud. Storms out of season never bode well."

"We only live a short distance away," Violet said, and Alex nodded his agreement. She turned to Mrs Harley. "Thank you for a lovely afternoon. We must have you to dinner soon."

"We should like that, your grace. The Abbey has been quiet too long, I think. It's time to open up again," Mrs Harley said, with a sidelong glance at Alex.

He was more concerned about the sky, though. The Harleys accompanied them to the carriage, again offering to house them until the storm blew over. But Alex was determined, and they were soon off. The horses sensed the sky's mood, and they needed no urging to keep a steady clip.

No matter how fast they went, however, the oncoming storm moved faster. Violet stared fixedly at the roiling, purple-black cloud, wincing whenever a particularly wicked flash of lightning arced down. The wind whipped across their faces in ever stronger gusts.

"I may have miscalculated this time," Alex muttered. "We'll get wet before we're home." They passed into a small copse of trees growing close to the road. They were like a tunnel of green in the summertime, but now the bare branches tangled into each other, and the black clouds made it as dark as twilight.

"Water we can endure. It's the lightning that worries me," Violet said.

He risked taking his gaze off the track for a moment, concerned at Violet's tone. "I should have left you with the Harleys," he said in apology.

She smiled at him. "Nonsense, I—" She broke off as a great flash of light illuminated the world, followed instantly by a tremendous clap of thunder that deafened them both. Violet screamed as the horses spooked, tearing at the reins.

Alex tried to pull the horses in, but another flash came, this time bringing a long cracking sound with it. He looked up, saw a branch falling, and before he even thought about what he was doing, he pushed Violet, propelling them both out of the carriage.

Cursed. The word flashed into his brain. And then, everything went black.

* * * *

Violet rose from the ground, stunned. She saw a massive tree branch about three feet in front of her. On the other side of it, several feet away, Alex lay on his side.

She stumbled toward him, hardly daring to breathe.

"Alex?"

He didn't respond, so she put her hand on his shoulder and pulled him toward her. He rolled onto his back, and then she saw his face.

The eyepatch he always wore had come off.

A weird pain shot through her when she saw the thick, white scar tissue over the sunken eye socket. She couldn't begin to imagine how it hurt. How did anyone endure such a wound? It seemed impossible.

Before she even knew what she was doing, Violet bent down and kissed Alex's cheek. "I'm so sorry," she whispered. Sorry it happened, sorry she didn't know how to help him, sorry she couldn't fix things. She searched the ground for the patch, finding it not far away. She did her best to put it back on. Alex would not like it if he knew she'd seen his wound.

"Alex," she said, when it was done. "I need you to wake up." She put a hand on his chest. He was breathing. He just wasn't responding.

Violet stood up, looking around helplessly. She couldn't move him. She couldn't leave him. Raindrops began to spatter on the cold ground, unconcerned at their plight.

But they were found only minutes later by a servant returning home from the village. Soon it seemed dozens of people were about, helping them back to the Abbey. Alex didn't wake up at all, and Violet ordered his doctor to be sent for immediately, regardless of the storm. The way the whole household jumped to obey every directive revealed how concerned they were about their master's fate.

Violet repeatedly assured everyone who asked that she was unharmed. True, her side ached from where she hit the ground, and she was chilled from the rain that still lashed at the windows. Dalby saw to it that she got dried off and then dressed her in a new, warm woolen gown. But Violet was only concerned with Alex.

She went to his main bedroom door and knocked. Alex's valet stood there, uncertain as to whether or not to let Violet in.

"Step aside, please," she said, relying on his instinct to obey orders.

He did step aside, and even announced her arrival to Dr Baldwin.

The doctor was at Alex's bedside, wrapping something around Alex's head. The layers covered his forehead and his missing eye.

"Is he awake?" she asked nervously.

Dr Baldwin turned. "No, your grace. That branch hit him quite a solid blow."

"Can I do anything?"

He shook his head. "We must wait for him to regain consciousness. It is possible he suffered the sort of wound that will leave him in a coma."

Violet moved to the bed. "I don't believe that."

"I hope you're right, ma'am." The doctor cut off the end of the bandage. "He should be kept warm, and someone ought to stay and watch."

"I will do that."

"It may be hours," Dr Baldwin warned.

"He pushed me out of the way," Violet said suddenly. "If he hadn't, I'd be the one lying unconscious. Or worse."

The doctor paused in his tidying up, uncertain what to say.

"I'll sit with him. It's the least I can do." She added, "I nursed my cousin in her last illness. Sitting by a bedside is nothing new to me."

"Very well, your grace. I'll give further instructions to the staff."

"Thank you. Will you come again in the morning?"

"Yes." Baldwin hesitated again. "Though I can promise nothing, his grace is a strong man."

"Have you been his physician long? Did you tend to him when he lost his eye?"

"He was injured while abroad, but I did tend to him on his return. A long and painful recovery. Learning to see differently, to judge distances correctly… He never complained."

"Did he tell you what happened?" she asked.

"No. He's a very private person. I got the impression though, that it was a dire situation. He had other wounds, too. Any one of them could have been mortal, if they'd bled a bit more or festered at all. He evaded death that time."

"Just as he will this time," Violet said, trying to sound confident.

"Let us hope so."

The doctor left her then, and once Violet settled what needed to be done, everyone else left, too. She pulled up a chair to sit near Alex's bed.

How strange, she thought. She'd never been in this bedroom before, but now she was alone with Alex, and the only thing she could do was watch helplessly to see if he woke or slept on.

Violet put one hand on his cheek. His skin was warm, she noted with relief. That was a good sign. But he didn't react to her touch at all.

He breathed steadily, undisturbed. Violet settled into the chair, and kept watching him, hoping to see a change. The stress of the day slowly dragged at her, though. By the time darkness fell, she was dozing in the chair, with only the light of one candle burning by the bedside.

* * * *

Alex woke slowly. His room was dark except for a single candle. He was lying in his own bed, and in a chair next to him sat Violet, dead asleep. Surprised, he gazed at her for a full minute. Her delicate features were enhanced by the strong shadows, and her hair glowed as the light picked out every strand. Seeing her in the golden light of the flame, he breathed in uncertainly, not sure if he had ever realized how beautiful his wife was. Also, why was she there at all, beside his bed?

"Violet?" he said aloud.

She stirred. "Alex?" Once she saw that he was awake, she burst into a smile that dazzled him. "Oh, Lord, Alex, I was so worried!" She reached out and took his hand. "Are you in pain?"

Was he? Alex paused and took stock of his condition. He had a headache, for certain. "What happened?"

"Don't you remember? We were riding back home when the storm struck, and lightning hit the tree..."

Oh, God. In a flash, everything flooded back. The storm, the crash, Violet's terrified scream. His last conscious thought that the curse had returned to mock him again. Alex shuddered. "I remember."

"Should I call for Dr Baldwin again?" She began to stand up.

"No." He stopped her with the pressure of his hand. "Are *you* all right?"

"Perfectly." She smiled, though her eyes were shadowed. "I was sure we were both going to die. When the carriage went down and I saw you on the road, I thought you *were* dead. The branch of the tree crushed the top of the carriage, and struck you." She shook herself. "But someone from the Abbey was riding back on an errand and found us only a few minutes later. Your people came straight away to help."

"How long has it been?"

"Several hours. The doctor said you're not to try to get up. Not yet. He'll come again in the morning."

He nodded. But he kept his grip on Violet's hand, unwilling to let her go. Had she waited for him to come to? Did she care that much?

Inspired, he said, "A kiss might help me heal."

Violet shook her head, wearing an odd smile. "I already gave you one earlier. You need to rest now." She left the room as fast as she could.

Alex could do nothing except wait for morning. Had she actually given him a kiss, and he missed it? How was that fair?

Partly because he was determined to not miss such an opportunity again, Alex healed remarkably quickly. He got out of bed as soon as he could the next day.

"You ought to rest longer," Dr Baldwin told him.

"I have things to take care of," Alex returned.

"You have a household of servants to attend to

things."

"These are things only I can do," he said.

That was true. Nothing made a man take stock of his life like a brush with death, Alex reflected ruefully. How had he deluded himself into thinking that his marriage to Violet could be a simple contract? And how could he have been so blind to Violet herself? He had to get to know her better.

* * * *

Over next few days, Alex spent nearly all the daylight hours around the estate, reassuring the household, the tenants, and the neighbors that absolutely nothing was wrong. Thank God Violet hadn't been hurt—the slightest injury to her would doubtless rekindle old rumors. But she seemed perfectly normal, the same quiet and polite woman every time he saw her. The distance between them was unbridgeable. Alex had once planned on that. Now he regretted it.

One evening, Alex returned to the house much too late for supper, so he went to the parlor, hoping to find Violet, who he knew stayed awake late. However, only Millie was there, reading a play out loud to herself, doing both voices in the scene.

"Sorry to interrupt," he said. "Where's Violet?"

"I don't know," Millie said with a pout. "She's probably outside."

"Outside? It's nearly midnight."

"I know that, Alex. But she runs off outside nearly every night after supper. Didn't *you* know that?" She rolled her eyes, disdainful of his ignorance.

Alex wouldn't let Millie see it, of course, but his temper was rising. "She may be outside now, but not for long. It's not wise to wander around at night, even on the estate."

"She's not *wander*ing," said Millie. "She's at her folly."

Her folly. Alex left the room, too angry to say another word. *Her* folly. Alex gave Violet the key to the place. It was *his* folly. In every sense. He trusted Violet, and for what? She wouldn't even let him touch her, but she fled out to the folly every evening?

Alex could only think of one reason why she'd do that.

He didn't even put on a coat. He just yanked open one of the French doors to the gardens and stalked outside.

He would catch Violet and whoever she was inviting to her little folly. Alex sneered at himself as he walked past the shore of the lake. Violet had been so clever, feigning sweet and shy around him. He genuinely thought she liked the folly for itself. He was an idiot. She probably had some lover before she even married him. She was twenty-five, after all. Perhaps she just had her lover follow her, and now they met every night on the estate grounds. It was hardly an inconvenience, especially since Alex was gone so often and so stupidly agreed to let Violet set the terms of their own marriage.

What a conniving, sneaky, two-faced woman. No one could be that sweet and adorable. It had to be an act.

Alex reached the door of the folly, and took a steadying breath. He found the door unlocked. What a careless lady, he thought. He slipped in and moved up the steps. They were stone, and therefore utterly silent.

At the landing, he saw the door to the room open a few inches. He eased it open further. The brazier was going, providing a steady warmth. But there were no lights, and the room was silent and empty.

He was actually worried for a moment, but then remembered the upper floor. Of course. He looked at the steps to the roof, and saw the hatch door open. He could take them by surprise.

Or he could just turn back.

Alex realized how little he wanted to find what he expected to find. The idea of Violet with another man sickened him. But wouldn't it be better to have it over? He walked up the steps.

Just before he reached the top, he heard Violet's voice.

"...moving through the constellation of Argo Navis. Magnitude brighter than last week's observation..."

Her voice was soft and lilting, as if she were speaking to herself while writing slowly.

As she undoubtedly was.

Be rational. This was *Violet*, he told himself. She was incapable of acting the way he'd pretended she was doing. Alex's gift for picturing scenes completely failed him this time. But still, what was she doing up here, at night?

"Violet?" he asked, not wishing to scare her by popping up like a ghost in a bad theater production.

The soft stream of words stopped.

"Alex?" she called uncertainly.

He climbed the last few steps.

She stood up from the little stool she'd been sitting on, and carefully stepped away from a telescope so as not to jar it, ruining the angle. She put the book she'd been writing in on the stone surface. "Alex? Why are you here?"

"I was looking for my wife," he said, feeling a little dazed.

"Well, you've found her," Violet said with a smile.

"Yes. What are you doing?"

"I'm stargazing. What else would I be doing?"

He laughed to himself. And at himself. "Nothing comes to mind."

"Were you worried about me?"

"I'm less worried now that I know where you are."

"But I told you I intended to set the folly up for this." Violet paused, tipping her head. "Actually, it's possible I didn't tell you. Are you angry? That I changed the folly around for my studies?"

"No. I was just…curious," Alex said. "I didn't know you owned a telescope."

"It was my father's," Violet explained. "He gave it to me because it had the best lens of all the ones in his collection."

"Looks quite heavy. You carry it up and down each night just to see the stars?"

"Yes. They mostly come out at night. Mostly."

He gave her a disgusted look. "There's no need to insult my intelligence."

"I wouldn't dream of it," she said.

"So what are you looking at? Specifically?"

"There have been sightings of an unknown object in the north sky," she said, enthusiasm kindling in her voice. "Possibly a nova, but much more likely a comet. However, it's faint, and some of the reports are conflicting about its location and movement. I'm tracking it."

"The telescope is that powerful?"

"It's better than most, though if I knew I was looking for a comet, I'd want a telescope with a shorter focal…ah, never mind. The point is, the conditions have been quite good over the past five nights. I've been able to identify it. Now if I can keep it in sight over the next few weeks,

118 ⚘ *Elizabeth Cole*

I'll know if it's moving like a comet ought to."

Alex nodded, but said, "I'm not sure I like the idea of you out alone."

"You said yourself this is probably the safest place in England."

"I wouldn't have said it if I'd known you were planning to come here at night."

"Please don't tell me not to come back," she said suddenly.

"Would you listen if I did?"

"I wouldn't like it." Then she said, "Would you feel better if you came to get me at the end of the evening? I'm almost always done viewing by about two."

"Do you ever sleep?" asked Alex.

"Yes. Usually around four or five in the morning."

"That leaves hours. What do you do before you fall asleep?"

"I try to fall asleep," she said practically. "That's about how long it takes."

"You could take something to help you."

"Thank you, but no. I've tried several options already."

"Nothing works?"

"Oh, some work quite well, but at the expense of my sharpness of mind. I'd rather be able to think and be awake half the night than live in a fog all my waking hours."

"I see." Alex looked around. "Well, if you'll permit, I'll walk you back now, since I'm here. May I carry that down for you?" He pointed to the telescope.

"Oh, I'll do it. If it should break, I want only myself to blame."

"If it breaks, I'll buy you a better one," he said.

Violet paused. "Very well. Thank you."

He carried the telescope down the stairs. It was not a lightweight object for a woman like Violet to haul up and down.

As they walked back toward the house, Alex had another minor revelation. Many of Violet's books must be on astronomy. Perhaps he could go through them and see if there was a sign or symbol that he'd missed. Or perhaps he'd see a pattern at last, and be able to prevent the next murder.

He almost asked Violet where to look, until he remembered how little he'd be able to explain. No, he had to work alone, as usual.

But it was reassuring to know what Violet was up to. When they passed by the lake, Alex said, "I'm glad you like the folly."

"Oh, it's perfect. Almost custom made for my needs."

"So it made the inconvenience of the marriage worth it," he observed, before he could stop himself.

"There is nothing inconvenient about my life here," Violet said calmly. Then she added, "Though to tell the truth, I'd have wed Bluebeard himself if it meant getting out of my aunt's house."

"To many women, the difference between me and Bluebeard is probably insignificant."

Violet sniffed. "Regardless, I'd have taken my chances, folly or not."

He couldn't tell if she intended the double meaning of her words, and didn't want to find out.

*

Once Alex learned exactly what Violet did most nights, he began a new ritual of walking to the folly at whatever time she told him. The hour varied from night to night, depending on exactly what Violet was studying. When he asked how she knew, Violet just said, "It's easy. The whole night sky is a clock and a calendar all in one."

Alex was profoundly relieved that it was the night sky —and not a lover—pulling Violet from the house. But he was also glad to discover something about her personality, which until then seemed rather opaque.

He also made a point of looking through her books, though he waited until she was otherwise occupied to do so. Explaining his interest would have been awkward at best, even if he was permitted to mention the Zodiac, which naturally was to be kept secret.

Alex paged through several titles. Most were histories or descriptions of very specific discoveries or theories and were of no use to him. But he did find one larger book that was more of a reference. It contained charts and tables of various constellations and other stars, including their signs, when they rose and set, and some of the details of their place in the sky. Alex noted several spots in the pages, jotting little notes to himself on scraps of paper as he went. He'd have to consult this book again, but he didn't want to remove it from the shelf, so he slid it back among the others when he was done.

He looked through a few more books in Violet's collection, then saw a small pasteboard box on the shelf. Curious, he opened the lid and found a stack of loose papers. These must be Violet's own notes about her stargazing.

He idly scanned some of the pages, not really reading. Most were rather dry, technical notes about the positions of stars or calculations of some kind. He unfolded one page near the top and found a sketch of a rough, cratered surface, filled with shadowed spots and empty fields of brightness. Something Violet viewed through her scope, he decided, studying the alien landscape.

Now intrigued, he kept sifting through the papers. As he went, he noticed the handwriting growing steadily more childish. No more scholar's notes; these were little passages and cryptic phrases, sometimes accompanied by a crude illustration.

He held up one page he dug from the bottom of the box, struck by what he saw. In the corner there was a line drawing of a robed figure he took to be Death, though instead of a scythe, it held a bright red serpent in both hands. The snake was as long as the figure was tall, and it looped and coiled menacingly over the page. Alex frowned. It seemed like far too gruesome an image for his Violet, especially as a child. He read the words near the drawing: *gift of death, thirteen, father after mother*. The words were jumbled together, as if written in dim light. None of it made sense. He saw one more phrase at the top, above a list of numbers: *the serpent handler*.

He put the papers back, and returned the box to its place on the shelf. What could possibly have inspired a young Violet to draw such a thing? He thought of her polite, endlessly sweet manner, and realized again that he didn't know her at all.

Chapter 10

♋

VIOLET WAS SITTING OUTSIDE ONE day, just after tea. The grasses on the lawn had turned green already, but she was enjoying the first shoots of the flowers coming up in the gardens nearest the house, the part most sheltered from the wind and cold. Her serenity was not to last, however. Millie swept up to her. The girl's cheeks were bright pink, more due to her anger than the brisk air.

"It's happening!" she announced. "Just as I said it would!"

"What do you mean?" Violet asked, patting the place on the bench to invite Millie to sit. But Millie was far too upset to stay still.

"I was just talking to Mrs Simpson. She'd been down to the village to speak to the grocer and *he* told her that everyone is talking about Marianne!"

"Who's Marianne?"

"Alex's second wife, remember? The one who drowned. They say her ghost caused the carriage accident. That she was trying to kill you!"

"Her aim was off," Violet noted dryly.

"How can you joke about this?" Millie asked. "It's appalling."

"What else can I do? People share rumors because they want to. The truth means little to them. The only reason that Alex was harmed was because we were unwisely driving through a thunderstorm. But people like reasons. Why blame a streak of lightning when you could blame a ghost?" Violet shrugged. "They'll grow bored soon enough."

"She's right."

Both ladies turned to see Alex approaching, a folded note in his hand.

He continued, "I've learned that no person can stop a rumor. But one can ignore it, and that's nearly as effective."

"But Alex," Millie protested. "It's worse than usual. People are saying Marianne's ghost is haunting the woods, and a woman in white can be seen nearly every night!"

"Well, if someone can catch Marianne's ghost, they're welcome to it," Alex said indifferently. "From what I remember, she never liked living here, so she's unlikely to remain here in the afterlife."

"You're not taking this seriously!" Millie said.

"Talk of ghosts and curses? I'm treating it with exactly the seriousness that's due, which is none at all."

"It's mortifying," Millie declared.

"It makes them look bad, not you, Millie," Violet tried to comfort her. "Just let it die down, so to speak."

"I don't understand how either of you can tolerate it." Millie walked off, savagely beheading old dried flower stalks on the way.

Violet let out a sigh. "So, she's a ghost now, this Marianne?"

"As you say, people like to talk." Alex shrugged. Then

he shifted. "But that's not why I came out here. I have to go to London again. Something is going to happen soon. I need to be there when it does."

"That's very mysterious."

"Yes, I suppose it is. Sorry I can't elaborate."

"Oh." Violet said. Well, at least he told her this time, instead of rushing off as he had before.

Then he said, "Actually, you should come with me. To London, that is."

"I should?" Violet asked.

"Yes. There are a number of things to take care of in town, and there's no point putting it off longer. You've got most of your gowns by now, haven't you?"

"Yes. There are a few still to be delivered. Ball gowns, mostly."

"They can be sent to the London address," he said. "You need to be presented as duchess. And you need to meet a few people."

"Of course." So it wasn't that Alex wanted her company. He just wanted to check items off his list. "When do we leave? Today?"

"Tomorrow morning will do. Dalby will need some time to pack for you. Tell her to plan for at least two weeks. And of course, she should follow in the other carriage. You'll have no lady's maid in town otherwise, and you'll need to look your best."

Violet nodded, accepting that meant at least two weeks before she'd get to look at the sky again.

Alex paused just as he was turning around. "You should pack some of your astronomy books to take with you. The general charts and references and whatever you're reading now. That way you won't lose time when you return."

"That's a good idea," Violet said, touched that he'd think of it. "I will."

* * * *

Not long before dawn, Alex woke suddenly. He reached out to the table by his bed, grabbing the eyepatch in a now instinctive move. He put it on without thinking about it, since he was concentrating on the sound. It was unmistakable, and had to be real. Broken glass.

He sat up, waiting to hear something more. Had someone smashed a window pane? The image of a thief came to mind, though the idea of someone sneaking all the way onto the estate to commit a robbery on the upper floor was absurd. If that was what happened, there would be footsteps, conversation. A clatter. Something.

When he did hear something, it wasn't what he expected. The sound was quiet enough that it would never have awoken him on its own. A sob.

Alex rushed through the connecting door before he had another thought. Violet's room was almost completely dark, the curtains all drawn. He moved toward the bed, but a piercing pain stopped him in his tracks just before he reached it. Stifling a curse, he looked down. He was standing in a puddle of water and glass shards. Violet must have knocked a glass off her nightstand. That was what woke him, and now he'd got a shard in his foot for his trouble.

Another small sound came from beside him as Violet tossed in her sleep. One arm was flung out, and he saw exactly how she must have knocked the glass over. He reached out to touch her, but she jerked away, her eyes still shut but her brow wrinkled as if she were in pain.

Alex heard that one shouldn't awaken sleepers having nightmares, but he didn't want to see Violet suffer.

"Violet," he said, shaking her shoulder gently. "Wake up."

"Don't," she whispered.

Alex said, suddenly more concerned, "Please wake up."

She stiffened, and then her eyes opened wide as she gasped for air.

"Violet," he repeated, willing her to look at him.

"Alex?" she asked, her eyes still wide, but now focused and awake.

"You were having a nightmare," he explained.

She looked him over, blinking. Alex was glad that he'd apparently managed to throw a robe on when he got out of bed. If Violet saw him naked in her room in the middle of the night, she'd probably prefer the nightmare.

"I was dreaming," she said, starting to shiver as she came to. "How did you know, though?"

Alex sat on the edge of the bed. "You knocked the glass over, and I heard it in my room."

"Oh, no. It will stain," she said, looking over at the mess on the floor.

"The mess is what concerns you now?" he asked incredulously. "This happens all the time, doesn't it? The nightmares are why you don't sleep at night. It has nothing to do with the stargazing. That's just how you occupy yourself for the hours you can't sleep."

She wouldn't look at him. "It's always been this way."

"You should have told me."

"Why?"

"Why?" he repeated. "You're my *wife*."

He leaned forward and pulled her to him. To his surprise Violet didn't pull back, though she didn't say a word. He held her as close as he dared.

"I don't like being kept in the dark, Violet." That wasn't what he meant, exactly, but then he never seemed to say the right thing around her.

"I'm sorry," she said, her voice muffled. "It never occurred to me that it would matter."

"Well, it matters now. So tell me. What happened in the dream?" Alex asked.

"I don't know," she said. "I can never remember. I know it's terrifying, but as soon as I wake, the details of the dream…just slide away."

"You've had this same dream before?"

"Yes. Or very similar ones. I've never slept well. I like it when you hold me," she added.

He sighed. Violet constantly surprised him. How easy it was, to hold her. "I'm happy to do it, Violet. You just have to ask."

She stiffened the tiniest bit, and he knew exactly why. "You don't have to ask me to your bed if all you want is this," he said, trying to keep his tone even. "I'll just hold you. Especially if it helps after a nightmare."

"It does help," she said, nevertheless pulling away then. She gave him a weak smile. "I'm sorry I woke you up. I feel better now. You can go back to sleep."

"Not likely." He shifted to look at his foot. "First I ought to take care of this, and then it will practically be time to get up anyway."

"Take care of what…" Violet made a little sound of dismay when she saw what happened. "Oh, Lord. You're bleeding!"

"Broken glass will do that."

"This is horrible. Every time I'm around you get hurt!

Lightning makes a branch strike you, you step on glass I broke…"

"That's only two times," he said. "And believe me, I've had worse."

"Oh, Alex." Violet reached out to take his hand.

Was that pity in her voice? Alex hoped not. He stood up, ignoring her hand. "Go back to sleep, Violet. We're still going to London. Perhaps a change of scenery will help you."

"Maybe." Her tone grew cooler. "You should get that bandaged before you bleed all over the floor."

"I should." He turned to leave.

"Alex?" Violet called just as he reached the connecting door. "Thank you. For coming to check on me."

"You're my wife," he said again, not knowing what else to say.

Violet nodded, but it wasn't clear whether she agreed with him or not.

Alex didn't go to sleep again. He got the glass shard out, and covered the wound. But the whole time he was thinking of Violet.

* * * *

In London, Violet discovered anew that Alex simply didn't live like other people. His townhouse was palatial, decorated in a heavy Baroque style so different from the more recent classical-inspired look. Violet could easily imagine generations of dukes residing in the place.

"This house is bigger than Hawebeck Place, and it's in the heart of London," she said to Alex. "You never even hinted at that."

"I don't really care for this house," Alex said. "I always feel as if the walls are pressing down on me."

"Well, the plaster is not to be ignored," she returned with a slight smile. "Why haven't you changed things more to your liking?"

"I don't know. Never found the time. And I'd rather work on the Abbey."

Violet was shown to the suite that must have belonged to all the previous duchesses. She didn't like it at all, with its dark colors, heavy molding, and massive, dark paintings on every wall. Dalby took one look and shivered, then steadfastly ignored the walls to concentrate on unpacking Violet's trunks.

"Who chose these paintings?" she asked the housekeeper, who had led her there.

"Lady Virginia," Mrs Malk said proudly. "She spent days selecting them and deciding where they would hang."

Violet wrinkled her nose. The scenes were dismal at best, and others were unsettling. The portraits were mostly chiaroscuro, with heavy shadows and startled, pale faces staring out from the canvases. There were also a few massive landscapes of dreary nighttime scenes. In one, a broken castle stood on a hill, and in another a storm-tossed ship looked about to be wrecked on a shore.

Violet couldn't imagine waking up to these. "Well, I think they're hideous. Have someone come and take them down as soon as it's convenient."

"Ma'am, you can't do that!"

"Why ever not? Who could sleep in a room with these faces hanging over you?"

Mrs Malk huffed. "You cannot simply come in here and change things that have been the same for years!"

"But it's *my* room, is it not?" Violet said.

130 ❧ *Elizabeth Cole*

"His grace would not approve!"

"Approve of what?" They both turned on hearing Alex's voice. He must have overheard the argument and come over.

"I want these paintings out of my bedroom," Violet said.

"Good," Alex said promptly. "I never liked them."

"But, your grace," Mrs Malk burst out, "the *duchess* chose them!"

Alex turned his attention to the woman, and to have the full attention of a displeased duke was never a comfortable experience.

"There is only one Duchess of Dunmere, and she is standing right here," he said in a level voice. "If Lady Violet gives an order, it will be obeyed—instantly and joyously. Is that understood?"

"Yes, your grace," the housekeeper murmured, dropping into a curtsey.

"Excellent. Her grace would be pleased to have these paintings gone by the time we return to the house. Come, Violet."

Violet asked Dalby to follow with a pelisse and things for outside. "Where are we going?" she asked.

"Out," he said. "I have a few items of business to resolve before...well, never mind. And now you evidently need new art as well."

"Blank walls are better than those paintings," Violet said. "There's no hurry to replace them."

"No, you should have what you want," he said. "Those paintings certainly won't help your insomnia, so they should go for that reason alone. Besides, I suspect Virginia chose those simply because she knew I'd hate them."

"Really?"

"By the end, she did everything she could to keep me far away, aside from simply asking me to stay away." He shrugged. "But she certainly was a favorite of Mrs Malk's. Do you want a new one?"

"A new what?"

"Housekeeper."

"She seems perfectly competent."

"Not if she dares argue with you, she's not."

"Alex. Please leave it. Why not tell me where we're going first?"

"You need jewelry," he said. "So we're going to a jeweler who can supply stones worthy of a duchess of Dunmere."

They were the only people at the jeweler's, and it was more like being invited into a private salon than entering an ordinary store on a high street. It seemed everyone did what Alex wanted them to do.

Violet stood for a moment, looking at collections of stunning, sparkling jewels on every surface. Violet was offered the opportunity to wear anything she liked, and Alex encouraged her to do so. Between them, they ordered many items. Diamonds, rubies, sapphires, pearls. Earrings, necklaces, bracelets, hair clips, and pins.

But Alex insisted it was all necessary.

"These jewels are so grand," Violet protested. She didn't say the rest of what she was thinking… They didn't suit her at all. But then, they weren't for *her*, they were for the position of duchess.

Her eye was caught by something. On a carved wooden form of a woman's neck lay a simple stone: a star sapphire set in silver, on a silver chain. It was lovely, with a special subtle gleam. But it was far too modest compared to all the things she'd just ordered. Violet sighed and returned to the task at hand.

"Your grace must have jet pieces in your collection," the jeweler murmured unctuously. "Any lady must, so that when mourning, she will still be stylish."

"Of course," Violet said dryly. She dutifully picked out several items of jet black. It would never do to sparkle at the cemetery.

"Millie would like this necklace," Violet remarked to Alex, after she took off the one in question. It was made of blackened metal rather than gold, and several jet teardrops hung from the chain.

"So she would." Alex told the jeweler to box it up separately. The rest of the jewels were to be cleaned and packed up for delivery. "Millie's birthday is only a few months away," he said to Violet.

"She'll be delighted." Violet sent another glance at the star sapphire.

"And you?" he asked. "You don't look delighted."

"Of course I am," she said, trying to sound excited. "I've just been draped in diamonds."

Alex looked unconvinced, but not long afterward they left the store, where the jeweler was no doubt at that moment ecstatically making out a bill.

"Are you sure you don't want anything else?" he asked on the street.

"I only have one head," Violet said. "I'll never find time to wear all those stones."

"There will be all too many opportunities," Alex assured her grimly. But Violet was no longer paying attention. "Oh, we're near Collier Street. I thought I recognized the neighborhood."

"You do?"

"Yes. We only came to London a few times a year, but I always visited this particular bookstore. May we stop in, Alex? Do we have time?"

"Nothing but time."

She led him down a few blocks and turned into a smaller street. Not far down, she saw the window of a small, familiar bookshop, where a number of volumes were visible on the shelf. "There it is!" She tugged eagerly at his arm.

Alex grinned. "I understand now. She refuses diamonds and begs for paper."

They entered the narrow shop. The owner recognized her immediately.

"Why, Lady Violet!" he exclaimed. "You are in town this Season after all? How good to see you again!"

"Thank you, Mr Turnbull. Though I am Lady Alexander now." Glancing at Alex shyly, she said, "Let me introduce you to the Duke of Dunmere."

The little man bowed immediately. "Your grace. I am honored to have you in my shop."

But then he looked back at Violet and beamed at her. "A marriage! My very best wishes to you, your grace. The stars have aligned, yes?" His tone was teasing.

She made a face. "What nonsense. Do you have any books on astronomy here? Or just useless ramblings of prognosticators?"

Turnbull laughed. It was an old joke between them.

Violet immediately put in a string of requests. The little man began scurrying about, fetching a number of books and apologizing profusely when some titles proved elusive. Alex was content to hover in the background, watching the exchange.

"Is that another edition of Laplace's *Mécanique*

Céleste?" she asked Turnbull at one point. "Oh, has no one translated it into English yet?"

"But your grace reads French," the shopkeeper said confidently.

"Yes, but he only wrote half of it in French. The rest is in algebra."

Turnbull laughed. "Maybe you will do the honors of translating someday."

"Or another woman will." Violet smiled, accepting the book. "I have always wanted a copy of my own." She turned to Alex. "It's quite a lot of books. Do you mind?"

"I can manage," he said wryly. "One could buy half the bookstore for a few of the necklaces I bought earlier this morning. I believe that's what's known as a tactical error."

"How so?" Violet asked, too pleased with the new books to really follow his comment. "You said the jewels were a necessary purchase, and now it's taken care of."

Alex made a sound of agreement, and she didn't pursue the question.

They left the store bearing a stack of volumes, none of which Alex ever heard of, by his own puzzled admission.

"There's no reason you should," she told him. "These are on the esoteric side."

"Those are all books on astronomy?"

"Yes, indeed."

"Not *astrology*," he said, with emphasis.

"No. Astrology is the worst sort of pseudo-scientific dodge." Violet sniffed. "It's all too easy to fool some people into thinking a few guesses are divinely inspired, rather than pure chance. Anyway, most so-called predictions are done in retrospect, using trickery to learn the right answers. But it's enough to establish some charlatan as a high priest of learning, and then what happens? He takes all their money and leaves gullible people destitute."

"So you do not believe in fortune telling."

"No. No more than I believe three unfortunate events constitute a curse, which was your real question, was it not?"

"I don't believe in any curse." Alex said firmly.

"But others *do*," she countered. "And you can't change their minds. You can't correct them."

"If they believe that, I want nothing to do with them."

"Sometimes you don't have a choice."

* * * *

Alex told Violet they would be attending a ball hosted by Lady Mathering, who was a sort of queen of social gatherings among the ton. It would be the first real chance for society to view the new Duchess of Dunmere, and Violet spent a long time conferring with Dalby over the right thing to wear. Violet understood without being told that her main role would be to appear *happy*. That is, she must look as though she was joyously married, and not in the least concerned about being joined to the Duke of Death. Dalby exerted herself to the best of her abilities, and finally pronounced Violet ready.

Violet cast a long look over her reflection. The new light blue evening gown she wore was considerably more daring than her usual wear. The high waist emphasized her breasts, as did the plunging neckline. She wore an extravagant diamond necklace Alex had insisted on purchasing. She hoped she hadn't forgotten anything. She desperately wanted to prove to Alex that she could be a duchess, not a mere country mouse. She looked the part tonight, with the modish gown, and the terrifyingly costly diamonds encircling her neck. Her hair was curled carefully, lifted and bound on her head in the current romantic style.

With Dalby's approval, she descended the steps from her room. Alex heard her coming and stepped into the hall from where he'd been waiting for her.

"Do I look all right?" she asked nervously.

"You look wonderful," he said, as if he didn't expect such an outcome.

She flushed. "You think so?"

"I wouldn't have said so otherwise."

He helped her into the coach, sitting across from her. Violet barely moved, afraid to rumple herself.

"Are you nervous?" he asked.

"Yes."

"Don't be. You're the one they're desperate to meet. A smile from you tonight will be the highlight of someone's Season."

"You're joking."

"Not a bit."

He turned out to be absolutely correct. Violet did her best to present a gracious, gentle face to the crowd, and she shoved aside her natural shyness as much as she could. Several gentlemen asked her to dance, and Violet accepted a few of them, deliberately choosing those who looked a little older or those who'd been introduced to her along with their wives. Violet didn't want to be seen with a man too close to Alex's age.

When she was standing to the side of the room, taking a few moments' rest, she heard "Violet," from a familiar voice.

Violet turned to find Judith standing there, along with

a lady and gentleman she didn't know. "I didn't expect to see you, Aunt."

"Such delight on seeing family," Judith commented. "I am so pleased."

"How are you?"

"Very well, now that your uncle and I have come to London for the rest of the Season." Funded, no doubt, by Alex's various payments to Judith.

"I am sure you will enjoy yourself," Violet said coolly. She saw Judith's gaze fix on her diamond necklace, and actually was glad she wore it. It was like a shield, or a mask. Even though Judith knew Violet as a shy little mouse, the diamonds seemed to turn her into a princess, and everyone forgot who was actually wearing the necklace.

Judith gestured to the lady standing next to her, who was lovely in a fragile way.

"Your grace," Judith began. "May I present to you Miss Susanna Gilroy."

Miss Gilroy curtsied to Violet. "How do you do, your grace."

Violet nodded a greeting, noting how quick the woman's breath came. She didn't want to be overly familiar, but her first instinct was to ask the woman if she was well.

"How do you know my aunt, Miss Gilroy?" she asked instead.

"Why, we have similar interests in the matter of the new sciences," the other lady replied.

"Ah," Violet said. So she was part of Judith's crowd, the ones who chased occult fads, picking them up and discarding them just as quickly. But something about Miss Gilroy kept Violet from making a sharper retort.

"You must enjoy living in London, then," she said. "Such a large city has something for every interest."

Miss Gilroy nodded with a pleased smile. "Indeed, your grace."

"And I wanted to introduce my good friend to you, as well," Judith said. "Mr Hanchett."

The gentleman who had waited patiently up to that point looked to be around the same age and station as Judith. He was tall and broad-shouldered, with dark hair untouched by grey. His clothes were extremely fashionable, as far as Violet could tell. This was a gentleman who lived among high society.

He bowed very properly. "How do you do, your grace."

"How do you do, sir," Violet replied. "Have you known my aunt long?"

"Since we were quite young," Hanchett said. "Though the years have separated us to some degree. I offer you best wishes on your marriage, your grace. Mrs Peake told me of it, and I must say I have never seen a woman so proud. You have honored your family."

Violet nodded. *Proud?* she thought. Judith was only proud of the deal she brokered. "Are you married, Mr Hanchett?" she asked, rather pointedly. He stood *very* close to her aunt.

"Not yet, your grace," he said with a laugh. He either didn't notice or didn't care about what Violet thought of his relationship with Judith. "But I'm confident that all will occur as the stars intend."

"Of course it will!" her aunt said. "And who better to read the stars than you?"

"So you are also a follower of astrology," Violet concluded.

"No," Mr Hanchett said promptly, causing both ladies to look at him in surprise. "I'm a *leader*," he clarified, with a quick smile. "Your grace is skeptical, and I don't fault you. Astrology has too often been the domain of fools and frauds. But it doesn't have to be."

"Don't feel you have to defend your pastime, sir." Violet looked around, hoping for an escape. "It doesn't matter to me in the least."

"But it should," said her aunt. "In fact, I was hoping you'd join me at a very special gathering later tonight. Our society—"

"Ah, there is my husband. You'll excuse me." Violet moved off. She didn't actually see Alex anywhere, but she had no interest in speaking with Judith or her friends further.

I'm becoming a rather duplicitous duchess, she thought. Who would have imagined it?

Luckily, she did run into Alex. "May I stay by you?" she whispered. "I fear whoever else I must have introduced to me tonight."

"Who did you meet to inspire that?" he asked.

"Oh, just a good *friend* of Aunt Judith's," Violet said, not bothering to hide her disbelief. "It was appalling the way they behaved."

"She's that public about it?"

She looked away, embarrassed at even discussing the idea. "Well, it was just an impression. Perhaps I'm wrong."

"Don't discount your impressions, Violet." He paused, then said, "One more reason to avoid her company. While I don't wish to order you to avoid her…"

"You don't have to," Violet assured him. "I am well rid of my aunt."

Alex had to leave her again, though, when he saw a gentleman in the smoking room he wanted to speak with. "I'll be back as soon as I can," he assured her.

Violet found herself in a group of ladies, all of whom were chattering and gossiping. The stress of smiling and appearing serene was starting to wear on Violet, who desperately wanted to leave. But duchesses didn't run away. So she stayed, hoping the clock would somehow speed up.

"You've met the ward then," one of the ladies said to her.

"Her name is Miss Sherwood," Violet said. "His grace's second cousin."

"Oh, that's what he calls her, is it?" One of the women laughed meanly. "Not what I heard," she whispered to her companion.

"Please share what you heard," Violet asked. Her heart was hammering, but she couldn't stand the look on the other lady's face.

The woman lost the smug expression, but only because she didn't have a good way to avoid responding to Violet's request.

"It's only a rumor," she said at last.

"What a relief," said Violet. "Then hearing it will be harmless. Do go on."

"I've heard..." the lady stumbled over her words. "I've heard she's the duke's bastard daughter."

Violet raised her chin. "Well, that is rather on the insulting side of harmless. I'm glad Miss Sherwood herself puts no stock in that lie. A less composed young woman might be hurt by the suggestion that the duke took her in for any other reason than charity."

"Oh, I had another reason." Everyone turned at the

unexpected voice. Violet felt a little shock as Alex slipped his hand around her waist, standing very close to her.

He went on, "Miss Sherwood's father is a drunk and a gambler. She was living on the edge of poverty with no support from her family after her mother died. I took her in as soon as I heard about her situation. And now that my wife has moved to Dunmere Abbey, Miss Sherwood has the family any young girl ought to. Odd that some people would choose to spread a falsehood instead of that truth."

Almost on cue, people turned and walked away in different directions. No one wanted to be anywhere near the Duke of Dunmere at the moment.

Except Violet, who was very happy he'd arrived. "I didn't think people could be so horrible," she murmured.

"Oh, that was a mild example of a London socialite's wit. I'm used to it by now," he said, his tone calm again. "You stood up well."

"Only because I knew what she would say," Violet admitted. "Poor Millie told me herself a few weeks ago."

"She's had a more difficult childhood than most people would assume," Alex said. "I've tried to shield her from the worst of the lies, but as long as she's living with me…"

"Millie said living with you was the best thing to happen to her," Violet confided. "All the black gowns notwithstanding."

He smiled at that, then said, "Would you like to leave?"

"I'd like nothing better."

They left the building together, both of them breathing the cool night air with relief.

"I thought that would never end," she said so only he could hear. "I felt as if I was being attacked by quizzing glasses."

"I noticed a few looks as well," he said dryly. "Hard to avoid with all the rumors swirling around my name."

"You shouldn't have to hear all that," Violet said. She did not want to think of the darker side of Alex's past any longer.

He helped her into the coach when it arrived, then sat across from her. The coach rolled slowly into traffic, and they both sat in silence. Then everything ground to a halt.

Alex made an irritated sound, then shifted to Violet's seat so he could see the driver from the window. "What is the hold up?" he called.

"Sorry, sir!" the driver called. "Jam up in the intersection ahead. I'll try to maneuver around."

"Just be careful," Alex called back. He closed the blind and settled back on his own seat. "You're still upset about what happened back there at the party," he guessed.

Violet sat back on her seat, sighing. "Yes. I'm not used to that at all. I'd much rather be stuck in a coach with you than stuck back in that overheated oven."

"What an endorsement," he said dryly.

"Oh, I didn't mean…" Violet put a hand to her temple. "I just can't think anymore."

Alex caught her hand as she brought it down.

"What is it?" she asked, slightly nervous.

"I have something for you," he said, reaching into a pocket inside his jacket. "I wasn't sure when to give it to you, but now seems like it might be a good moment, if I might distract you from your mood."

He put a small velvet pouch in her open hand.

"What's this?" she asked.

"Best way to find out would be to open it," he suggested.

She undid the little button that held the envelope together, and tipped the pouch over. A star fell into her hand. "Oh!"

It was the star sapphire necklace she admired at the jeweler's. "Alex, I didn't tell you I wanted this."

"But you kept looking at it," he said. "So I got it when you weren't paying attention."

"Thank you. It's beautiful."

"Put it on," he urged.

Violet reached up to unclasp the diamond necklace she was wearing, but fumbled at it with her gloved fingers. "Bother," she muttered.

"Here, let me." Alex moved to her seat and quickly undid the clasp, then lifted the diamonds off her neck. He dropped the necklace into the empty seat.

He took the star sapphire from her hand. Once it was on, he leaned back to admire the result. "It looks good with your gown."

"The stone is so pretty," Violet said, picking it up and tilting it to see the star shift in the stone.

"It suits you better than the diamonds, I admit," he said.

"Diamonds are expected, though," she said.

"You are continually unexpected." He reached for her hand again, asking, "I have your permission to hold your hand, do I not?"

Violet laughed. "Yes, of course."

It was rather nice, actually, with Alex just sitting by her, holding her hand in his.

But nothing with Alex was ever simple. He plucked idly at the fingers of her glove, pulling it off. "And I have your permission to hold your bare hand, do I?"

"Yes," Violet said. Nothing could happen with just her

hand.

He held her hand in his own for a moment, just caressing. Then he raised it to his lips. At the touch of his mouth on her skin, Violet felt a little stirring of heat. He smiled. She couldn't see it, but she could sense it.

He kept her hand there, turning it to kiss her palm. Violet felt a much stronger sensation then. Her hand and arm tingled. "Alex," she said in a tiny voice.

"So you like me at least a little bit," he said.

"It's not a matter of not liking you," she began to explain.

She had to stop because he took one fingertip in his mouth, biting gently.

Violet wanted to squirm, or twist, or dance. But she was also afraid to move, lest he stop. "Oh," she whispered.

"So you'll let me continue?" With his free hand, he put one fingertip in the center of her palm, then drew it down to her wrist and in a line down the inside of her forearm to her elbow.

Violet didn't think such a simple thing could feel so intriguing. "Yes. Please."

He laughed once, a low sound. He bent to kiss her neck.

The touch of his mouth, and then his tongue against the pulse point at her throat started a slow fire in Violet. She tipped her head instinctively, and sighed when his kiss deepened.

He still held her hand in his, and she tightened her grip, somehow afraid he'd get away. Then she took a deep breath, suddenly aware of how dangerous his few moves had been. "On second thought, I think we should stop."

"Why stop?" he murmured.

What a good question. His kiss felt very good, and warm, and confusing, and rich.

"Because...because we're in a carriage," she finally said, after probably too long of a pause. He'd think her addle-brained.

"So we are. But soon we'll be home."

"I should go to bed immediately, then."

"Not a bad plan. You'll need help to take off the gown." He slid a hand up her back, to the buttons at the top of the gown. He undid the first one, and Violet felt the bodice loosen a tiny bit, which somehow didn't help her breathing at all.

"Alex," she said, putting a hand on his chest.

"I'd be happy to help you with the rest later," he said. "Nothing more than that. Unless you want more, of course."

"No," she said. "Later is better. I mean, not tonight. That is, thank you, but not yet." She stumbled over her words, torn by entirely contradictory feelings. "I'll go to bed alone," she said. "I think."

He pulled away.

"I'm not ready."

He said nothing.

When the carriage returned to the townhouse, Alex helped her out without a word. Violet struggled to think of something to say—an apology to start—but her throat closed up at the idea of speaking at all. She knew she offended him, which she didn't mean to do, but he had surprised her.

Alex walked into the foyer behind her. He dropped the diamond necklace into the hands of a startled maid. "See that gets back to her grace's jewelry case," he said.

"Yes, sir!" the housemaid said, plainly terrified to be

holding such a priceless object. "I'll get it to Dalby as soon as..." She looked to Violet. "Ma'am? Should I give it to you?"

Before Violet could respond, the maid turned again when Alex would have gone for the stairs. "Oh, wait, your grace! A letter came for you not long ago. The man who delivered it said it was imperative!"

Alex stopped. "Where is it?"

The maid dropped the necklace into Violet's hand, then dashed to a side table. "Here, sir," she said breathlessly.

Violet saw how fast Alex broke the seal, and wanted to either yell or cry.

"Tell the driver I'm leaving now," he directed the footman nearest the door.

Violet found her voice. "You're going out again?" she asked.

Alex looked over at her, as if he'd completely forgotten she existed. "What?"

"You're going out again?"

"Yes." He started to put the letter down on the table, then changed his mind and slid it into his pocket. A very odd, bitter smile crossed his face. "Don't wait up."

Then he went outside, leaving Violet in the foyer, her hands full of diamonds she didn't want.

Chapter 11

♋

ALEX FELT AS IF HE was fleeing his own house, but the words on the note couldn't be ignored. There'd been another murder. And this time, he would arrive at the scene soon enough to learn something useful.

He rushed to the spot listed on the note, and moved toward the small crowd gathered at one edge of a public square in a quiet neighborhood.

Comments and questions filled the air as onlookers speculated about what occurred. Alex was able to get the gist just by listening.

A man had been found lying on the ground, near the base of a massive sycamore tree. Alex could see the body, now covered with a white cloth. Officers of the law were keeping people away from the immediate area.

"Stabbed right through the heart," one woman gasped. "Right here, while people were walking to and fro."

"Does that mean someone saw the attack?" Alex asked, directing his question to no one in particular.

"That man says he did."

He followed a pointed finger to where a middle-aged man was speaking to another pair of men, likely the law.

Alex would have to learn the witness's name as soon as possible.

One option was to slip into the persona of some authority figure in order to get closer. Alex had done that plenty of times in the past, though he preferred to have a little time to prepare. Saying the wrong name or claiming to come from the wrong parish would destroy the illusion. Just as Alex was about to chance it, he felt a light touch on his arm.

"Sir," said someone who'd sidled up next to him.

He looked over to see a young woman with curly black hair and a bright, round face. She wore a cloak that conveyed little about her station.

She didn't look at him, but murmured, "I'm Ivy, sir. I've been keeping an eye on the scene since I got here about two hours ago."

Alex let her lead him a bit away from the main crowd. He didn't recognize her face, but he guessed what she was. He asked, "Disreputable?"

A brief smile colored her face. "Aye, sir. As soon as word came through that this happened, someone sent you a message, and sent me here." She paused for a moment, then said, "I don't write things down, sir, but I remember everyone I saw and heard."

If she was one of the Disreputables, like Rook, Alex trusted her confidence. The Disreputables were all former criminals who had since become trustworthy domestic servants who were now thoroughly reputable—but they liked the "disreputable" moniker better.

Alex looked the young lady over. She probably worked as a housemaid when she wasn't aiding the Zodiac. "Do you know who I am?" he asked.

"Not by name, sir," she said, "But I could tell you

weren't just a random passerby so I knew you were the one they sent for."

He turned back to where the witness was standing. "Is it true that he saw the attack?"

She turned as well. To anyone watching, they appeared to be another pair of idle spectators. Ivy said, "Not sure. He was here when I arrived, that's certain. His name is Parker. He's a grocer in the neighborhood. No reason to think he's lying."

"How'd you learn that?"

"I have sharp ears," Ivy said. "And I got very close in the beginning. They let pretty girls get away with things," she added, with a pleased note.

"Good. Having the name means I can track him down later. What about the body?"

"Found dead tonight. Stabbed, though no weapon remained. Someone either stole it before the authorities could arrive, or the killer kept it. Not much interesting about that, of course. But there was a mark made in blood next to the body." She held up her hand. On the palm, she traced two lines curved toward each other, crossed by a short bar.

"Pisces," he muttered.

"Is it?" she asked. "We were told to be alert whenever a mark made in blood was found. Is this a thing you're after?" She nodded toward the body.

"I fear it's exactly what I'm after. I don't suppose anyone recognized the victim."

"Not his face. But those men found a notebook in his pocket. I overheard them say his name was Warner Mason."

Alex breathed a sigh of relief. Knowing that immediately would help him in his investigation.

Ivy related the rest of what she'd seen and heard so far, including the people who seemed most interested. She was precise and matter-of-fact.

The body was about to be taken away, finally, and there was little reason for him to linger. Ivy told him where he could send for her, if he needed to. Alex would come back the next day, when he could see more in the light.

He returned home very late, but he wasn't tired. There was far too much to think about. Alex went into his study and wrote steadily for another hour.

The murders certainly weren't random in their occurrence, though Alex still had no idea how the victims were connected. But the dates were starting to form a pattern. What had Violet said? *The whole night sky is a clock and a calendar.* Her innocent statement nudged his own thoughts. The killer was using astronomical symbols, so he must be planning his murders by the same method.

He was glad he suggested Violet bring her reference books to London, since he feared he'd need to look at them again for just this reason. After cross checking several tables in one of the books, Alex found something that might fit. One night early in the period that a new sign along the path of the Zodiac crossed the point of the sun's rising, somebody died. Then the killer moved the body to the chosen place, and used the victim's blood to paint the matching symbol by the body. But the dates still didn't fit perfectly, which frustrated Alex no end. He tried several calculations to force an answer to appear. He got no further than a guess. The next murder would happen between the thirteenth and sixteenth of April. London was a big city, though. How could he possibly be in the right place at the right time to prevent the next death?

Drained, Alex walked slowly upstairs. The house was silent in the small hours, but when he passed Violet's door, he saw that a light was burning. He almost knocked, but remembered what she said in the carriage. Violet didn't want him anywhere near her bedroom. And in any case, what could he say?

* * * *

Alex left the house very early the next day. He didn't want to encounter Violet, not after she repulsed him last night. Every time he thought he was getting a little closer to her, she closed up, unwilling to accept him. He didn't think it was physical—she hadn't seemed disgusted by his touch at all. It was something else, and he couldn't be sure what.

Why had he made that promise to not bed her until she asked him to? His shy Violet would never ask. Hearing her react to a simple touch in the carriage was intoxicating, and her first, unguarded response to his kiss made him think of a thousand other things to do to her. He could barely sleep that night, even after she'd flatly refused the idea of continuing the perfectly harmless practice of him undressing her.

Lord, how did a man go about seducing his own wife?

Solving a murder seemed easy by comparison.

He returned to the scene from last night, in the square. It wasn't cordoned off or watched. There was nothing left to protect. Alex walked slowly around the area where the body lay. He saw the bloody mark of Pisces still there. Now it was brown, and drying out in the dirt. It would vanish with the next rain.

He looked harder at the ground, recreating the event in

his head. There was no suggestion of a struggle, no digging of heels into the ground, nothing disturbed.

"He knew the victim, and the victim knew him," Alex said to himself. Mason would never let a stranger get so close. He could have easily run toward the safety of others if he got frightened. Instead, he let someone get very close indeed.

Energized, Alex went to find the grocer who'd spoken as a witness last night. He was easy to find, and even easier to speak to. He held court in his place of business, telling everyone who passed by about his great adventure.

Thus, Alex learned how the grocer was returning from his favorite pub, crossed the square, and nearly stumbled over the prone body of the victim.

"Still warm, he was," the grocer said. "I yelled for help, but the man was dead as could be. I looked all around, and I saw this figure staring back at me. Huge, hulking figure, with eyes cold as death!"

"Dressed as Death?" Alex asked casually. "Robe? Scythe?"

"Oh, you may chuckle, sir, but you wouldn't have if you'd seen 'im. Dressed like any other gentleman, in black coat and hat. But he had the knife in his hand! No scythes in the city, see? Death comes prepared!"

Alex nodded. So the killer kept the weapon. He wasn't scared to be found with it. Nor did he leave it behind because he was flustered. Though vague, the description fit with what he knew about Galbraith's and Lyle's killer, a calm, methodical man who was fully in charge of the situation, every time.

Alex walked to the nearby river and sat on one of the benches overlooking the water. His mind was far away, churning though the facts he'd learned. He searched his pockets, trying to locate the note he'd made about the dates of the killings. He couldn't find it, though, to his frustration. Had he dropped it somewhere? Was his concentration so off?

He was startled when a shadow moved across him.

"Want some company, sir?"

He looked over to see a woman in a tawdry dress. "What?" he asked, jolted out of his musings.

She smiled, showing white teeth. "I said, do you want some company? You look like a man with a lot on your mind. I can take it away, for a few minutes at least."

Alex surveyed the prostitute. She was young, and actually quite pretty. But the expression was painted on, feigned interest pretended only to make a few coins off his need.

He should need her. It had been a long while since he'd bedded a woman, and the last few times were deeply disappointing. Even though he paid a fair amount for the company of a very talented and well-trained woman each time, the event was barely tolerable, mostly because he spent the time assessing whether the girl was disgusted by his face or not. He concluded that she was, every time.

So he should be interested in this offer. More so after he discovered a lust for Violet that seemed as if it would never be fulfilled. Kissing just her hand made him nearly lose his mind. If only she'd let him go on. If only she let him near her.

"You interested?" the whore asked, peering at him.

"No," he said after a moment. "No, not remotely."

It probably wasn't an answer she heard very often. She was unsure whether to ask again, to convince him to go with her.

"How much do you charge for your company?" he

asked abruptly.

She named her price, and he pulled twice that out of a pocket and handed it to her. "Thank you for your company," he said. "Now leave me alone."

She took it with a professional smile. "Pleasure doing business with you, your lordship," she said.

Alex didn't even notice which direction she walked away. His gaze was out over the river again, and his mind was full of stars, and murder, and Violet.

* * * *

Violet rose very late. When Dalby came in, Violet said, "I thought I told you to never let me sleep past eleven."

"Well, you did, ma'am. But you seemed rather distraught last night, and I know you were up late reading…"

"Never mind. I suppose his grace has left."

"Quite early, I believe."

Violet sighed. Just as usual. Well, if she refused Alex's attention, she could hardly complain when he turned his attention to other things. If only she had said the right thing last night, maybe he wouldn't have left.

She wished she could talk to him. She'd slept badly and thought up a hundred questions about what a duchess should know, about what he wanted from her. If she could learn how to behave as a duchess, she'd feel more confident when Alex did all those things that made her so turned around. How should she respond? Should she be eager? Compliant? She ought to not refuse him—which she had, though she didn't intend to hurt him with her words. She just didn't know what to say.

It was all so confusing. Instead, she went to the study

and did some work on her own, which was comforting in its familiarity. At Alex's suggestion, she'd brought several of her most used references in a small trunk. Though she didn't have her telescope with her, she could plan for the next viewing when she returned. Violet opened her book to recall the expected rising times for the star Vega, which she was using to help locate the much fainter comet.

When she flipped the pages, a piece of paper fell out. She recognized the writing as belonging to Alex. She had to read the note several times before it made any sense.

15 January: Capricorn, Randolphus Lyle, mark on church steps

15 February: Aquarius, James Galbraith, mark on ground near body

14 March: Pisces, Warner Mason, mark in dirt by body

14/15 April: Aries? Who will die? Where?

Violet sat down, reading the words over and over, trying to suppress a chill. Why would Alex be recording the details of killings? And why would he put such a note in her book? There were a number of scratched notes, attempted calculations as if he wanted to choose the next date.

She looked at the dates and times more closely, then she got up and checked a few charts. The chill wouldn't go away. She paced around the study, thinking hard. She tried a few calculations of her own. One in particular seemed to fit the dates, like a key sliding into a lock.

Alex must have left the note there by accident. He certainly didn't intend for her to find it. She tucked the note carefully away in a pocket of her gown and replaced the book on the shelf.

Alex returned after dinner was over, but Violet made

sure she was in the parlor, reading, so she knew when he came in. She wore the star sapphire around her throat, and played with the stone as she read.

When he came into the front hall, she put the book down, waiting patiently. Would he come in, or pass her by? He hadn't spoken to her since she put him off last night in the carriage.

He came in. "They said you were in here," Alex said. "If you're occupied…"

"If I wanted privacy, I would have retired to my room," she said.

"Oh." Alex seemed uncertain, which was unusual for him.

"Since you're here," she said, "you could clarify something for me. I'm a bit confused."

"Yes?"

"You left this note in one of my books," she said, handing him the list of killings.

Chapter 12

♋

ALEX TOOK THE NOTE, NOT realizing what it was until he was reading the words. And reading through Violet's eyes, the list looked damning. Particularly since it was written by a man often called the Duke of Death. He exhaled. "I wondered where I left that."

"Perhaps you'd like to explain it to me."

"Why?" Did she think he was a killer? Why not? Everyone else was happy to debate whether he'd murdered his previous wives. What was another few strangers on the London streets? "Why should I tell you?"

"So I can assist you in finding what you're looking for." Violet's tone remained perfectly calm, that even tone he was beginning to think of as her duchess voice.

He chanced a look at her, and noticed the stone hanging around her neck. She wouldn't wear a gift from him if she thought him a murderer, would she? "What do you think I'm looking for?"

"I think you're looking for a killer," she said. "Though I can't imagine why *you're* the one doing the looking. Someone must have asked you to do it. And it must be someone who has the authority to ask such a thing." She tipped her head to the side. "I couldn't think of many people with that authority, and all my guesses seemed absurd."

"You're doing quite well so far," he said, actually impressed as hell. "Why not share your guesses?"

"You're a duke," Violet said slowly. "So only another man of your rank or higher would technically be able to order you to…investigate such a matter. The king could do it, obviously. Or far more likely the prime minister or a member of the cabinet with clout and interest in a series of murders."

"Go on," he said. Violet had given this a lot of thought.

"Or," she said, speaking slower, "it's something less… direct. A friend, or a favor. You may have a bond to someone that goes beyond mere duty." She watched him steadily as she spoke, searching for a reaction.

He sighed. "Violet, you're considerably more dangerous than you appear. That's a compliment."

"Thank you," she said evenly. "But I'd prefer the truth."

"The truth," he began carefully, "is quite close to your guess. I offer my services to the government as an…investigator, you might say."

"And you investigate murders?" Violet asked.

"Not just that. I pursue whatever lines of inquiry I'm instructed to. It's complicated, and not all appropriate for a lady's hearing. Let's just say I investigate crimes."

"What crimes require a duke to get involved?" she asked, sounding a bit skeptical now.

"It's not my title they want," Alex said. "It's my brain."

"And your brain is currently pursuing three murders?"

"Three murders, but all connected. One killer, and three victims so far. There will be more if I don't find him."

He told her some of the details, and saw her face clear after a moment.

"So that's why you left when those letters arrived? I wondered." Then her delicate brow wrinkled. "But that still doesn't explain how they selected you in the first place. I don't imagine someone walks up to a duke with such a proposal."

"No, it was less direct than that. I can't tell you. But I was selected partly for who and what I am. I can go places others cannot. Or sometimes, the issue is too sensitive to trust to a public bureau."

"So they ask you to help?"

"Well, someone does. Forgive me if I don't go into details. I am not permitted to say anything about the organization behind this."

"So there's an organization," she said.

"Please don't pursue this, Violet," he said. Lord, he'd have to step carefully around her now. The Zodiac did not like others to know about it. "I must ask you to trust me."

"I do," she said. "And I do think I can actually help you."

"How so?"

"As you know, the dates of the killings aren't random."

He said, "I've been trying to determine what the trigger is. I thought it was the full moon, but that was just a coincidence. I looked at the Zodiac signs, because of what was found at the crime scenes. But it's off by nearly a week."

"Only in the Ptolemaic system," said Violet. "If you

use the sidereal dates—that is, what the Babylonians used, then dates coincide with the first day that the sun enters a new sign of the Zodiac. The next killing will occur on the fifteenth of April—counting the day as beginning just after midnight, that is."

He said nothing for a long moment. Then, "And you found this note only this afternoon?"

Violet smiled. "It wasn't that difficult for me, considering my background in astronomy, and considering you only listed the relevant dates. I imagine you had to sort through far more...confused details."

"That's one way of putting it." He sighed. "Do you have any other insights?"

"I'm not sure. Do you think January was the first killing?" she asked.

"It's the earliest one I can find that seems to match. Why?"

"Capricorn isn't the first sign of the Zodiac. And it seems odd to begin anywhere but the beginning." She tipped her head. "I don't suppose you have their dates of birth."

He'd thought of the same possibility. "I do for two of them. The signs don't match."

Violet shook her head. "Well, it was an idea. I don't have much else to say. I only have questions, not answers."

"You know how I feel then."

"Hardly. You've been pursuing this for weeks, haven't you?" She walked over to him. "You were thinking of these deaths, some of them, all while dealing with a wedding and a new wife and quotidian life. How do you manage?"

"Badly, considering how I've dealt with you," he said

glumly.

"What do you mean?" Violet asked.

But he just said, "I might go mad if I keep at it."

"No, you won't," she said firmly. "Madness lies in whoever is committing the crimes. But if you follow logic and reason, you'll figure out the answer."

"Provided I actually have enough facts."

"I think you will." Violet gave him a tiny smile. "From what I've seen, you don't give up."

* * * *

Violet was relieved by Alex's explanation, partial as it was. She never believed his actions were nefarious, though they certainly could have been interpreted in a less flattering light. At least he wasn't seeing a mistress after all. Violet didn't know how relieved she was to realize that until she heard it. At least Alex didn't leave because he hated her.

He did tell her that over the next few days, he'd be virtually useless on a social level. Investigating the new death would take all his time.

She told him to do what he had to. "I'll stay here and put my new title to good use."

As far as Violet could see, her role was still to be his duchess, and to present a calm, composed face to the ton. She accepted callers and made visits over the next few days. She remained polite and quiet as much as she could. Before, she'd been called shy. Now she was "enigmatic." Everywhere she went, people stumbled over themselves to treat her as if she were a princess. Those same people would not have been home to her a few months ago. What a difference a title made.

One afternoon, she was startled by the card brought in on the tray. "My aunt is here?" she asked the maid.

"Yes, your grace."

Violet didn't want to invite her aunt into the parlor, but she also didn't want to turn her away completely. Instead, she rose and went to the foyer.

"Aunt Judith!" she said with false pleasure. "What a surprise. I have just decided I need some air. You may join me on a walk around the park."

Her aunt grimaced, but nodded. Judith hated to exert herself.

Violet was dressed for the outdoors, and the two ladies walked out, one of Violet's grooms following at a discreet distance.

"How are you finding London?" Violet began.

"The country is dull at this time of year, while London is the center of life." Aunt Judith gave her a sharp look. "You seem to be enjoying yourself, with your new extravagant life."

"You were the one who chose it for me," Violet pointed out. "So you can hardly complain."

"I didn't complain at all," Judith said. "I hoped you'd come to a dinner with me this Saturday evening. My good friend Mr Hanchett—you met him—would like to make a better acquaintance." Judith drew out a sealed paper from her reticle. "You'll come?"

"I'll consider it," said Violet, taking the invitation. "It is a rare evening that we are not expected somewhere. I've never appreciated how different my social schedule would be as a duchess."

Violet asked after her uncle then, more out of politeness than affection.

"Oh, he is the same as ever," said Judith. "Couldn't

come to call today, of course. Sleeping late…just like you."

"But for a different reason, I imagine." Soon enough, Violet said she had to return home, and she bid Judith farewell in the park, cutting off any attempt of the other woman to come back to the townhouse with her.

When Violet was alone again, she looked at the invitation. A Mr John Frobisher was the host of the dinner, even though it was Mr Hanchett who she was supposed to be excited about meeting. She sighed. How tedious, to indulge her aunt in this madness.

Then she thought of Alex. He would never attend such a thing if he didn't want to. He told her that she was to act like a duchess and not a country mouse. Violet flung the invitation into the fireplace, then burst into laughter. What fun, to act like a duchess. All she had to do was what *she* wanted.

Alex would be so proud.

Chapter 13

♋

ALEX WAS GLAD HE COULD put off his social obligations for a bit. He needed to learn everything he could about the most recent victim, Warner Mason, who was a clerk with the War Office. The man was thoroughly respectable on the surface, but Alex thought something more had to be going on.

However, it was imperative that he not be connected to this part of the investigation in any way. The War Office was full of people who might recognize him as the Duke of Dunmere, or worse, people who might start wondering what organization he represented.

So he'd have to break in at night, he decided cheerfully. Alex *missed* that part of being an agent. The challenge of slipping into the well-guarded offices of a building run by the War Office was simply too inviting. Alex dressed in his favorite outfit for such activities—dark, nondescript, and excellent for running in—and made his way to Mason's old office.

After he watched the place for a half hour, Alex was not impressed with the War Office's security. Two guards patrolled the grounds, but they weren't coordinated, so it was easy to slip across the yard when both were on the other side of the building. Alex had a bit of trouble with the lock on the door, but even that gave way after a few moments. He got inside and pushed the door shut just as one guard rounded the corner of the building.

Inside, the place was dark, except for a glow far away, which he assumed to be where the night watchman was resting. Alex moved silently through the halls, searching for the place where Mason had worked. He knew the details of the man's employment from his previous research, so it wasn't long before he found the office that held Mason's desk. It looked like he had shared the room with several other clerks. Now, the top of Mason's desk was conspicuously empty, and a few boxes were stacked nearby.

Packing up, Alex thought. Good thing he got here tonight, before everything was gone. Alex opened the curtain of the window nearby, which let in enough light so he wouldn't need a lamp.

A quick look through the boxes revealed only files of notes, memoranda, and some dull-sounding bureaucratic papers. Alex memorized the names in some of the most recent documents, but he doubted that they were what he needed to find. Using his skills again, he picked the exceedingly simple locks on the desk drawers. Apparently no one else had opened them yet. Papers were jammed inside, and nothing was sorted. Alex shifted the papers carefully, seeking something out of place or interesting, or ideally both.

Soon enough, something caught his attention: a paper marked with several familiar symbols. He pulled the paper out of the drawer and read it. It appeared to be astrological advice meant for Mason specifically. He read the last entry.

Venus occluded on the day of 15 Mar heralds a time of sacrifice without fame. Perform a worthy task on this day. Though no one will applaud your act, it will bear fruit when the moon passes through Scorpio.

The serpent bearer seeks only the brave and unflinching, as shown by the constellation's position over the next three weeks. Follow the design of the heavens to prove your worth as the true sky dictates.

Alex put the paper into his jacket pocket. "A great omen," he muttered, with derision. That was the day Mason died, and Alex would bet that the man would have preferred some hint of that cosmic design, rather than some bromide about proving one's worth.

But the fact that the paper existed at all was significant. It meant Mason was interested in the occult, and since the killer used similar signs, the two certainly could have known each other for that reason. Alex kept looking through the desk, and found a little notebook shoved toward the back of one drawer. It appeared to be written by Mason himself, and it was also concerned with astrology. Alex pocketed that, too.

He decided not to press his luck further. He put everything back and relocked the drawers. He had just pulled the curtain shut again when he heard a sound in the hallway. The night watchman was on his rounds. Alex held still, praying the man wouldn't open each office door.

He didn't. The footsteps faded away. Alex moved to the door and slipped through. He retraced his steps, but just when he reached the stairway, a voice called out.

"Stop there!"

Alex didn't feel like obeying that order. He bolted down the stairs to the ground floor. The night watchman was not an idiot, though. Rather than chase Alex, who had a head start, he opened a window and yelled an alert to the outdoor guards. They were already converging on Alex when he yanked open the door to the yard.

But he was in no mood to get caught. He barreled past the guards, neatly avoiding one's bat. They gave chase, but Alex didn't let them get close. He ran like a thief and outdistanced the guards well before he had to stop to catch his breath.

He dove down a narrow alley when he was sure he was out of sight. A quick breather, then he adjusted his clothes to be as presentable as possible. He walked out the other end of the alley and ambled down the street. He was not entirely surprised when a few minutes later, one of the guards ran past him, offering only a shouted apology for nearly knocking Alex over.

He shook his head, and then hailed a coach to take him home.

"People always expect thieves to be running," he said to himself, sitting back in the seat.

He took out the notebook, and saw a street direction inscribed on the front flap. Inspired, he called out to the driver to take him there instead. He *was* already dressed for it, he thought.

Mason had rented rooms in a neighborhood that Alex would have thought too expensive for a mere clerk. Breaking in was almost too easy, and Alex pushed the front door open very gently, reasoning that Mason might well share accommodations with someone to help with the rent.

But the whole place was utterly silent, and seemingly undisturbed.

Alex walked through the rooms, noting how well-appointed everything was. The furniture was quite new. Paintings and mirrors hung on the walls, and the only unpleasant thing in the place was the sour tang of rotted food. No one had been here since Mason's death. No one but mice and rats, he amended, seeing little dark shapes flee at his approach.

There was little evidence that Mason took his work home. The only papers Alex found were personal letters. Most seemed to be from a sister who wrote every week, to judge by the dates. There were a few other letters as well, some kept carefully in a little cardboard box, as if they were special. Alex opened the first one and read it in the dim light by the window.

"My darling," he muttered. A love letter? If so, it was a dangerous one to keep in the open. The writing was decidedly masculine, and the sender signed the note with *Forever, Daniel*.

That didn't necessarily mean much for Alex's investigation, though. Mason didn't appear to have worried about exposure. And he wasn't short of money, to judge by the place. So he wasn't being blackmailed by someone who thought they might exploit his romantic preferences.

Unless Mason *was* the blackmailer. That might explain how he could afford to live beyond the means of a clerk's pay.

Alex quickly went through the rest of the place, pocketing all the documents that interested him. Then he left, using a window like a thief.

* * * *

Though it was quite late, Violet was awake when Alex returned to the townhouse. She heard his distinctive footsteps below. Though she didn't want to bother him when he was working, she was also rather curious about his progress.

So she descended the steps, looking for him. The study light was on, and she knocked softly on the door. "Alex?"

There was a pause, then, "Come in."

Violet stepped into the room, and gasped. "You look terrible." He wore dark clothes that were a bit ripped and torn. But more than that, his face was haggard.

"That makes sense," he said. "I feel as if I've got no sleep for days."

"That's because you haven't," she said, "unless you're sleeping somewhere else." She bit her lip. "I didn't mean that how it sounded."

Alex just looked at her for a long moment, then said, "It sounded as if you're slightly concerned about my well-being."

"Oh," Violet said, relieved that she hadn't accidentally started a new argument. "In that case, I meant it exactly as it sounded."

"You're not asleep either," he said then. "The usual reason?"

"More or less." Violet moved further into the room. "I shouldn't bother you now, either. You're working, aren't you?"

"If breaking into a victim's home to find out who they were counts, then yes, I've been working."

Violet thought of her well-born husband acting as a common thief. It was surprisingly easy to picture. "I suppose," she said, "that if one waited for the law to do everything, it would take too long to get to the answer. Did you learn anything?"

"I think so. But not enough. There are more questions than answers at this point." He pushed what he'd been reading aside. "And of course, I do still have to act like everyone else. There's some event tomorrow evening, isn't there?"

"Yes, but if you're pursuing…"

"No," Alex said quickly. "We'll appear as expected. A few hours among society won't kill me."

Violet laughed. "I think your notion of what's dangerous has got skewed, Alex. Society isn't asking you to sneak into buildings and chase murderers."

"Not directly. But someone has to."

She shook her head, saying she'd leave him to work. She could tell Alex wanted to say something else, but she turned away before he could. Violet wouldn't get in the way of his pursuit. She knew that it was important, and he'd made his priorities quite clear.

* * * *

As she warned Alex, the next night brought another event to attend. They reached the party when it was already packed with guests. Alex said he hoped to put in an appearance and then leave as soon as possible.

Almost as soon as they entered, an absolutely gorgeous woman hailed them. No, Violet corrected, she hailed Alex, and Violet just happened to be in the vicinity. Alex led her over to the woman with a speed that made Violet even more suspicious.

"Your grace," the woman murmured. She was even more stunning up close. Her very dark hair was cut quite short, though on her the style seemed perfect. Her eyes fairly smoldered. It didn't matter that her mouth was a little small or that she was actually rather skinny. The deep burgundy silk of her gown rustled whenever she moved. And her smile was far too…knowing.

"Didn't know you'd be here tonight," Alex said to her. "May I introduce you to my wife?" Without waiting for a response, he said, "Violet, this is Sophia, Lady Forester. She is the wife of my friend, the Viscount Forester."

"How do you do, your grace," the other woman said. By her accent, she was obviously French by birth. Something in her expression made it clear that this was a woman who expected the world to turn around her.

But then she smiled, and Violet found herself smiling back.

"I've heard quite a lot about you, your grace," Lady Forester went on. "I suspect some of those things may even be true."

"You have faith," Violet said quietly.

Lady Forester's smile deepened. "Does it seem so? Tell me, are you staying in London long?"

"A couple of weeks, I expect. My husband is much in demand."

"The irony of his position," Lady Forester said, with an understanding laugh, and a glance toward Alex. "My own husband finds himself in much the same position, and I am left all alone to pine for his return." The last part was said in a deliberately theatrical tone, making both Violet and Alex laugh.

"I must entertain you while his grace is occupied," she went on. "You will come to my home tomorrow for the afternoon."

Violet almost agreed without even considering it. Such was the power of this woman's voice. "I may have a prior engagement," she hedged.

"I hope not," Lady Forester said smoothly. "You would enjoy the day, I think. Only intelligent women are permitted over my threshold, and gossip is considered terribly boring by my guests."

"Are you inviting me to Utopia?" Violet asked before she thought better of it.

Lady Forester laughed delightedly. "You will come. I know that you will."

"You should, Violet," Alex added. "No sense in you being bored at home while I'm away."

"Very well, then."

Alex then sighed. "I think I see one of my cousins. Damn. I'll have to speak to him now. Please excuse me."

Lady Forester also excused herself, saying that she had to locate her own husband, saying, "He's probably trying to climb out a window. He hates parties." Then she left, after reminding Violet of the invitation to her home.

At moment later, a man with dark hair and very well cut clothing came up to Violet. He was quite handsome—a little too handsome, actually, in the sense that he was quite aware of his looks. He bowed to her, with a touch more drama than necessary.

"Excuse me, your grace. That is, you *are* the Duchess of Dunmere, is that right?"

"Correct," Violet said.

"I saw you across the room and knew you had to be her. You must be a particularly *daring* woman, to brave the curse."

"I do not believe in curses," she said flatly.

He merely smiled. "Do you believe in love at first sight?"

"Excuse me?"

"I'm only testing the range of your beliefs, your

grace," he explained easily. "Do you believe in dancing, for example?"

"I believe it exists, if that's what you're asking," Violet said, uncertain.

"Excellent. Prove it to me." He took her hand with the obvious intention of taking her to the floor. "I am Derek Holbrook, by the way. You may have heard of my father, Lord Leconbury. Shall we dance?"

Violet wasn't sure she wanted to do that, but a quick glance around didn't help. Alex was nowhere to be seen.

"Very well," she said, even as Derek led her to the dance. One dance couldn't possibly hurt.

* * * *

Alex thought the evening was going surprisingly well. Violet looked even more lovely tonight than ever before. She was wearing a white gown with touches of blue and purple embroidered all over it, and she wore another necklace from her new collection—this one featuring a large amethyst as the center stone. With her hair up in a mass of curls, the whole effect made her look both innocent and tempting. Or perhaps Alex was reading a little too much of his own desires into her appearance. Either way, she was certainly the most beautiful woman there tonight.

But she also seemed to be missing, or at least he didn't see her. He asked a few people, and heard from one that she'd been dancing with Derek Holbrook. His cynical, investigative side immediately created a mental image that set his teeth on edge. Derek was notorious for chasing newlywed women. He saw their presumably blissful state as a challenge to his talents as a seducer. And Violet, of course, was completely innocent. If Derek set his sights on her, Alex would likely end up in a duel tonight, one way or another.

Alex had to find her. But before he could get very far, it seemed half of London had to come up to him and tell him things he didn't want to hear.

He avoided as many of them as he could, but some people were more persistent.

"I must say, she looks better than the rumors would have it," a Lord Morley was saying to him.

"What rumors?" snapped Alex.

"Ah, there are rumors that the duchess haunts the grounds like a ghost, wandering at all hours and scaring everyone half to death."

Alex took a deep breath. He said, "Tell me. Does the duchess strike you as someone who haunts anything?"

Lord Morley looked sorry he brought it up. "No."

"Good. I hope that puts an end to any discussion of a rumor that's patently stupid." Privately, Alex resolved to find out exactly how the reality of Violet's insomnia got blown up into this wild tale. Some servant must be to blame. There were over a hundred on the estate, and it was impossible to get all of them to hold their tongues.

But first he had to find Violet before she got into trouble.

* * * *

Violet was getting into trouble. Derek seemed harmless enough at first. He was a good dancer and made her laugh more than she thought he might. But after the dance, he'd drawn her well away from where he'd found her. Indeed, he drew her well away from the crowd. While it was a relief to breathe in the less congested room near the gallery on the upper floor, she did not like being alone with the gentleman, or his increasingly uncomfortable conversation.

She didn't want to be rude, so she tried to simply ignore the man's words at first. But when he touched her arm and made an unquestionable innuendo about temptation, she had had enough.

In a voice as cold as winter, Violet said, "I do not find you tempting, my lord. I find you tedious."

Derek, who must have been slightly drunk, took a moment to digest her words.

"I refused you," Violet added helpfully. "Get out of my sight immediately, and I shall not press the matter. The stairs are that way." She pointed with her closed fan, hoping she wouldn't have to use it as a weapon.

He didn't say a word, but instead huffed and turned around. The sound of his boots faded rapidly down the corridor in the other direction.

Violet snapped open her fan, and felt the beginnings of a sob in her chest. Why should she feel so embarrassed when it was the man who behaved so terribly? But Violet should have known better than to let it get so far. She been taught that it was a lady's responsibility to guard her own virtue and keep any hint of scandal away. If anyone discovered that she'd been alone with the gentleman for even a moment, it would reflect badly on Violet. Alex would be furious, she thought. Her first impulse was tell him all about it, for some reason. But he was always cognizant of what society would say, and he'd likely blame her for getting into the situation.

Nevertheless, she should return to him as soon as possible. Still overheated and feeling ashamed at the whole encounter, she stepped out of the room and made her way back to the crush.

It took a moment to find Alex among the many guests, but she finally did and made a beeline for him. "Alex, I'm so glad I found you."

"Was I lost?" he asked. His voice was joking, but he put one hand around her waist as if he worried about her slipping away. She stepped as close to him as she dared, wordlessly seeking his protection from the likes of Derek Holbrook.

"There are some truly awful people here," she confided in a soft voice meant for him alone.

His hold tightened fractionally. "Anyone in particular?"

"I..." She paused. "It's partly my fault. I should not have been wandering through the house, and I didn't expect him to follow...never mind."

"We can leave if you'd like," he said, noticing her flush.

"I would like."

In the carriage, she stayed quiet, though she felt much better than she had in the house. Alex clearly knew something had upset her, though he didn't ask her questions about it. He sat across from her, politely looking out the window at nothing.

"Please sit beside me," she said suddenly.

He shifted to accommodate her request. Violet reached for his hand in the darkness, and he squeezed hers in response.

"Would it be possible to return to the Abbey soon?" she asked in a small voice.

"Do you not care for London?"

"Not especially," she responded, her eyes pricking.

What a country mouse she was after all.

"We can leave soon," he said. "A few days. Certainly less than a week."

"Are you sure? Will your work keep you—"

"I don't want to talk about that now," he said.

She looked up at him, feeling unshed tears in her eyes. "It's good we left."

"Violet, if anyone back there did anything to make you upset, I swear…"

"No! Please, don't." She sighed, exhaustion creeping over her. She laid her head on Alex's arm, and he quickly lifted it to draw her against his chest. She felt the fine weave of his linen jacket on her cheek, and thought it was surprisingly comfortable. "I just want to go home soon. There might even be swans on the lake by now," she added in a soft, almost dreamy tone.

"You said home," Alex said after a moment. "You think of the Abbey as your home now?"

"Of course I do," she said.

"Oh," he said, exhaling. "I'm…I'm glad to hear that."

Violet sensed he was not merely glad, but she was too tired to pursue it, and really it was pleasant to have Alex to lean against, his warmth surrounding her and easing her into a doze. She had no idea when her eyes closed, but she'd rarely felt so safe in her life.

* * * *

Violet rose early the next morning. Dalby came in when she rang.

"Good morning, ma'am. If you would like, you could take breakfast with his grace. He just walked down a moment ago."

"Oh, yes. Find me a morning dress and don't fuss about my hair."

Dalby had her dressed in no time and sat her at the vanity to brush her hair quickly.

Violet studied her refection, thinking of the previous night. "Dalby, do you happen to know how I got inside last night? I remember falling asleep in the carriage, but I don't remember waking."

Dalby giggled. "Well, you didn't, ma'am. I was waiting up, of course, and I saw out the window when the carriage pulled up. His grace carried you inside. All the way up the stairs and to the bed. Then he said not to wake you if I could help it, since you have such trouble sleeping. Then he left. You woke a bit when I helped get you out of your gown, but you dropped off right after. You must have danced forever!"

Violet was interested in only one detail of the previous night. "He carried me in? All the way?"

"Yes, ma'am." Dalby clearly thought the whole thing was rather romantic. Perhaps she was right.

"Well, finish my hair then. I should certainly thank him for it."

Chapter 14

♋

ALEX SAT IN THE DINING room, now flooded with sunlight. He was perfectly dressed to go out, in a dark blue coat over grey pants tucked into his black hessians. But he wasn't in a rush, and he was reading from a set of handwritten notes when Violet came in.

"Good morning," she said.

"Good morning to you, Violet." He looked up and smiled.

She walked over to him. "I heard how I returned to the house last night. You are very kind to me," she said softly, and bent to kiss him lightly on the cheek.

"Any gentleman would have done the same," he said, striving for nonchalance but not quite succeeding.

"I suspect not," Violet disagreed, in such a gentle tone that it would be rude to argue the point. She smiled at him for a moment, then turned her head at the sound of a maid coming with more coffee.

With Violet distracted by assembling her breakfast, Alex caught his breath. He remembered his original intention to keep their marriage an arrangement of convenience, one that would not entangle either of them emotionally. What a fiction that was turning out to be. Her kiss had affected him, *far* more than it ought to have.

"I will be out most of the day," he said abruptly.

Violet looked at him over her coffee cup, her eyes calm. "Of course. Remember I have been invited to luncheon at Lady Forester's home. That is all right, I hope?"

Alex nodded. "Yes, of course. Not a bad person to know in London," he added.

"Good to hear," she said. "But in any case, I expect that I shall be here all evening."

"I'll see you tonight then."

When he got outside, the day was bright enough to make him more hopeful than he'd been in quite a while.

"Never mind the coach," he said to the driver. "I'll walk instead."

"Yes, your grace."

Alex was in an astonishingly good mood, he realized with a jolt. He was knee-deep in murder, there were rumors swirling around both him and Violet, but he was in a good mood. And it was largely Violet's fault. He remembered her sleepy comment about the swans, and smiled to himself. If she truly thought of the Abbey as her home, then there was hope for their marriage. He also felt much better now that Violet knew about his real work, even if he only told her part of it. He hadn't thought much about how his constant going to and from London would be viewed—in fact, he hadn't considered Violet's feelings much at all. But he would from this point forward. Especially since she had been so rational about it all. Then again, rationality was Violet's pride. If he asked her, she'd probably offer to help with the investigation.

He smiled again when he thought of her little kiss over breakfast. It was casual and anything but passionate. But it was natural, and that made all the difference. He liked

Violet's kisses, and he'd do what he could to actually earn them. He wondered what he'd have to do to get that every morning…aside from carrying her inside the house every night, which might get redundant after a while. He'd been stupid to think that she'd just accept him because they were already married.

He arrived at the Whitby Club at precisely the time Lord Forester had requested. He assumed it had something to do with his investigation, since Forester was also a sign of the Zodiac. Alex remembered how surprised he was when he learned that. He'd met the Lord Forester, Bruce Allander, several times socially and liked him. Forester was also deeply interested in his own estate, and he and Alex found plenty to talk about that was of more interest to them than the Season's gossip. When he was told that Forester was also a sign, Alex didn't believe it. Bruce just didn't look much like a spy.

Then again, no good spy did.

The tall, black-haired man came up to him at the club, a serious look on his face. "Dunmere, I'm glad you made it. Might I have a word?"

Alex nodded at him. "Of course." Then he recalled something Violet had said earlier. "I believe my wife is at your house right about now."

"Sophie mentioned that. She has a soft spot for those who don't quite have a circle yet. I think she wants to take the duchess under her wing while she's in town."

Alex knew about Lady Forester's capabilities, and thought that under her wing would be a very safe place for Violet to be.

"Let's move upstairs," Bruce said. "I'd prefer a private conversation."

Dunmere followed him up a wide, carpeted staircase

to a smaller room on the next floor. When they both entered, Bruce shut the door.

"What's this about?" Alex asked. "Did Aries tell you to do something related to my assignment?" He wasn't upset about the idea. The Zodiac agents worked together more often in recent years than before. But some warning would have been appreciated.

Bruce shook his head. "I wish it were that, but I haven't got the slightest idea what your assignment is. No, this is more personal."

"Go on."

"I should tell you this, but please don't think it's an insult or ill-meant."

"That doesn't bode well," Alex said slowly. He couldn't imagine Bruce doing any such thing.

"I just don't want you to call me out," Bruce said with a slight grin that was anything but happy.

"Please tell me. I've never made a practice of shooting the messenger," Alex said, on tenterhooks now.

"I overheard a comment at my other club the other night. Purely by chance, and I can't say for sure who spoke it."

Alex's heart sank. "About me, I suppose? What scandalous, horrible thing have I done now?"

"It's not about you. Not directly." Bruce took a breath, and then said, "Apparently, there's a pool going somewhere, betting on how long your wife will live."

"*What?*" Alex asked in disbelief. This was beyond the pale, certainly worse than anything he expected to hear.

"Steady," Bruce warned in a low voice. "Understand I didn't hear details. But I felt it better that you hear it from a friend rather than otherwise."

Alex clenched his fists, trying to suppress the rage that

was building. Betting on Violet's life? He had the urge to break some man's legs.

"Who?" he asked.

"I didn't see who spoke." Bruce seemed anxious to avoid bloodshed. He'd seen the look in Alex's eye and knew exactly what it meant.

"Can you repeat the words?"

The other man paused, remembering. Then he spoke, in a different tone: "I've put my wager on Dunmere's wife at six months, two weeks. The furthest out is a year and a day." His voice reverted back to his customary tone. "Another man then asked about the odds."

"What club were you at?" Alex pressed.

"Asters. Obviously, the pool is not one the club would ever countenance. It's simply some stupid prank by one of the less reputable gaming hells around."

"I'm going to find out where," Alex muttered, already thinking about his contacts, who he could extract information from. "You'll excuse me." He nodded curtly, turning on his heel.

"Dunmere." Bruce's tone cut through the rage in his brain for a moment. He looked back at the other man. "When you find out who's responsible, I'd be honored to be your second."

Alex paused, then nodded. "Thank you. Not merely for the offer, but for the honesty."

"You're welcome." Bruce took a breath, and a new look flashed across his face, something savage. "If I'd heard something like this about Sophie, I'd be sharpening my swords right now." He paused. "Then again, so would she."

"Maybe I'll ask her to be my second." Alex smiled without mirth and left the building, leaving the other spy behind.

* * * *

Blissfully ignorant of the darker habits of London, Violet was enjoying her time at Lady Forester's home. A number of other women were invited for the afternoon, as well. In contrast to the various parties and evening events, where Violet felt exposed and constantly examined, this seemed remarkably casual. As promised, the ladies were all intelligent, and the discussion was anything but gossipy. No wonder Lady Forester wasn't at home to other callers that day.

At one point, Sophie pulled her aside. "It is as promised, yes? Not a trial like all those events with the ton?"

"This is lovely. Thank you."

"You looked a little lost when I first met you. How are you settling in, cherie?"

"To London?"

"And to married life." Sophie lips curved. "Myself, I found it quite an adjustment." She laughed at something only she remembered, then sobered. "Of course, I did not have to contend with a host of idiotic rumors, either. I have heard many of them, you know."

"They will fade," Violet said, trying to be practical. "I am sure people will grow bored."

"It is so heartening to know you are Dunmere's wife now. I do not mean to gossip, but…"

"I have heard some details of the previous marriages," Violet said.

"Then you know that Dunmere had all the trials of marriage, without the joys." She sighed. "It is unfortunate so many noble unions do not take the wishes of the couple into account."

"Ours did not either," Violet noted. "I only met him on the day of the wedding."

"Perhaps, but fate has certainly made up for that. How lucky you are to have love in your life."

"I am not sure I do."

Sophie said, "Well, men are not often good at saying what's in their hearts. They express it in other ways. Usually in the bedroom," she added with a knowing little laugh.

Violet felt her cheeks flame. "I wouldn't know," she said, before she thought better of it.

Sophie put a hand on Violet's arm. "Cherie, did I understand you? You were married last month!"

"Yes. Technically. Just not…completely."

"You have still not consummated it?" Sophie asked gently. "*That* is something to keep secret, or some mother will work to have it annulled in order to have her own daughter made duchess."

"Is that a risk?" Violet asked miserably. "According to what I've heard, I was the only woman in England who dared brave the curse—not that I even heard about it until after the ceremony."

"I thought you didn't believe in curses."

"I don't!" she said.

"But?" Sophie asked. "You weren't finished."

"I *don't* believe in curses," Violet affirmed. She took a breath. "But if there *was* a curse, it shouldn't matter whether I believe in it or not. And if we're not completely married, perhaps that's keeping the curse at bay."

Sophie guessed, "You're afraid of dying?"

"No, of course not."

"That is the curse, is it not?"

"Well, yes, but that's not what worries me."

"What, then, if not your death?" asked Sophie.

"The curse isn't on me," she began. "It's on Alex. If I die, I die. Everyone does at some point. But he'll be alone again. I couldn't bear to think of him like that." All at once, her muddled feelings made much more sense. She knew what she had just said was true. She couldn't stand the idea of Alex alone. She wanted to be with him.

"So you love him."

Violet flushed, shy again. "I…hardly know."

"I think you do." Sophie leaned forward and gave her a little kiss on the cheek. "And it sounds as though fate may have played a hand after all. For the best, this time. You just need to trust yourself, cherie."

When Violet left Sophie's home, the other woman's words still echoed in her mind.

* * * *

Alex returned to the town house in a far worse mood than he'd left it. He was livid over the news of the bet, and he felt very much like ripping the city apart brick by brick so he could exterminate all the rats in it.

How dare someone involve Violet in their vice?

Unfortunately, he hadn't been successful in learning more about the wager. For obvious reasons, people were extremely unwilling to talk to him about the details. To a man, all his potential sources either professed complete ignorance or could only relate the barest details. Alex learned almost nothing over the course of several hours. He tried to convince himself to ignore the whole thing. It was an insult, but he was used to insults now. It would all soon blow over. It had to. But it was much harder to put aside an insult to Violet, and the anger continued to simmer inside.

He saw the light in the parlor still burning, so he pushed the door open to see his wife sleeping in a chair by the fire. Violet must have been reading a book, but despite the tea by her side, she eventually dozed off, the book falling unheeded into her lap.

He didn't want to wake Violet, considering how she seemed to struggle with sleep. Her porcelain skin looked almost pink in the glow of the fire, but there were faint shadows under her eyes. His anger faded as he looked at her, a new emotion replacing it, something more protective. Violet shouldn't be subjected to the gossips of the ton. She'd asked to return to the Abbey. After the day he'd just experienced, he realized how much he would like to return there, too. A few more days, a week, and then they would.

Feeling rude for staring at a sleeping woman, Alex reached out and gently touched Violet's bare arm. She jumped at the contact, her eyes opening wide before they focused on him.

"Oh, Alex! You've come back!" She smiled then.

"Where else would I go?" he asked wryly.

"Did you have a good day?" she asked.

His expression tightened. "No."

"What's wrong?" Violet asked, seeing his face.

"Nothing for you to worry about. I had some unpleasant dealings today, that's all. I hope your day was better."

"Lady Sophie is so marvelous! I feared I would stay too long, but she almost wouldn't let me go. She routinely asks a small number of ladies to join her for luncheon every month or so. She calls it her *petite salon*. They were all very charming."

"I'm glad. Violet, you should be in bed. You'll hurt your back if you sleep on this thing all night."

"I'm surprised I fell asleep at all," she said.

"Can I walk you upstairs?" he asked. "Or I could carry you," he added, deliberately keeping his tone light.

Violet blushed, looking down. "You don't have to do that."

"I wouldn't mind at all."

"You may walk me up, and that will do very well."

At her door, he said, "Let me kiss you."

"Oh."

"Just a kiss good night," he clarified. "We started this on the wrong foot. That is, I did. But I want to set things right. One step at a time."

Violet looked astonished. "I'd like that." She took a step toward him. "You may kiss me."

He felt as if he'd been given some great gift. He bent and kissed her lightly on the mouth, not daring to push for more. "Good night, Violet."

She was smiling when he pulled away enough to see her face. "Good night, Alex," she said softly. "I'll see you in the morning."

When he reached his own room, he realized his rage had dissipated completely.

* * * *

In the morning, Violet made a special effort to wake early enough to join Alex for breakfast. She had resolved to be a proper duchess, and that meant keeping more appropriate hours so she could do all the sorts of things around the house and among society that needed to be done.

The walls of her bedroom were now bare, since the offending paintings had been removed. She felt much better waking in the mornings, and thought that the addition of mirrors instead of art might improve it further. With nothing more serious on her mind at the moment, she went downstairs to find Alex.

She found him in the breakfast room, just finishing his meal. "I always feel I've just missed you," she said, annoyed at herself. "But I am trying to wake earlier."

"Not your fault," he said. "I never set a particular time. Do you want me to sit with you?"

"Oh, no, you don't have to, if you've got things to do."

Alex did sit with her for a few moments, but rose when a footman announced that several letters arrived. "They're in your study, sir."

"Off to work with you," Violet said cheerfully. "What events do we look forward to this evening, by the way? I can't remember."

"Ah, nothing too horrible," Alex said from the door. "A dinner, I think. Just wear what you like. You always look lovely."

He left to take care of his correspondence.

"This came for you, ma'am," said a maid, bearing a box in from another room. It was about a foot square. "Just left at the side door. The boy who delivered it ran off. Didn't even wait to ask for a tip."

Violet took the box, which seemed very heavy for its size. "I don't recall ordering anything. There's no note?"

"Maybe it's inside?" the maid asked, with a little shrug. "The boy just gave your name."

Violet opened the box, curious as to what it could be.

She pulled the lid off and saw only thin shreds of patterned paper, which must be protecting whatever was underneath. Before she could pull it aside, another maid came in, bearing a few letters.

"These just came for you, your grace," she said.

Violet turned to take them from the tray, automatically sorting through them to see who'd written.

"Ah, Lady Forester did write after all," she said, pleased. "I was hoping to get the name of..."

The maid's shriek snapped Violet's attention around.

"There!" She was pointing to the table.

Violet looked back, where the box had fallen onto its side. No, not just fallen. Something *made* it fall. She blinked, trying to put sense into the strange, circular, coiling pattern...

"It's a snake, ma'am," the maid shrieked again, tugging desperately at Violet's arm to pull her away.

Violet didn't shriek. She didn't say a word. She was frozen with terror.

The maid's scream kept echoing in her ears, but she didn't register anything other than the snake's coiling body. It oozed out of the box, foot after foot of black scales and thick white bands. It slithered onto the table and then onto the floor, where it recoiled and reared its head up.

It started to edge toward Violet. She took a step back, helped by whoever now grabbed her by the shoulders and yanked her farther away.

The snake hissed madly, sensing a new threat. But it sensed it far too late.

Alex brought his foot down hard onto the thing, crushing its slender body. The snake snapped into violent death throes. But then it lay in nearly two pieces on the floor, a wild bloody mess in the civilized space of the house.

"Violet." Alex was there, looking at her with concern. "Violet, are you all right?"

"It was a snake," she said, shocked into dullness.

"Violet, did you get hurt? Did it bite you?"

She shook her head mutely, tears streaming down her face. Alex took her by the shoulders and steered her into the room on the other side of the foyer.

She heard him giving clipped orders to the servants. "Clean it up. The whole rug. Just roll it up and have it burned. I want everything gone. Now."

He sat Violet down on the wide chair she liked to read on, then crouched in front of her. "Violet, are you all right?" He ran his hands up and down her arms, looking for any wound.

"I hate snakes," she whispered, pushing tears off her cheek. "I hate them."

"I know," he said, his voice deliberately calm. "But it's dead. It can't hurt you."

"Ma'am!" Dalby rushed into the room. "I just heard what happened! Do you…" She faltered on seeing Alex as well. "Excuse me, sir."

He said, "Have someone bring her grace something to drink. And pack up her things. We're leaving for the Abbey as soon as we can. Today."

"We are?" Violet asked, finally coming out of her shock. "But you have important things to attend to…"

"I'm attending to you," he said shortly. "And I want you safe at the Abbey."

Chapter 15

♋

THE COACH WAS ON THE road out of London within an hour. Alex appeared calm, but Violet could tell that he was actually on fire with anger at whoever was behind the prank. She told herself over and over that it was a prank, because she didn't want to think it might be anything worse than that.

The recollection of looking over to find those living, shifting coils made her shudder again, and she rubbed her arms to get rid of the bumps that rose on her skin.

"Are you all right?" Alex asked, seeing her move.

"I will be," she said.

"I'll find out who sent it," he said grimly.

"How can you?" she asked helplessly. Then she shrugged, trying to avoid any more thought of it. "It was just a nasty trick."

"Was it?"

"What do you mean?" Violet looked over at him, aware that his rage was more focused than simply being offended at a prank that scared his wife.

"It could have been venomous."

"Ugh!" Violet shook herself. "That's hideous. Who would do something like that?"

"Someone who might not like me investigating the murders."

"So they'd kill *me*?" she asked.

"Perhaps it was meant as a warning."

"Will you stop investigating?"

"No. But I will take steps to keep you safe. And that means staying at the Abbey."

"I prefer it there anyway." She paused. "I'm glad you're not giving up."

"I'll just add this as a matter to investigate. Who sent that to you, and how did they plan for you to open it?"

"Everyone likes opening mysterious packages," she said. "If it was ordinary, or had a name on it like the milliner's, a servant would have handled it instead of giving it to me."

"I should have saved the thing to identify what it was."

She said, "It was a black snake with white bands. It must have been at least six feet long, and it was very slender for its size."

"You remember all that?"

"I just have to close my eyes to see it." She laughed at herself. "And to think I was just resolving to sleep better at night!"

Alex leaned forward. "Can I ask you something?"

"Of course."

"Who knows about your fear of snakes?"

Violet blinked. "I don't know. Dalby. Uncle Roger and Aunt Judith. My cousin Madeline knew, but she's gone. That's all. None of them would have sent it!"

"Probably not," Alex conceded, though he didn't look convinced. "But it can't be coincidence. I remember how you reacted when you saw that harmless little snake at the

Abbey. Someone must want to exploit your fear."

"Maybe. I used to have nightmares about them. I slept in the same room as Madeline when I first moved to Hawebeck Place, and I'd wake her up because I'd be screaming in my sleep."

"Lord," he said, appalled.

"I suppose I'll forget it in time."

"Well, I don't know if this will help at all," he said, pulling a slim package from his jacket. "But I do promise it's not a snake."

"You got me a present?" Violet asked.

"I did. Open it."

She did, and found a pamphlet by a French astronomer. "Poisson's new work on the movements of the planets! This was just printed."

"I went back to your Mr Turnbull and asked what a stargazing duchess would like best. He said you'd want this."

"I was asking about it, and it hadn't come in yet." Violet smiled at him. "Thank you. This helps." She put her hand out and he took it, lifting it up to his lips.

Violet felt that instant shyness come over her, but he didn't let her retreat.

"I meant what I said last night," he said seriously. "I started this all wrong. I don't know what I was thinking... no, that's not true," he corrected himself. "I was thinking that I could pretend it was nothing more than a business arrangement. That you were someone who knew exactly what you were getting into, and we'd just endure each other to get what we wanted."

"You still married me, thinking that?" she asked.

"It was the only way I could. And then I found out you were different, in the best way possible. Can we start over?"

"I'd say we've already started over," she said, hoping to make him feel better about it.

"So you'll give me another chance?"

"What do you want me to do?"

"Just be you. I'm the one who has to do things differently. I'll spend time with you, and talk to you. I insist on at least one kiss good night, every night."

Violet nodded quickly. "May I insist on something as well?"

"Yes."

"Please tell me when you're going into London to work. And tell me if I can help you in any way. If there's something I can do, I want to do it. Especially if...if someone insists on involving *me*." She shivered again at the memory.

"I'll try," he said seriously. "I'm not allowed to promise more than that. But at some point there might be a way to help. I know there's some connection between these victims that I'm missing. A pattern that's not all revealed yet."

* * * *

After they returned to the Abbey, Alex saw to it that no one in the household would allow Violet to receive any packages or mail larger than a letter unless someone opened it first. He also forbade any unknown visitors, and told the household to report any strangers on the grounds. He didn't think anyone would dare come onto his property. But then, he wouldn't have guessed someone would send a snake to the townhouse either.

The morning after their return, Alex came into the

breakfast room to find Millie already there, dressed in black as usual. Unsurprisingly, Violet was still in her bedroom.

"What are you planning to do today?" he asked his ward.

"I'm going to read up on my Norse myths. Ones about Odin, to be specific."

"You are? Why?"

"Well, he reminds me of you. One-eyed and all that."

Alex put his fork down, irked. "You know, Millie, you don't have to eat with me. You can have a tray brought up to your room."

"But I thought I was supposed to learn how to converse and hone my wit."

"There's a difference between wit and insult," he said.

"It's not an insult to compare someone to a deity! Anyway, you were the one who told me I ought to prepare to enter society. *And* you didn't get me copies of any of the new plays when you were in town, which you promised to do."

"I was a bit distracted," Alex muttered. Then he remembered something he wanted to ask. "Millie, has Violet ever mentioned astrology or fortune telling to you?"

She frowned. "In a manner of speaking. She berated me for tossing an apple peel over my shoulder on the last full moon."

"What?"

"Alex, don't you know anything? If a maiden peels an apple and tosses it over her shoulder on the night of the full moon, the peel will form a letter, which is the first initial of the man she is to marry."

"That's ridiculous."

"That's exactly what Violet said."

He put his head back, considering. "What letter did you see?"

Millie pursed her lips. "Well, it was a little difficult to discern. I'm fairly sure it was a T. But it also looked like it might be a J. Or an L."

"And is it the first name or the last name that is mystically revealed?" he asked, with a serious face.

"Oh, stop teasing me!"

"I'm not," he protested, though he couldn't stop a smile breaking through. "You're my ward. Wouldn't it make my task easier if I knew I could automatically turn away any potential suitor not possessing a T or J or L name? Should I make allowance for an I?"

Millie crossed her arms. "It's all very funny to you. You don't understand."

Violet walked in just then. "Good morning. Oh, am I interrupting?"

"Not at all," said Alex. "We were just discussing the universe's plans for Millie's upcoming marriage."

"Stop it!" Millie said. "All I want is to know what's in my future, and instead I'm completely in the dark. Why shouldn't I try to find out? It's only the rest of my life!" She stormed out of the room, leaving Violet looking after her with large eyes. Then she turned back to Alex. "What was that about?"

"Apple peels."

Understanding colored her face. "Oh, yes. She seems quite interested in any method of divining her future husband's name." She tipped her head. "She's not pining after anyone in particular, is she?"

"Lord, I hope not. I have enough problems."

Violet smiled a bit. "I know."

He stood up, walking over to her. "It helps that you

know," he said quietly. "I never wanted to lie to you, but I've grown used to not telling anyone what I'm involved in."

"Don't tell me details," she said quickly.

"I won't. But it's good to speak to someone about it," he confessed. "I talk to myself more than you might think."

"Well, you can talk to me," Violet offered. "I may not be a…whatever you are…but I can sometimes see patterns as you do. One has to in astronomy. If you don't know where the fixed stars are, there's no hope of finding a new one."

"Will you look tonight?"

"I hope so," Violet said. "I couldn't stargaze in town, and I don't want to miss anything."

* * * *

However, early that evening, the sky seemed to drop all at once. Torrents of rain hit the flagstones, the gardens, the grounds, the roof, the windowpanes. Lightning and thunder added to the chaos. There was a frightful din, and several maids screamed at the noise.

"Well," said Violet staring out the window into the blackness beyond. "I suppose you'll tell me it's a poor night for stargazing."

Over by the fireplace, Alex laughed. "It's a poor night to be out at all. You can't possibly want to leave the house."

"Not in this weather." Violet let the curtain fall back into place, then turned to face the room again. With the windows all covered, the storm wasn't quite so intimidating. The fire pushed a warm glow throughout the room, and the candles on the walls all burned steadily. Alex didn't ever have to worry about spending too much on light. It was a subtle difference from her old life, but one that Violet wholeheartedly appreciated.

A maid came in with a tray and placed it on the tea table in the center of the room. Violet nodded to her. "I'll pour. You may go."

When the maid withdrew, Violet moved to pour herself a cup. "Do you want some?" she asked Alex, indicating the teapot.

He shook his head, lifting up the glass of brandy in explanation. But he moved to sit by Violet a moment later.

Before he could say a word, Millie opened the door and stepped in.

"I say," Millie began, then stopped on seeing them seated together. "Never mind." She turned and closed the door behind her.

"Oh, she didn't have to leave. Should I go tell her?" Violet half rose, but Alex put a hand out.

"Don't. She either thought she was interrupting, or she's still a bit embarrassed by this morning's conversation."

"That sounds more likely," said Violet. "Did she bring it up then?"

"No, I did."

"Whatever for? You know it's all a lot of nonsense."

"I was curious about why *you* think it's a lot of nonsense."

"Because it is."

"Yes, but why?" he pressed. "You're far more vehement on that topic than others. What led you to decry divination so loudly?"

"I've told you. At best, it is a mindless diversion without intellectual merit, and at worst it is a fraud."

"Yes," he said patiently. "Now tell me why you think that."

"Because it's true."

"I meant why it strikes so close to you. And don't tell me it's the mere defense of your science."

Violet put the teacup down. "It's not important."

"Then you shouldn't mind telling me." He paused, then said, "Why does it matter to you? You're too clever to get caught."

"Yes,." Violet said. "But my father wasn't."

Alex reached over and took her hand. "Go on."

She gripped his hand tightly, glad that he was there. "It just makes me angry. My father was the person who taught me astronomy, and how to use telescopes. But he was also very interested in…more fanciful aspects of the stars. He corresponded with several people who shared his interests, and over time, he seemed to fall under their influence. He would consult star charts to decide when to travel, or how to invest, or what to buy on a trip to London. I was young, but I could see that Mama didn't like it at all. She thought the occult was too close to the Devil. But he wouldn't stop, and after Mama's death—which no chart predicted, by the way—he turned to his friends for solace."

"Not you," Alex guessed.

"Of course not me. I was very young. It wasn't that I expected…I don't know. But he forgot me completely. After Mama died, he just vanished. Always off on his own pursuits with his friends, and he sounded half-mad when he did come home and spoke to me about anything. Aunt Judith was one of them, and he'd believe her if she said the sun would rise in the west next morning."

"Your aunt was interested in that?" Alex asked. "She doesn't seem the type."

"She's more complex than she appears. She always was. And for whatever reason, my father listened to her."

"How did he die?"

Violet swallowed, her throat gone dry, despite the tea. "He was convinced—and I mean that someone convinced him—that some new star was going to appear in the heavens, and those who could see it and put it into the right star chart according to the correct formula would be able to predict…well, everything."

"I take it he didn't see it."

"He drove himself mad looking for it. He wouldn't come inside until dawn. He set up five different telescopes on the balcony, looking through each one in turn. He cursed the clouds, saying they were trying to obscure the truth. And ultimately he died of pneumonia, brought on by exposure to the winter nights." She sighed, feeling drained, but rather relieved to share it at last.

Alex didn't respond, other than to keep holding her hand.

"I moved to the Peakes a week or so later," she said. "I didn't realize how long I'd be there, or I'd have cried the whole way."

"Was she the one who proposed taking you in?" Alex asked suddenly.

"I don't know. It was logical enough that I'd go to the Peakes—they are my closest relatives, after all. And their daughter Madeline was close to my age. I never questioned it." Violet looked over at him. "Why?"

Alex gave a shrug. "No reason."

"You always have a reason."

He smiled briefly. "Do I? Well, when you first came here with them, I couldn't believe you were in the same family. That first dinner…"

"Don't even talk about it," Violet said with a little groan.

"They were both loud and drunk and querulous. And you were this quiet, contained lady who barely spoke above a hum."

"I couldn't speak because I was mortified."

"No one blamed you for their behavior."

"It didn't make the evening any easier," she confessed. "I didn't know a thing about you then. I'm not sure I know much more now."

"You know me better than anyone else."

"Is that true?" Violet asked skeptically.

"Yes."

"That can't possibly be. I hardly know you at all."

"Ask me something." He drained the last of the brandy, then put the glass aside. He let go of her hand, and Violet missed the contact.

"You know," she said suddenly, "when you went to London all those times, I thought it was because you had a mistress."

"Interesting." His expression didn't reveal anything, making Violet think that he must work quite hard at that skill.

She hoped her blush wouldn't be ridiculously evident in the dim light. "I know why you went now, but…*do* you have a mistress?" she asked after a moment.

"I don't," he said immediately.

"You're not just saying that to humor me?"

"No. I used to have one, years ago. Never at any time I was married. But it was far more effort than it was worth, and after I was injured…" He shrugged, perhaps deciding that he'd already said more than he wanted to. "Let's just say my priorities changed." He looked over at her. "I'll admit I never thought you'd ask about such a topic."

"I never thought you'd answer the question."

"Do you have any other questions you think I won't answer?"

She shook her head.

"Not my eye?" He said it like a challenge.

But Violet refused to accept it as one. "I assume that it would only serve to reawaken bad memories. If you ever want to tell me, I will listen. But I have no claim on your past."

He turned his face toward the fire, not saying anything for a long moment. Violet was worried she'd offended him.

But then he sighed. "Thank you," was all he said.

Their conversation shifted to slightly less grave topics, and Violet realized how much she craved Alex's company, even if it was just to talk.

When she announced that she would retire, Alex walked her down the hall at a pace slow enough to let Violet know he certainly wasn't rushing to leave her.

At her doorway, he turned her to face him. "May I kiss you good night?"

"You don't have to ask each time," she said, blushing a little.

"Nonetheless, I will." He pulled her a little closer. "So?"

"Yes, please." Violet tipped her head up in expectation.

He bent to kiss her, and Violet felt the now familiar

surge of longing he instilled in her. One kiss would not suffice, and he must be counting on that, Violet thought.

He pulled away slowly, and Violet leaned toward him in her desire to not break off the kiss. "Alex..." she breathed.

He had her in his arms, but he didn't kiss her again. "Good night, Violet."

"Good night," she echoed, wishing she dared say something else.

But she didn't, and he released her. Violet closed her door before she could notice if his expression was anywhere near as confused as she felt.

* * * *

The next morning, Violet woke up with a smile on her face. Sunlight burst through her window and a delicious fragrance wafted through the air. Wondering what it was, she opened her eyes to find a bouquet of exquisite white blooms on her dressing table. A note was tucked in among the flowers. Curious, she quickly slid out of bed. Putting her dressing gown on as she crossed the room, she saw the flowers were jasmine and orchids.

She opened the envelope and withdrew the little card. *For my duchess. Alex.*

Mouthing the words silently, Violet fingered one of the jasmine blossoms, which triggered an explosion of scent. On an impulse, she pulled one stem out of the vase. Ringing for Dalby, she mentally ticked through her wardrobe, deciding what gown she wanted.

"Good morning," Dalby said as she entered. "My, those smell wonderful in the sunshine!"

"Yes, they do. Dalby, will you bring out the white

muslin with the little green embroidery, and I'd like you to put some of this jasmine in my hair."

Dalby's eyes lit up. "Oh, yes, ma'am."

Violet entered the breakfast room, clad in the diaphanous white gown, with white flowers tucked into her soft hair. "Good morning!" she called out cheerfully.

Alex nearly dropped his coffee cup when he saw her. "You look beautiful," he responded, after a moment.

Violet laughed, happy at his reaction. "I just wanted to keep smelling the lovely flowers. I know this dress isn't meant for a day at home."

"Isn't meant for?" Alex rose from the table and advanced toward her as if drawn by an invisible power. "Violet," he said as he took her hands in his own. "You are Duchess of Dunmere, and you shall wear whatever you want, whenever you want. You look beautiful," he repeated.

"Thank you." She looked down shyly. "And thank you for the flowers. They are gorgeous."

"You enhance them," he said seriously, reaching to touch the jasmine in her hair, releasing the fragrance. The scent of the jasmine mingled with the coffee that clung to him. The effect was strangely intoxicating.

"You must be hungry," Alex said, stepping away. "There are strawberries. First crop from the glasshouse."

"That sounds perfect." Violet said. She was more than hungry, she was ravenous. She took a scoop of little red strawberries and ate them with her fingers, getting juice all over her lips.

She looked up to find Alex watching her with an interested expression.

Violet licked her lips, tasting sweet red juice.

"That's not helping," he said.

"It's not?" Violet felt a rush of nervousness. He wouldn't kiss her in the middle of the breakfast room, would he? Did she want him to? "What should I do, then?"

He stood up. "You should enjoy your day, beautiful. I'll see you for dinner. And don't forget our agreement."

He left, and when Violet spoke to the housekeeper about the meals, she directed her to include fresh strawberries as part of the dessert course that evening.

Alex thanked her for doing so when he kissed her at her door that night, and Violet nearly floated the last few steps to her bed.

The next day, she found flowers on her bedside table again—roses, this time. The bouquet was all soft pink blooms that filled the air with their heady scent. There was a card again: *For my duchess.*

Alex found her at the table sipping coffee not long after.

"Good morning," she said. "Thank you for the roses."

"You like them?" he asked, almost absently. "If you have a moment now, it would be good if you could join me," he said.

She stood up immediately, putting her hand on his arm when he offered it. "Certainly. You look very serious."

"Do I?" He walked her down the hall, not saying more. Then he stopped at the door to the blue parlor. "I want you to keep your eyes on the floor. Understand?"

"Yes," she said, drawing out the word. He took her by the hand and led her in, turning her to face a particular wall.

Violet waited, keeping her eyes down on the floor. Alex moved to stand beside her.

"All right," he said. "Look up."

She looked up into the faces of her mother and father. The portraits from Hawebeck Place were now right here at the Abbey. Without warning, Violet's eyes welled up.

"Oh, my Lord," she whispered, the portraits going hazy through her tears. "Oh, my Lord. You brought them here for me."

Alex took her by the arm and swiveled her around to him. "Violet, this isn't a crying moment."

"No," she agreed. "Or yes. I'm happy. Truly. I just wasn't expecting… Thank you." She threw her arms around him. "This is wonderful. I don't know how you did it."

He said, a little awkwardly, "I had the idea a few weeks ago when Herbert happened to mention seeing the portraits at your home. So I told your aunt via letter how much I'd pay for them, and had them wrapped up and shipped over."

"I never thought I'd see them again."

"If I known how you'd react, I'd have just demanded them to be delivered on the day of the wedding." He paused. "That would have necessitated knowing you, though, which means everything would have been different in the first place." He disentangled himself from her arms. "I'm sorry, Violet."

"Don't be! This is a marvelous gift."

"I'm glad you like it. I chose this room because you seem to enjoy reading here. If you want the paintings moved, just say."

"No, this is perfect. Thank you." Then she laughed. "Oh, my. The roses were just a decoy, weren't they? So I wouldn't suspect."

"Roses are never a decoy," he protested. "Besides, I wouldn't want you to wake up thinking I'd forgotten you."

"I don't think that's a danger."

Alex reached out to touch her cheek. "The roses were a little bit of a decoy, actually. I have to go back to town. You're to stay here—no arguments. The household knows to check any package or item before you can receive it. And never leave the property alone. Take someone along for events. Only ride with a groom. Understood?"

She nodded. "I promise."

"Good. I'll be back as soon as I can."

"I'll...I'll miss you," she said suddenly, not even aware she was thinking that until the words were out.

He smiled. "I hope so."

Chapter 16

♋

ONCE BACK IN LONDON, ALEX'S first order of business was somewhat personal. He would find out who sent the snake to Violet, and why. If it was connected to the murders, it meant that the killer was aware of Alex, which was a terrifying prospect. But he had to know the truth in order to protect Violet.

So Alex headed out into the damp, dank night. He took the coach as far as one of his clubs, then told his driver to wait. "I may be a few hours."

"Yes, your grace."

The expectation was that Alex would stay in the club for the whole time, but he barely stepped in before he left again—pausing long enough to have a single brandy. Where he was going, liquor on the breath was a requirement.

He returned into the night, and paused again in a doorway a few streets down to adjust his clothes. He'd deliberately worn extremely basic pieces, dull in color and unremarkable in quality. After he shifted a few things to make himself look a bit disheveled, he continued on toward a much darker part of the city. Rain spat down intermittently.

Half an hour later, he slowed his pace as he walked down the main thoroughfare of the neighborhood, which was lit up by lanterns at the doors of the many restaurants, taverns, and gaming hells jammed together. Despite the rain, the street was teeming with men and women of all classes. Some were dilettantes, sampling the seedier part of the city, looking on at the denizens with disgust and fascination. Prostitutes strolled up and down, all smiles and brazen glances. Pickpockets were hard at work, as well, he noted, marking the progress of one coming toward him.

The scrap of a girl chose her victims carefully, picking the drunks and the lecherous first. They got a feel of her body when she "accidentally" bumped into them. In return, she snatched coins, watches, rings…anything small enough to palm.

The pickpocket's face grew wary as she surveyed Alex from about twenty paces away. She was trying to decide if he was drunk enough to brush up against. Alex aided her decision-making by shoving open his coat, as if he was too warm. Her eyes brightened. Easier access to his pockets was too tempting to resist.

Her pretended fall was quite authentic looking. Alex grabbed her arm, just as she intended. "You all right, miss?" he asked.

"Oh, yes, sir," she said, her face sweet and innocent looking. "I am so sorry to have troubled you."

"No trouble," he said, not releasing her arm. "You can keep the money you just snagged from my left pocket if you answer a few questions."

She dropped the innocent act. "For a man with one eye, you're damn sharp," she hissed.

"Thank you. Your fall would have fooled nearly anyone." He kept his voice calm, not wanting to spook her.

She nodded in wary acknowledgement of the compliment. "What do you want? I ain't for sale. Other girls would get angry anyway."

"I only want to know where Short Henry might be tonight." He let her go, certain she wouldn't run by that point.

The girl's expression changed again, showing interest. "You know him?"

"I just asked for him by name, didn't I?"

"Aye." She glanced up and down the street. "This time of night...try Roddy's pub. The one with the awnings. Mind you, I ain't seen Henry tonight. But he's never liked the rain."

"Thank you," Alex said. "Best of luck in your business."

"That's all?" she asked. "You ain't going to make a fuss about the coins?"

"You'll put them to good use, I'm sure." Alex watched her go, then went on toward the place she mentioned.

Roddy's public house was crowded. The smells nearly knocked Alex off his feet. Curry mingled with smoke and ale and sweat, all made stronger with the damp air. He looked around, asked after Short Henry, and was directed to a smaller dining room toward the back.

Short Henry was sitting in state near the coal-burning stove in the corner. A few others were with him, laughing and joking over drinks. The man was called Short Henry due to the physical deformity that made him legless, and thus only about three and a half feet high. He made up for his inability to walk by the use of a sort of rolling platform which he propelled with his arms. His appearance was shocking to most people, and he made a good living as a street beggar. He made an even better living as an informant.

Henry was actually sitting on top of the table, so he saw Alex enter. A slightly evil grin crossed his face.

"Good evening, *sir*!" he called out. "Sent you back here with the other unfortunates, did they?"

"Evening, Henry," Alex said. "Wonder if I might have a word."

"It's called a public house for a reason, friend. Anyone can have a word here."

Alex came closer. "Profitable day?"

"Not bad," Henry said, taking a swig of whatever he was drinking. "Made enough to stop in before I make my way to my humble abode."

"Care to make a bit more before you go?"

Henry's grin widened. "Everyone with two legs and two eyes step out!" he ordered the group. "When this man leaves, you can come back, and the next round will be on me."

The room emptied instantly.

Alex pulled out a few notes from an inner pocket. "That means the next round is on me," he said. "This should cover the drinks."

Henry took the money. "Good thing you made it in here with that load of blunt."

"Oh, I already had a discussion with a bright young lady who stumbled into me on the street. She got the money I wanted her to get."

"Ah, you met Meg, did you? Sharp thing, she is. Wouldn't surprise me if the girl goes far in life—assuming she's not killed or transported first." Henry took another drink. "Now, to business."

"Tell me who in the city might sell snakes."

"Interesting," Henry said, not expecting that question. "It's a big city, of course."

"Come on, you know all the circus types and freak shows in the city."

"Well, for that sort of animal, you'd want to speak to Sardo. He's got a place near Fleet Market. He deals with all kinds of creatures imported from the East and the darker parts of Africa and whatnot. He'd have snakes to sell for charming acts, or dancers and the like. All safe to handle, of course."

"What about those not safe to handle?" Alex asked.

"Poisonous, you mean? Sardo wouldn't stock those. Why buy a prop that might kill you?"

"Well, I may go see him. But first, tell me who would sell a venomous snake."

"You might try some doctors or near the medical schools to begin. There's a use for venom among that crowd, I've heard." Henry gave a single shudder. "Don't know how they manage. I'd never get near one of those creatures. Heard the worst stories from blokes come back from India—can't step into the trees there without one of those things attacking you."

"Tell me where exactly this Mr Sardo is."

"No mister, accent on the *do*," Henry corrected. "He's very particular on that point."

Armed with the directions to his next place, Alex bid Henry good night. He got a mocking half bow in return. He was never sure if Short Henry knew who he really was, but he suspected the man knew Alex was far higher in rank than he behaved. But like most informants, Henry knew when to speak and when to stay silent.

Despite the hour when Alex reached Sardo's place of

business, which was also his home, light streamed through the front windows of the narrow building. The door was answered by a woman with shining black hair and smooth, dark skin. She wore a jewel between her brows, but her outfit was completely Western.

"May I help you, sir?" she asked in strongly accented English.

"If the hour is not too late, I wish to speak with Sardo," he said, remembering how Henry said the name.

She nodded in approval at his pronunciation. "Step inside, sir, and I shall see if my master is receiving. Who shall I say is calling?"

"Mr Kenyon," he said, supplying one of his favorite aliases. "It is a matter of business—the possible sale of a snake."

She was gone for only a moment, and then he was beckoned to follow her into a room heavily decorated in what seemed to Alex an exotic fashion, though he supposed it was perfectly mundane to the owner. Heavy silks covered the walls, and candles burned in lanterns paned with many-colored glass, reminding him of Violet's red-paned stargazing lamp. Was India where the idea had been born? Too bad he didn't have time to think about that.

"Welcome, Mr Kenyon," said a voice.

Alex saw a small, slight man sitting on a couch against the far wall. "Sardo," he guessed.

"Please come closer, sir," Sardo said. "You will forgive me for not getting up. My legs are not what they used to be."

"I apologize for the unexpected call," said Alex, "but you were recommended as the best vendor of animals, including snakes."

"You need one tonight?" Sardo asked, with a little

chuckle. "What sort of emergency requires a new snake? And what sort of snake would you like?"

"Six feet long, rather slender for its length. Black body, with white bands about every half foot."

Sardo lost his pleasant demeanor. "You describe the krait. A dangerous creature, and one with no value to performers. I do not sell it."

"Has someone else asked you about one recently?" Alex asked.

"Why?"

"One was delivered to my house," Alex said honestly. "The sender hoped my wife would be bitten."

"What! Where is that snake now?" Sardo asked.

"I killed it. Before anyone could be hurt."

"Good." Sardo gave a little sigh. "The krait is one of the most deadly snakes in India, and very liable to bite. If one was in your home, the danger was real."

"Will a bite mean death?"

"Almost certainly." The other man shifted in his seat. "The bite itself is not always painful, or so it is reported. Some who are bitten while sleeping do not even wake up. But the effect is dire. Victims are slowly paralyzed, dying in a matter of hours, unable to move or speak or breathe. They die silent and wide-eyed, and there is nothing to be done."

"I trust that you don't sell it," said Alex. "But I need to know who might. Surely you've heard of another merchant who imports this snake. You called it a krait?"

"Krait," Sardo confirmed. "Yes. There is a man. His name is Rakesh. He deals in medicinal products. Plants, herbs, oils...and a few animals which are used in making such medicines. He is a good man," Sardo said. "He would be horrified to hear that someone took advantage of his trade to harm someone."

"I'll keep that in mind." Alex learned where he could find Rakesh, though he was told that the next morning was the earliest he would be able to speak to him.

The housekeeper showed him out, and Alex took a deep breath of the damp London air. He was getting closer to learning the answer to one mystery, he told himself. The person who sent the krait to Violet was hoping to kill her, but Alex had to know why. Because they hated Violet? Because they feared Alex's investigation?

Alex met with Rakesh the very next day. What the merchant told him was disturbing. He'd sold one krait to a dark-haired man who seemed to be a gentleman—well spoken and well dressed. He claimed the purchase was on behalf of a doctor who couldn't come himself. But the timing of the sale was exactly one day before the snake was delivered to Violet. The unknown gentleman had to be the same man who wanted Violet dead. But once again, the trail ended.

* * * *

After inquiring about the snake, Alex spent a few days looking deeper into the matter of the killing of Warner Mason, sending a few feelers out through the city for additional information.

Mason was certainly a follower of astrology. He joined a few different societies and groups dedicated to the notion, and Alex recorded them all, intending to track them down as time allowed.

It also appeared that Mason was selling confidential information linked to his work, based on what Alex found in his investigation. Several contacts in the underworld knew the name. He'd been doing it for years as a way to supplement his legitimate income. Alex breathed a sigh of relief when he realized that threat was gone. Though it would have been better if Mason could have been apprehended rather than killed, at least he was no longer exposing state secrets.

Alex worked hard to trace Mason's connections. He met with a man who remembered Mason talking about a friend named Daniel Galbraith, though he recalled nothing else. Still, the similarity in name was enough to send Alex back to his old sources for the murder of James Galbraith.

After speaking to a few more people, he learned of a Daniel Galbraith in the family. He was remembered as a charming young man, but a bad lot, always edging into trouble. The family lost track of him nearly twenty years previously, and nothing was known now. Alex managed to get a hold of a small portrait of the man. But it was so old that if he was still alive, he'd not look anything like it.

Still, it was something. And the name linked the murders of Warner Mason and James Galbraith.

When he was sure of the connection, he went to the Zodiac offices.

"You look terrible," Julian said when he arrived.

"Yes, I've heard that recently. But it's for a good reason."

Julian was extremely interested in his progress, though the actual killer remained unknown.

"It seems Mason was working with someone on the outside to sell some secrets that he acquired through his work," Alex explained. "A clerk doesn't make much of an income, and from the look of his home, he lived beyond his means. And it's also likely that his lover—the one who signed his letters *Daniel*—was also the man who he delivered the goods to. In fact, I'd bet that their relationship was business first, then became more personal."

"Was it the lover who killed him?" Julian wondered. "An attack of conscience? Or Mason got greedy and wanted too much money?"

"Until I find out who this Daniel was, and whether he's the same person as the Daniel Galbraith related to James, it's impossible to know."

"So what will you look for next?"

"What I need to know is the future," Alex said. "I need to know where the next attack will occur, and who is likely to be the target. This city is too large to chase after a murderer. I have to anticipate him in order to catch him."

"Shame you can't have a fortune teller help you out."

Alex straightened up. "I wouldn't trust an astrologer, but I do have an expert nearby."

"Who?"

He grinned. "That's confidential." Alex had no intention of letting anyone else know about Violet's interest in astronomy, and he wasn't keen to admit to any member of the Zodiac that he'd half-revealed the group's existence to his wife. No, Violet was to be kept safe, and that meant keeping her well away from the case. But he could consult with her about dates and stars. He needed someone to read the sky, and Violet could do that.

Chapter 17

♋

DAY AFTER DAY, VIOLET DISCOVERED another gift from Alex as soon as she awoke. Even while he was gone, he arranged for some small thing like flowers or a book to come to her.

Every gift came with a note. *For my duchess.* Violet, though delighted by her husband's thoughtfulness, nevertheless began to feel strangely sad when she read the inevitable words. They began to feel wrong, as if something was missing. But she did not know what else she could possibly be to him. She was his duchess. Why could she not be content with that?

One morning, Violet was reading in the room with her parents' portraits when Millie found her.

"Do you know how many gifts and letters you've got?" the younger woman asked.

"From Alex, you mean?" Violet asked.

"Not those. I meant the things the household wasn't to let you have till it had been checked."

"What?" Violet rose when Millie beckoned her at the doorway.

"It's a pile, and it's so intriguing. I think we should

look!"

Violet walked through the halls with Millie. "But it could be dangerous."

"Oh, I heard about the snake. How dramatic!" she added critically. "I read a play where that happened, and it seemed so overdone. Cleopatra should stand alone in the category of death by asp, don't you think?"

"I certainly don't want to join her," Violet said.

They reached the butler's retiring room off the kitchens. Millie demanded to see the "suspicious presents," as she called them.

"His grace order them to be kept here," the butler said.

"Then we'll look at them here!" Millie countered.

Grudgingly, he stood aside and let Millie and Violet enter. "Call out if you need anything, your grace," he told Violet. "We've checked everything, but just in case…"

"I'm sure it's safe," Millie said airily, with the confidence of the young. "Come, Violet. It's fascinating."

Violet stared in amazement as Millie showed her a stockpile of little gifts and letters covering one table in the room. She touched a few bouquets of flowers in jars, a set of gloves, a few knickknacks, and several letters.

"These were all sent to me?" she asked.

"Since you came back to the Abbey. Alex was very firm about no one letting you get them, though, in case it should be another nasty surprise like that snake."

"These are just…violets," said Violet, looking at one bunch of flowers. "How could they hurt me?"

"I've no idea. Perhaps Alex is just jealous. *I* think you have an admirer."

Violet picked up one of the folded sheets, reading a short poem. "Not exactly a passionate declaration of love," she said.

Millie plucked the paper away to read it herself. "Odd," she agreed. "He compares you to a *dread queen*. Sounds like he'd be scared to actually meet you."

"One should not send love letters to a married woman. Or flowers." Violet touched the gloves, unconsciously comparing them to the ones she owned. This pair was cheaper, rougher. "He can't have much money. I hope he stops sending things, if only because he can't afford it."

Millie gave a sigh. "It's rather romantic, though. He must have seen you from across a room, and been love-struck! He'll waste away with love, since you're a duchess, and married to another, and so far above him."

"If he's as young as you're making him out to be, he'll get over me quickly enough," Violet said.

"Ugh. I hope not. It's much more pleasant to think of a young man with some constancy in his affections. That's how it should be."

Violet shook her head. "It still doesn't make sense."

"Love doesn't have to make sense," Millie said.

"This isn't love," Violet protested. "This is…theater. Anonymous notes. Odd gifts. I would much prefer he stop. And I don't wish to know if he sends anything else."

"But he'd be even more heartbroken. Maybe he'll be so upset that he'll send a snake, as well."

"There aren't two people in England mad enough to mail me a snake," Violet snapped, upset at Millie's continued defense of the sender.

But Millie's eyes rounded. "That's it!" she cried. "These are *apologies*!"

"Why? If he sent a snake at first, why would he want to apologize? Wouldn't he hate me?"

"I don't know," the younger girl admitted. "It's very confusing. Perhaps it's because men are so terribly confused themselves. In every story or play I read, they never know what they want until it's too late."

* * * *

Late on a sunny afternoon, one of the maids entered the room where Violet was reading. "His grace's carriage was just spotted at the head of the drive, ma'am."

Violet looked up, happy at the news. "It was? Then I shall come down to the front doors immediately."

She had no time to change, not that it mattered much. She looked presentable, especially since Dalby had spent extra time that morning experimenting with a new hairstyle that left ringlets trailing down her neck.

Violet reached the foyer just as Alex walked in. "You gave no hint you were returning today!" she said as she came up to him. Indeed, while he had sent her a short letter nearly every day, none suggested when he'd be back.

"I thought I'd surprise you," Alex replied. He looked pleased to see her, and Violet wondered if she ought to embrace him, but the moment for that seemed to have passed.

Instead, they walked toward the wing of the house where their bedrooms were, since both had to change for dinner. They went slowly, each sharing news of what happened during the time apart.

At one point, when they were alone in the upper hall, he stopped, then reached out and touched the ivory hair comb she'd found on her dresser that morning.

"Lovely. Who gave you that?" he asked, teasingly.

Violet laughed. "You did, and you know it. Though I'm still not sure why."

"Do I need a reason? Other than wanting to adorn you the way you deserve to be?"

Violet looked down at the floor. She was not up to countering his banter, especially when she couldn't tell how seriously he meant it. She suspected this might be what it felt like to be courted, but she and Alex were already married.

Alex interrupted her reverie. "Could I ask for your assistance with something I'm studying?" he asked, his voice more serious.

"Of course. After dinner?"

"Not till tomorrow. To be honest," he confided. "I need a bit of a rest. Chasing after shadows and meeting with people who don't particularly want to see me does take a toll."

His words were casual, but his intent was not. He was once again letting her see a part of his life that no one else could.

She shook her head. "That sounds rather dangerous. Daring, but dangerous."

"It was necessary."

"Well, I should hope it wasn't merely for amusement," she said, then put her hand out. "I can only treat this lightly because you weren't hurt."

He took her hand, squeezing it in reassurance. "Not a bit. Just a little tired, and hungry."

"Excellent. Dinner is in less than an hour. We wouldn't want to keep Herbert and Millie waiting. Also, I was thinking I'd go out to the folly tonight," Violet added. "You could come by at half past two. The comet I'm measuring will only be visible until then."

"I'll be there. Both for dinner and later," he added with a smile.

* * * *

The evening meal was lively. Even though their group was small, talk was animated. Millie in particular was eager to explain her new theory of—as she termed them—"the *other* gifts." Though Alex was initially upset when he heard how many little gifts arrived, he listened carefully to Millie's idea.

"He's terribly sorry, you see," Millie was saying. "He's madly in love with Violet, and so he was struck by wild jealousy. He thought if he couldn't have her, no one could, and he sent the snake to the house so Violet would be killed. That way she would be lost to all men. If he was going to lose, no one would win!" By the end, Millie had gotten so carried away that she stood up at the table, brandishing a butter knife.

"If he was going to lose," Alex echoed, as if to himself. Then he asked, more sharply, "Why the flowers *afterward* then?"

"Because he realized the depths of his depravity, Alex." Millie gave an exasperated sigh. "Honestly, do I have to explain everything? He knew he'd done a great evil, and he now wishes to express his remorse. His is a heart capable of great range, from high to low."

Herbert bit back a laugh. "Sounds like me at eighteen. Though the deadliest act I ever committed was to write some extremely dire verse. There is a certain madness among the young."

"I'm not mad," Millie objected, sitting down again.

"No, you're not. Just a tad morbid," Alex said. "It's an interesting theory. And like all theories, it would need to be examined."

"Exactly," said Millie, content in her reasoning.

After dinner, Violet went out to the folly. The sky was clear and the spring air was soft against her face. She lost track of time as she worked, and when Alex came up to the roof, she nearly jumped in surprise.

"Is it so late?" she asked.

"Half past two," he said. "That's what you told me."

Then he stepped up to her, putting his hands on her shoulders. "Time to go back," he said gently. "You may not have noticed, but you're shivering."

She had not noticed until then. Instinctively, she slid her hands under his jacket until her arms were wrapped around him.

After a moment, Alex embraced her, tucking her head under his chin. "Does that help?" he asked.

Violet nodded, already feeling warmer. "Thank you," she said, hardly loud enough to be heard. "I don't know why you indulge me so much. You come out here in the middle of the night. You get me presents for no reason…"

"I have a reason," he said.

"What?" She tipped her head up to see him.

"It's not obvious?"

Alex kissed her then, and Violet tightened her hold on him. She could feel Alex's body tense beneath the shirt, but felt no inclination to pull away.

When the kiss ended, she asked, "What do you want?"

He touched her face, but then said, "I want to walk you to your room so I can kiss you goodnight."

"Oh." Violet smiled, but inwardly wished he'd said something else. *Don't be such a mouse*, she told herself. *He promised to let you decide.* She sighed. That meant she had to say the words. And something in her was still fearful. She wasn't afraid of Alex, she realized. She was afraid *for* him.

What if she became another part in his tragedy? How would he deal with that?

Violet didn't say much as they walked back to the house. But she wrapped her hand around his arm very tightly, as if she could keep him safe from fate.

He noticed. "Violet, what's the matter?"

"I care about you," she blurted out. "I do care, and I don't want anything to happen—"

He put a hand on hers, stopping her words. "Lord, did I scare you with my comment today? I wasn't in danger. I shouldn't have mentioned it."

"It's not that. Not exactly. I know you're involved in something that you can't tell me about. And I don't want you to violate that trust. I don't need to hear details. But just know…that I care."

He said nothing for a moment, then kissed her lightly on her cheek. "Thank you, Violet."

They resumed their walk back, Alex saying that he had to get her safely inside before she truly took a chill.

At her bedroom door, he kissed her goodnight. This time it was almost painfully sweet, and Violet wanted nothing more than to hear him ask to come in.

But he didn't, because he promised. Violet whispered goodnight instead of what she wanted to say, and both of them went to bed alone.

* * * *

When Violet came down for breakfast late the next morning, she was surprised to find Alex still in the room, sipping a cup of coffee and reading a newspaper. The smell of the coffee teased her nose, being particularly fresh and strong for some reason.

"Either I am remarkably early or you're unusually late for breakfast," she said.

"Perhaps both," he said. "I had a lot of work to catch up on, and I put off the meal for a while."

Violet assembled her breakfast from the sideboard, choosing bread and honey and some cheese. She filled her own coffee cup and joined Alex at the table.

She ate a few bites of food, while Alex went back to his papers. She looked around, and blinked when she saw a large wooden crate on the floor by the table. How had she missed that? She practically tripped over it to get to her seat.

"What's this?" she asked.

Alex glanced up. "Hmm? Oh, that crate? Perhaps you'd better find out."

Frowning, Violet got up and examined the crate. Her name was indeed on the label, along with the name of Dunmere Abbey. She ran a hand along the lid and noticed two rope handles. It looked as though she could tug the lid right off.

She turned to find Alex watching.

"I assume this is safe to open," she said.

"Yes. Go on," he said, no longer pretending to read the paper.

"This is your doing," she accused.

He gave a little, helpless shrug that would have fooled no one.

With a huff, Violet turned back and grabbed the handles. The lid was tightly fitted, but a strong tug released it, and the intense aroma of roasted coffee wafted out. "What…"

She leaned over the crate, inhaling the scent. The crate was absolutely filled with nothing but heavy burlap bags of coffee beans. She plunged her hands in, felt the peculiar weight and heft of beans, and then she was laughing, elbow deep in coffee smell and utterly undone. "Alex, you got me *coffee*."

"Well, diamonds don't seem to impress you," he noted mildly. But when she turned, he was smiling, unable to pretend nonchalance. "Do you like it?"

"Yes!" Violet stood up. She rounded the table and leaned over to embrace him. "Thank you. I shall drink every drop."

Alex put one hand up to keep her there. "Kiss me," he said.

She did, tasting coffee on his lips.

He released her with a show of reluctance. "I almost don't want to bring up my next request."

"What is it?"

"Can I ask you something about astronomy?"

"Oh, yes."

"Come with me to the study," he said. "I'll show you there."

He shut the door and settled Violet into a seat by the desk before he said another word. Then he pulled his papers from a locked drawer. "This represents what I've learned, at least in terms of who the victims are, and when and where they were killed.

"I need to know what's coming," he said seriously. "I don't have enough information to know who the killer is, but I think there are enough puzzle pieces that we can guess where he'll strike next. And when. If we can narrow that down, I can see to it that those spots are watched at the time. It might be sufficient to save someone's life."

"Well, I can hardly refuse to help after that argument."

"I don't like to involve you in something so

gruesome."

"Alex, someone tried to kill me not long ago. I am involved. So let's begin work, shall we?"

As Alex laid out his notes, Violet read them all closely, chewing thoughtfully on her lower lip.

"Do you have a map of London?" she asked.

"Somewhere." Alex dug through his papers until he found one. "Try this."

"May I write on it?"

"If you're solving a murder, you can do whatever you like to it."

Violet actually laughed as she unfolded the map flat on the desk. "Never thought I'd hear that in my life. All right. List the locations of each murder, in the order they occurred."

He did, and Violet dutifully marked each one on the map. She inscribed the symbol found next to each body on the map as well.

"See a pattern?" Alex asked.

"Not yet." With her finger, Violet drew a line from the first to the last murder. "It could be a circle, like the Zodiac. And these are the first three signs the killer used. They're in order…"

"But?" Alex could tell she didn't like her theory.

"As I said before, Capricorn is the first sign he used, but it's not the first sign of the Zodiac. So why start in the middle? It makes no sense."

"Murder doesn't always make sense."

Violet shook her head. "But you think the victims were chosen carefully. So there is *some* logic. Perhaps…" She looked thoughtful. "Perhaps the pattern—if it is a pattern—is a constellation. One murder for each star."

"That's dark."

"Agreed," said Violet. "I'll look through my books to see if these three points correspond to any particular constellation. Though three points isn't much to go on."

"That sounds impossible," Alex objected. "You've got a whole night sky to choose from."

"I don't think so," Violet said. "I'll look first at the constellations along the ecliptic—that is, the signs of the zodiac. If our murderer is painting such symbols on the ground, it fits that he could also be recreating something on a larger scale."

"The whole city is his canvas."

"Well, if he's aiming to kill twelve people, he's got grand plans," she noted. "Perhaps he believes that the whole city is the canvas he deserves."

Violet moved to the door. "I'll be back in a moment with my books. Unless you'd prefer to work alone till I find something of value?"

He shook his head. "Hurry back."

She did, and sunk into a chair in order to flip through her books of stars, trying to match the scanty evidence of three little dots in a crooked line to a real constellation.

She plotted out a few possible patterns based on what they knew. "If the killer is making a circle of signs, just like the zodiac, the next one should occur near here." She marked that spot on the map.

"There's a park close by," Alex said. "I've been there. A good spot to lure someone. I can make sure the park is under watch. What if he goes the other direction?"

"The signs have been consecutive so far. The next sign should be Aries. And *if* he's making a circle, it should continue on a counterclockwise arc, like so." She traced the imaginary circle on the map. "The last one, Sagittarius, would occur here, in December."

"Let's hope it doesn't take me that long to catch him."

"Or her," Violet suggested.

"One witness described a big, younger man…and the victims were all held before being stabbed in the chest. It would have to be a very strong woman."

Violet shuddered. "Forget I mentioned it."

"No, I don't think I will. You made me realize something. I was assuming the murderer acted alone. There's nothing to say it couldn't be *more* than one person. A woman could certainly be involved in some way."

"Perhaps she got the victims to follow her. They wouldn't be scared of a woman." Violet tried to picture a lady who could be so callous. She automatically thought of her Aunt Judith. Perhaps it wasn't so farfetched to think there could be other women like her aunt. So determined to get what they wanted that they would stop at nothing. Not even murder.

"That's logical," Alex said in agreement.

"Yes, well." She relied on logic…most of the time.

As they worked for the next few hours, Violet kept looking over at Alex. He was so dedicated to his work, just as he was dedicated to his estate and his family. He did all of it without complaint. And until he married her, he'd done all of that virtually alone for years.

She was glad that he trusted her enough to let her see a tiny sliver of his life. She wished she could do more.

Well, she *could*. Violet took a slow breath. Alex hadn't married her for help in his investigations. He married her because he wanted an heir. And Violet knew that, to be a true wife, she had to accept the entire role.

She chanced another look at her husband. Her very kind, extremely compelling, and decidedly *not* cursed husband.

"What?" Alex asked. He'd noticed her gaze.

"Oh!" Violet jumped in her seat, embarrassed to be caught staring, particularly considering her line of thought. "I was just…distracted."

He consulted the clock in the room. "No wonder. We've been in here for hours. Let's get some air."

Violet stood up. "That would be very welcome." She'd ask tonight. Somehow. Her stomach was tying up in knots as she contemplated how to do it.

Alex took her outside on a brief walk, but Violet was by now so preoccupied that she couldn't focus on the conversation. Could she actually speak the words that she knew she had to? Or would she shrink away from it again? At the door to the house, she actually said out loud, "Of course I can. They're just *words*, after all."

"What?" Alex sounded confused. He'd been talking about something completely different, and she hadn't registered a thing.

"I'm sorry," she said. "It's just that I need to rest before dinner. Please excuse me. I'll see you then."

"Very well." Violet knew he watched her until she got all the way up the stairs and turned the corner toward her room.

* * * *

After Violet left, Alex had no idea how to occupy himself until dinner. Returning to the grisly work of investigating the murders was too much to bear at the moment. Especially if he had to work alone.

Instead, he thought of his perplexing wife. Despite the genuine pleasure he felt in simply being near Violet, a gnawing sense of frustration had set in. Granted, she seemed much more comfortable with him than she did at first. She was even affectionate, never hesitating to touch him or take his hand. He remembered when she rushed into the foyer when he got back to the house, looking as if she'd run from wherever she was. He couldn't recall anyone looking that happy to see him lately. He almost kissed her right in the foyer, though something held him back, some fear that she'd refuse a kiss where others—even just the household—would see. Although she certainly hadn't refused his kiss when he walked her to her room after stargazing that same night. He almost asked her to let him in. But pride shut him up in time, and he reluctantly let her go. He promised, and he'd keep the promise.

He paced in his study, thinking of his supposed curse. He knew that lay at the root of the matter. His previous marriages, the gossip, the fear. On some level, he was sure, Violet believed that if their marriage remained in name only, the curse could be avoided.

They had dinner as usual, though Violet still seemed a bit distracted. Afterwards, she said to him, "I'm heading out to the folly. There's, ah, a meteor shower I'm quite interested in. Might I ask you to come by a bit after midnight?"

"Isn't midnight early for you?"

"Oh, if you'll be disturbed…" she began to say.

"No, not at all. I just have some reading to do in the library. I'll come for you after midnight."

Violet did not reply, other than to kiss him lightly on the cheek. "I will see you later then," she said, an odd catch in her voice.

Alex headed directly to the library after supper. He dismissed everyone, saying he did not wish to be disturbed. Pouring a glass of brandy, he settled down by the fire to read, but found himself distracted and malcontent. He could not focus on the task at hand. His mind was full of Violet.

The clock ticked toward midnight. He kept glancing up, wishing the hands would move faster. Finally, the chimes for midnight sounded. He couldn't wait any longer.

At the garden door, he flung on his greatcoat and shoes. He walked past the lake and though the wet grass. He glanced up, and noticed heavy clouds. Violet could not possibly be stargazing tonight. But she would have stopped in the library and told him if she came back early. Perhaps she'd fallen asleep.

The door to the folly was unlocked, just as always. He went in and up the curving stairs, moving quietly so as not to disturb Violet.

He reached the upper landing, where the dull red glow of her special lantern spilled out under the door. There was no noise, so he assumed she had fallen asleep. But when he opened the door, Violet was sitting near the brazier. She wasn't reading or writing, just sitting. She stood up quickly.

"I'm glad you've come," she said, her voice very soft.

"You asked me to."

"Yes. But tonight, especially. I worried that you wouldn't."

He moved closer to her, now worried himself. "Violet, is something wrong?"

"Yes," she replied intently. She came up to him, reaching out to take his hands.

"What is it?" he asked.

"We are married in name only," Violet whispered. "And it's long past time to change that."

At her words, his body temperature seemed to double.

"Violet…" he began, but she cut him off by stretching up and kissing him quickly. He kissed her back, his mind suddenly filled with visions he'd tried so hard to suppress for the past several weeks. "You want me."

Chapter 18

♋

VIOLET WAS RELIEVED SHE'D FINALLY said something. "Yes," she breathed, her voice trembling slightly.

He reached out and took her by the waist, pulling her to him. "Then let me take you back home."

"Here," she said quickly. Then she bowed her head. "I'd like it to be here…this time. Away from the house."

"Why?"

"I'm comfortable here. It's my place."

"Don't be scared, beauty," Alex said, cupping her face.

"I'm not scared," she said. "Not exactly. I just don't know…well, anything. I was told that it hurts. But that it will all be over quickly. And I'm just to let you do what you like."

"To begin with, all three of those things are wrong," he said quietly.

"They are?" Violet felt a little stab of remorse. What else was she wrong about?

"Yes," he said. "I have no intention of hurting you. It will certainly not be over quickly. And we are going to do what *we* like."

"But I don't know what I'd like."

"Well, it's time to find out." He smiled. He bent his head and kissed the side of her neck, lightly at first, but then with increasing intensity. Violet gasped, then moaned very softly, her body quivering with her response.

"Just like that, darling," he murmured. "Tell me if you like what I do." He licked her neck then, making her gasp.

"I like it," Violet managed to whisper. "I like it."

"Good, darling. Just keep telling me what you feel. I've wanted you for so long, and now you're mine."

"Yes," she said, awed by his intensity, wondering what would happen next.

He didn't take long to show her. He worked his way slowly from her neck to her shoulder, always holding her fast, always giving her just enough that she knew she wanted more.

"Speak to me, beautiful," Alex murmured as he loosened the ribbon of her gown, then undid the buttons at the back.

He easily lifted the gown off, leaving only the loose chemise. He laid a kiss on her chest as he pulled the fine lawn down over her breasts, the nipples now hard with anticipation. "Do you like this?" He bent and laid a series of featherlight kisses across her breasts and down the valley between them.

"Yes," she said, the word turning into a sigh. Her back arched, and he caught her head in his hand, baring her neck and shoulders. He chose to sweep her with his tongue, setting her skin on fire.

"Alex," she gasped. Everything was happening at once, threatening to overwhelm her. She wanted to be overwhelmed.

"Yes, sweet. Tell me everything."

"If you didn't mind…you could kiss me like that

everywhere."

By his smile, he was delighted to oblige her. His hands made quick work of the chemise, easing it down her body until it lay in a puddle at her feet, and bent again to kiss her.

"Wait." She laid her hands on his chest. "Take off your clothes, too. I want to see you."

"When did you get so bold?" he asked, with a low laugh. He began to remove his jacket, and then his shirt. Then he paused. "Ah, you're not really that bold yet."

No, she wasn't. Violet was torn between peeking at him from under her lashes and keeping her eyes closed.

"Look at me, darling," he directed. "Better yet, help me."

"Are you sure?" she asked, even as she reached out to hold his shirt, now halfway worked out of his breeches.

"Very sure." He grinned as she tentatively pulled the rest of the fabric out. He quickly pulled the shirt over his head, revealing the skin underneath. Violet gave up peeking and simply devoured him with her eyes, though it was so dim in the room that she caught hints rather than the full sight of him.

Alex took her hand, guiding her to the waist of his breeches. "Help me."

Violet found the cord and loosened it, and Alex stepped out of his clothes, finally as naked as she was.

Her eyes widened when she finally saw all of him, his desire for her made plain. His skin turned into shadows by the meager lamplight, highlighting the muscles honed from riding and working outdoors. His broad shoulders tapered to a narrow waist and hips, and Violet shyly placed her hands on his torso, feeling the warm skin and the fine hairs that covered him.

"What should I do?" she asked, looking up at his face.

"For now, just let me know what you like," he said roughly, taking her very firmly in his arms and bending to kiss her mouth.

Violet melted under his kiss, giving up her natural modesty to accommodate his wish that she *tell* him how she felt. She tried to tell him without words, by twining her arms around his neck, opening her mouth at his tongue's urging, accepting that she was his entirely.

Alex kissed her as if he'd never get enough of her. At last he pulled back slowly, ending by sucking gently on her lower lip, sensing how ragged her breath was. "Did you like that?"

"Yes," she whispered, her eyes heavy and her mouth swollen. "Did you?"

He laughed, a low rich sound. "I could eat you whole, darling."

"Will you?"

"Perhaps," he shifted his weight, pressing her body to him, letting her feel how hard he was. She gasped a little, but didn't try to pull away. Then he backed her into the chair, making her sit down.

"There's a bed involved at some point," she said nervously. "Correct?"

"At some point. Not this point. We're going to take our time." He knelt on the floor, placing himself between her knees, spreading her legs.

He began by simply running his hands up and down her body, feeling how she reacted to his touch. He watched her face as he explored her, and when she gasped or closed her eyes, he touched her again, finding the sensitive spots, sometimes following up with a flick of his tongue.

Feeling shy and exposed at first, Violet found herself quickly succumbing to his methodical, wonderful assault on her senses. Over and over, he asked her if she liked what he did, and she nodded helplessly, too nervous to speak.

Then his hand moved between her legs. "Just tell me if you like it, darling." He was watching her with an intensity that thrilled her. "Or if you don't."

Then gently, so gently she wasn't sure when it started, he began to stroke her below the curls, where her body had grown so warm. Violet wanted to tell him that it was fine, it was lovely, but she could only moan his name, unable to put the exquisite sensation into words. His lips curving as he listened to her response, he delved deeper, seeking the center of her heat.

Violet unconsciously pushed her hips forward on the chair, spreading her legs further, allowing him freer access to her body. She sighed as a heaviness took her, a strange feeling of something building within her, a fire coaxed into being by the subtle magic her lover worked inside her. She put her hands on his shoulders, as she flexed her whole body in the rhythm he created.

"Do you like this, darling?" he asked.

"Yes, I... Please don't stop," she managed to say.

He did not. He pulled her down from the chair, still cupping her center, but taking her closer to him, skin to skin. She knelt with him, allowing him to plunder her, feeling his hardness against her inner thigh, knowing that whatever he was doing, it was still only a prelude. But still, he lingered over her body, *playing* her, giving her such incredible feelings that her breath almost stopped.

Just when Violet thought she couldn't stand anymore of the pressure, everything broke. With a soft, shuddering cry, she collapsed against him, her muscles weak.

Alex's smile turned a bit savage. Wrapping his arms around her silken, satiated body, he lifted her up.

"This will hurt a little, love," he whispered. He brought her down onto him. She was so slick and hot that there was little resistance at first, only a new pressure that she welcomed.

Alex closed his eyes, gripping Violet tighter. "Relax, my beauty. Let me in." He pushed hard once, and she felt the wall break. Violet gave a little cry, more surprise than pain.

"You're all right," Alex said.

She wasn't sure if it was a question or a reassurance, but she nodded and quickly lowered her head to kiss him. "You didn't hurt me. Play me, please, Alex. Play me. However you like."

"I don't have time for what I'd like," he nearly growled.

She dimly understood what he meant, aware of how excited he was to have her at last. It took only a few rough thrusts to hurl him over the edge. Violet locked her arms tight around his neck, her body still quivering with the reaction he caused in her. She wished she could see more of him, but it was too dark to catch more than an outline.

After a moment, he gathered himself to his knees, and bent forward to lay Violet down on her back on the thick rug on the floor. She murmured a protest as he slipped out of her, but he moved to lie beside her and wrap her in his arms.

"You said a bed would be involved," she noted sleepily.

"Another time," he promised.

She cuddled into his chest and fell asleep, utterly content. Equally satisfied, Alex quickly followed her into oblivion.

* * * *

Alex woke up when the clock struck four in the morning. The coals had sunk to glowing embers, barely enough to see by. Looking over at the exquisite woman lying beside him, he wondered briefly if he was still dreaming. She murmured sleepily when he stroked her hair. With a shock, he recalled they were still in the folly. The servants would be up and about the house in a few hours.

Alex rose and quickly put his clothes on. He found Violet's chemise and gown.

"Sweetheart," he said quietly. "Wake up."

Violet blinked awake, her eyes widening when she realized where she was. "Oh," she said, looking around.

"We should go back to the house," Alex said. "Here. Stand up."

She rose, and even in the dim light, he could tell that she was shy all over again. He slid the chemise over her body, letting the skirt drop to the floor, and then followed with her gown.

"Don't bother with the buttons," Violet whispered. "I can get back to the house like this." She slid her feet into her slippers.

He locked the folly door behind them. He suddenly didn't want anyone to be in this place besides him and Violet.

He took her hand and they walked silently back to the house. The clouds had moved off, but the sky was still a velvet blue black, with stars twinkling madly overhead. The east had just begun to turn slightly lighter, but it would be well over an hour until dawn.

They slipped into a garden door that Alex knew was unlocked. Still not speaking, they moved silently up the stairs through the house where not even a single sound broke the quiet.

At the end of the hallway, she refused to release his hand when he would have gone to her door.

"I want to stay with you," she whispered.

He wondered if she was completely awake. He had never spent an entire night with a woman, even his previous wives. It was not the way of society marriages. It had never occurred to him to stay. Certainly, no one had ever asked him to.

Until now. He headed to his own rooms, keeping hold of Violet's hand. Once inside his own bedroom, he needed no light to show Violet to the bed, already turned down for the night. Before she climbed in, he stripped off her gown again, and she let him, her face serious in the dim light.

She snuggled down between the covers, and Alex wasted no time in joining her, shedding his clothes in an instant. Despite his sleepiness, he found himself reaching for Violet again, drawn like a magnet to her. She responded sleepily, her limbs heavy but inviting. He kissed her softly, urging her silently to wake and kiss him back. She did so, her mouth opening and her sweet tongue soon darting and eager.

He grew hard within moments, remembering how good she had felt around him. He almost thought he imagined the feeling, but he soon realized that Violet was actually touching him, making his heart pound.

"We're married now," she murmured against his ear. "At last."

"Violet," he moaned. "If you keep doing that, I can't promise I won't take you."

"Why shouldn't you?" she asked.

"Darling, you're sore now…"

"But do you want me?" She squeezed him slightly harder, her half-awake state making her strangely bold.

"Oh yes," he gasped.

"I want you, too. Is that wanton, to ask again so soon?"

"I don't want to hurt you, love."

"You could never hurt me," she promised.

He searched the mound of tight curls at her thighs, and felt her legs fall open at his first hesitant touch.

She moaned when his fingers slipped inside her. She was still slick with her own juices and his seed.

Sleep gone, he rose to his knees. Spreading her legs wide, he settled himself above her, pressing her into the bed. Something in this shy, quiet woman brought out the savage in him. He felt a moment of doubt.

But then, as if she had lain with him for years, Violet shifted so her body fitted perfectly to his. He felt her glorious tightness sheath itself around him, slick and hot. Bracing himself on his arms, he began to thrust slowly, possessively, feeding off her excited gasps.

She reached up to twine her arms around his neck, threading her fingers through his hair, whispering to him how he made her feel, her shyness burned away by the heat of their lovemaking. Driven on by her wild honesty, he urged her to meet him. She lifted her hips and began to push against him, a counterpoint to his thrusts that brought a new wave of sensations to them both. Violet cried out at the new feeling, and Alex knew he'd never get enough of her.

The pressure between them built quickly, leaving them both hot with sweat as they struggled to match the other's rhythm. Alex, determined to give Violet what she needed, reached down to touch her sensitive nub with his thumb, even as he continued to thrust within her. At his touch, she gave a low, delighted laugh that was all the encouragement he needed.

Breathing hoarsely, he gave himself up, and thrust even more deeply. She contracted around him, triggering his own completion, breathtaking in its intensity.

"You're mine now," Violet whispered as he lay on top of her. She slipped her slender arms around him, holding him to her, holding him inside her.

"Always," he said, turning his head to give her a lingering kiss. They drifted to sleep again, as one.

Chapter 19

♋

VIOLET WOKE UP SLOWLY, UNWILLING to leave her pleasant, dreamy state and the warmth that enveloped her. She stretched, and suddenly felt the heat of another body next to her. Alex, as naked as she was, and still asleep, his features no longer cold as stone, but peaceful, warm. It made him even more arresting. All at once, the memory of last night rushed back to her. She blushed, remembering how boldly she had acted and how eagerly she had responded to Alex's touch. And she was in his bed this morning.

He wasn't asleep, after all. In a low tone, he said, "If I had known how it would feel to wake up with you, I would have insisted on it earlier."

"You don't mind?" she asked meekly.

"Darling," he laughed. "How could I?" Turning to her, he smiled as he kissed her forehead, and then reached out to tip her face up to his.

Then someone knocked at the door and entered. "Your grace, I'm afraid there's a problem. Her grace is missing."

"Missing?" Alex asked, with a laugh, while Violet ducked her head, as if that would conceal her.

"Yes, sir! Dalby is concerned. She's not in her bed,

and she's not at her folly…oh." The valet stopped short on seeing Violet in the bed.

Alex smiled. "Thank you for telling me. But she's quite safe where she is."

"Yes, your grace." Stammering apologies, the valet left the room as quickly as he could.

Everyone below stairs would talk about how Violet was in Alex's bed. Mortified by the thought, she recoiled, her body becoming tense. Alex sensed the change in her. "Violet?"

"Yes," she whispered.

"Come here." He held out his arm and she instinctively curled up to him, burying her face in his shoulder.

"They'll all know," she whispered, her cheeks stinging red.

"So?"

"They'll think I'm a—"

"Wife?"

She raised her head the tiniest bit. "I hate the idea of being talked about."

"I understand that completely. But Violet, we're at the center of this world. They exist because we do. It's natural that they'll know what's going on."

"But they'll judge me. For waiting so long."

"It doesn't matter."

He kissed her mouth, softly at first, but with increasing force as he came fully awake. He took advantage of her nakedness to run his hands possessively over her skin. "How do you feel?" he asked urgently. "Tell me the truth. Did I hurt you at all?"

"No," she assured him. "I liked it. All of it."

"Good, but I still think I might have been too rough."

"I would have told you so."

"Would you?" Alex worried. "When we first met, I told you that I never heard you say no."

"You didn't know me at all," she pointed out, regaining some of her previous ease. "I promise you I would have said if something felt wrong."

He sighed and held her closer. Violet welcomed it, reveling in how affectionate he was toward her. She closed her eyes, enjoying the warmth they made under the bedcovers.

They must have fallen asleep again, because Violet blinked and saw that the light was different. Much brighter.

Alex was no longer in the bed. He was standing by the window, wearing only a robe tied at the waist, the sort of intimate detail that made her very aware that she was truly a wife now.

Her stomach growled then. "Oh! I think I'm hungry."

"So am I," Alex agreed. His smile made it clear that he wasn't talking about breakfast. He returned to the bed, lying down next to her. He stroked her body lightly, before reluctantly wrapping the blanket around her. "Why don't you go to your room and ring for your maid? Or do you want me to carry you?"

She laughed. "It's a walk of thirty paces. I think I can manage."

"Yes, but I rather enjoy carrying you."

Violet sat up. "Another time. I'll see you after I'm dressed."

"What a shame," he commented, then sent her on her way.

In her own room, Violet rang for Dalby, hardly knowing what she'd say to the maid, who had been with her for years, and certainly since before Violet ever contemplated being married.

But Dalby was so matter of fact and efficient that Violet didn't have a chance to be embarrassed.

A bath was prepared while Violet nibbled food from a tray Dalby thoughtfully brought up before Violet could even ask. Her coffee was perfectly strong and scalding.

Only when Violet was up to her shoulders in bath water did Dalby chance a personal comment.

"Did you enjoy your wedding night, then?" she asked, not looking at Violet.

"Yes." Violet hoped the heat of the bath water masked her blush. "Even if it was a bit later than usual."

"Better a late honeymoon than none at all," Dalby said with a giggle. "If he kept you in his room for a week, I wouldn't care, ma'am. Just so long as he makes you happy in your marriage."

"I am, Dalby. I didn't think I would be when I came here. But I am now. Even before last night."

"That's good then." Her maid nodded once, quite satisfied with the situation.

* * * *

Alex found he didn't want to let Violet out of his sight. The day, despite starting very late for both of them, seemed to take too long. Alex was also delighted when a cloudbank rolled in, though he didn't say so. Over dinner, he couldn't stop looking at Violet. Dessert was probably exquisite, though neither of them really tasted it. After the meal, when they would normally spend an hour or two having a drink, or chatting like civilized humans, they both kept looking at the clock.

Finally, Violet left off pretending to read her book and

walked over to him.

"Alex," she said, her eyes downcast. "You...that is, if you like..." She took a deep breath and then said in a quiet rush, "You may come to my room tonight."

"May I?"

"Yes. Please. If you want to."

"I do." Lions couldn't keep him away.

"Oh." She smiled shyly. "Very good, then."

He stood up too. "And I still insist on walking you to your door."

Her smile widened. "I'd like that."

At her door, he gave her a teasing kiss made more effective by what he'd learned last night. Leaving her at her door half-seduced might become his new favorite game.

"Good night, Violet," he murmured. "I promise."

"Please," she returned in a whisper.

Of course, Violet would still have her nightly ritual of summoning her maid and preparing for bed, just as she did nearly every night. Alex had his own rituals, though he was terribly aware of the ticking of the clock. He heard when the door in the hall opened and closed. Dalby was leaving for downstairs.

Alex felt an unfamiliar nervousness when he reached the connecting door. It made no sense. He'd already spent a whole night with Violet. But then, he hadn't been anticipating *how* he'd be spending his night when he walked to the folly. The surprise of Violet asking for him prevented any possible second thoughts.

But tonight was the first time she invited him to her room as his wife. How proper. How expected. What if she started behaving like a proper wife now, all duty and no passion? What if the spark between them wouldn't last?

"Don't be an idiot," he told himself.

He knocked at the door, and heard footsteps flying toward it almost before he took his hand down.

She was smiling at him as if she hadn't seen him in weeks. "Hello," she said a little breathlessly.

Violet had changed into her dressing gown and had Dalby take the pins out of her hair, which now fell in loose waves around her shoulders. He surveyed every inch with approval. He had also changed out of his evening clothes, and now only wore a robe.

Then Violet noticed the small box in his hand. "What's that?" she asked.

"I meant to leave this for you this morning, before you altered my plans." He smiled, remembering how marvelous it had been to wake up with her in his bed.

"For me?"

"Who else?" He gave her the little box.

She untied the ribbon and lifted the cover to reveal a beautifully worked enamel pin in the shape of a crescent moon.

"Oh, it's beautiful. You don't have to give me things, you know." She looked up at him seriously. "They are all so lovely, but I don't need them."

"I want to give them to you," he insisted. "Consider it compensation for the way I neglected you before."

"You never neglected me."

"Violet, I was beastly to you, both before and after our wedding. Refusing to meet you, then treating you like a… a—"

"Contract?" she asked softly.

"I acted like a cad."

"No, you were always kind to me."

Kindness was not the word. Violet simply had no basis

from which to judge how men and women should interact, or how families should behave. Her life before their marriage was a joyless one. He owed it to her to make the rest of her life better.

"Turn down the light," he said.

Deciding that actions would speak louder than words, he chose to show her how he wanted to make her happy. From the satisfied moans, she had no complaints, and when they slid into sleep on Violet's bed, he had none either.

Alex only dozed, and when he woke, he slipped quietly out of Violet's room. It seemed like a miracle that she was asleep before dawn, and he didn't dare disturb her, not even for the kiss he wanted to give her.

He found his own bed depressingly cold, but it seemed a small price to pay for having Violet in his life.

Chapter 20

♋

OVER THE NEXT SEVERAL DAYS, anyone watching would have assumed the couple was just beginning a honeymoon, which was partly correct. Alex still took pride in sending Violet flowers at odd times, and finding excuses to give her gifts as though he were still courting her. Never mind the fact that he ended up in her bed every night.

Violet noticed he always waited until she asked him to her room. One night, she hadn't actually said the words, and he dutifully stayed away until she knocked on the connecting door and demanded an explanation.

"Why do you wait? We're married, and you can do whatever you like."

"I like to hear you ask for me," he said easily. Somehow, those words made Violet want to melt.

"I think about you constantly, love," he went on, "but I want to know it's mutual."

"I...I..." Violet tried to speak, but she felt shy and awkward again. "I think about you, too."

"That's good," he said, dipping his head to kiss her.

Violet opened her mouth, eager for him. How had she become addicted to this so quickly? But it had started much earlier, she knew. The day she'd gone riding without permission, when he'd shown that he cared very much if she lived or died. The first afternoon at the folly, when he'd kissed her so passionately.

Violet, for her part, was awed by the change in her husband. Every look he gave her was filled with emotion, and his distant exterior seemed to have melted away. Was this what it took for him to finally reveal himself to her?

Because in a very real sense, he had revealed himself to her. Even before she finally accepted him in her bed, Alex let her know about his work. And now that they were together at last, he shared even more, becoming more open about his thoughts, his plans, even his work, though he kept a wall around the details of exactly who he worked for.

"Not because I don't trust you," he said once. "But it's safer."

"I don't need to know," Violet assured him even though she worried that the work would pull him away from her when she needed him most. She was certain he lost his eye due to his work. What if he lost his life?

Violet maintained her practice of going to the folly on clear nights, and Alex started to accompany her for the whole time. He seemed fascinated by the telescope and her measurement of the stars, even her years' worth of careful notes. He found the notebooks on the shelf in the room of the folly, and read through some of them one evening, when a sudden squall forced Violet to curtail her stargazing. Alex had barely got the telescope inside ahead of the rain.

"You have a whole library here," he said, holding one notebook. "Just with what you've written."

"About fifteen years of work," Violet agreed. "I should hope I've left some mark."

"Would you share it with others? It must have value to

other astronomers. Or is it a closely guarded secret?"

She smiled, a bit sadly. "I don't consider it secret. But I don't know who would be interested. I'm just a woman. And I didn't think you would like your duchess dabbling in scientific circles."

"Why not?"

"Well, I know you don't like the ton to talk about your name."

"There's a difference between getting tormented with old misfortunes or lies and hearing you discussed as a genius."

"I'm not a genius. I just have the patience to watch the sky for hours."

He reached out to touch her. "That's not all you have patience for. You dealt with me being insufferable."

"A misunderstanding, and all past us now." Violet smiled to reassure him.

"Well, I think you should look into how to publish some of your findings. You can use a pseudonym, if you prefer. But your work is valuable. You've helped me."

"That was a very specific request," she said with a laugh.

"All the same. Who knows who you could help next?"

"I'll worry about that after your task is finished."

"If I finish," he said, dispirited. "No matter how many pieces I pick up, they don't seem to amount to anything larger."

"They will," Violet said. "Surely you've been at a similar point before in your investigations."

"Similar. But knowing that there's another death coming, every month, makes it worse. I'm to blame every time another person dies."

"No, you're not," Violet said sharply. "No one is to

blame but the killer himself. And you will find him."

"I hope so."

* * * *

One clear night in early April, Alex came up to the top of the folly when Violet was working. He could tell how intent she was on her measurements, so he simply sat down on the stone floor, waiting for her to acknowledge him.

Violet tipped the red-paned lantern carefully toward the notebook as she jotted down the night's numbers.

"I very much doubt it's a nova," she said finally, as if they'd been discussing it all along. "There is a slight but significant movement westward over the weeks. It's a comet, though who can say if it's going to return in our lifetimes, or ever. It's so strange, to think of this rock flying through the night, too far away to be anything but a speck to those who will see it, and destined to either fly off into darkness unending, or perhaps crashing into the sun itself. It makes me wonder if we—mankind, that is—will ever have the chance to get close to one." She glanced at him. "You don't mind my speculating about it? It must sound mad—traveling into space."

"Not at all. I like to hear about anything that doesn't involve death." He stretched out, his body flat on the stones. "I'm sick of thinking in circles."

"But the universe works in circles," Violet said. "The moon circles the earth, the earth circles the sun, and the sun spins against the background of space. That comet's path might be a cosmically massive circle, too big for us to see. And that's why the stars seem to spin in a circle, and why the Zodiac signs return every year at just the same time."

"So it's inescapable," said Alex, watching the stars. "I think I feel the earth spinning now, which I prefer not to."

"I've always found it reassuring. The music of the spheres."

Alex raised his head slightly. "Your aunt used that phrase once."

"Well, she's terribly interested in the stars, as I said. But she doesn't use it in the same sense that I do."

"Did you ever get along with your aunt?"

"She wasn't always so...abrasive. It got worse after Madeline took sick and then died. I tried not to blame her. Judith was distraught. But she changed, all the same. We barely spoke after a while. She offered dictates, and I obeyed her. That sufficed, for the most part."

He laughed. "But you let her know you didn't agree with her."

"She doesn't listen. She invited me to one of her little parties again while she was in London—where the future is revealed," Violet added in a dramatic tone. "Exactly the same sort as the ones my father went to. So she's never stopped her nonsense, no matter what I said."

"What happens at these parties?" he asked, curiously.

"Oh, I only remember them hazily, from peeping over the railing when my parents thought me asleep. Just like any party, I suppose. But there's more talk of the future, of star charts. They chat about how uncannily accurate the last one was...or why it was their fault they misread something from last month."

"Convenient."

"They want to believe in something, something tangible to plan their futures."

"I understand that," he said. "I spent years assuming

that ever worse things were going to happen to me, or around me."

Violet sat down and leaned over him. "Good things happened, too."

He reached up, running his fingers along her cheek. "Finally. I wouldn't have believed anyone if they told me I'd fall in love again."

"You…you love me?" she asked, her heart glowing brightly.

"Yes. Have I never said?"

"Not in words," she replied, "though you've certainly expressed it in other ways."

"I love you," he said, stumbling very slightly over the words, as if it was a long-forgotten phrase. "I love you."

Violet opened her mouth, but he said, "You don't have to say anything, Violet. I'm not expecting a declaration from you."

"Why not?"

"It's not that simple."

Violet paused, then said, "I've never been in love before, so perhaps I wouldn't know the signs. Tell me what to expect."

"Are you serious?" he asked.

"What could be more serious than this? Tell me."

"When…if…you love someone…"

"You," she said firmly. "When I fall in love with you, how will I feel?"

"Happy. Deliriously happy. And scared."

"Why scared?"

"Scared to lose what you've just found. You'll forget to eat. Sleeping won't matter. You'll feel dizzy."

"Are you describing love or a fever?"

"Well, one is often mistaken for the other." Then he

laughed.

"You never joke like this when other people are around," she said. "Is it because you're always thinking of serious things?"

"The truth is that I haven't been particularly amusing to be around for the last several years."

"You could have fooled me." She lay down beside him. The stones were cold as, well, stone. But she didn't care, especially not when Alex pulled her close.

"Alex, I have to tell you something."

"What?"

"Based on what you've just told me…I'm definitely in love with you." She kissed him. "I'm afraid you'll just have to accept it."

"Yes, your grace." Alex kissed her back so soundly that she was left breathless for a moment.

They walked back to the house hand in hand. Alex came to her door moments after Violet readied herself for bed.

"May I?" he asked, though with a smile.

"Don't waste a moment," Violet ordered.

He obeyed. When he reached her bedside, he leaned over to blow out the lamp flame.

"You don't have to do that," she said.

"I prefer it."

"Do you?" she pressed. "Or do you think *I* prefer it?" Violet was getting quite curious about seeing her husband more completely. She guessed why he always kept the room dark, though she didn't bring it up till now.

"I prefer it," he repeated, without elaborating. Then he was sliding into the bed, under the covers and reaching for her. Violet put aside the discussion, quite content to let Alex distract her again.

Chapter 21

♋

VIOLET TREAD CAREFULLY THROUGH HER newfound happiness, lest it vanish like dew under too bright a sunbeam. It had been a very long time since she last felt anything close to it, and she didn't trust it. Not that she didn't trust Alex, of course. He maintained his usual, indefinable aristocratic mien in public, but when they were in private—either alone or just with family—he was open and, at times, silly. He revealed an absurd sense of humor Violet would never have guessed he had, making her laugh till she hurt.

Even Millie lost her serious attitude around Alex now. Violet watched the two of them, noticing how much Millie modeled her own behavior on Alex's...cool when he was cool, smiling when he was smiling. Alex was probably more of a father figure to Millie than he suspected, and Violet was grateful for it.

Now if only she could give Alex a child of his own. The thought had been weighing on her more heavily over the past few weeks, though she knew it was far too early to wonder if she would have difficulty carrying a child. What if she was too old? Or just barren? What if she'd fail at the one duty she was expected to carry out as duchess?

"What's the matter?"

Violet jumped at the sound of Alex's voice. She'd been so lost in thought that she hadn't heard him come into the parlor where she was reading.

"Oh! Nothing."

"You looked quite troubled over nothing," Alex countered. He sat down in the chair across from hers. "What's on your mind?"

"In three days," she said, thinking quickly, "the sun will pass into a new sign."

"I know." He cursed under his breath. "That means I have to return to London. I was putting it off," he added. "I didn't want to leave the Abbey…or you."

"Well, I'll come with you."

He paused. "You'd be safer here."

"But not as useful," Violet argued. "It's just a matter of being careful. And I really believe I can help." She smiled at him. "Please."

"All right," he said. "Having you closer might help me think."

* * * *

When they reached London the next day, both Alex and Violet found a stack of invitations and letters waiting for them, having accumulated while they'd been gone.

Violet picked up one invitation, contemplating it. "My aunt is persistent, I'll give her that."

"She was certainly persistent when it came to arranging the marriage," Alex noted. "What does she want from you this time?"

"One of her ridiculous astrology meetings. She's been

pestering me to join her."

"Her and your uncle?"

"No, Uncle Roger wouldn't bother to come, and Judith never encouraged him to." Violet remembered Aunt Judith's friend Mr Hanchett and thought she could guess why. "But she wants me to join the fold."

"But she knows you're a skeptic, doesn't she?"

"There's a vast gulf between someone telling Aunt Judith something and her actually hearing it," Violet said, rolling her eyes. "She thinks I'll be convinced once I go."

"Well, go once and prove otherwise," Alex suggested. "Sometimes that's the best way."

"You told me you preferred that I not see my aunt."

"I was probably overreacting," he said. "You're not responsible for her foibles, and she is family. What harm could it do, other than being a little tedious?"

"Perhaps you're right."

Thus, Violet did the previously unthinkable and wrote to her aunt that she would attend the party the next evening. She had no doubt her aunt would faint when she received the message.

* * * *

While Violet was occupied with her family, Alex enlisted help to solve a problem that had been gnawing at him ever since he heard Millie's idea about Violet's "admirer." What if the snake had nothing to do with the murders, but rather that offensive wager he heard about?

He contacted Lord Forester again, and explained the issue. Bruce declared that they'd have to go deeper into the demimonde to get real answers. So he and Alex met that evening, and Bruce led him to another establishment in the city.

This place was decidedly less stuffy than some of Alex's clubs. In fact, it was on the edge of scandalous, a place where wealthy men could find diversions of all types. Whether it was gambling, women, or other forms of vice, a discreet payment was all that was needed.

Alex hadn't been in this type of place for years, unless his work took him there. He forgot how seamy it could be. The light was low, thanks to guttering candles, and tobacco smoke hung thickly in the air.

Bruce led Alex through room after room, seeking someone in particular.

"Ah," he said finally. "That's who we're here to meet." Bruce gestured to another man standing several feet away, accompanied by a beautiful woman in a rich yellow gown. The similarity between the two men was not obvious at first, but it was there. The other man had the same black hair and dark eyes as Bruce, though his features were more regular. He wasn't nearly as tall, nor as big. Bruce used his size to get what he wanted; this man didn't have to.

When they reached him, Bruce said, "My brother, the Honorable Ashley Allander."

Smirking, the other man offered a hand. "He left out the 'disreputable, younger brother' this time." He grinned at Alex. "A pleasure to meet you, your grace."

"You, as well, regardless of the setting," Alex said.

"Ah. Forester may not have told you that I have a most scandalous reputation."

"I don't have to, Ash," Bruce broke in sourly. "All of London knows about you."

"Lord, I hope so," Ash said carelessly. "I spend enough time tarnishing the family name. Be a shame if nothing came of it." He then turned to his companion, and his expression, though still sly, softened a bit. "I trust you're both acquainted with the incomparable Miss Fox."

"I have not yet had the pleasure of making the personal acquaintance of the duke," the lady in the golden gown said. She smiled warmly at Alex, dipping her head in acknowledgement. "Your grace."

"Miss Fox," he returned, unable to keep from smiling back. Regina Fox was a courtesan, notorious throughout London and beyond, with the talent for charming nearly any man. "You need no introduction."

She laughed prettily, with a slight edge of sadness that made the sound even more enchanting. "You are kind to say so, your grace. May I congratulate you on your recent marriage?"

"You may," he said. "Thank you."

"Tied the knot again?" Ash asked, with considerably less reverence. "Brave of you."

He let the multiple meanings of his words sink in, not caring in the least who he might insult.

Regina made a face at him. "Lord, Ash. You're terrible."

"As advertised." He looked at Alex, then over at Bruce. "Are you gentlemen just enjoying the various delights of the city, or was there a particular item to discuss?"

"Yes," Alex said. But he couldn't form words, once again furious at the situation.

Bruce broke in, seeing his difficulty. "The issue is this." He told about the wager on Violet's life, and how high the stakes seemed to have risen.

Ash looked coldly at his brother. All mannerisms of the carefree playboy were gone. "That's disgusting," he said. "You actually think I'd wager on such a thing?"

"I didn't mean to imply *you* bet on her death," Bruce explained hurriedly. "I hoped merely that you might know the sort of places where such a pool might exist. Places that would take one look and shut *us* out immediately."

"I need to know who's involved," Alex added.

The flinty look in Ash's eyes retreated a bit. "Well, as a matter of fact, you're right. I do know of some places. Benefit of my dissolute life." He paused. "I'll ask around."

"I'd be grateful for whatever information you could find," Alex said, his voice tight.

"I expect you would be." Ash suddenly laughed. "What exactly do you need to know? Just the name of the bookmaker?"

"Yes, but mostly so I can shake him down to get the names of the bettors, and the dates of death they chose."

"Matter of honor? Offended some men would make a profit over bad luck?"

"Someone doesn't seem content to leave it to luck." Alex explained, very briefly, how the krait appeared in the house and the danger it brought with it. Regina let out a gasp of horror when she heard, and even Ash's expression turned sympathetic.

"Well, that's not very sporting," he said, though his light tone sounded forced this time. "I'll do what I can, then bring the information to Bruce, who can pass it to you. No sense sullying a man's good reputation with rumors of my company."

"Bring it to me directly," said Alex. "What's one more rumor around my name?"

Ash grinned. "Very well, if you insist. And I promise to not sell it for profit first."

"Ash," Bruce began.

"Let's not get into a discussion about family honor," Ash said, forestalling him. "We all know that you're the brother with all the good qualities, leaving the rest to me. Just as well you get the title, too!" He offered an arm to Regina, who slipped her hand around it, just as ladylike as could be.

"Well, we're off," Ash drawled. "Detecting to do, and all that. What very exciting lives you gentlemen must lead…whatever it is you really do." With that rather too perceptive comment, Ash left the room, the incomparable Miss Fox beside him.

Alex watched them go. "Will he look, do you think?"

Bruce nodded. "Ash talks like a hedonist, but he's more reliable than he pretends. So is Miss Fox, for that matter. He'll do his best to find answers…if only because he wants to confound expectations."

"I hope he finds them soon."

* * * *

Violet wasn't sure what to expect in terms of formality, so on the night of the party her aunt invited her to, she had Dalby dress her in an understated gown of midnight blue wool. She wore a simple strand of pearls at her throat, avoiding any of the extravagant jewels she now owned.

When she arrived at the house, she told the driver to wait. She certainly didn't want to be stuck if the mood of the gathering made her uncomfortable or would reflect badly on her.

But inside the home, there was little to distinguish the gathering from any other small party in London that night.

If anything, it was a little on the dull side. A dozen people stood about and chatted. Wine glasses clinked in the candlelight, and the conversation flowed easily, punctuated by laughter. Only the odd phrase jumped out at Violet, reminding her that this was not quite a normal gathering. Talk of signs and the coming of the serpent made her shiver, but it was otherwise quite innocuous.

She met almost everyone there within the first quarter hour. Most were dazzled by her title, but a few guests were gentry as well, so it was an illustrious company. The surprisingly young Mr Frobisher was the host, and he seemed anxious that everyone enjoyed themselves. He spoke to everyone, his expression earnest. Someone told Violet that John Frobisher was until recently an officer in the army. He'd sold his commission a few years ago, intent on finding a less martial path in life. Looking at his broad frame and ramrod straight posture, it was easy to picture him in a uniform.

If Frobisher was the host, Mr Hanchett was clearly the center of the group. When he spoke, others listened. He took several people aside, into a little study, for a few moments each.

"What's happening in there?" she asked her aunt.

"Oh, Mr Hanchett is drawing up star charts of everyone for the month."

"Is he?"

At that moment, the dark-haired man emerged with a guest and caught Judith's eye. She took Violet by the arm. "Come. It's your turn. How exciting!"

Violet wasn't at all sure she wanted to know what Hanchett saw in the skies for her, but she trailed along.

"Come in, your grace," Mr Hanchett said. He stood up, his broad shoulders and courtly manner making him appear noble. "Mrs Peake will wait outside."

"My aunt will remain with me," Violet said firmly. "I insist." The idea of being alone with Mr Hanchett repelled her.

"It is customarily between the reader and the querent," he said.

"If it is a star chart," said Violet, "then literally anyone can see my fate. My aunt remains, or I go."

"Very well." He cast a look to Judith, who looked quite pleased to stay. "I have taken the liberty of drawing up your chart, based on the birthday provided by your aunt."

"And it reveals what is to occur in the near future?" she asked.

"This star chart does, because I have plotted out the movement and the location of the planets according to my own—secret—calculations. No other astrologer will be able to match it precisely. That is the great advantage of being a member of the Society of the True Sky."

"That's why Daniel is always correct in his prognostications," Judith began.

But he silenced her with a look. "I must tell you, your grace, that you were destined to come here tonight."

Easy prediction to make once she was here, Violet thought. But she said, "And I am here. What next?"

"It is vital that you listen to my next words, your grace. The stars do not lie, and there is a great darkness hovering over you. Your marriage was predicted by the rising of Venus in the sign of Gemini, and as predicted, it came to pass. But your husband is concealing something from you, which could destroy your marriage."

Violet frowned at Hanchett. Did the man really think he could frighten her with these vague implications? She could tell that he wanted her to gasp and beg to know more, using her presumed insecurity to convince her of his methods.

"That is a bold claim," she said.

"It is not my claim, but that of the stars."

"What is he hiding? A mistress?" Violet remembered the conversation she had with Alex about it. She believed him when he said he didn't have one. But if she hadn't dared to ask…well, that was an easy point to touch in a wife's consciousness. She also couldn't stop the tiniest doubt. What if Alex had lied to her? She had known him for such a short time.

"A mistress? Nothing so mundane," Hanchett assured her. "It is stranger and graver than that."

"What, then?"

"He is haunted, your grace. Haunted by a past that will not let him go. And that past will most certainly seize him and take him from you beginning when the Great Warrior is ascendant." Hanchett tapped another constellation. "There will be nothing you can do to save him."

"Then why tell me?" she asked.

"Because you can do something *now*. You must join our society. If you listen to the stars' plans carefully, and follows the proper path, both you and he may avoid the darkness. You can live in peace and happiness."

"How reassuring." Hanchett didn't appear to notice her sarcasm. He tapped a point on her chart where several lines crossed. "The moon is now passing into Libra, both bodies highly significant of water and sleep. Your sleepless nights and restless dreams will cease if you divest yourself of the doubts you carry." He handed her a small bottle. "This is water charged with the power of the full moon. Drink three drops in wine every night before bed for the next seven nights. By the seventh night, your sleep will be like a child's again."

Violet took the little bottle, thinking Judith must have told Hanchett of Violet's insomnia. And he gave her this ridiculous, false medicine to cure it.

Unless it was meant to kill her instead. Violet recalled the krait. Someone did want her dead, after all. Perhaps this was another attempt.

But Hanchett only rolled up Violet's star chart and gave it to her. "You may study it as much as you wish, your grace. If you have a question, simply send for me and I will answer it."

"Thank you," she said. At least the star chart was something she could verify to see if the man knew where the planets should be in the night sky!

When Violet left the study, Judith followed, anxious to ask her what she thought of Hanchett's words.

But Violet thought quickly enough to distract her aunt.

Susanna Gilroy sat on a chaise in the corner, looking even frailer than she had the last time Violet had seen her. Frobisher hovered near her, having just fetched a warm throw, which she accepted with a soft thanks. Then he reluctantly left to speak to someone at the door.

"Are they betrothed?" Violet asked Judith, hoping the question would work as distraction.

"I don't think so," Judith replied. "He is most assiduous when near her, though. They met last year. Mr Frobisher invited her to our gatherings. She's come every time," Judith added with approval.

"She's ill, isn't she?"

"Yes, but she keeps her spirits high, and she does not give up. Fate will smile on her. I've no doubt she'll recover completely!"

Violet saw the fragile way Susanna moved, and the disturbingly pale tone in her cheeks. She didn't have Judith's confidence that Susanna would triumph over whatever sickness plagued her.

Drawn to the other woman, Violet approached her. "May I sit by you?" she asked.

"Oh, your grace, I would be honored," Susanna said. "Your aunt has told me so much about you. She is so happy you're here tonight."

"Yes, I imagine," Violet said dryly. But then she smiled at Susanna. "It sounds as if you don't miss a meeting."

"I wouldn't dare."

"Why not? The stars still spin, regardless of whether we leave the house or not."

Susanna put a hand to her mouth to hide a smile. "That's a little blasphemous."

"Is it? Do I apologize to the stars? Or Mr Frobisher?"

"Oh, he's not the leader. We don't have a leader, as such."

"Mr Hanchett once called himself a leader."

"Mr Hanchett is, of course, very important to our society's success," Susanna said, though it sounded as if she was trying to convince herself. "He's the most accomplished at the star charts, and he's just uncanny when telling the future. But we avoid titles when among believers. We are all under the same sky, are we not?"

"Indisputably. Are you very interested in…all this?" Violet waved her hand to indicate the party.

"I want to know the future," Susanna said. Her eyes tracked Mr Frobisher, who was on the other side of the room. "I used to lie awake at night, so scared of what would happen. Then I met these people, and learned how to reveal some of the future. It helps me."

"I have trouble sleeping, myself," Violet said.

Susanna reached out to touch Violet's arm. "Then you must tell Mr Hanchett! He'll draw up your chart, and tell you what to expect. It's ever so comforting."

"He just told me his conclusions," Violet admitted. "What did he tell you, if I may ask?"

"To be patient. To have faith." The lady's eyes were again on Frobisher. "The future belongs to those who grasp the serpent unflinching."

The quote echoed one that Judith used frequently, but Violet remembered something older, something her father told her once. What had he said about a serpent? She struggled to recall the words, but then saw someone approaching.

"Mr Frobisher is coming over here again," Violet noted. "Shall I leave you alone?"

"Oh, you must get to know him," Susanna said. "He's very kind."

Mr Frobisher was quite happy to speak with Violet, though he was more interested in Susanna. He never dared to touch the lady, but it was clear that he hung on her every word.

After a few moments, Susanna sagged back against her chair, coughing weakly. "Excuse me, I've spoken too much."

Frobisher said quickly, "Can I get you anything?"

"I need a few moments' rest. Why not take her grace for a turn? I'll feel much better in a bit."

So Frobisher rose and offered to escort Violet around the gardens. She accepted, hoping to speak to her host alone for a minute.

"Miss Gilroy is such a charming lady," she said, once they stepped out of the house.

"She is a jewel," he agreed, his blue eyes catching the light from the house. "And possessed of such perfect faith."

"In the stars?"

"In the stars' plan for us all," he said, vehemently. "The music of the spheres is always there—"

"—for those who listen." Violet finished the half-remembered phrase she heard her father say so many years ago. Odd how everything was coming back to her now.

Frobisher beamed at her. "Exactly. I can see why Mrs Peake wanted you to join us. She says you have studied the stars for years on your own."

"In my way," Violet said modestly. "As my father taught me to."

"Mrs Peake's brother, correct?" Frobisher seemed well informed. "Of course the whole family would be enlightened. You are very lucky, your grace."

She thought of Alex and smiled. "Yes, I suppose I am. But I wonder, sir, if you could tell me a bit more about your Society of the True Sky. I am very curious about what you hope to accomplish."

"Has Mr Hanchett not said?"

"Not yet. We have not had much chance to speak. But I know of the serpent handler." She added the last phrase in almost unconsciously. That's what her father spoke of! Perhaps the mention of it would make Frobisher think she knew far more than she did.

It worked better than she expected. Frobisher stopped and turned toward her. "You know about Ophiuchus?"

"Of course," she said. "I remember my father's words quite clearly." His half-mad words, spat out on his deathbed. But she didn't add that.

"Daniel—Mr Hanchett, that is—will be most impressed. Only the most devoted learn about the thirteenth sign."

"You obviously know, so you proved your devotion."

His expression changed to one of worry. "I can only try. As do we all. Just as I work to keep Susanna's spirits up. She's been so downcast lately. I won't say she's a doubter, but…" he trailed off.

"It must be very hard for her," Violet said sympathetically. "With such an illness to contend with. It would try any person. At least she has you. You clearly care for her."

Frobisher actually looked bashful. The expression was charming, turning the big man into an overgrown boy. "She is—"

"A jewel." Violet echoed his word from before.

"Yes. I hope someday—"

Before he could add anything, they were interrupted by the sounds of another couple approaching them. The laughter and low, confidential tones made it sound like a pair of youngsters, so Violet's eyes widened when she saw Judith and Mr Hanchett turn the corner. Hanchett was holding Judith scandalously close to him, and his lips were brushing her ear in a way that made both Violet and Frobisher stiffen in shared embarrassment at what they witnessed.

"Hello, Aunt," Violet said.

"Violet!" Judith gasped and stepped away. "I didn't know you were outside!"

"Mr Frobisher was kind enough to take me for a turn about the gardens. Just as Mr Hanchett did for you, I *assume*."

"Yes, yes of course. Daniel…Mr Hanchett is most…

ah."

"Words fail me as well." Before her marriage, Violet would not have dreamed she could speak like that to her aunt. Indeed, she had been so sheltered that she wouldn't dream of a lady being with any man but the one she married. But now, Violet knew quite a bit more about both herself and the world. And she no longer feared Judith's wrath.

"The hour is getting rather late," Violet said then. "I think I should call my carriage."

"You must stay for the ceremony, your grace," Hanchett said.

Violet didn't try to hide her disgust. The nerve of the man, to think she'd linger. "Oh, I'm quite sure of my immediate future, and it involves a carriage home." She turned to Mr Frobisher. "Would you please walk me to the front hall? And then you should return to Miss Gilroy. You can convey my goodbyes to her."

"Indeed, your grace." Frobisher gave a look to the other couple, one that was both disturbed and rather offended. But he said nothing about it until they reached the front hall.

"I hope, your grace," he said carefully, "I hope you will return for the next gathering, regardless of… That is…" He was plainly appalled at the scene.

"I will consider it, Mr Frobisher. I did meet some people I'd like to see again."

"Oh," he said. "That's good."

"Give Miss Gilroy my best," Violet added when the coach pulled up. "I am sorry she wasn't feeling well tonight."

"I will tell her, your grace." Frobisher helped her inside the carriage. "May you return safely to your home.

The streets of London seem more dangerous every month."

That was all too true, Violet thought as the carriage rolled away toward home. She hoped to talk to Alex about the meeting, but she knew that he was going to be out—likely all night, since he was certain the murderer would strike again.

* * * *

According to Violet's estimations, the next murder would occur on the fifteenth of April. Thus, Alex made Violet promise that she would be home well before midnight. He didn't plan on getting home before dawn.

Alex had enlisted some of the Disreputables to help that night. Ivy, the dark-haired girl from before, acted as a sort of supervisor, and Rook was eager to join as well. Through some mechanism Alex wasn't privy to, Ivy sent various people to the locations Alex thought might attract the killer. He was still guessing, though, and he had a sour feeling in the pit of his stomach that told him he would fail again.

He tried to ignore it as best he could. Ivy got regular updates from the other Disreputables scattered around the city. A young girl of about ten years appeared quite often to give Ivy little slips of paper.

"Thank you, Sally," she said, opening the latest. She read it, then announced to Alex, "Still no word of a murder. Perhaps our luck will continue."

"It's early," Alex muttered. The bells had just chimed two in the morning. He and Ivy were strolling a section of Hyde Park. Alex chose it as the most likely place.

But in reality, there wasn't much Alex could do. He

just didn't know enough about the killer. A dark haired, well-built man who was strong enough to keep his victims quiet and drag bodies as far as he wanted to. That could be almost anybody.

Alex needed more. He would prefer not to get that information in the form of another dead body.

"Someone's coming. Looks like Jem," Ivy said suddenly.

He straightened up. Someone was hurrying toward them. It was a young man, running toward them from the road where a carriage waited.

"It happened," he said. "Rook's still there, keeping an eye on things."

"Where?" Alex asked.

"Other side of the park, close to the river. I have a rig."

They reached the scene of the crime minutes later. It was an out of the way spot, unlike the other murders. That helped to keep spectators away, as did the later hour. Only two people stood near the body. One looked like an officer of the law, but the other was the young lad Rook.

Alex chose the direct route, addressing the young officer as if he had every right to do so. "What happened? Report."

"The boy found a body," the man said nervously. "I stayed to make sure nothing happened, and sent him to get help... Though he found you?" He looked at Alex, trying to decide who he was.

Alex didn't let him get far. "Keep everyone else at least thirty feet from the body. There's four people here. Spread out. Make a square, and don't let anyone pass. I'll look at the scene."

Everyone obeyed, and Alex was free to walk to the

body, which had been covered with a coat.

He looked first at the ground around the body. The sign was there: the symbol of Aries drawn in dark blood, just above the head of the body. He expected to see it, but that didn't make the fact any less horrible. Heavy footprints of a man's boots were evident, as were the smaller prints of a woman's shoes.

That was his first hint of the victim. Alex knelt and pulled back the cloak. A woman stared up at the sky above. Hair spilled out around her face, making a fuzzy halo. Alex closed the blue eyes gently. He then pulled the cloak back further. He noticed that the body looked as if it was arranged after the kill. There was no way the woman fell back into such a neat pose, tidily on her back, arms folded over her chest. The other victims were face down, or in a heap.

The killer must have taken some time to arrange the body so neatly and draw his symbol nearby. Why? Because he finally got someone in an out of the way place? Was she special? Was the killer a chivalrous sort? He certainly wasn't scared of getting caught.

Alex saw a small bag near the body. He looked through it, finding coins and bills undisturbed. He also found a letter, which he put away for the moment. He'd examine it more carefully when he wasn't bending over the victim.

A quick search of the body revealed only a single knife wound in the chest. At least the lady's death came fast.

Alex heard a few voices around him, as spectators started to gather. But the officer and the Disreputables did an excellent job of keeping others well away, and the sounds faded once people realized there was nothing much to see.

As Alex was thinking, the officer appeared by his side. "Um, sir?"

"What?" Alex said irritably.

"You're the one investigating this crime?"

"Appears that way, doesn't it?"

"I didn't catch your name, sir."

"There's a reason for that," Alex said coldly. "Your name?"

"Maxwell, sir. Arthur Maxwell."

"Good. I'll make sure to mention your good work in keeping the crowd away."

"What happened?" he asked. "Looks as if she was robbed and killed by a madman."

"Not robbed. Her reticule is there, with money. And a letter addressed to her, so I know who she is—or I will, once I look further into it." He cleared his throat. "Did you find the body?"

"No, that lad did." The officer pointed to Rook. "He called for help."

"Did anyone actually see the attack?"

"If they did, they didn't stay."

Alex grunted. Of course his luck would stay bad on that score. He stood up. "Well, I've got plenty of work. Carry on, Maxwell. You know the procedure."

Rook approached. "I can help!" he said eagerly. "Let me stay, sir!"

"Very well. You can assist Maxwell," Alex declared, as if he had the authority to deputize the boy. He gestured to Ivy and Jem and started to move off. "You'll hear from me soon, Maxwell. Good luck."

Maxwell didn't dare leave the scene to chase after Alex, who was able to get himself and Ivy to the carriage the young man Jem had been driving.

"I'll tell the others that there's nothing left to watch for tonight. And I'll pass on whatever Rook learns," Ivy said. "Where are you going, sir?"

"To the address on the letter in her bag," said Alex. "My work's not done tonight."

"I'll drive you there, sir." Jem pointed to the carriage. "No time like the present."

Chapter 22

♋

VIOLET HEARD ALEX RETURN HOME as dawn was just coloring the sky. She didn't even pretend that she'd been sleeping. She came into the dining room where he was devouring some cold meat and bread brought from the kitchen.

"What happened?" she asked. Then she said, "No, eat first. You must be ravenous."

He nodded briefly. When he cleared the plate, he said, "Lord, I needed that."

"How are you?" she asked.

"Exhausted." He looked worse than that.

"Would you like to go to sleep and talk later in the morning?"

"No. I need to talk now. Come with me." Together, they went up to Alex's bedroom, and sat by the small fireplace. Alex sagged back in his chair, lines etched on his face. "So there's been another death."

She expected to hear that, judging from his attitude. "The same as the others?"

"In most respects. But this victim was a woman. And, I suspect, a lady."

That sent a little chill through Violet. "Who was she? Do you know yet?"

"A Susanna Gilroy. She lived here in London with her family."

Violet gasped. "No! I just saw her."

"You knew her?" Alex straightened up in his chair, alert now. "How?"

"She was an acquaintance of Aunt Judith's. I met her at one of the first events we attended here in town, and again at Judith's little party last night. Only for a few moments, but she seemed like such a gentle woman. She was ill," Violet added. "Very frail. I could tell."

"I'm sorry," said Alex.

"This means she was killed just after she left the house," Violet said. She didn't add the next logical thought. Violet herself could easily have been the next victim, if she had stayed longer.

But Alex seemed to read her mind. "We don't know why she was chosen. I have to find out more about her."

"This is horrible," Violet said. "Susanna was a very sweet lady. From what I could see, everyone liked her."

"Evidently, someone didn't." Alex then looked at Violet closely. "Did you sleep at all?"

"No, but neither did you."

"You need to sleep," he said.

"After this news, I'm not sure I can."

"No arguments." He walked with her to her bedroom, and put her into the turned down bed after she changed into a simple shift.

Seeing the bottle on her bedside table, Alex picked it up. "What's this?"

"Oh, that," Violet said. "Mr Hanchett gave me that at the meeting. He claimed some utter nonsense about it being moonlight water to help me sleep."

Alex's expression went cold. "He gave this to you and told you to drink it?"

"I didn't!" she assured him. "I'm not a fool."

He pocketed the bottle. "I'm going to find out what it is."

"Are you going to bed?" she asked.

"Soon," he assured her, bending to give her a kiss. Violet was asleep before he left the room.

* * * *

The next few days were strange for Violet. Judith called on her the day the news of Susanna's death became public, and for once the two women had no animosity in their conversation, only a shared shock of losing someone unexpectedly.

"I know she wasn't well," Judith said, "But there was no hint that death would come like this. Of course, the star charts are meant for the individual. But she had no fear the night she died. How could that be?" Judith looked so upset that Violet took pity on her.

"Perhaps it's better that way," she said to her aunt. "What comfort is there in knowing about such a fate? Apparently her death was very quick. She was suffering before, but this death ended that suffering."

Judith nodded slowly. "It would explain the reading she got. She didn't die of her illness—but of something else."

"That's true," Violet said.

"So the stars were still correct. As always, the fault lies in human fallibility. The sky is still true."

Violet said nothing, unable to share Judith's relief.

Who cared what Susanna's star chart predicted when it so obviously wasn't a violent end like this? But she didn't want to pick a fight at this point.

"How is Mr Frobisher?" Violet asked. "Have you heard?"

"Devastated," Judith said baldly. "He's not even accepting callers, poor man. I heard he shut himself up in his rooms. I knew he cared for Susanna, but..." she trailed off.

"I hope he'll recover," Violet said. "And Mr Hanchett?"

Judith frowned. "He was not available this morning. I'm not sure where his business took him. He'll be back for the funeral."

But as it happened, the funeral did not occur in London. Susanna's family insisted on taking the body to their home in the country.

A few days later, Violet called on Mr Frobisher. She expected that he would not be at home to anyone, so she would simply leave a card. But to her surprise, the maid said Frobisher would receive her.

He looked terrible when Violet saw him in his parlor, as if he'd not eaten since news of the murder. A little bottle sat on the table near him. It was identical to the one Hanchett gave Violet the other day.

"Thank you for calling, your grace," Frobisher said. He blinked slowly as he registered her presence. Then he said, "Forgive me! I should stand."

"Don't trouble yourself," she said quickly. "This is not the usual social call, is it?"

"No," he agreed, his gaze dropping again.

"I wanted to convey my condolences," Violet told him. "I knew her only slightly, but she was the sort of woman who engendered affection instantly."

"Yes, she was," Frobisher said. "Yes, she was."

"And it happened so suddenly," Violet added.

"She left before I could escort her home," Frobisher said, his voice quiet. "I wanted to. I should have left *with* her."

"Oh, you mustn't blame yourself," Violet said.

But he wasn't listening. "One makes so many little decisions in life," he said. "One after another. Perhaps you greet someone…or you don't. Perhaps you turn a corner…or you don't. How can you know which is right? You don't know which decisions have meaning until it's too late…"

Violet's heart ached in sympathy. She understood exactly what he meant, yet she had no answers. Instead, she quietly made her way out the door, leaving Frobisher to his grief.

When she returned home, Alex was actually there. He'd spent the last few days out of the house, seemingly constantly chasing lead after lead.

"I didn't think you'd be here until tonight," she said.

Alex sighed. "I may have exhausted my reserves. What have you been doing?"

Violet related the news of Frobisher and the others who were affected by Susanna's death. Alex nodded absently.

"And what have you learned?" she asked.

"About Miss Gilroy? Only that she doesn't fit."

"Doesn't fit what?"

"The expectation of the victims. The others were all men. She was a woman, with no political connections or odd activities or anything to explain why someone would want to hurt her."

"Perhaps she does and they're not obvious. A father or brother could be a politician like Galbraith."

"I've already done some inquiries. There's no connection I can identify. I'm waiting for the family to return."

"You must have learned something."

"I learned that what Hanchett gave you in that bottle was opium."

"Harmless, then."

"Hardly," Alex said. "Have you ever seen someone far gone on opium? They don't even eat at the end."

"I suppose you're right. Mr Frobisher must have had some right before I saw him, because he could barely focus on me. I saw a similar bottle at his home."

"That reminds me," said Alex. "With all the other news, I forgot to ask about the meeting itself. How was it?" he asked, once she was sitting in the parlor with him.

"Tolerable until it was not," she said. "Most of the people were perfectly pleasant. Mr Frobisher—the host—was most accommodating, and of course quite well then, since it was before anything bad happened. He saw me to the carriage when I left."

Something in her voice made Alex say, "And why did you leave?"

"I saw Aunt Judith and this Mr Hanchett together. Again. And this time there was no mistaking the nature of their relationship. She called him Daniel, just as if they were alone together."

"Awkward," he commented.

"I know it's not uncommon," she said, "But knowing that is quite different from seeing it in one's own family!"

"I'm sorry you had to deal with it."

"Mr Frobisher was just as embarrassed as I was…on my behalf, I'm sure. And yet they all wanted me to come back. As if the Society of the True Sky needed me!"

"You called it what?"

"That's what they call themselves. The Society of the True Sky."

"I've heard that before." Excited, Alex found his notes and went through them quickly. "Here. It was referenced in Mason's things. He had several star charts and fortunes written out, along with the reference to the True Sky."

"So he was part of the group?" Violet asked. "Why did no one say?"

"They probably didn't want to bring it up, and certainly not to a potential recruit."

Violet sighed. "That does explain why there was an empty spot for me."

"Daniel Hanchett," Alex said then, slowly. "Was that always his name?"

"What do you mean?" Violet asked. "What else could it have been?"

He took a breath. "I have one very good guess. I'll let you know if I'm correct. And until I say so, avoid Hanchett. Don't go anywhere near him."

"Should I tell Aunt Judith to do the same?" she asked.

"No. I don't want to alarm anyone. And there's a possibility I'm wrong. It could be coincidence."

Violet actually laughed. "Coincidence? At this point?"

"Well, then perhaps the stars have it all planned out."

Chapter 23

♋

BECAUSE ALEX ASKED ROOK TO watch the Gilroy home, he got a report when the family was back in London. So a few days later, he dressed like an ordinary gentleman and went around to the house.

"I have some questions about the death of Miss Gilroy," he told the maid who answered the door. "It's important."

"Oh," said the maid. "I'll see if Mrs Gilroy is at home. Please wait in the parlor, sir."

Alex walked into the room she indicated, and stood by the fireplace to wait. Would the mother speak to him? Or would she send him away without even seeing him? It was hard to guess. Alex wasn't using his title to gain entrance, and his official standing to investigate was murky at best.

But five minutes later, the maid reappeared in the door, her arm around the waist of an older lady dressed entirely in black.

"Mrs Gilroy," Alex said, bowing politely.

"How do you do…Mr Kenyon, is it?" She sat down on one of the chairs, and indicated that Alex should be seated as well. "Marie tells me you wish to speak to me about my Susanna."

"Yes, ma'am. I realize it's a difficult time."

"What is your interest in her death?" she asked bluntly.

Alex took a breath. "In short, I hope to prevent another death."

"Is that so?" She turned to Marie, who hadn't left yet. "Bring some tea in for our guest and me."

Marie left, and Mrs Gilroy turned her attention to him again. Alex felt her appraisal. She saw his eyepatch, his clothes, his demeanor, and she was certainly alert enough to notice that he was not official at all.

"Who do you hope to save?" she asked.

Alex could have explained the truth. He only had hints and guesses and he had no idea who the next victim would be. But that would not matter to this woman, who was in deep mourning for her daughter. He had to make this story personal.

"I'm married," he began slowly. "And my wife may be in similar circumstances to your late daughter."

"Oh, dear," Mrs Gilroy said, her expression disturbed. "Has she been to the moon doctor as well? Is she a believer?"

"I'm...I'm not sure," said Alex. "Can you tell me a little bit about the moon doctor?" Including, he hoped, what the devil a moon doctor *was*.

"Doctor Fermier, he calls himself." The lady sniffed. "Every full moon—and new moon too, I think—he gathers his patients and conducts his so-called cures. Pure quackery! And not godly in the least. My Susanna had been ill for months, and even as it got worse, she returned to Fermier again and again, convinced that he could cure her. He said it was science, of course. He'll produce any number of drawings and proofs that look very impressive and explain absolutely nothing. I went the first time, and never set foot in his office again. But Susanna was convinced that the skies could save her. She refused to listen to reason, though I pleaded with her to stay home and trust in Providence."

"My wife draws pictures of the moon," Alex said musingly.

Mrs Gilroy shook her head sadly. "Then she is likely under the spell of this doctor, too. You must keep her from attending the next cure! Susanna was killed on her way home from one of those gatherings. The authorities said it was just bad luck—a drunk or a madman who seized the chance to steal from a lady. But then why was there that hideous mark left beside her body? It's connected. I *know* it, but the authorities won't listen to me. They see only a grieving woman, and dismiss my words."

"They won't dismiss mine," Alex said firmly. "And if there is a connection between the killing and this so-called doctor, I'll make sure he never practices a cure again."

"Bless you for trying. I never trusted him!"

"You think she might have been followed from Fermier's office?" Alex asked. "Perhaps the doctor's customers are known to be wealthy."

"I don't know. All I know is that my loving, precious child became a nervous wreck in the last months of her life. Obsessed with the phases of the moon and the stars in the sky. Is that true of your wife?"

"She stargazes every chance she gets," Alex said, with complete honesty.

"If you care for her, you'll get her well away from London," Mrs Gilroy advised.

"As soon as I can," he promised. "But now I'll go to this Fermier's office and learn who he really is."

Mrs. Gilroy gave him the street name of where the doctor practiced his trade, and implored him to be careful. Alex left the house and went toward the shabbier part of London, where his next quarry was.

It was not hard to find Doctor Fermier's place of business. He had large posters pasted on the walls of his building, advertising the "moon cure" for nearly all ills. *Safe! Scientific! Praised by the royal houses of Europe!*

Alex sneered. He doubted very much that any royal would dare put their name to this man's work. He knocked loudly on the door, then pounded on it again after a moment. "Open up!" he ordered.

The door jerked open, and a short, stooped-back man peered up at him. "What is the matter with you, sir! I do not have office hours until after three."

"I'm here now," Alex said. "So now is when you'll talk to me."

"Can't fix your eye," the man said. "Sorry!" He tried to close the door.

Alex put his shoulder in the way, and the man stumbled back from the force. "My eye does not concern me. Shall we go up to your office?" He stepped in and turned the key in the lock.

"Very well." Fermier led him up a narrow staircase and down a short hall to a large room.

Alex stopped short, not expecting what he found. The room wasn't shabby like the rest of the building. It was bright, with a glass frame set in the ceiling, where the sun shone down by day and the moon would do so at night. The rest of the ceiling and the walls were beautifully painted in a rich, dark blue to mimic the night sky. Little white stars lay scattered across the surface. It was lovingly done, and extremely effective.

The room contained many chairs, all arranged in circles around the empty center of the room. A few couches were pushed against the walls.

The doctor walked to the center, and swept his hand around. "Sit anywhere you like. On the night of the full moon, it's standing room only."

"This is where you conduct your cures?"

"Yes, yes." The doctor crossed his arms. "What brings you here? You're no believer."

"That obvious?" Alex asked. "I'm here to ask about Susanna Gilroy."

"Dear Lord," the doctor said, with a sigh. He sank down onto a chair. "Have you not heard? She's dead, the poor child."

"Her mother says she was killed immediately after attending one of your gatherings."

"Oh, no!" The doctor glared at Alex. "I held no gathering on the night she died. It wasn't the full moon, or the new moon!"

"But she attended here on those days?"

"Yes, yes. But it's useless to pester me. I couldn't save her from the disease that she suffered from, and I certainly had nothing to do with the madman who killed her on the street. Horrible business."

"What disease?"

"A murmur in her heart, I suspect. One that worsened as she aged."

"Are you a real doctor, then? Licensed?"

"I attended medical college in Paris, but I became disgusted with the practices of modern medicine. Treating a person as a mere machine, with no attention to the many influences on a human life that affect health. So I left. But I still recognize signs of illness when I see them."

"So you diagnosed Miss Gilroy."

Fermier shook his head. "She already knew when she first came here. And before you ask, she'd been to several other doctors, who could do nothing more for her, despite their scalpels and pills. So don't look at me and call my practice barbaric!"

"I didn't."

"Ah, but you would. I can smell a skeptic from a hundred paces. They sneak into my gatherings, prepared to laugh and mock. But I've helped my patients!"

"How?" Alex asked him.

"You want a detailed explanation of the link between the moon, gravity, and the tides of the world as well as within the human body? I doubt it. But there is an established pattern of human physiology and the moon's phases. By balancing and adjusting these tides, tremendous progress can be made in patients. Particularly for those who suffer from diseases of the mind and spirit, which no scalpel can cure. Melancholia, manias, nightmares…I have cured people of all of these."

"For a hefty price," Alex guessed.

"Three pennies per person, per gathering." Fermier wrinkled his nose. "I'm a doctor, not a thief."

"Did you believe you could cure Miss Gilroy?"

"I believed I could ease her suffering. I don't claim to offer immortality. She came here for several months, and she felt better when she left. Is that not worth three pennies?"

"How exactly does the cure work?" Alex asked.

"You may attend the next gathering and see for yourself. I have no time to educate you in my methods."

"Mrs Gilroy calls you a quack. She thinks you were after money."

"People will believe what they like. But if she feared for her daughter, she would have done better to confront Mr Hanchett."

Something in Alex went cold. "Tell me about him."

"He's a fortune teller in town, with some sort of club for those who pay," Fermier said. "Miss Gilroy went to him, as well. Not for a cure, but to know her future, poor girl. She was fearful of death, and Hanchett must have told her something she wanted to hear, because she went on and on about him."

"You called him a fortune teller. I should talk to him," Alex said.

"Oh, now you want your cards read?"

"I want to know what he told Miss Gilroy, and why he didn't predict her murder."

"Good question!" The doctor snorted in derision. "Those frauds give people like me a bad name! Come back and tell me what he says."

"So you didn't encourage her to go to him."

"If she wanted to give her money away, she could have distributed it to the poor. Better use of it, I say."

"One more question. Was one of your patients a man named Warner Mason?" Alex remembered the papers on astrology Mason owned

The doctor frowned. "The name is not familiar. But that may not mean much. Many times, people come to the gathering but don't introduce themselves."

Alex described him, but Fermier just shook his head. "No, no. That's too general. I'm not saying he wasn't here, mind you. But I can't recall that name or face."

If he was telling the truth, which Alex thought he was, the connection between victims was not their interest in the moon cure. Alex thanked the man and left. He almost laughed at how irate the moon doctor was at the idea of fortune tellers. It seemed everyone was convinced that their own ideas were perfectly logical, while everyone else was deluded.

Yet wasn't that exactly how all people thought? No one ever embraced an idea they thought silly. And no one liked to admit that they made a mistake. So they looked at the moon and the stars, desperate to find the answers to their questions.

And then there were the people eager to help answer those questions, like Hanchett. Alex was getting a very bad feeling about the man. Though he had no hard evidence, he suspected that Hanchett was the key to the whole mystery surrounding these deaths. Maybe he wasn't the killer, but it was time to learn more about him. As soon as Alex got some rest.

He went home to Violet. She smiled at him in a way that made up for nearly all the frustrations of the past days and weeks.

"I waited for you," she said. "I hoped you'd dine with me, and stay in tonight."

He returned her smile. "As it happens, that was precisely my plan."

"Excellent." Violet stepped up to him. The star sapphire shone at her throat. She put a hand on his arm, drawing him closer. "Everything has been so odd, and I know that you have so much on your mind. But Susanna's death in particular has made me realize how very happy I am right now. I don't want to forget that, no matter what is happening in the world." She gave a little sigh. "Would you put the investigation aside, just for tonight?"

"I will try." Alex put his arms around her. "Until tomorrow, I won't say a word about it."

Chapter 24

♋

ALEX WOKE UP IN THE night. He'd been invited to Violet's bed, but they did nothing more than slide into sleep together. Alex fought sleep for a few moments after Violet nodded off, her head on his shoulder. He adored holding her, still marveling in the newness of knowing this woman wanted him near.

Something had made him wake up in the middle of the night. Moonlight streamed in one window, where the curtain hadn't been drawn fully. The pale light washed over everything, turning it silver.

With a jolt, he realized what felt different. His eyepatch had come off while he slept. He didn't want Violet to see him without it. If his wound disgusted him, it would terrify her.

He felt around his pillow, but couldn't find it. He grew a little more frantic, sitting up to look for it, hoping she wouldn't wake.

But she did. "Stop fretting, Alex," she said, her voice mellow. "I found it."

"Give it to me," he said urgently. *Fretting?* He didn't fret.

"No."

"No? Give it over."

"No, Alex," she said. "You don't need it."

"I do. I don't want you to see me."

Violet shifted, rising onto her side. "I've seen you, love. You know that? I've seen you night after night."

He held one hand over the ruined part of his face. "It was dark then."

"Not that dark. Don't pretend with me. I married all of you."

"Give it back," he repeated.

"I will when you accept that it doesn't matter, and that I'm not in the least repelled by your lost eye."

He couldn't say anything, because he flatly didn't believe it.

"I love you. All of you. If you'd lost an arm, I'd love you. A leg. If you had a legion of scars. I will still look on you with adoration, because I know you like no one else does."

He squeezed his good eye shut, unwilling to look at her. "Please give it back."

"No." Her lips were on his then, her hands pulling his own from his face.

Alex rarely felt as weak as he did then. "Don't do this to me."

"I will." His shy Violet suddenly had iron in her voice. "It's long past time that you admitted this. You are not unlucky, you are extraordinarily lucky. You *survived*, Alex. You never have to tell me what happened to you, but I'm sure that most men would be dead. You survived. You came home."

"I'm lucky," he echoed. "But only because I somehow got you."

"Good," she confirmed. "Now, revel in it. We are together, in bed, and you would push me aside because of this little scrap of cloth?"

He saw at last the black eyepatch in her hand. She flicked it in an arc, away from the bed.

She turned back to him. "Enough. Make love to me. I am your duchess and I insist."

He had run out of objections. He had to admit that he really was lucky.

She sat up and straddled him, her hands resting on his chest. She bent down and kissed him once, a long, slow kiss that warmed them both.

"Let me see you," he said, pushing her up again. He stared at her for a long moment, reaching up to twine his fingers in her hair.

"What do you want?" she asked, smiling.

It was suddenly difficult to speak. "You. On your back," he got out.

Violet obligingly lay down next to him, drawing him over her. She watched him with avid eyes.

Without speaking, he settled himself between her legs and just nudged her center, finding her shockingly ready for him.

"I need you, Alex," she said, her own voice a little raw. "I need you."

He entered her, and Violet sighed. Her eyes closed briefly, but then she opened them again, smiling at him.

Was this what being needed felt like? Alex loved it. Violet gasped when he thrust once within her. She instinctively began to rock her hips.

"Not yet, love," Alex warned, his hands restraining her. He continued to push slowly, achingly slowly, rocking her body with his hands, waiting until her breath came in ever faster moans, until she was begging him to release her. When he paused, she held still, waiting but never taking her eyes off his face. When he told her to rise, or shift, she did, accepting his words with a delighted eagerness.

At last she gasped out, "Alex, please, I can't stand it..."

He kissed her again, as he quickened his movements. His own breathing changed, became labored as he held her to him. Even as she let out a final cry, he felt his whole body stiffen, his seed surging into her. She sighed, her arms slipping loosely around him.

When he moved to lie next to her, his hands lingered on her belly for a moment, feeling a naked longing. He desperately wanted a child with her, though he'd never told her how much it had been on his mind. He didn't want to bring it up, not when everything between them still felt so new.

"Alex," she whispered as he cradled her on his chest. "I love you."

* * * *

He told her then, about what he'd done for years. The more active work, the risk, and the rewards. The only thing he kept back was the name of the Zodiac, and the precise details he couldn't ever reveal. But he told her enough so she understood.

"I suppose I started to get lazy," he said finally. "I wasn't alert when they cornered me in Paris."

"They? What exactly were you doing in Paris?"

"I was there to find a man who was a deserter from the British Army. He knew a number of valuable secrets, and he was making his way toward the French command, hoping to sell what he knew."

"You were after a traitor?"

"In short, yes."

"So what happened?"

"I have a number of contacts in France. I've been there many times," he added carefully.

"As a spy," Violet finished. "You can say the word out loud, you know. You are a spy."

"I was," he corrected. "I don't know what I am now."

"Go on."

"While I could never be sure, I think one of my contacts sold me out, either for money or a sense of loyalty to the nation. When I got some information about where this traitor was, I went there, but it was a trap."

A little frown crossed her face. "He wasn't there after all?"

"Oh, he was, in fact. But he wasn't alone. There were a half dozen men with him. They were probably with the French Army, or working for the Emperor in some capacity. They cornered me before I could get away."

"But you're here now," Violet said, putting a hand on his chest. "So you did get away."

"Eventually. I tend to get angry when I'm cornered," Alex explained delicately. "I didn't go quietly. I also was rather intent on not letting the traitor get away from me. I should have let him go," he said. "It would have been the prudent move."

"But not the right move. He had information that shouldn't be shared."

Alex gave a little shrug. "That was my reasoning. I went for him, which surprised the group. And him."

"He died," she guessed. "You don't have to go into details, if you don't want to."

"He died," Alex confirmed. "But I was unable to fend off the others. One of them—the man in charge, as it turned out—was quite upset. He wanted some revenge."

"He was responsible for your eye?"

"Yes. His plan was to take both eyes, then kill me and leave me to be found where Britain would get the message: no one could look too closely at France's intelligence and not pay the price."

"That's horrible."

"It's war," he said, "which is never as grand as the stories pretend."

"So what happened?"

"I was held down. It took five to do it. And he stabbed me in the eye."

Violet winced, even though Alex said it in a matter of fact way.

"Sorry," he said. "I can stop."

"No," she said. "I want to know."

"There's not much more to it. He wasn't prepared for my reaction. No one was. I wasn't. I don't even know what I did, exactly. But I do know that I got out, and there were five bodies behind me."

"So two got away."

"Evidently," he said, thinking back. "I stumbled off, and managed to find someone who helped me. I remember church bells. None of my memories are visual."

"I suppose they wouldn't be."

"There were other wounds besides the eye. I had to hole up in Paris for several days before I could get a ship to take me back to England. I didn't leave my room for about a month," he added.

"Well, I'm surprised you recovered that quickly!"

"It took much longer to recover," he said. "I had to

learn how to see again. It's different now. The light seems so strange. Everything is a little flatter. And every day, I had to face waking up again. Alone. Without a future in the one thing that I was good at. I couldn't be an agent any longer, not in a real sense. Though they did convince me I was still useful."

Violet tightened her arms around him. "They were right."

"I suppose. But it took a very long time before I felt anything like myself again. Till you, to be honest." He kissed her.

After a few moments, he felt her relax. Then she asked, "Am I mistress of this house? May I make a demand?"

"You're asking permission to make a demand?" he asked, amused. He was even happier that he could feel amusement so soon after telling that story. Maybe he was recovering after all.

But Violet wasn't smiling. "Please don't tease, Alex. This is difficult for me to ask."

"Go on. Demand."

"When we are in the same house, can we sleep together...until morning? Don't leave me in the middle of the night."

"I didn't want to bother you."

"No, I like it when you're near."

"Then that is a demand I'll happily obey." He tightened his arms around her. "I'm never going to let you go, Violet."

"I don't want to be let go," she breathed.

Chapter 25

♋

VIOLET WANDERED THROUGH STREETS IN a city she didn't know. The lanes split and twisted, but she followed the spots of blood on the stones. Alex was ahead of her, somewhere, and he needed her help before things got out of hand. Violet continued her walk, moving with the slowness of dreams, her steps taking very long despite the rapid beating of her heart. Where had Alex gone, and had he met her father yet?

She wasn't sure why the idea of Alex meeting her father made her worry. But she was quite certain that both she and Alex were heading to the same destination.

And there she was, finally, at the base of the folly, though as she tilted her head back, the tower soared upward until she could barely see it.

"I must fly," she deduced sadly, even as her feet left the ground. She rose up and up. Surely her father was at the top. She ought to say something about Alex before the men met. But what?

As she rose, she heard Judith giggling inside the tower, though there were no lights. Someone else spoke, too, the words lost as she passed by a window. As she continued to rise, she noticed signs of the zodiac marked in dark paint on the outside of the tower windows. At each point, a body slumped over the windowsill. Violet wasn't flying fast enough.

But at the top, Alex reached out and caught her by the hand. "I waited for you," he said.

Violet looked across the tower floor. Her father stood by a telescope, peering into the viewfinder.

"My child," he said excitedly. "Come here and see! I've found it, after all this time! Everything will be different now. Once the world knows, fear will shrivel away. All will be known and there will be no more darkness, only starlight…"

He gestured urgently for Violet to come. She let go of Alex's hand reluctantly, then gazed into his dark eyes. "I must listen to my father," she said. "He tried so hard to find the answers."

Alex turned away. His jacket was red with blood.

"Come, child," her father said again. "The stars are spinning! You must look now!"

Violet bent to the scope, hoping to see what her father wanted her to see.

But there were no stars. Only a circle of people, and a figure at the center. It was robed, holding a serpent in both hands. The figure raised its hooded head toward Violet, laughing. Then it flung the serpent directly toward her.

Gasping, Violet sat upright, flinging her arm up to ward off the thing attacking her. But she encountered nothing but empty air. She was in bed, Alex asleep beside her.

Her heart was beating wildly, her skin felt clammy,

and she thought she might be sick to her stomach. But she *remembered.*

She slid out of bed, trying not to disturb Alex. She walked to the desk in the corner of her room, though she kept an eye on the door to the conveniences. Yet as she began to write down everything she remembered, her nausea subsided, lost under the flood of emotions and ideas coming to the forefront of her mind. Some were long buried memories, others were connections just illuminated. But for once, she wasn't blank with fear. She was full of knowledge.

It was light enough from the moonlight in the room that she didn't need a candle. When she stopped, her hand was trembling, but she felt relief.

She turned back to the bed.

"Alex," she said urgently. "Alex, wake up."

He shifted, then woke. "What is it?"

"I remembered something," she said, holding the pages out to him. "I wrote it down as soon as I woke."

"Now? What time is it?" He sat up, more alert. "What did you remember?"

"One of my nightmares, the one I have over and over. Right before I wake, I see a man who is holding a serpent in both hands, just like Ophiuchus does in the constellation. These past few weeks have brought it all back. I first thought it was just my mind making the constellation real. But that's not it. I was a child, living in my father's home. I woke up very late one night, disturbed by some strange sound. I got out of bed and followed the noise outside. There were people standing in a circle, there on the lawn. Twelve people, and a thirteenth at the center, a hooded man holding a serpent. He was saying, 'The future belongs to those who grasp the serpent unflinching.'"

"I've heard that before."

"Judith says it quite often. Susanna Gilroy said it the night she died. It was one of the sayings of the society my father joined all those years ago. The one Aunt Judith encouraged him to join. It's been over a decade, but Hanchett has revived it. Not just the part about predicting the future in a more accurate way, but the *rituals* of it. All the nonsense about Ophiuchus. These murders are all linked to that idea."

She doubted she was making sense. But Alex slid out of the bed as well. "Let's see what you've written." He stooped to pick up the eye patch, fixing it where it usually was.

"Now?" Violet asked.

"We're both awake, are we not?" He reached for his robe. "No time like the present."

So they moved to Alex's small study. Alex started a fire and lit the lamps, making the space bright and cozy. They both set to reading through her hasty notes.

He looked at the pages carefully, reading each line and tracing each little drawing with a finger. "I've seen this before," he said, pointing to one sketch of a robed man, "in a box of your old papers."

"Yes, it wasn't from my imagination. It was this memory that frightened me so badly."

"This figure…" Alex said slowly, "is a real person?"

"Yes." Violet took a deep breath. "I think I know what this is all about."

"Go on."

"Do you know what precession is?" she asked.

"No," Alex said. "Should I?"

"Not unless you're an astronomer. Or possibly a navigator." She walked to the side of the room to pick up a decorative quartz sphere resting on a stand.

"Imagine this is the earth. It rotates on its axis once per day." She spun the ball around once. "But the axis isn't real. It's a mathematical construct. The universe isn't perfect as the ancients thought. The moon isn't perfect, because it has craters. The stars aren't perfectly fixed, because new ones are born and stars must die like any other thing outside of heaven."

She spun the ball again, shifting her hand as she did so. "The earth doesn't rotate perfectly either. There is a very slight wobble. If it were perfect, the ends of the axis would drill a single point into whatever is beyond. But instead, the ends of the axis trace a little circle in each polar sky—both north and south. And that means that the stars along the zodiac are sometimes in a slightly different place than they ought to be, according to Ptolemy's equations. They might rise a little later or a little earlier."

"Does that make such a difference?" Alex asked, watching the sphere tilt in her hand.

Violet said, "In practice, the wobble is so slight it doesn't to most. But precession matters to two types of people—astronomers hoping to identify and record exact details of a celestial object's location and trajectory, and astrologers drawing up star charts to predict the future. If precession means a star chart can be wrong, then if you correct for it, you should be able to predict a better, more accurate future than anyone else."

"Is that what your father believed?"

"It is, among other things. He lost his mind trying to prove that the zodiac needed to be updated via the arrival of a new star, which ultimately led to his death. What if someone is now hurting others for a similar reason?"

Alex frowned. "Someone is killing people just because a star chart is off by a bit?"

"Yes." Violet shook her head. "I can't believe I didn't remember this until now. When I was at that gathering, Mr Frobisher even got me talking about Ophiuchus!"

"What's that?"

"Ophiuchus is a constellation that lies along the zodiac, between Scorpio and Sagittarius. The constellation is also called the Serpent Bearer, because it's of a man holding a gigantic snake. Some people think that, due to precession, Ophiuchus should be considered the thirteenth sign of the zodiac—and that a truly accurate, scientific star chart will incorporate Ophiuchus into the calculations."

"A more scientific astrology," Alex said.

"Exactly," Violet said. "What's more appealing than magic wrapped in the trappings of logic? People who think themselves very modern suddenly have permission to believe in ancient myths because it seems to be mathematically sound to do so."

"You don't agree, I gather."

Violet shook her head. "The zodiac is established, and has been since before the Greeks even glanced skyward. Just because a set of stars lies along the elliptic doesn't mean the whole system should be changed. Twelve divides perfectly into 360. There is no reason to complicate the mathematics on account of one arbitrary constellation. And in any case, Ophiuchus is not the only constellation to cross the zodiac without being a part of it. It's just one that catches people's fancy, reviving this old debate." Then she gasped. "Oh, no."

"What?"

She waved an impatient hand. "Wait."

She hurried to the desk. Dipping pen into ink, she

hastily drew a rough figure on the paper, then dotted several points across its surface. "This is what the killer is making! See, here's the first four points. There are about ten stars in the constellation officially, but it varies. The killer will have no trouble adding a few. It's the thirteenth sign. That's why the points marking the location didn't fit any of the real signs of the zodiac. He's making a new one."

"It's all connected," Alex said, nodding slowly. "Hanchett's the one the moon doctor told me about. The one who persuaded Susanna Gilroy that she wouldn't die. But she did die, immediately after she left Hanchett behind."

"But what possible reason could he have to harm her? She was a patron!"

"Perhaps she stopped believing what Hanchett sold. Or she learned something dangerous."

Violet put her hand up. "The only way to discover that is to talk to him. I can do it. I was at the last gathering. They want me to return for the next."

"Absolutely not." Alex stood up. "That is the last place in the world you should be. Are you forgetting that someone sent you a venomous snake? And the only people who know about your phobia just happen to be in a cult that's known for colorful phrases such as *The future belongs to those who grasp the serpent unflinching*?"

"Aunt Judith would never have sent that!"

"But she might have mentioned your fear to Hanchett. It sounds like there's very little she'd keep from him. How else did he know of your insomnia?"

Violet bit her lip. "But if I don't go to the next meeting, how will we find out what he's up to?"

"I'll go talk to him, as soon as possible."

310 ❧ *Elizabeth Cole*

"You?"

"Of course. Your skepticism he'll start to suspect, but they know nothing about me...other than the rumors of my curse."

"Would he believe that the curse troubles you?"

"Why not?" Alex said. "Everyone else does."

Chapter 26

♋

SEVERAL DAYS LATER, VIOLET WOKE up to sunlight. Though the day was beautiful, especially now that spring was in full bloom, Violet was restless. She wanted Alex back at home, though she understood his commitment to solving the case as quickly as possible. He was pursuing more information about Hanchett, so that he could be as prepared as possible when he actually met the man. That meant he was out nearly every day and sometimes into the night.

Over the past week or so, she'd felt unbalanced, nervous. Whenever she had too long a moment alone, she thought of the danger Alex was putting himself into, making her stomach grow queasy and her heart race.

When the door opened, she was grateful for the distraction.

"Good morning, my lady," Dalby chimed. "Your coffee. And some ham, with a croissant and fig preserves!"

Violet smelled the breakfast tray Dalby brought in, but her stomach suddenly turned. "Oh. Thank you, but no. Not today."

"Are you not feeling well?" Dalby asked.

"I'm not sick. Just not hungry. Perhaps toast. Plain,

dry toast."

The maid's eyes widened. "You didn't finish your breakfast yesterday, either."

"No. But I ate a lot at supper," Violet said. "I don't feel ill."

"Ma'am," Dalby said hesitantly, daring to sit at the very edge of the bed. "If I may ask, when do you expect your courses next? Or are you late?"

Violet understood immediately. "Oh. Oh, Dalby."

"Are you late?"

"I'm...not sure." Violet told Dalby to fetch a little notebook on her desk. She had neglected it, to be honest. The last few weeks were so out of the usual that she quite forgot about it. She flipped through the pages, noting the dates she wrote down. Violet had tracked her courses over the past three years. At first it was simply out of curiosity. Did the cycle really match the moon's, or was it a convention? She'd found that she bled regularly, but that her cycle was consistently 32 days, and thus varied considerably from the moon's cycle.

She was horribly flustered, trying to decide if she was really weeks late, or if she'd simply forgotten to record the last time she bled. But no, she was long overdue. "Oh, my God."

A smile pulled at one corner of Dalby's mouth. "So you are."

"Oh, my God." Violet put her hands to her face. Could it be possible? Then again, why shouldn't it be possible, considering just how...*attentive* Alex was. "I think you might be right."

"Oh! This is so exciting!"

Violet reached forward to seize Dalby's hand. "You must not breathe a word. Not till I can be sure one way or the other. I must find a doctor, who can be completely discreet. I could not stand it if he heard good news, only to…" She stopped short. It would be cruel. She must not even hint at the possibility until it could be confirmed.

Dalby nodded, her eyes wide. "I won't say a thing, ma'am. But tell me if you need anything. Anything at all. I'll get you some toast right now."

"There's no rush. I'm not truly hungry." That was true. How could she think about food when she had *this* to consider?

* * * *

Later that day, Alex was at his club, waiting for Ashley Allander to arrive. Bruce's younger brother apparently had done some sleuthing after all. He saw the man come in. Even across the room, it was obvious what gifts Ash had for putting people at ease. He wasn't a member of the club, and his reputation was such that most gentlemen wouldn't want to be in the same room as him. But there he was, turning the majordomo into an ally and being treated like an old friend.

Eventually, Ash made his way to Alex, who'd deliberately chosen an out of the way corner.

"Evening, your grace." Ash dropped casually into the chair opposite.

Alex instinctively compared Ash's build and movements to Bruce's.

"Measuring me up for something?" Ash asked, noticing the perusal.

"Without seeing you both together, it's impossible to believe you and your brother are related."

"Only by blood," Ash responded. "Bruce doesn't have

a lot of use for me...until he does." He gave a slightly bitter laugh.

"Well, this time he was only doing a favor for me," Alex said. "You found something?"

"Yes, I've had some luck." Ash lost his jovial air. "The man running the wager is a bookmaker named Farley. He operates out of a gaming hell near St James."

"How did you find him?"

"Oh, I have some familiarity with the sort of gambler who'd be excited by that wager. I once bet on which of the Kalman twins would fall from grace first. All bettors were barred from...ah, influencing the outcome, of course."

"Did you win the bet?"

Ash smiled. "As it happened, no one won. Don't you remember that scandal? The twins ran off to Italy with some marchese. The bet was off, for lack of conclusive information."

"Shame," Alex said sarcastically.

"It was years ago. But I'm still considered that sort of gambler. I asked around and learned the name. I told Farley I was interested in placing a bet, so he led me to his office. I asked about the odds, and the payment, and then insisted on seeing who else had wagered before I would place my own bet."

"He let you see the list?" Alex asked. He was incredulous. Bookies usually guarded that with their lives, for any number of reasons.

"I can be very persuasive when I choose to be." Ash pulled out a sheet of paper, handing it to Alex. "I memorized the names—I do have a few talents. Accept, with my compliments, a complete list of those men willing to gamble on your wife's longevity."

Alex read the list over slowly, taking in the names on it. "Half these men are gentry," he said in disgust.

"Oh, a few are higher born than that. A couple illustrious names there. If I were inclined toward blackmail, that would be a most lucrative place to start." Ash shrugged. "Blackmail seems like such a lot of effort, though. But even if you acted from the most noble intentions, you'd have the means to destroy those bettors. Simply tell their fathers what they've done."

"Tempting," said Alex. "But first I need to find out who on this list might be tilting the odds in his favor." He looked up. "I'm in your debt."

"Consider it an apology," Ash said, waving it away. "After all, I did have to place a bet, as well, to keep the charade going."

"What was your wager?" Alex asked curiously.

"Fifty years." Ash rose, preparing to leave. "I'm not a complete monster, after all. Congratulations on your marriage. And may each year be better than the last."

"Thank you." Alex waited until Ash had left to examine the list in more detail. All the names on it were offensive to him, but only one truly mattered. If one of these men tried to have Violet killed, he just had to find out who it was.

Chapter 27

♋

THE DATE OF THE NEXT expected death neared. Violet could tell how it weighed on Alex, even though he now had a good idea of some of the players involved. Alex shared much of what he learned about Hanchett over the past several days. He said the man deserved to be imprisoned even if he hadn't murdered anyone.

"I can trace his name to any number of shady deals… I just have to find out where to start."

Alex also said that he had to attend the next meeting of the Society. He absolutely refused to let Violet go.

"It's too dangerous, love. You are brilliant and clever, and I'm grateful for everything you've done. But if you think I'll let you take one step further toward a killer without any protection, you don't know me."

Violet shook her head. "You're just saying that because you're a trained spy with a decade of experience and skills I can't hope to match."

"Well, yes, that's all true. But I'm mostly saying it because I love you and I can't stand to lose you."

"Oh, that was clever. Now I can't argue against you at all."

"Good." Alex smiled.

"To be honest," she said then, "Mr Hanchett doesn't *seem* much like a killer. Then again, I suppose I have no basis to judge."

"I do," said Alex. "That's why I need to be invited to the next meeting. Getting your Aunt Judith to tell Hanchett I'm harmless is the best way to do that. You're not going alone."

The worst part of the plan was that Violet had to pretend that she wanted to see her aunt again. But Alex insisted it would seem more natural if they were both there.

"If I just showed up on her doorstep, asking about Ophiuchus, she'll suspect a trick. But you're going to steer the conversation toward it. Let *her* bring it up. She won't suspect a thing if she thinks inviting me is her own idea."

"All right."

He leaned over to give her a kiss. "Don't mention anything about the murders."

"I wouldn't dream of it."

"And be prepared," he added in warning. "I'm going to say several things you won't like. I'll seem like I'm not myself, perhaps. But just let me do that. You don't have to look pleased—if fact, it would be a bit suspicious if you were."

"You're going to let her think she's convincing you?"

"Yes. Just enough to get to the next step." He kissed her again. "You have to trust me."

"Of course I do."

"Good. Then let's go pay a social call."

They went to the rooms Judith and Roger rented in town—though Roger was out somewhere, and thus only Judith was waiting for them. The call was initially less awkward than Violet feared. The ostensible reason was for Violet to check in on her aunt, to see how she was doing in the wake of her friend's death.

Judith was on her best behavior, which helped. In fact, she was obviously trying to be as charming as possible to Alex. Worse, it seemed to be working. Alex was rather aloof at first, but by the second course, he'd thawed considerably.

"Violet told me a bit about her evening with your group, but she then had to go run off to look at a meteor or something."

"Oh, is she still stargazing?" Judith asked.

Alex nodded indulgently. "Every night she gets the chance. I see no harm in it—one silly hobby is just like another. Don't know what she thinks she's looking for, but as long as it provides diversion..." He shrugged.

Violet felt stung. Yes, Alex warned her that he'd say things she wouldn't like, but he sounded so convincing. "There's great merit in what I do," she said, unable to keep silent.

"Oh, indeed?" Judith spoke. "And what great insight have you gained, Violet? What mysteries have revealed themselves to you? It's just like I've always said. You look, but you don't *see*."

A slight pressure on her foot kept Violet from snapping back. Alex was warning her as subtly as he could. But she was not prepared for this after all.

"I saw a comet," she said. "I tracked it. I charted its path through the sky. That's something, Aunt Judith." Tears pricked at her eyes.

"It's nothing," her aunt said, her voice oddly gentle in its condescension. "Not compared to seeing the future."

That was more than Violet could tolerate. She stood

abruptly. "Please excuse me. I need some fresh air."

* * * *

Alex watched Violet turn and walk away. He ached to follow her, yet he couldn't, not without destroying the opportunity he spent the whole time crafting. He had Judith on her own now.

"What do you mean about seeing the future?" he asked. He strove to balance the casualness of his question with a bit of curiosity.

Judith turned to him, already eager to share. "She hasn't told you, has she?"

"Told me what?"

"I saw her marriage to you, your grace. In the stars—it's all there, for those who know how to look. Why do you think I was so bold in negotiating the matter? I knew she was destined to be the next Duchess of Dunmere."

"She is an excellent duchess," Alex allowed. "Though I admit I would never have guessed that on the day of the wedding."

Judith was smug. "The stars have a plan that is not readily apparent to mortals. One must study them with great dedication."

"Isn't that what she does?" Alex asked, gesturing to where Violet had gone off.

"She only gazes at the surface! The music of the celestial spheres is deeper than that, more mysterious."

"Even to see the future?" Alex asked, putting more urgency into his tone.

"Yes. Do you want to know what yours holds?"

"Doesn't everyone?" Alex pulled back, regaining a bit of his original demeanor. He didn't want it to be too easy for Judith.

"Ah, but you have more reason to question than most, your grace. Fate seems to have taken an interest in you."

"Perhaps." Alex suddenly wanted to walk away. Judith's needling disgusted him. But instead, he leaned forward. "I need to know…"

"Yes?"

"Violet," he said. "I need to know her future."

Judith smiled slowly. "I have a way to help you with that, your grace. I will tell Mr Hanchett that you are interested in joining our little society." The briefest frown crossed her face. "After all, we do have a recent opening."

Alex left Judith as soon as he could. He walked outside to where Violet was waiting. She stood in a small garden between the house and the street.

"Are you all right?" he asked.

Violet ignored the question. "What did she say?"

"I'm going to meet this Mr Hanchett. If I pass muster, presumably I'll get to attend the next meeting, whenever it is."

"It will be at midnight, the fifteenth of May," Violet said. "Exactly as the sky demands."

Alex reached out to take her arm. "I told you that I'd say some things you wouldn't like to hear."

She nodded once. "You did. If I didn't know you better, I would have believed them."

"You looked very offended."

She gave him a tiny smile. "It convinced Judith, did it not?"

"It worried me, as well," Alex confessed. "All right, let's move on before anyone can see our touching reconciliation."

"As my husband commands," Violet said. Her voice

was as demure as it had been the day he first met her. But Alex heard all the nuances in it now, and marveled how he ever could have missed them.

He saw her home and then left again. He only had a few days before he would confront Hanchett, so time was precious. He consulted with the Disreputables and arranged to use them again on the night of the fifteenth. Then he met a few more people, settling a few last details of Hanchett's past—including the fact that he'd been born Daniel Galbraith.

Alex was eager to get back to the townhouse that night. He couldn't fathom one more hour without Violet. He didn't want to disturb the household as they completed their usual tasks before turning in. He used his own key to come in the side door. He shrugged out of his greatcoat while listening to the servants' idle chatter in the room beyond. Most were the typical end of day exchanges, but he picked up on a word, and then a phrase, that seemed out of place and was quickly hushed.

Doctor. Her grace. Ill.

Alex went cold. Had something happened to Violet, despite all the steps they taken to keep her safe?

One of the footmen happened to step out into the hall at that moment. He saw Alex and jumped in surprise.

"Dear Lord, your grace! Thought you were a ghost." He recovered quickly. "Take your things, sir?" He reached for the coat and hat.

Alex judged his expression and saw no fear in it. "Where's my wife?" he asked in a low voice.

"She retired over an hour ago," the footman said. "Dalby is still awake, should you have a question for her."

"Was she the one who called for the doctor to see her grace?"

"Oh, yes, sir," the footman said. Then he drew up as he remembered there was no way for Alex to know that. "How did…"

"Never mind. I'm going up."

Alex left the hall, taking the stairs two at a time. A doctor had come for Violet. The only thing he could think was that someone made the curse real after all.

His rational side intervened before he slammed open the door to Violet's room. If she was in danger, the household would never be so calm, and he would certainly be told. And yet…

Slipping in through the narrowest crack of the door he could make, he tiptoed to her bedside. Violet was asleep, her breathing light and even.

The room was illuminated only by the remains of the fire. He wondered if he dared wake her. But he couldn't stand not knowing. He reached down to touch her shoulder. "Violet?"

She stirred immediately, and gave him a sleepy smile. "You're back," she said. "What time is it?"

"Just after midnight." He sat on the bed. "I heard a doctor was called."

She frowned. "I told Dalby to stay quiet about that."

"Stay quiet?" He leaned forward. "This is important, Violet! If someone tried to hurt you again—"

"Alex! That's not what happened!" She sat up in bed, her eyes now wide.

"Then what? Are you ill?"

She shook her head slowly.

"Then what?"

"I have something to tell you, Alex, but I needed to find a way to say it so you wouldn't be concerned or upset."

"What is it?" he insisted. "Christ, if you're sick…"

"No, Alex." She put her hand on his arm. "I just don't want you to be upset if it's a girl."

It took a moment for her words to sink in. "A girl?"

"Because we can try again, of course." She smiled now, unable to hide it.

Alex reached out, putting his hands on her waist and drawing her closer. "You're with child?" His heartbeat suddenly went erratic.

She nodded happily. "It's very early, but the doctor says it's as certain as can be. I was going to wait a week or so, to spare you if I was wrong. But I know something's changed." She leaned in closer and whispered, "Are you pleased?"

Alex could barely breathe. "Violet," he said, wrapping his arms around her.

She kissed him sweetly, then said, "Because *I'm* pleased."

"I love you," he said, not at all sure what else he could say. "You must be careful. Your health, I mean. No more riding. And you need to sleep regularly…"

"Oh, Alex," she said, laughing gently. "We'll get the doctor to tell me all that. I just need to know you're happy about it."

"Of course I am." He kissed her again.

Her arms twined around him eagerly. "I missed you," she said.

He missed her. He wanted her. But her news made him uncertain. "I can't risk hurting you, love."

"Silly," she said. "You wouldn't even know if I hadn't told you. Just be gentle."

He was. He very gently laid her down and kissed her and put his hands on her body. Now that he knew, he was sure she had already started to change, very subtly. Her breasts were a little fuller, her skin pinker.

"You're beautiful," he said, in awe. "You're everything I ever wanted."

She said, "I've been waiting for you to come home. Not just to tell you, but for you."

He found that she had been waiting for him, and he slid into her body as she sighed contentedly.

He went slowly, enjoying her warmth and her breathing and her delight more than ever. She ran her hands all over him, as if reassuring herself he was there. He came swiftly, but without any urgency. Violet smiled at him, wrapping her arms around his shoulders. "That's enough," she said. "That's all I want. But you must stay with me tonight. I missed you so much."

As if he'd leave. He lay next to her, his hand on her belly. He could stay like that for hours.

"I'm turning lazy," he said out loud. "All I want to do is be in bed with you."

"Hardly lazy," Violet returned. "Isn't this why you married me? To secure an heir? You're doing exactly what you're supposed to do. And being quite productive at it." She laughed a little.

He nodded, but then said, "That's why I married you, but it's not why I love you. If we never have children, I'm lucky to have you."

"Alex," she said, putting a hand on his face. "There's no need to say it. And we *will* have children. You aren't compromising."

"No, I'm not." He put his head down, wanting to sleep. Then he remembered the list Ash gave him, and got angry all over again.

Violet caught Alex's expression. "What is it?" she

asked, suddenly aware that something was amiss.

"I don't want to worry you," he said.

"Well, now you must tell me."

"I know," he said. "I've been debating. Keeping you unaware in the hope that you'd be happier…"

"I'd rather know," she said. "No matter what it is."

He nodded. "All right. When someone sent that snake to the house…"

"You're not bringing up the curse again."

"No. Nothing mystical caused that." He explained the pool and the bets, and the amount it had grown to.

Violet looked appalled. "Someone tried to kill me so as not to lose a *wager*?"

"That's my fear. Which is only slightly less horrifying than my original theory, which was that the killer was aware of my investigation and tried to kill you in revenge. The timing didn't match up for that, thank God. But it matches all too well for this pool."

"Don't kill anyone," she warned.

"No promises," he said. Then he abruptly pulled her into his arms. "Everything in the world seems aligned against us."

"You're forgetting our child."

"Certainly not," he said, with a sigh. "Promise me to be careful, and keep someone near you at all times when you're outside the house itself. No more stargazing, Violet. Not till this is done."

"I'll promise that if you promise not to kill anyone in connection to this wager."

He sighed. "You have my word."

Chapter 28

♋

THE NIGHT OF THE NEXT meeting arrived. Violet dressed for the evening's excursion in a dark blue gown, and then went down to join Alex, who had indeed relented in his opposition of her attending. She had campaigned persistently—though gently—to go, telling him that if there were the slightest chance her knowledge of the stars could help him capture a killer, the risk was worth it. He capitulated.

Alex looked so handsome. So aristocratic. She had to remind herself that she was actually married to him, and everything they were doing tonight was an elaborate charade to draw out a murderer.

"Ready?" he asked her.

"Not as such," she replied. "I can't help thinking this is all a bad dream. I've certainly had enough of them to know the feeling."

"It will end tonight," he promised.

They arrived at the meeting. Alex was greeted with

enthusiasm by all. Hanchett himself looked smug, as far as Violet could tell.

"I'm so happy you joined us, your grace," he said to Alex. Hanchett gave a little bow that might have been mocking.

The evening proceeded normally enough. Violet saw no difference in how people spoke or acted. Mr Frobisher, who was wearing black, seemed much more somber than the others, which she understood. But the meeting was otherwise unremarkable.

Violet did her best to behave as if she believed everything Hanchett and the others said. She didn't even smirk during the exceedingly silly ceremony at midnight—which involved candles and a lot of chanting. She was careful not to look at Alex, lest she burst into laughter. Even the knowledge that someone here was a killer didn't lessen her disdain for the false ritual.

At the close of the evening, Alex told her that she was going home.

"You're not?" she asked in a low voice.

"I'm going wherever Hanchett is going," Alex explained. "But you are to go directly home. The people driving you are extremely trustworthy. They'll keep you safe along the way."

Violet studied Alex's expression. "You think I'm Hanchett's next target," she guessed.

The way he reacted told her she was right. "Let's just say that I want you as far from Hanchett as possible."

"While you get as close as possible. Be careful," she said.

"I will."

Mr Frobisher came up to them both. "Excuse me, your graces. Your carriage is at the front."

"Good," said Alex. "Please walk her grace to it. I must have a word with Mr Hanchett."

Frobisher bowed. "Certainly." He offered an arm to Violet, who took it.

She glanced back at Alex, wishing she could say a more private goodbye.

At the carriage, the driver said, "Home, ma'am?"

"Yes, Jem. Directly."

Frobisher saw her into the carriage, and then, unexpectedly climbed in after her.

"I thought I might as well see you all the way home," he said. "His grace seemed concerned about you. And I know all too well how it feels to regret."

The carriage was already in motion, so Violet saw little point in objecting.

Frobisher looked down at his hands, folded on his lap. "I wanted to thank you," he said. "You were very kind to call on me, after Susanna…" He took a deep breath. "We weren't betrothed, and not many people knew what she meant to me. If I'd been stronger, I'd have asked her to marry me when I met her. Things would have been different."

"You can't blame yourself."

"I can and do," he said. "I'll never go a day without thinking of her."

Frobisher pulled a piece of cloth from his pocket. Violet blinked, trying to clear her head, which suddenly felt a bit strange.

"What is that—" She got no further before Frobisher leaned forward and caught her as her vision swam.

"I'm sorry, your grace," he said, his voice lower than usual. "But I've been ordered by the Serpent Handler to act on his behalf."

"Don't—" Violet sagged back onto the seat as she inhaled whatever the cloth was soaked in. She felt weightless.

Frobisher said something else, but his voice came out impossibly slurred and slow.

"Your grace!" someone shouted then. "Your grace! Wake up!"

Violet stirred. As she opened her eyes, the face of the driver hovered over her.

"You fell asleep, your grace," he said. A younger boy, the footman, peered in worriedly.

"Where's Mr Frobisher?" she asked.

"Who?" Jem said.

"The gentleman who got in the carriage with me! To see me home."

"No one else is in here, your grace. Do you mean that man got in the carriage? He looked as if he was only helping you in."

"It was unexpected…" she began. As she remembered the last thing Frobisher said, the truth dawned on Violet with a speed that left her breathless. "Oh, my God," she said. "We must turn around! Take me back to the house we left."

"But you're home now! And his grace was quite adamant that home was the only place you are to be."

"He needs to be warned," she said. "And I need to see him. Don't argue with me. Just go!"

Jem nodded, though unhappily. "Very well."

The carriage wheeled about and headed back, where Alex waited in vain for the wrong person.

Violet knew the truth now. John Frobisher was the killer. And he was closer to reaching Alex than Violet was.

330 ❦ *Elizabeth Cole*

Jem drove dangerously fast, but Violet only wished for more speed. At their destination, she didn't even wait for the door to be opened. She dashed out of the carriage into the house with Jem on her heels.

She heard a commotion in the hall before she reached the large room where the ceremony had been. She kept to the side of the hall, pulling Jem with her.

"Ma'am," hissed Jem, "what do you think you're *doing*?"

"I need to find something in the next room," she said, anxiously. "Do you hear that?"

"Sounds like a battle over there. How could I miss it?"

"Go do what you can to help."

The young man nodded, looking completely unfazed by the idea of jumping into a fight. "And you?"

"I'll think of something."

"Think of it far away from any actual danger, ma'am," Jem warned. Then he dashed off.

Violet took that moment to slip into the room where the ceremony had been held. It was quieter here, since the tussle was in the hallway around the corner. There must be something there that she could use to help Alex.

She turned around, not seeing anything useful, until she noticed a small door at the end, half-hidden by a curtain. She hurried to it, exposing a small room full of odds and ends.

Inside, she stifled a shriek. There were snakes inside, each one in a little bamboo cage. She stumbled, accidentally grabbing and pulling a pile of fabric down to the floor with her. She found herself half buried in soft grey velvet, the hissing of snakes in her ears.

Then she understood what to do.

* * * *

Alex spent several minutes trailing Hanchett around the house, who seemed unaware that Alex remained. Judith was with Hanchett, and the couple was definitely up to something, to judge by how they both scurried around and kept exchanging quick words. Eventually, both of them went into a room next to where that silly ceremony had taken place.

Alex remained where he was. He knew the door Hanchett and Judith had gone through. Hanchett would have to come out eventually.

But minutes went by, and there was nothing. Just as Alex got up to try the door, he felt something in the air change.

A second later, a huge weight seemed to drop on him. Someone was attacking. Had Hanchett slipped around behind him?

Alex twisted out of the grasp of whoever it was. The edge of a knife flashed past his face.

"Damn it!" The voice didn't belong to Hanchett. It was Frobisher.

Since Alex didn't have the luxury of surprise, he ignored the revelation and focused on not getting killed.

"You planning on scrawling Taurus next to my head?" he said, hoping to throw Frobisher off balance.

"You know about the others?" the man asked, his breath fast.

Alex didn't answer, other than to seize Frobisher's arm and twist, hard.

The other man didn't shout out, or even seem particularly fazed. He was a big man, after all. *Fits the description perfectly*, Alex thought. And by coincidence, he looked rather like Hanchett from a distance.

The fight wasn't easy. Frobisher was a worthy opponent. His military background must have included actual fighting, because he moved like a cat.

Alex used every trick he knew to wear Frobisher down. At last, he got in a hit that caught Frobisher on the chin. He staggered, off balance just long enough for Alex to swing again and knock him out briefly.

He used those precious seconds to disarm Frobisher, who found himself unable to fight back when he came to a moment later.

"You should tell me why you tried to kill me," Alex said. "Personal?"

"I'm following the instructions of the serpent handler."

"Who?" Alex asked.

"The avatar of the sacred sign! The hidden one. Ophiuchus!"

"Oh, Mr Hanchett, you mean? He told you directly to kill me?"

Frobisher's eyes were bright with anger, and possibly some drug as well. "I've heard his voice, you know. The voice of the serpent handler. When his sign rises next in the heavens, he'll take his rightful place among the sacred. All will be accounted for. The darkness will fall away and we'll see the pattern and the path laid out before our feet!"

"The path seems a bit bloody," Alex said.

The other man's face went cold. "You wouldn't understand the sacrifice required. All must happen in time to the music of the spheres. I was willing to do that terrible work. I didn't like it—not one bit." He shuddered, looking down. "Especially not Susanna. But their names were chosen. Their fate was sealed."

"*Who* told you their names? Be honest."

"Ophiuchus himself. Robed and hooded, bearing the red serpent in his hands. Every month, he spoke to me in the shadows, told me my task. I could not disobey."

"Drugged," Alex muttered to himself. "Your mind made suggestible. I've seen it before."

But the other man wasn't listening. "I must carry out his orders. If the next sacrifice is not made by dawn, the celestial clock will be wrong. The serpent handler will be angry."

"The serpent handler was a trick," Alex said flatly. "The so-called sacrifices were all people chosen by Hanchett himself. And his reasons were anything but heavenly."

"He said there would be liars coming." Frobisher spat on the floor. "You are one of those. That's what he told me tonight. Kill Dunmere—he'll speak out against me."

Alex had no idea how to convince the man. He was so deep in the spiral of lies that he wouldn't believe anything. Hanchett anticipated a confrontation, and told his lackey just the right things to keep him obsessed.

"I only want to prevent another death." Alex tried to keep his voice calm.

"Death is inevitable," Frobisher said. "Trying to prevent it is like trying to stop the sun."

"It might be inevitable, but you don't have the right to hasten it!" Alex said, his frustration rising. "Why listen to anyone who tells you to kill?"

"He said only I was strong enough." Frobisher's voice was quiet. "He said he didn't trust the others. They were weak…"

"Hanchett used you."

"It wasn't Hanchett!" Frobisher suddenly stood, enraged. "It was—"

"—Ophiuchus." The new voice chimed out from the darkness at the end of the hall. Both men looked over. Alex strained to see who was there, but Frobisher had no doubts.

The other man dropped to his knees, his head bowed. "I never doubted you!" he cried. "No matter what this man said, I believed you!"

A figure emerged from the darkness. It was robed in dark grey, a solid shadow in the deeper shadows. No hint of a face could be seen below the hood.

"Why did you believe?" the figure asked, in a thin, ghostly voice. "What did I promise?"

Frobisher began to respond, but faltered when the figure held out one arm. From its hand dangled a small but ornate cage on a chain. And in the cage was a bright red snake, coiled on itself.

"Don't hurt me," Frobisher begged. "I swear I obeyed your every word!"

The figure approached a few more steps, and held of the cage closer to Frobisher. "The future belongs to those who grasp the serpent unflinching."

The invitation was clear. Frobisher reached forward to open the cage door. But he faltered, flinching back at the last second. "It will bite me. I'll die."

"No, you won't," said the figure.

But Frobisher huddled now, undone. "I failed you."

The figure placed the cage gently on the floor, than dropped the chain with a soft metallic hiss. It then leaned over Frobisher and pushed its hood back with one hand.

Violet's soft brown curls tumbled over the collar of the robe. Her gaze flickered over Alex. But she touched

Frobisher's shoulder with one hand.

"You didn't fail," she explained. "You were used by someone not worthy of your trust."

Alex was ready to move, his muscles aching with the effort to stay still. His wife was facing a murderer four times over.

But Frobisher only stared at her in amazement. "I left you in the carriage. But you're here! Who are you?"

Incredibly, she smiled at him. "I'm just the one who found this robe and that snake among Hanchett's things, in that little room off to the side of the main room you held the ceremony in. The same place where he told you to go alone to hear from Ophiuchus."

"How do you know about that?"

"I only guessed, from what I saw in the antechamber. Hanchett had everything set up—the lighting, the timing, even the rope to pull at the window when he wanted the candles to gutter out. He staged it all, and you were his audience. Just you. He said that Ophiuchus might reveal himself to the faithful."

Frobisher nodded dumbly.

"But it was Hanchett himself who ordered you to hurt those people, and his reasons were entirely selfish."

At her words, Frobisher sank to the floor.

Alex moved near Violet, not willing to trust Frobisher so close to her any longer. "You held that snake," he said, astonished.

"It was in the cage. That helped a bit." Violet looked back at the cage, and shuddered. "I tried not to think about it."

"That was brave of you," he said in a low tone, "and it was the only thing that snapped him out of his delusion."

"I didn't want you to kill him," she responded.

336 ◆ *Elizabeth Cole*

"He is a killer."

"He was the weapon. Hanchett's the killer. He must have realized you were onto him and decided you were the next to go," said Violet. "You have to find him."

Alex looked at Frobisher. "Maybe he can help after all."

They approached the huddled man again.

"Mr Frobisher," Violet said. "We need to speak to you. It's important."

"Leave me be. He tricked me."

"Susanna would not like to see you as you appear right now. She didn't give up when she knew she was ill. Neither should you."

"He made me kill her. To prove my loyalty."

"Then prove your *real* loyalty," Violet said. "Avenge Susanna by telling us where Hanchett is."

"He tricked me," Frobisher said again, getting used to the idea. Each time, he sounded both sadder and stronger.

"Do you know where he might be now?" Violet asked.

After a moment, Frobisher nodded. "I think so." He pointed. "There's an exit through that room. The door is hidden behind a curtain, but it leads outside."

"Tell me," said Alex. "So I can stop him."

Frobisher told what he knew, his voice broken. At the end, Frobisher said, "I'll come with you. Let me help. Hanchett is expecting me anyway. Now I know why he always found a reason to meet with me after I…" Frobisher broke down again.

"No," said Alex. "You're in no condition to be out."

Alex turned to the Disreputable who'd driven Violet back. "Jem, he should be watched. Take him somewhere safe."

Jem nodded. "Done."

"Wait," Alex said. "Frobisher, give me your coat and hat."

"Sir?"

"No questions. Just do it."

The authoritative tone worked, and Frobisher shrugged out of his coat. Handing it over to Alex he said, "Be careful."

Then he was led away, unprotesting.

Alex watched them go, then took Violet aside. "I'm going to follow his directions. It's the best chance to catch Hanchett. We don't have much time. But you need to go home."

"You expect me to simply wait at home? Not doing anything?"

"You've done so much already. You got us here. You knocked some sense into Frobisher when I couldn't. But you are done for the evening, love." His voice dropped to a whisper. "If you want to help me, go home and take care of our child. I need to know you're both safe."

She smiled, despite everything that had happened. "All right. But you must come home to me."

"Always."

Chapter 29

Alex rushed to the place Frobisher told him about, trusting the other man was telling the truth, either out of remorse or a sense of duty.

He stood in front of a church still under construction, the very same church where the murder of Randolphus Lyle occurred. It now seemed as if that first killing was only for practice, and where else but a building Hanchett knew well?

The nave was mostly done, and the tall tower that was likely the belfry loomed over the property. Hanchett financed some of the building, Frobisher had told them. The broken man confessed he thought it was a sincere desire to invest in the church. But Hanchett likely had another reason.

"He never used a bank, he didn't trust anyone with money, not a coin," Frobisher had said.

So Hanchett probably kept all his money in a hidden spot in the building. It was a clever choice. No one looked for treasure in a church, and no one would expect to find anything in a building still being built.

Alex saw just a flash of movement, but that was enough. Hanchett was there, hiding somewhere up above.

He took a deep breath, then moved out into the open. In Frobisher's borrowed clothing, Alex had to trust that he looked enough like the other man from a distance that Hanchett wouldn't shoot him in the back.

Following the instructions he'd been given, Alex walked to the place where the altar would be. A lantern stood there, and Alex stooped to light it, just as Frobisher said he was told to. It was a signal that Hanchett would be watching for. A way to tell him that Frobisher had carried out his task. Now, Hanchett should be confident that all was going according to plan.

Alex actually smiled when he turned to the staircase up to the tower. He couldn't wait to meet Hanchett this time. The staircase to the top of the tower was newly built, but felt rickety all the same. The wooden risers squeaked with every step. Hanchett would hear him long before he could be surprised. Once again, he had to trust that wearing Frobisher's distinctive coat would fool the other man long enough for Alex to get close.

At the top, he held back for a moment.

"Frobisher, are you finally here?" Hanchett's voice filtered around the corner where Alex waited.

"I've obeyed the serpent handler's orders," Alex said, trying to match Frobisher's voice.

"Took you long enough," Hanchett grunted. "But then, Ophiuchus would never give you a task you weren't capable of completing. Come up here. I've got something for you to take."

"Yes, sir!" Alex said.

"And hurry. I can scarcely lift this." That voice was feminine. With a jolt, Alex recognized it as belonging to Judith. He hadn't been counting on that.

But there was little he could do at this point. Alex kept

his head tilted down. The hat's brim would shield his face for a second longer.

He stepped into the doorway.

Hanchett and Judith stood outside, on a narrow walkway that ran the length of the roof's peak. At both ends of the walkway was a door. Hanchett must have concealed the money in the front bell tower, which was only accessible from the roof. And Alex now blocked the way out, down the only staircase to the ground.

Both man and woman were burdened with heavy canvas packages.

"Come, come," Hanchett said impatiently. "There's another load in the tower still. We must—"

Judith's scream interrupted his words. "He's not Frobisher!"

"You noticed," Alex drawled.

She pulled the bags toward her again, ignoring the weight she was just complaining about. "You can't take this from us! We earned it!"

"I earned it," Hanchett corrected, with a dark look at Judith.

"Oh, and I didn't help?" she snapped. She looked at Alex. "Why are you here?"

"She doesn't know?" Alex asked Hanchett.

"Know what?" Judith demanded.

"Your lover instructed Frobisher to kill me. Just as he did for the past four victims. You probably remember Mr Mason. And you definitely knew Miss Gilroy."

"Mr Frobisher would never hurt his Susanna!" Judith said, disbelieving.

"Her death weighed on him the most," Alex said. "But he remained loyal to Ophiuchus, the Serpent Handler. As it turned out, Ophiuchus was just Hanchett, using a mix of coersion and trickery to make a troubled man into a useful tool."

Judith looked back at Hanchett. "He's lying, Daniel. Isn't he?"

"Of course he is," Hanchett said quickly.

"Doesn't explain why Hanchett chose this night to move all his money from its rather good hiding spot. What's changed?" Alex turned to him. "Why didn't the stars tell you that I was coming? Or that Violet never believed a word you said?"

Hanchett growled, "Get out of the way."

But Judith was caught up in Alex's revelation. "Violet told you something?"

"Violet told me everything she remembered about her father's involvement in the society, and how it led to his death, and she remembers it all now, thanks to you."

"What will we do?" Judith asked Hanchett. "If the Duchess of Dunmere says something, people will talk."

Hanchett snarled. Whatever plans he had were ruined now. Alex could almost hear him thinking of new ways out.

"Frobisher will speak against you," Alex said to Hanchett. "And Mrs Peake's involvement will certainly destroy her socially. Unless," he said to Judith, "you can help me."

"I'll tell you everything he told me about where he got his money. I can tell you how he found new people to join!" She stepped closer to Alex, anxious to make herself useful.

In her haste she dropped the bag she carried. It fell to the roof and then tumbled over. Hanchett yelled at her. "You idiot, you lost it. Go fetch it back!"

"Back?" Judith stared at him. "It's on the *ground* now.

What do you want me to do? Fly down?"

"Oh, hell." In disgust, Hanchett pushed Judith hard to the side.

She had no warning, and no chance to catch her balance. Before anyone could reach her, she fell. She didn't even scream as she tumbled to the sloping roof, slid down, and tipped over the edge. Only when she disappeared from view did a short, thin wail rise up, only to be silenced a second later.

Alex was completely stunned for a second. "Not much to be gained for those loyal to you," he managed.

"She was loyal to money first." If Hanchett regretted what he'd just done, it didn't show.

"So you killed her?"

"Well, she just threw something of mine away, didn't she?" Hanchett growled. "Get out of the way, or I'll send you over, too."

"I won't go alone," said Alex.

Something in his voice made Hanchett hesitate. Then he shrugged. "Move back. You don't want to risk death."

"You don't know me very well."

"Think of your wife, then." Hanchett warned, more anxiously, "Move back, and I'll let you live."

"Let you walk away?"

"Why not?" Hanchett said. "What harm have I done you personally? I arranged for you to marry a new bride. I just got rid of—let's admit it—a rather annoying relative. And I never actually stole a pound from you. Let me vanish, and everything will be forgotten."

Alex took one step back. Hanchett mimicked it.

"There," he said. "Just walk back."

Alex took another step, balancing despite the narrow walkway and the height of the building. Now was a terrible time to remember that his depth perception was not to be trusted. A straight line is a straight line, he reminded himself.

Hanchett moved whenever Alex did, never getting too close. But as Alex got closer to the doorway, the other man tensed up, giving Alex one second of warning. Hanchett couldn't stop from taking a deep breath. Then he was hurtling himself at Alex, intent on shoving him aside to follow Judith down the roof.

Alex ducked down, flattening himself as low as he could. Hanchett shrieked, missing his target. Instinctively, he spun around to get another chance at Alex. But he misjudged his own balance. He fell, clawing madly at the roof tiles. He got hold of something, and kept himself from falling.

"Help me," he gasped out.

"Not inclined to," Alex said, getting up.

"Please! I'll give you anything you want."

"Everything you have to offer belongs to someone else."

"You won't let me die! You're not that kind of man!"

"You know nothing about me."

"I know you wouldn't have come all the way up here only to come back empty handed! Please!" Hanchett lost his grip with one hand, scrambling to get hold again. Two more bags of money went skittering down the slate roof tiles, lost in the darkness below.

"I suppose it's easier to take you down the stairs than pick you up from the ground." Alex shifted. He reached Hanchett and put one hand out. "Take hold," he said.

Hanchett was too desperate not to. He allowed Alex to haul him up and inside the belfry. Hanchett lay on the wooden planks, breathing heavily.

"Let's go." Alex didn't want Hanchett to get his breath, or have time to think up new mischief.

"I can't walk," Hanchett protested, though with a sly look on his face.

Alex moved toward him. Hanchett sprang up, anticipating him. But he wasn't ready when Alex slammed his fist into his face. Hanchett dropped to the floor again, unconscious.

Alex took a few breaths. Then he dragged his catch down the stairs like a sack of flour. The bruising might prove instructive.

At the bottom, the Disreputables Jem and Rook were waiting, along with two more men Alex didn't recognize.

"We came as soon as Frobisher was safely put away. What's needed?" asked Jem.

"There's a body outside on the south side," Alex said. "Along with a few sacks, likely filled with money. And I need to get this man to a place where he can't run away."

He got into the carriage with Hanchett, who was just beginning to stir.

"What will be done with me? I'll hold my own in any court of law, you know."

"Possible," Alex agreed, "but we're not going to a court of law. At least, not officially. In the meantime, why not tell me how it started?"

Chapter 30

♋

THE ZODIAC OFFICES BLAZED WITH light. Alex could barely stand it, so he shielded his one eye with his hand.

"Sorry," Chattan whispered once as she passed near him. "There's a lot that needs looking at."

That was all too true. More Disreputables had been deployed to retrieve all the materials they could get from Hanchett's home before anyone knew he was gone. They retrieved the money, and one of the Disreputables was counting the total, looking as if he saw that amount of cash every day.

Meanwhile, Alex had been explaining everything he deduced himself and learned from Hanchett's confession. Frobisher had also confirmed several points.

"Hanchett was mostly a con man and a trickster," Alex began. "He didn't resort to violence unless he felt it was necessary. But he also had some bigger plans. When he met John Frobisher, a man who was outwardly strong but mentally fragile, Hanchett got a wild notion. He knew Frobisher was a believer, prone to accepting authority, whether that was in the military or in a society dedicated to astrology. Hanchett encouraged Frobisher's use of opium, even supplying it to him. But his real hope was that

Frobisher could be manipulated into doing the sort of act Hanchett was afraid to do himself. Frobisher was a soldier, after all. He'd killed on orders before. Perhaps he'd do it again.

"So Hanchett worked at him, over months. He used the star charts and the trappings of their little society to prepare Frobisher's mind. And in January, he decided to test his idea.

"Hanchett chose a victim named Randolphus Lyle. He was living on the streets, an old man with few friends. In Hanchett's eyes, Lyle was a perfect choice. No one would care if he died or disappeared. And no one would connect Lyle with Hanchett because there *was* no connection. He was just unlucky.

"After the January meeting of the Society of the True Sky, Hanchett got Frobisher to stay in the room where they held their ceremony. He used some basic stagecraft to appear as Ophiuchus, and Frobisher—who had been given a dose of opium earlier—bought it. He did just as the seemingly godlike figure told him to do. Lyle was killed that same night, and the symbol for that month's sign marked next to it. Hanchett was delighted, even more so when Frobisher appeared to forget the whole incident.

"If he stopped there, no one would have ever noticed anything. The symbol was not picked up on, so the Zodiac never heard of the death. But Hanchett wanted to use the weapon he made."

"So James Galbraith was killed in February," Chattan said.

Alex nodded. "James Galbraith held a large but private debt over Hanchett. Hanchett had been paying it back on time, and with interest, so Galbraith had no reason to be upset. But Hanchett saw an opportunity to avoid paying the balance. He repeated what he'd done the last month, but told Frobisher a new name."

"He must have been quite confident," said Julian. "If he miscalculated, Frobisher would have denounced him. That's a huge risk to take."

Alex shook his head. "If Frobisher wasn't receptive that time, Hanchett would have laughed it off as a joke, or a misunderstanding. But he knew Frobisher very well, after months of close contact. Frobisher was more…suggestible than he appeared."

Julian frowned. "So the fact that Galbraith was a politician didn't have anything to do with it?"

"No. It was entirely personal. Very personal, since Daniel Hanchett was actually born Daniel Galbraith. He changed his name years ago when his criminal activities made it prudent to disappear for a while. But he was still in touch with some of his family, and that's how he got the loan from his relative."

"But he had his family killed to save on the repayments."

"Yes," said Alex. "Hanchett isn't particularly sentimental."

"Go back to the murders," said Julian. "Mason was next."

"Yes, in March. Warner Mason wasn't the simple clerk he seemed to be. He was interested in the occult for years, but when he met Hanchett, his interest became more…ah, intimate."

"In what sense?"

"In the sense that Hanchett quickly discovered Mason's romantic preferences and exploited that to earn Mason's trust. Mason was privy to cabinet secrets, and Hanchett used his influence to learn some very important ones. But Mason made a mistake—probably giving Hanchett a document he shouldn't have. He started to feel guilty about what he'd done. Mason was going to admit his mistakes to his superior. Hanchett persuaded him to wait until after that month's meeting. But of course, Frobisher killed him on the way home, just as he was ordered to by the so-called Ophiuchus—who was just Hanchett in a robe."

Once again, Alex felt a stab of remorse for his failure to act quickly enough to prevent the next murder. He said, "Susanna Gilroy was a believer, until she had second thoughts when Hanchett pressed her a little too hard for money. Why encourage her to make out a will when he told her her disease would be cured? She was starting to doubt him, and he had her killed next—before she could disentangle herself completely. That was a huge mistake on Hanchett's part. Frobisher loved Miss Gilroy, and though he did kill her on Hanchett's orders, he was severely damaged by it, and secretly started to doubt everything, though on the surface he became more devoted than ever."

"He was trying to convince himself," Chattan said.

Alex shifted in his seat. "Yes. Of course, that was when I started pulling threads together, though I had no idea what the connections were yet. There were some other mistakes on the part of Judith Peake and Hanchett. When they tried to bring Violet into the fold, there was an unintended consequence. Violet remembered events from her past, and she also had the background in astronomy to know exactly what the new group was doing. She told me what she knew, and I finally knew *where* my killer was."

"The Society of the True Sky."

"Yes. Hanchett had been the man pulling the strings of

the group for a very long time—he knew Judith Peake for years, back when the idea last enjoyed popularity. Apparently, that last incarnation really was just a group of astrologers who thought they'd found a secret. Hanchett's new version was more of a source for fraud, as he tried to recruit people most likely to give him money he asked for.

"He thought Violet was a timid, easily controlled person, because that's how Judith Peake saw her. But Violet is nothing like that, and furthermore, she has always been highly skeptical, as a result of seeing her father's gullibility."

"But Mrs Peake didn't know that?" Chattan asked.

"She refused to acknowledge it," said Alex. "It's an example of someone so convinced of their own beliefs that they'll ignore all evidence to the contrary. Hanchett thought he'd get a wealthy duchess to tap for funds. Instead, he got a mess—a woman skilled in astronomy... and by coincidence, a husband skilled in detection."

"So he wanted you dead purely to stop the investigation?"

"Exactly. I was a little too inquisitive, and Hanchett got suspicious when he heard from an associate that a man with only one eye was asking about him. Things were getting a bit out of control."

Julian said, "The killing of a duke would have ignited the country. Did he not think of that?"

"He was against the ropes," said Alex. "He didn't have a lot of choice. He basically hoped to outrun the problem—with the money he'd been hoarding. He would let Frobisher take the fall."

"That's a terrible plan."

Alex shrugged. "He was holding too many threads at once, so he got tangled up in them when I appeared. I knew what he was at the end, and that made it nearly impossible for him to trick me in the small amount of time he had. So once I cornered him, I was able to stop him. Easy."

"I'm a bit confused by your definition of *easy*," Chattan noted dryly.

"So there was never a threat to the nation, in the sense of foreign agents being involved," Julian said.

"No," said Alex. "Every death was due to Hanchett's own life. He was a confidence man and a fraud. But only for himself. There's no hint he worked for or with another government."

"So... That's a relief?" Chattan asked.

"Is it?" Julian gazed up at the ceiling. "The only reason the Zodiac got involved was coincidence! I was sure those zodiac symbols had to be a message or a warning of some type. But it was just chance."

"Well, Mason was selling confidential information," Alex said, "and now he isn't. That's indisputable."

"And our Zodiac is still a secret," Chattan said with a little laugh. "Thank the stars."

Alex stood up. "I think that's enough revelation for tonight. I'll write all this up, of course. But now, I'd like to go home."

Chapter 31

♋

AFTER HE RETURNED, AND SHE saw he was safe, Violet had a long discussion with Alex about the events, and in particular about her aunt's death. Though Violet never got along with Judith, the news still shocked her.

The official story would be that Judith was hit by a runaway carriage when crossing a dark street. Alex saw no point in implicating Judith after her death, and the group he worked for was all too happy to comply with the request.

"The fewer questions, the better," Alex said. "Will her husband believe the story?"

Violet nodded. "My guess is that Uncle Roger will toast to her death and then keep drinking. They were not exactly a united couple."

But she was unable to speak to Roger in person. By the time she went around to the rooms the Peakes were renting in London, the landlord informed her that Mr Peake was gone.

"Took the coffin back to his home for burial," the landlord said. "Terrible thing."

Violet couldn't agree. She didn't want to celebrate any death, but she couldn't imagine many people mourning

352 ❦ Elizabeth Cole

Judith Peake. The woman had only seen most people as stepping stones. Violet had been a bargaining chip for marriage, and Roger was an easy source of income. She had no love for anyone but herself.

So Violet returned home. Alex was waiting for her when she entered the parlor. "I'm glad you're back, love," he said, his expression serious.

"What's happened?"

"Remember when someone sent you a deadly snake, hoping you'd be bitten? Well, now I know who is responsible. And I want to have a chat."

Violet watched her husband, calculated the likelihood that he'd kill whoever it was, then concluded that she'd better come along to prevent bloodshed. She pulled off the pretty, tulle-wrapped straw hat she'd been wearing and put it on the table.

"Well, then. What's the plan?" she asked.

* * * *

A few days later, Violet waited in her carriage, scanning the passersby. The day was warm and bright, after a morning rain shower left diamonds all over the leaves and grasses of the park, washed the windows clean, and cleared the walkways of dirt. The sunshine required ladies to shelter under wide-brimmed hats. It seemed half the city was walking today, many under lacy parasols in pastel shades. The overall effect was that of an ambulatory garden.

But Violet was not enjoying the spectacle, since she was too occupied in searching for a particular person.

Then she saw him. He was walking with an older couple, undoubtedly his parents. After taking a deep breath,

Violet exited the carriage and walked toward the trio, and managed to drop her fan as she passed the young man.

She turned a few steps beyond. "Oh, excuse me, sir. My fan is at your feet."

The young man glanced down, and immediately bent to pick it up. He bowed very politely to Violet and offered it to her with a smile. His mother looked on proudly, content that she'd raised a model son.

"Here you are," the boy said.

"How very kind," Violet said gravely. "Thank you."

"You're most welcome, my lady."

"The correct form of address is your grace," she added gently. "I am Lady Violet, the Duchess of Dunmere. But you know that, don't you, Geoffrey? Or else why would you have sent the krait to me?"

The young man's face went completely white, and Violet was afraid he'd faint. Geoffrey stepped away from her, stammering apologies that were almost incoherent.

"What are you going on about?" his father demanded, embarrassed at the scene.

"He's apologizing, Mr Crisholm," said Alex, who chose that moment to join the little group. "You see, he tried to kill her grace as the result of an unwise wager."

The older man blinked, not comprehending the word in connection with his son. "Kill?" he echoed.

"Perhaps we should not discuss this on the street," Violet said.

Naturally, Alex had already decided on a location to move to. In a private salon of a hotel nearby, the Crisholm family sat with the Duke and Duchess of Dunmere. Alex gave a brief account of what happened.

"How did you find out it was me?" the young man asked.

Alex shrugged. "Did you imagine you were terribly clever?"

"No."

"Good. Once I learned the names of the bettors—and believe me, every one of them will regret it—all that remained was to look at the dates of the predicted death, combined with the amount wagered. Your large bet combined with the earlier death date made you the prime candidate, though a few others were close."

"So you just guessed it was our boy," his father said, seizing on the last remaining hope.

"No," said Alex. "I eliminated the other possibilities. I knew it was you, Geoffrey. But I'd like to hear the details. What made you do it?"

Geoffrey cleared his throat. "I was stupid to wager so much. But I had just received my annual allowance as a single payment from the bank. Some of my friends wouldn't blink at the sum, but to me... Well, the truth is that I lost my head that night. We went out for the evening. A few drinks, a dinner somewhere, then a few other, um, diversions."

He cast a guilty glance toward his mother, but then continued. "Anyway, we ended up in this hell near St Giles. I was drunk, and happy. Everyone was having a good time. I only heard about the wager when one of my other friends placed a bet. It was absurd. Betting on the date of a death! Everyone was laughing about it, and trading stories about the rumors. It all seemed like a joke. I don't even remember when I decided to stake. I didn't think about it at all. But the man wrote it all down and I felt rather...proud. No one else dared to make such a high bet."

"I wonder why," his father nearly spat out.

Geoffrey looked down at his hands. "The next morning, I finally stumbled home to my rooms in town. After I realized the insanity of what I'd done, I tried to go back to the bookmaker and explain that it was a mistake. But he wouldn't hear of it. Told me that *true* gentlemen stood by their word and that he had a responsibility to the others who staked. He couldn't give back the money—all the stakes were held for the winner, as a way to get even more men to bet. He laughed at me and sent me packing."

"You could have come to me," his father said.

"And told you what?" Geoffrey burst out. "That I'd placed real money, my whole allowance, on the death of a peer? You'd have disowned me then, just as you will now. I couldn't tell anyone in a position to assist, or risk losing all respect. No, I had to do it on my own."

"So you decided to nudge the odds in your favor," Alex said. "What gave you the idea to use a venomous snake?"

"It wasn't my idea," Geoffrey said. "After I realized how stuck I was, I spent the rest of the day and night getting completely drunk. There was this man. He'd come up to me in a tavern—the same one where I'd placed the bet. He got me talking, and I told him everything. But he didn't laugh at me. He said he would help me."

"This stranger suggested death by snake?" Alex asked, already guessing who the stranger might be. Hanchett.

"He told me that it would be the safest way. Said he heard of the duchess and knew she hated snakes. She'd be frightened to death just by seeing one. The man even told me where to go to get one, and what to say. All I had to do was…" The boy stopped talking, his face going red.

"Do what?"

"Split the winnings with him. I'd already told him my

name, and he could have ruined me if I didn't go along. So I agreed."

"You trusted him?" his father asked incredulously. "He'd have blackmailed you for the rest of your life!"

"I couldn't think straight," Geoffrey explained. "I was desperate, so I did what the man said. On the day my wager was supposed to come due, I had the box with the snake inside. It was terrifying. I didn't even open it. I addressed it to her grace and paid a boy to deliver it."

"So you couldn't kill in person, but you were happy enough to kill from a distance." Alex's tone was one of complete disgust.

"I didn't know what else to do!" The boy appealed to Violet. "I didn't know you, your grace. I'd never seen you. I knew nothing about you. It was just a name on a paper. I told myself that if this curse was real, then it wasn't my fault. Maybe Fate was using me to its own ends."

"Everyone has free will," Violet said coldly.

"I know," he said, downcast. "I know. It was just a thing I told myself. When I heard nothing, I knew that the plan hadn't worked. The snake must have been killed, or never reached the house, or something. I was glad to realize I failed," he added vehemently. "I didn't know how much I hated myself until I heard that the wager was still wide open. The duchess lived and the curse had yet to claim her."

Geoffrey stared at the floor. "I'll be ruined, and I've mangled everything. But I don't want to be a murderer. Believe me, I'm so sorry it got that far. That's all I did," he swore.

"You sent the flowers and the gifts afterward," Violet said. "Why?"

"To apologize," he said miserably. "I didn't know what else to do. I never tried anything else to harm you. I promise."

"Once seems quite enough," Alex said, unmoved by the boy's confession.

"Why didn't you just call me out?" Geoffrey asked him. Duels were no longer the preferred method of settling debates between gentlemen. Indeed, their legality was now rather murky. But no one would have been shocked if the duke demanded one in this instance.

"We will find justice another way, *not* through death," Violet said. "Mr Crisholm made a grave mistake, which I think he recognized immediately."

Geoffrey's father stood up. "Still too late! How can we possibly live this down? I'll disown him, your graces," he said. "But by God, this will tarnish the Crisholm name for generations." He glared at his son.

"There is another option," Violet said. "While Geoffrey Crisholm certainly must work to reestablish his worth in the eyes of his family, there is little benefit to public shame that would harm even more people."

"What do you suggest, your grace?" Mrs Crisholm had a wild, hopeful look in her eyes.

"A change in circumstance may help," said Violet. "If you purchased your son a commission, he would be removed from his old crowd and he would learn how to live a more disciplined life. His troubles, I think, have come from trying to be something he is not."

She looked at Geoffrey. "Your current friends are rather capricious with their money. They can afford to be, while you cannot."

"That is true," he admitted. "They do anything they desire, and they liked me, so I got to join them on their carousing. But I could never really match them."

"Would you consider the army as a career?" she asked. "The idea means nothing if you don't accept it willingly."

"I would do anything your grace asks," Geoffrey said sincerely. "But the debt I owe means I couldn't afford the commission."

"I'll pay," said Alex. "Both the debt and the commission. Not officially, of course. But let me know how much you need, and I'll see you get it. *And* you may be sure that I'll keep well informed of your activities."

"Yes, your grace," the boy said quickly. "Anything you say. I'm at your service."

He turned to Violet. "I beg your forgiveness, your grace. You've already shown me more mercy that I deserve, but I swear that I could not feel any more shame and remorse than I already do."

"You beg my forgiveness," Violet echoed. "A good first step toward redemption. I will not answer you now, but I will most assuredly see you again."

Geoffrey bowed even lower, accepting that. After promising that he'd follow all the instructions, he left with his parents.

"An awkward ride home, I'd imagine," Alex said afterward.

"He made a mistake," said Violet. "There should be consequences. But he is young. Perhaps it will make him better than he would have been otherwise."

"No doubt new rumors will spread about the mercy of the Duchess of Dunmere."

Violet sighed. "I can't imagine they'll speak of it at all. It's too shameful."

"Not of the event, but I saw how that whole family

looked at you when you proposed your alternative. If you'd demanded veneration, they'd have made you a saint."

Then he stood up, and took Violet's hand to help her up as well. "Now let's get home. I'm nearly done with London."

"What else do you need to do?" she asked, curious.

"Just need to speak to a few people," he said. "Nothing for you to worry about. I promise no blood will be drawn. Not by me, anyway."

* * * *

Alex took great pleasure in using his standing to scour a certain part of the London underworld. He used the threat of the law to shut the bookmaker down. It was, he argued, very likely illegal to coerce a seventeen-year-old boy into making a bet, particularly as the bet itself was so morally questionable. The local authorities agreed.

Then Alex used his social connections to spread the word of the other bettors. True, word had got around the various clubs of London already, in a quiet way. But that was very different from the scandal provoked when the rumors hit the salons and tea tables of polite society. Suddenly, the name of Dunmere was being mentioned in a most sympathetic way, and the names of the bettors might as well have been curses themselves.

"Can you imagine wagering on a woman's death?" said the influential Lady Mathering. "And in particular that of the duchess, who is clearly a most virtuous woman! I've scratched all those names from my books. They'll never come to one of *my* parties again!"

As the same time, Sophie made it a personal mission

to direct the rumors according to her own designs. Soon, the curse of the "Duke of Death" was utterly forgotten, as the love of Alex and Violet became *the* story of the Season among romantically minded ladies. Poetry even appeared in the newspapers celebrating the triumph of love over the curse.

True, the poems were terrible. But it was the sentiment that mattered. It was simply destined, proclaimed Lady Forester.

"Destined?" Alex asked her one evening, during a small dinner party.

"You don't have to believe a thing to *use* it," Sophie said airily. "What does it matter if people believe in destiny, so long as they are on your side instead of against it? You're the man of the moment, your grace. Trust me, if you strolled into the House of Lords right now, they'd listen to every word you say."

"Funny you should mention that," Alex said.

Sophie looked extremely interested. "Oh?"

"I've nothing to say now, my lady. But you'll doubtless be among the first to hear."

"Well, I should *hope* so." Sophie's voice was practically a purr. "What's the point of being a spy if one doesn't learn things before everyone else?"

* * * *

Finally, Alex went to the Zodiac offices again. Several days and nights of hard thinking—made easier by talking with Violet—led Alex to make a long-delayed announcement.

Miss Chattan let him in, and ushered him into Julian's office.

"How are you?" Julian asked, his eyes intent. "Seems your assignment was the least of your worries. We've heard any number of tales in the past few days."

"I imagine," said Alex. "Would you be interested in the truth?"

"The truth has always interested me," Julian responded. "But first, may I ask what the body count was?"

"Violet made me promise not to kill anyone in connection with the bet." Alex recounted all that happened with the young Mr Crisholm, concluding, "In the end, the boy's punishment, if you can call it so, is likely to make far more of an impression than anything I could have meted out."

"Good to hear," said Chattan, who'd been listening in.

Alex cleared his throat. "That brings me to another matter. My retirement."

"What?" Julian asked.

"I'm proud of what I've done over the years, but my life has changed dramatically. My injury restricts me to certain assignments. And I've neglected my personal life too long. There's a responsibility to being duke. I need to focus on that for my family, because no one else can." Alex took a deep breath. "It's time to pass the sign on to someone new."

The words didn't hurt nearly as much as Alex thought they would.

Julian watched him, not seeming terribly surprised in the end. "I trust you've considered this for some time."

"Yes. I'll lend advice, or assist in a particular matter if you absolutely require it," Alex said. "But I intend to become more active in politics—both domestic and foreign. I can probably have more effect in that sphere than I ever could in the Zodiac."

"Perhaps," said Julian. "It's a different world."

"Not that different," Chattan interjected with a knowing smirk. "If you're giving up the sign of Cancer, your grace, perhaps you'd consent to another code name. You can join our little group of supporters, such as Pandora and the others," she said, mentioning another recent addition.

"What do you have in mind?"

"Ophiuchus has a certain ring to it," said Chattan. "And as we all agree, it's definitely *not* an official sign of the Zodiac."

"I could use that," Alex said, with a smile. "Mind you, I'm retiring as an agent. I won't be running around the city all the time."

"We'll not strain you. And in truth, if I'm to lose an agent, I'd much rather it be to retirement than to death. So that's that," said Julian. "After all, it sounds as if you'll be quite busy with domestic bliss, your grace."

"Try to say it with less contempt next time," Chattan advised her companion. "Just because *you* live and breathe espionage doesn't mean everyone has to."

Julian gave her a slight smile. "So says the one who's *always* here with me."

Alex stood up. "Well, I'll leave you both to your domestic bliss. Send word if you need anything. Not too soon, mind."

He left the Zodiac offices and then the whole building, feeling as if he'd left a great burden behind him. He'd return to the town house, and then he and Violet would return *home*. Together. He couldn't wait.

Epilogue

☊

January 1810

WINTER WINDS BEAT AROUND THE wing of the Abbey. The weather was foul, the sky cloudy, and the light dull. But no one cared about the weather, least of all Alex. He paced rapidly in his study. He tried to carry on conversations with Herbert, who'd returned from Bath in the company of Alex's mother. But in general, Alex was a wreck.

"Don't run yourself down," Herbert advised. "After all, Violet might need you later."

"I hope so," Alex muttered. The alternative—that Violet would be beyond all need—was too painful to think about.

Her pregnancy didn't cause any problems until a month prior, when she began having pains nearly every time she stood or walked. The doctor ordered complete bed rest, forcing Violet to retire to her rooms for the last weeks. She kept her spirits up with visitors and games and books. Millie was with her most days, and Alex spent every moment he could with her.

But the last few days were brutal. Violet seemed so weak, so delicate. Alex never felt more fear than when he thought of his slip of a wife delivering a child. He prayed for the first time in years.

When the labor began, Violet kept Alex with her for the first hours. She reassured him that all would be well. But he could tell she was in tremendous pain. Then the doctor sent him out, saying he'd only be in the way. Millie and Dalby stayed on as helpers, which seemed quite unfair.

"I'll see you very soon," Violet whispered to him, her face streaked with sweat after the most recent contraction. "Kiss me."

He kissed her, wishing he could do more than simply wait. "I love you," he said, his voice raw.

"I love you," she responded. "Now go. It won't be long."

But it was long. Hours. Perhaps days. Possibly forever. Alex had no sense of time.

"Your grace?"

Alex jumped. He'd been so lost in thought that he didn't hear anyone come up.

"You may go in, your grace." The doctor stood in front of him, looking tired but not terrified.

"How is she?"

"You wife is resting comfortably. She did very well."

Those few words let him breathe again.

The doctor smiled. "I wouldn't have thought it to look at her, but she's very strong. You can go see her now."

Alex raced to Violet's room. One the way, it occurred to him that the doctor hadn't mentioned the baby. What if Violet lost the child? All that pain, for nothing...

But then he heard a laugh from the other side of the door. He knocked and was summoned by Violet's sweet voice.

When he opened the door, Violet lay in the middle of the bed, propped up with pillows. She was holding an infant in her arms, smiling beatifically at it.

Millie was in the room as well. She'd been at Violet's side for nearly the whole lying-in. She was also holding an infant in her arms. Alex blinked. He was so knackered that it took him a moment to understand.

"The doctor didn't say a word about twins," he said, his voice thick.

"I swore him to secrecy," Violet said. "I wanted to surprise you."

"I'm surprised." In fact, he might need to sit down.

Millie stepped up close to Alex, beaming happily. "Meet your son Alexander!"

He stared at the baby, not entirely sure what to do.

"You can hold him," Violet prompted from the bed.

Millie offered him the wrapped up infant. He took the baby, holding him like a very fragile thing. "Hello, Alexander," he said quietly. The baby looked at him with large, calm eyes.

"I think we might use Xander for him," Violet said. "You're Alex already. He needs to make his own mark."

"I'm sure he will," Alex said, sitting down on the edge of the bed.

Violet held the other bundle closer to her breast. "And this is our daughter Celeste."

"Oh, God. A son and daughter. She's going to be beautiful. Like you."

"We'll see about that." Violet smiled at him. "I am certain she'll be loved. By us and *all* her brothers and sisters."

"That's extremely optimistic," said Alex. "I like the way you think."

ABOUT THE AUTHOR

Elizabeth Cole is a romance writer with a penchant for history. Her stories draw upon her deep affection for the British Isles, action movies, medieval fantasies, and even science fiction. She now lives in a small house in a big city with a cat, a snake, and a rather charming gentleman. When not writing, she is usually curled in a corner reading...or watching costume dramas or things that explode. And yes, she believes in love at first sight.

Find out more at: elizabethcole.co